HARD *to Hold*

The Walkers of Coyote Ridge

Caine Cousins

By Nicole Edwards

The Alluring Indulgence Series
Kaleb
Zane
Travis
Holidays with the Walker Brothers
Ethan
Braydon
Sawyer
Brendon

The Walkers of Coyote Ridge Series
Curtis
Jared
Hard to Hold
Hard to Handle

The Austin Arrows Series
Rush
Kaufman

The Bad Boys of Sports Series
Bad Reputation
Bad Business

The Club Destiny Series
Conviction
Temptation
Addicted
Seduction
Infatuation
Captivated
Devotion
Perception
Entrusted
Adored
Distraction

The Dead Heat Ranch Series
Boots Optional
Betting on Grace
Overnight Love

By Nicole Edwards (cont.)

The Devil's Bend Series

Chasing Dreams
Vanishing Dreams

The Office Intrigue Series

Office Intrigue
Intrigued Out of the Office
Their Rebellious Submissive
Their Famous Dominant

The Pier 70 Series

Reckless
Fearless
Speechless
Harmless

The Sniper 1 Security Series

Wait for Morning
Never Say Never
Tomorrow's Too Late

The Southern Boy Mafia/Devil's Playground Series

Beautifully Brutal
Without Regret
Beautifully Loyal
Without Restraint

Standalone Novels

A Million Tiny Pieces
Inked on Paper

Writing as Timberlyn Scott

Unhinged
Unraveling
Chaos

Naughty Holiday Editions

2015
2016

HARD TO HOLD

The Walkers of Coyote Ridge, 3

NICOLE EDWARDS

Nicole Edwards Limited
PO Box 806
Hutto, Texas 78634
www.NicoleEdwardsLimited.com

Cover Image: © Wander Aguiar | wanderbookclub.com
Models: Zack Salaun, Genevieve Consoli, Jacob Cooley
Interior Image: © Ying Feng Johansson (14217504 – 123rf.com)
Back Cover Image: © Lindsay Helms (36305261) | 123rf.com

Cover Design: © Nicole Edwards Limited
Editing: Blue Otter Editing | BlueOtterEditing.com

ISBN (ebook): 978-1-939786-80-7
ISBN (print): 978-1-939786-79-1

Ménage Romance
Mature Audience

Dear Reader,

This story contains elements of domestic abuse. If you or someone you love is in an abusive relationship, please seek help.

National Domestic Violence Hotline
1-800-799-SAFE (7233) | 1-800-787-3224 (TTY)

1

WHAT WAS THE saying? Hell in a hand basket?

Yep. That was exactly where this night was going.

And fast.

Wolfe Caine had felt the prickling at the back of his neck as soon as he stepped into his favorite watering hole half an hour ago. That itchy feeling got worse when his cousin joined him a few minutes after.

Never failed that when the pair of them got together, the shit tended to hit the fan. What it was about them that made stupid cowboys want to throw down, Wolfe didn't know, but it seemed he couldn't spend a Friday night out without getting his knuckles scraped a little.

But he wasn't bitching about it. Sometimes, after busting his ass all damn week, a little scuffle was just what his inner redneck needed.

"Y'all wanna do this?" Lynx growled, his intimidating glare causing the two smartasses to puff out their chests.

Yep. And that was Lynx for you. The man had never met a ranch hand he didn't want to punch.

"Son of a bitch," one of the old men sitting near the back grumbled. "Why the hell do you dumb fuckers wanna start shit all the goddamn time? You ain't learned your lesson yet?"

That was the question of the hour.

He knew the old man wasn't talking to him and his cousin. Shit. Just a few minutes ago, Wolfe had been shooting the shit with him. Minding his own damn business, at that.

"Hear that, fuckers?" Lynx growled.

"You talk a lotta shit, you know that?" Dumb Ass Number One goaded, his words aimed at Lynx.

With a resigned sigh, Wolfe set his beer down on the scarred table and moved to stand beside his cousin.

A couple of the patrons opted to move to the far side of the room.

Wolfe could admit they were an intimidating pair. Always had been. At six foot three, the two of them tended to draw attention whenever they walked in a room. Add to that the tattoos Lynx had decorating a large portion of his body and they could usually part a crowd right down the middle. Didn't help that they took the bait every damn time.

"I'm gettin' too damn old for this shit," Wolfe muttered under his breath.

With the big three-oh looming in the very near future, Wolfe was starting to wonder if it was getting close to time to retire his weekly bar brawl action. And Lynx was no spring chicken at twenty-eight.

"You wanna do this? Let's take this shit outside," Lynx suggested. "I'll lead the way."

Of course he would.

"Anyone feel like they're in a zoo?" Dumb Ass Number One questioned.

Funny guy.

The dumb ass even chuckled at his own failed attempt at a joke. No one else did.

Wolfe had heard plenty of that shit growing up. Their fathers—brothers with less than two years between them—thought that it would be amusing to make a bet that each of them could not convince their wives to name their firstborn son after some sort of wildlife. Their sister Iris had insisted they were out of their minds, but, of course, being as competitive as they were, it was on at that point. Thanks to that drunken wager, Wolfe and Lynx had gotten used to the teasing during their childhood. Granted, as they grew up, that hadn't happened as much. However, there was still one dumb ass in every bunch.

"No new material?" Wolfe asked.

"Takes brains to come up with somethin' new," Lynx noted. "I think it's safe to say they're fresh outta smart."

"You're just as fucked up as your old man," Dumb Ass Number Two grumbled, his bushy eyebrows darting down.

Wolfe grinned, chuckling. "Who you talkin' to?"

Wolfe assumed the smart-mouthed cowboy was probably talking to both of them. The Caines had laid down roots in Embers Ridge nearly a hundred years ago and they'd been starting shit for just as many. And their fathers—Cooter and Calvin—were some of the wildest in Caine history.

"Pick one." Dumb Ass Number One cackled like a fucking girl, peering over at his buddy. "They're all fucking crazy."

Lynx glanced over at him. Wolfe was tempted to roll his eyes. These boys weren't in any hurry, obviously. And their stand-up comedy routine was seriously lacking.

"Since my old man ain't here to defend himself, why don't you take this up with me?" Lynx taunted. "I'll rip your ass a new one just as fast as he would, you dumb fuck."

Everyone in town knew that ol' Cooter Caine was as crazy as they came. After all, he had barricaded himself up in his compound on the outskirts of town and hadn't left the place in ten years. Not once since Lynx's mother had died in a car wreck on her way home from work. Sure, Cooter was a little out of touch with reality; however, ask anyone and they'd tell you that Lynx's old man wouldn't hurt a damn soul. As for Lynx, that was a different story altogether.

As for Wolfe's old man … Calvin Caine was probably the sanest in the long line of Caines before him, although that was debatable at times. The man lived in a small apartment above their furniture store just a few blocks south of downtown Embers Ridge. After Wolfe's mother passed away two years ago from pneumonia, Calvin had taken to spending all his time in the store. While Wolfe and Lynx were responsible for making the furniture, Calvin had taken it upon himself to sell it. Of course, he and Lynx were often pulling double duty to help out with the heavy lifting.

"Both of 'em are nuts," Dumb Ass Number Two said.

Yep, this was going nowhere fast.

"Come on," Lynx growled. "You wanna knuckle up, let's take this shit outside."

Lynx took one step toward the door, but the two dumb asses didn't move.

"We can do this right here," Dumb Ass Number One noted, obviously opposed to a little fresh air, maybe a broken nose.

"The hell we can," Wolfe grumbled. "You see that girl behind the bar? She's got a shotgun back there. You throw down in here, that first bullet'll have your name on it."

Granted, Wolfe knew that Reagan had yet to fire that bad boy up in here. She was a little on the defensive side, but so far, she hadn't proven to be crazy. However, that could change at any time.

Lynx chuckled, but there was no real humor in it. "I don't know 'bout you boys, but I'd like to live my life without any bullet holes."

Wolfe leaned toward Lynx. "You've already had one."

Lynx glared back at him, then rolled his eyes. "Without any *more* bullet holes," he amended. He lowered his voice. "And that didn't count. It was squirrel shot."

"Still hurt, didn't it?" Wolfe mumbled back.

Lynx's answer was in the form of a one-shoulder shrug.

Regardless, the statement got the two dumb asses glancing behind the bar. Wolfe didn't need to turn around to know that Reagan Trevino—the sweet girl who owned this beer bar—was standing there, one hand on her hip, the other twitching at her side. There *was* a shotgun behind that bar and the woman wasn't scared to use it.

"Reagan," Lynx called out as he started toward the door. "Corral these fools outside, would ya, doll?"

The sound of a shotgun being cocked echoed in the otherwise silent space.

Wolfe nodded toward the door. "Let's go, boys. My beer's gettin' warm."

It was a gamble turning your back on a couple of drunk good ol' boys, but what the fuck. Wolfe didn't have nothing else to do tonight. Nothing more than relax with a beer and chill with his cousin, anyway.

But this would work, too.

Once they were outside, the balmy July breeze slapped him right in the face.

“This is bullshit,” Lynx groused. “I just wanna drink my beer, chill for a bit. Maybe play some pool.” He shook out his hands. “Shit. My hands still hurt from the last damn fight.”

Seconds later, the two cowboys came barreling out of the bar. Likely having dealt with Reagan calling them a couple of pussies. She’d been known to taunt the fools who wanted to act like idiots.

“Come on, boys,” Lynx goaded. “Let’s get this shit over with.”

“Crazy, I tell you,” Dumb Ass Number Two mumbled, stumbling down the steps to the gravel lot. “Why can’t you Caine boys just—”

Obviously tired of chatting, Lynx launched himself at the dumb ass, landing a solid right hook to the fucker’s jaw. Another swing came, then the two were tangled together, their boots scrambling for purchase on the gravel. When it looked as though the other dumb ass was going to come to his friend’s rescue, Wolfe shot a look heavenward. There was no getting out of this one.

Wolfe figured the fastest way to get back inside to his beer was to offer his assistance.

So he did.

AMY MANNING—KNOWN to everyone in this town as Amy Smith—stood stone still when the two cowboys headed toward the door, following the Caine cousins. When they stepped outside, she glanced over at Reagan, watching as the woman wielded that shotgun like she was on a first-name basis with the thing.

Shit.

This place got stranger and stranger the longer Amy stayed.

Not so surprisingly, everyone piled out of the bar and into the parking lot. Seemed Friday night's entertainment was being held out there. Again.

When there were no more patrons to wait on, Amy went to the bar and peered over at her boss. "What do we do now? Wait?" That was what they'd done the last couple of times this had happened.

Reagan smiled and the move made the woman even prettier than she already was. She was short, like Amy, with dark brown eyes, also like Amy. Their similarities pretty much ran out at that point. Reagan had a cute little nose, perfect breasts, and her hair was long and looked like dark chocolate silk—similar to Amy's *before* circumstance had made her become a bottle blonde. Amy missed her dark hair, wishing she'd never been dumb enough to hit up the drugstore during one of her panic attacks. However, she had to admit, it did help to alter her appearance. Some.

"Yep. They'll be back. Won't take long."

Having been in this tiny town of Embers Ridge for all of three months and working in this small bar for only a third of that time, Amy clearly didn't understand the dynamics. Seemed there were a few consistencies though.

One, Wolfe and Lynx Caine did show up every Friday night without fail. Usually Saturday nights, also. Two, someone—typically a drunk cowboy—provoked one or both cousins and ended up out front.

Three, someone was usually bleeding by the time they all came stumbling back inside. And four, at some point tonight, the sheriff was going to make an appearance.

Seeing the sheriff wasn't high on Amy's priority list, even if he was nice to look at. Rhys Trevino's piercing blue eyes saw too damn much as far as she was concerned, which was the very reason Amy was keeping her distance.

The door opened. The sound of the fight and some rowdy onlookers floated into the empty room, then was quickly cut off when the door closed again.

Nope, they weren't done yet.

Amy leaned against the bar and glanced at the clock on the wall. It was only nine thirty. She had two and half hours to go, and that seemed like an interminably long time. Especially if she had to spend half an hour waiting for everyone to make their way back inside.

What she really wanted to do was go home, take a long, hot shower, and then fall asleep while reading. She'd recently discovered some rather intriguing books—a popular genre known as erotic romance—that had taught her a few things that she … uh … hadn't known. In fact, they'd taught her a *lot* of things she hadn't known. Needless to say, she looked forward to reading. It was what she'd been doing for the past year. Ever since … the hospital. Thanks to an extremely kind nurse who had clearly taken pity on Amy, she'd immersed herself in fiction as a way of escape.

Admittedly, she was getting comfortable in her new life.

The door opened and Amy's gaze instantly swung over to see who it was.

Okay, so maybe she wasn't exactly *comfortable*. She was still rather twitchy, but there was good reason for that. When one was running for their life, hiding out in a small town, and watching over their shoulder every second of every day, one tended to be jumpy.

"That Lynx Caine's somethin' else," the newcomer drawled as he headed toward an empty table on the far side of the room.

Amy preferred Wolfe to Lynx, but she had no idea why that was. Perhaps she'd had more interaction with him. And even that was extremely limited. There was just something about his deep voice, his black hair and green eyes, the scruffy jaw, and the…

Yeah. Okay. So she'd been thinking far too much about Wolfe Caine.

Not knowing what to say to the old man, Amy opted to pretend not to have heard, instead choosing to offer him a beer.

"Yeah, thanks, darlin'. Coors Light if you don't mind."

Amy turned back to the bar to find Reagan grinning as she pulled out a longneck and twisted the top off, passing it over to Amy.

It didn't take a lot of effort to keep the clientele in this place happy. Since there weren't many options for recreational activities in Embers Ridge, someone could stop into Reagan's for a beer or head over to Marla's Bar for something a little stronger, or even a hamburger and fries. Of course, they could stop in at the diner if they wanted down-home comfort food. Anything more than that would require they head out of town a good twenty miles to the nearest chain restaurant.

That was one of the many reasons Amy liked Embers Ridge. It was small, the pace was relatively slow, and the people were nice, if not a little nosey. The curiosity was the hardest part to deal with, but so far Amy had managed to evade most of the questions by pretending to be shy.

Since she'd moved into the small farmhouse originally owned by one of the town's founding families, Amy did tend to get a lot of questions. Most of them she couldn't answer since the only thing she knew about the previous owner was that the woman had gotten married and decided to sell the place. With just enough cash to get her settled in, Amy had forked it over. The process had been quick and easy, which was what she'd been aiming for.

"Get these boys some beers," an older man hollered as he stepped into the bar, holding the door open.

Amy turned in time to see Wolfe and Lynx being hustled in by another group of guys.

Her gaze instantly zeroed in on Wolfe. There was something about the man that drew her attention. Could've been the way he carried himself with more masculine grace than a big man like him should possess. Whatever it was, Amy found it difficult *not* to stare like a schoolgirl with a crush.

"Sheriff's on his way," the old man noted.

Shit.

The last person Amy wanted to come face-to-face with was the sheriff. She'd managed to stay off his radar thus far; she didn't see any reason to tempt fate.

Then again, if she really wanted to play it safe, perhaps she should rethink working at Reagan's on Friday nights.

RHYS TREVINO KNEW the call was coming in before he actually received it.

It was Friday night, after all.

But just like the sun rising in the east and setting in the west, they could always depend on some good Samaritan calling in to let the Lee County Sheriff's Department know that the Caine cousins were throwing down outside Reagan's. Never failed.

After responding to dispatch, letting them know he was in the vicinity and that he'd take care of the disturbance at Reagan's, Rhys turned his truck around and put his foot on the gas.

He knew what he would find when he arrived. It wouldn't be an emergency, unless one of the Caine cousins had gone off the rails. So far, their weekly brawls had yet to send anyone to the hospital. One of these days some smart-mouthed cowboy was going to push Lynx too far though. Rhys figured it was only a matter of time.

And now it was time to check it out.

He only hoped they'd wrapped it all up, because the last time he'd had to intervene, he'd sported a black eye for a fucking week.

Afterwards, he would stop for a cup of coffee, because if this call was anything to go by, tonight was going to be a long one.

Fifteen minutes later, Rhys pulled up to the bar. All looked quiet from the parking lot. Since he knew Reagan—the woman was his sister, after all—there was no way they'd been throwing down in the bar, so it appeared as though someone had wrangled all the misfits back inside.

Thank God for small miracles.

Getting out of his truck, Rhys grabbed his hat and shoved it on his head, then slammed the door shut and took a quick look around.

Other than the ruckus coming from inside the bar, all was quiet. The stars seemed extra bright tonight, too. Sighing, he resigned himself to dealing with these boys for what he hoped was the only time tonight.

When he stepped inside, his gaze instantly traveled through the room, categorizing all that was going on. The Caine cousins were seated at the bar, Reagan was telling one of her many stories, two younger guys were back near the pool table, another couple were playing darts. There were several tables off to the right that were still empty while the jukebox played an old Garth Brooks song.

His eyes stopped on the pretty blonde wiping down one of the tables.

Technically, he didn't think Amy Smith was a true blonde, nor did he think the color was a fashion statement. Her dark eyebrows and dark roots said the carpet probably didn't match the drapes. Not that he knew firsthand. In fact, Rhys didn't know much about the newcomer yet. Well, nothing more than the fact that she'd come to town three months ago and quickly gotten settled into McKenzie Catlay's old house after paying cash for the place. She started working at the diner a couple of weeks after that, and she'd been waitressing at Reagan's for the past month. Yet no one knew much of anything about her. Despite the fact she spent her time in the heart of town, mingling with customers, the woman did a damn good job of keeping to herself.

He'd been tempted to look into her, but even a small-town cowboy like himself could tell that Smith was likely not her real name, and if he did a search, he'd probably come up with thousands in the state of Texas alone.

"Hey, Sheriff! What brings you down here tonight?" Reagan crooned from behind the bar.

Rhys turned toward his sister and the two men holding down the barstools nearby. "Just checkin' on a disturbance call."

He noticed the Caine cousins didn't bother to turn around.

"You wouldn't know anything 'bout that, would you, Wolfe?"

Rhys sidled up to the bar beside the cousin closest to him.

"Nope," Wolfe muttered. "Sure wouldn't."

"So, the bleedin' knuckles…" Rhys nodded toward the hand currently wrapped around the beer bottle in front of Wolfe.

"Work."

"Right." It wasn't farfetched, although Rhys knew it for the lie it was. Since Wolfe and his cousin were in the furniture business, scarred hands were par for the course. However, this looked fresh, never mind the gravel dust on their jeans and hats.

"You wanna beer, Sheriff?" Reagan offered, smiling.

Rhys cocked an eyebrow. Reagan knew he was on duty, but it never failed; she always offered and he always refused. "I'll take a Coke."

"Comin' right up."

Turning around, Rhys leaned against the bar, still standing beside Wolfe.

"Who started it?" Rhys asked, keeping his voice low enough no one other than Wolfe could hear.

"Coupla dumb asses," Wolfe said. "They didn't come back inside. If you hurry, you could probably get 'em for a DUI."

Tempting. Especially if it meant keeping the residents of his small town safe. However, he knew Wolfe was trying to get him out of there.

"No one hurt?" Rhys turned and faced Wolfe, studying the man's profile.

Rhys and Wolfe were never what people would consider friends. Not in their small town, anyway. Although Rhys was accepted by the Caine cousins as good people and vice versa, they didn't run in the same circles. Being that Rhys's family was a longtime rival of the Caines, it would've been frowned upon. Didn't mean they weren't civil to one another though. And since they'd grown up here, gone to the same schools, Rhys knew everything there was to know about them.

Reagan passed over the Coke and Rhys tipped his hat. Turning back around, he caught sight of Amy moving toward the back. There was something about that woman. Rhys couldn't quite put his finger on what it was. It could've been the fact she always seemed to be looking over her shoulder, or even as simple as his underlying attraction to her. Whatever it was, Rhys had decided a couple of weeks ago that he'd see how things went before he approached her.

"She doin' okay in here?" Rhys asked Wolfe, again, keeping his voice low.

Wolfe shifted, his arm brushing Rhys's when he did.

Damn, the man smelled good. Always. It was a combination of cologne and the sexy scent of an alpha male, Rhys had determined.

"From what I can tell, yeah," Wolfe confirmed. "She's a little jittery."

Yeah, Rhys had noticed that, too. Whenever the door opened, she was always the first one looking. And it wasn't a casual move, either. It was as though the cute little waitress was expecting trouble to waltz right in through the double doors.

She must've sensed they were talking about her because Amy's attention turned to them. When Rhys met and held her gaze for a second, the woman quickly looked away.

Truth was, Rhys was curious about her and not necessarily in a law enforcement capacity. The only information he'd been able to get had come from his sister. According to Reagan, Amy was twenty-six, single, and not at all interested in sharing details about herself. From what Rhys could tell, Reagan knew Amy Smith better than anyone else in town.

Still, Rhys wanted to get to know her better.

It'd been a long damn time since he'd met a woman who captured his interest. Hell, it'd been a long damn time since *anyone* had captured his interest.

"Don't even think about it, Sheriff," Wolfe grumbled.

Rhys stood tall and turned to Wolfe. He held the man's stare, daring him to finish the threat. He knew Wolfe was warning him off the woman, and he even knew why.

"Jealous?" Rhys didn't look away. Wolfe knew exactly what Rhys was talking about and it only had a tiny bit to do with the cute little waitress.

A smirk curled the corner of Wolfe's mouth. "She's too sweet for your games."

"Games?" They both knew that Wolfe was referring to the fact that Rhys was bisexual, and he didn't necessarily keep his interactions separate. A man, a woman, both at the same time, he was open to all possibilities. And no, he didn't air his personal business around town, but word got around. Still, Rhys wanted the man to say it out loud.

Then again, Rhys wasn't sure he could handle it if he did. After all, their families might've been at odds, but that didn't mean Rhys felt the same way.

And he damn sure didn't feel that way about Wolfe Caine.

"Don't play dumb," Wolfe growled. "It's not becoming."

Rhys cocked his head, studying the man for a second.

Figuring now was not the time and here was definitely not the place to hash this out with Wolfe, Rhys nodded, then set his empty glass on the bar, glancing over at Reagan.

"If you have any more trouble, holler."

"Will do, *Sheriff*," she answered sweetly.

Rhys turned and met Amy's curious gaze once more. With a quick tip of his hat, he kept his expression masked, not wanting to send the woman running.

Wolfe was right about one thing. She was definitely jumpy.

Rhys was certainly curious as to what or who might've caused it.

One day he hoped to find out.

2

"ARE THEY BROTHERS?"

"No. Cousins. Their dads are brothers."

"And they grew up together?"

"Yup."

"Who's the oldest?"

"Wolfe. By almost two years."

"Who named them? And why're they named after animals?"

Honest to God, Amy had heard a million different variations of this very same conversation ever since she started waitressing here at the small diner just two short months ago. At least once a shift, someone started talking about the two men who'd clearly caught and held the attention of every female in a twenty-mile radius. And yes, women were always the culprits. They could be a gossipy bunch, no doubt about it.

"What do they do for a living?"

"They make furniture. Have an office building and everything."

"Oh. They own the Cedar Door?"

Yep, they did.

And the woman was right, along with the store not far from Main Street, they also had an office, although calling it that was probably a little more than it deserved. Based on the details Amy had been privy to, it was nothing more than a massive metal building with a few rooms inside that they used more for a workshop than anything.

Personally, Amy didn't know Wolfe or Lynx because she was relatively new in town, but that didn't mean she hadn't met them. Not only had she waited on them at Reagan's, they were also regulars at the diner, coming in almost every morning for a cup of coffee and the house special—two eggs, two slices of bacon, two pancakes each. Every day, they ordered the same thing. Every day, they left a more-than-generous tip. And every day, they made her wonder if she should pick up and move on before they figured out that she was hiding out in their backwoods little town.

"Is it true that they"—Tank Top With Pearls Chick lowered her voice a little—"share their women?"

Boobs nodded excitedly. "Oh, they do. They definitely do. They've been that way since they were young."

Yep, another rumor hot off the gossip mill press. As to its validity, Amy didn't know that, either.

"How young?"

Boobs shrugged. "I don't know. Teenagers, probably." The woman obviously didn't get all the details, but that didn't stop her from assuming, apparently.

However, that was how Amy had come to understand it, too. At least, according to the rumor mill, which she happened to be quite knowledgeable about since no one seemed to care that she was walking around, pouring coffee, taking and delivering orders. They treated her as though she didn't have ears most of the time, which worked well for her. It helped to pass the time.

Truth was, Amy didn't know the first non-rumor detail about the Caine cousins, but she was as curious as the next person, she wouldn't lie. When they dropped by, they rarely spoke, and never at length about anything, yet she wouldn't say they were exactly unapproachable. Just quiet.

They had a specific table they sat at, which allowed both of them to keep their eyes on the door. It also prevented anyone from sneaking up behind them. Well, maybe that wasn't the *real* reason they chose to sit there, but it was the reason Amy had made up in her head.

Evidently, she wasn't above making shit up, either.

The two cousins looked remarkably similar, although different at the same time. Both had jet-black hair. Lynx's was more of a Mohawk, while Wolfe sported the shorn sides, but not the spikey thing. Granted, they wore cowboy hats most of the time. And if they didn't have on Stetsons, they were wearing John Deere caps—yes, those were apparently a thing. Both usually had that sexy scruff on their jaws and emerald-green eyes that saw far too much.

For the most part, they seemed friendly, not at all menacing despite the intimidation factor, but Amy had gotten the feeling that they worked hard to pull that off.

"Is it true that they're ridiculously tall? Like six seven or something?"

Amy coughed to cover up a laugh.

"Oh, definitely," Boobs assured Tank Top. "Wolfe definitely is. I think Lynx might be taller."

Amy wondered if this was how fishermen's stories got so warped and twisted. In a minute, she figured the two women would claim the Caine cousins had penises as long and thick as baseball bats.

Amy rolled her eyes as she grabbed a fresh pot of coffee and continued her rounds. Yes, the two men were tall, sure. Above average, definitely. But not record-breaking heights by any means. They were significantly taller than she was. At five five, Amy had to look way up at them. Since they were usually sitting when she was around, that wasn't much of a problem.

"The sheriff does it, too," Boobs noted.

"Does what?" Tank Top questioned.

"Shares his women." The woman's voice lowered slightly.

"Shut up! I heard he was into men."

Boobs offered a one-shoulder shrug.

Amy had no idea where that story had originated, but she'd heard a variation of it as well. Of course, she did her best not to pay attention. What the men in this town did in their spare time was none of her business.

Boobs sipped her coffee. "I don't know anything about that."

"No?" Tank Top's eyes were skeptical. "Wouldn't that be hot?"

Amy put the coffeepot back on the burner, then grabbed a towel to clean the two tables that just cleared out.

"It would." Boobs giggled. "I'd definitely like to watch me some man-on-man action."

Wow. Okay.

"I want to know more about the sharing thing," Tank Top declared.

"No, you wanna know if what they say about Wolfe is true. If his mouth's as dirty as they claim. Or what about Lynx? I hear he's worse—or better, I guess you'd say—than Wolfe."

"I'm not partial," Tank Top said with another giggle. "I'd be interested to find out about the sheriff, too. They say the quiet ones are the dirtiest."

Who said that? Amy had never heard a single person say that before.

Sheesh.

Amy shook her head in disbelief. Every *single*—as in unattached—woman who had walked through those doors wanted to know what the Caine cousins were like in bed. At least one, if not both of them. Hell, one group of women had talked about taking Wolfe *and* Lynx on at once.

"I hear Wolfe likes to watch," Tank Top said.

"And to be watched," Boobs noted. "And I've heard he even watches—"

The bell over the door jingled at the same time Boobs stopped talking. Amy stood up straight, grabbing the two empty glasses from the table, and turned in time to see none other than Wolfe sauntering in the door.

One of the women giggled. It was rather embarrassing for all of womankind.

"Hey, Amy," he greeted as he passed by the counter on the way to his table.

His voice was like dark velvet. Smooth and warm and…

God, he smelled good.

Yeah.

After everything Amy had been through, she should've been completely immune to the seduction of his voice and the sexy scent of him, yet…

She shook off the thought and grabbed two coffee mugs—she knew Lynx would be along any second now—and the pot of coffee, then made her way over to their table. Without making too much eye contact, she poured the black liquid into the cups. "I'll have your food out shortly."

Like clockwork, the bells jingled and in walked Lynx. He tilted his hat in Amy's direction, then headed directly to Wolfe.

And now that they were here, it was time for Amy to fade into the background, or blend in with the wallpaper as was the case here. The Caine cousins might be a hot topic surrounded by a lot of speculation, but Amy had her own secrets to deal with. Ones she had to protect in order to survive. Including her identity.

Otherwise, she was as good as dead.

Shoring up her nerve, Amy returned to the counter and looked for something to do while she waited for their food to be ready. The place was practically empty this morning. It was during times like this that she got fidgety, hating that she could feel the Caine cousins' eyes on her, but she didn't know what they were thinking. It was as though they'd practiced the art of being expressionless. Even their eyes held no secrets. Not that she let herself look for long. She preferred to be invisible and that was an art form in itself.

One she'd mastered and fully intended to keep it that way.

HE KEPT THE car running as he sat in the parking lot of the small diner. From his spot, he could see her, watch her as she moved from one side of the diner to the other, helping customers, smiling even. He knew she couldn't see him. And even if she did glance out the window, even if she could see past the glare of the sun glinting off his windshield, she wouldn't recognize him.

But he recognized her. Even though she'd attempted to lighten her hair, even though she'd lost quite a bit of weight. He *still* recognized her. He would always recognize her.

He had to admit, the new look wasn't a good one for her. She was too fucking skinny and the blond hair did nothing for her. At first, it had pissed him off to see that she'd tried to alter her appearance. Of course, he doubted the weight loss was intentional. That was most likely due to the injuries she'd sustained, the time she'd spent in the hospital, the months she'd spent on the run.

But he still sat there.

He still watched her.

Biding his time.

One day he would make his presence known.

He would finish what he should've finished a long damn time ago.

"WHERE THE FUCK did the weekend go?" Lynx griped when he joined Wolfe at the table.

Wolfe peered at his cousin, trying to decipher his mood.

"Hell if I know," Wolfe replied, although he suspected the question was rhetorical.

Wolfe knew where *his* weekend went. He'd spent most of his time working on a ridiculously oversized twelve-foot dining room table for Mrs. Stephenson. She'd told him there was no rush, but the woman obviously didn't know what that meant. The fact that she'd been dropping by—not an easy feat for a woman who lived thirty minutes away—every day had forced Wolfe to insist she hold off until he was finished. Of course, that had only incentivized her to call at least twice a day to check on his progress. Since they'd lost their office manager two months ago when she decided to up and marry one of the ranch hands out at the Double D, Wolfe had been dealing directly with their customers. Hence the reason he'd finished up the table over the weekend. The only thing left was the chairs and he fully intended to knock those out soon. He got the feeling Mrs. Stephenson's surprise visits and frequent phone calls were getting a little more intimate than they should.

"Amy's an angel," Lynx noted, picking up the coffee cup that was waiting for him.

Wolfe didn't respond, but he did glance over at Amy.

He'd long ago learned to have coffee on hand when Lynx showed up anywhere. Apparently, Amy had figured that out, too. Didn't matter the time of day, although mornings were the most critical. The man would've been better suited with the name Bear, especially on mornings he didn't have his caffeine. "What'd *you* do this weekend?"

Lynx cast a sideways glance at him, then looked around the room as he set his coffee mug on the table. "I had to go see Tammy."

Wolfe put down his cup and turned to his cousin. "And?"

"It's done. I got her to sign the papers."

Shit.

Wolfe sat up straight. "Please tell me she didn't get anything else outta you."

Taking a sip from his mug, Lynx shook his head. "She tried. But I refused this time."

Tammy was Lynx's soon-to-be ex-wife. Their six-month stint at wedded bliss had failed miserably, and it had taken the same amount of time for them to put an end to it. They'd been doing this song and dance for the past four months, and every time they thought Lynx was getting that much closer to finalizing it, Tammy would throw a wrench into the works, insisting that Lynx give her something else. Why Lynx was even entertaining the notion of giving her anything at all was beyond Wolfe.

What Wolfe really didn't understand was how Lynx had hooked up with Tammy in the first place. For most of his life, Lynx had had a major thing for Reagan Trevino. Not that the woman had given him the time of day—not that Wolfe knew of, anyway—but it was obvious the man was into her. Needless to say, they were all stunned when Lynx popped up in town after a weekend hiatus letting everyone know he'd gotten hitched. To a woman no one had even met yet.

"So, it's over?" Wolfe wasn't sure how all that worked, and he hoped like hell he never found out firsthand. If and when he ever got married, it would be the forever kind. Which was part of the reason he was still single at twenty-nine.

"I ran the papers over to my lawyer last night. She's gonna file them this mornin'. Then it's a waitin' game."

A clatter sounded from the kitchen, and Wolfe jerked his head over in time to see Amy startle, her hand covering her heart. The woman was easily spooked, and he couldn't help but wonder why that was.

She seemed to catch herself and quickly reached for a coffeepot, wandering over to their table and topping off their cups, her hands trembling.

Wolfe did his best not to stare at her because he knew it made her nervous. From the very first moment he'd seen her, he recognized the fear in her eyes. The kind that caused her to instinctively back away from strangers—mostly men—although Wolfe wasn't sure she realized she was doing it. She was even doing it now, despite the fact that she was relatively familiar with him and his cousin.

Then again, Wolfe had always been told he made people nervous. He was nothing more than a good ol' boy, living his uncomplicated life on the edge and enjoying every damn second. Sure, he tended to get himself into trouble from time to time, but that was how it worked. And because of his past behavior, his actions had been talked about on more than one occasion.

Of course, there were plenty of rumors about him and his cousin running rampant through this town. No telling what Amy Smith had heard about them. They kept to themselves for the most part. The house Wolfe had built with his own two hands sat on the very outskirts of their small town, secluded on his family's land. If he didn't come into town and you wanted to find him, it would take some effort. But that was the Caine way and always had been.

He was sure Amy had heard plenty of the rumors, probably believed half of them. Hell, *he* sometimes believed half of them although he knew they were mostly fiction.

As he waited for his food, Wolfe allowed himself to watch Amy as she moved around, stopping to hand out checks, grabbing dishes from deserted tables. Honestly, he couldn't quite figure the woman out, and he was typically rather good at it. It was clear to him that she was running from something or someone, yet she came into this diner several times a week to work. She was right there in front of every person in this small town, talking to them, getting to know them. And they were doing the same with her. Embers Ridge was like any small town, full of gossip and conjecture. Not to mention, nosy fucking people. For a woman who had a secret, she hadn't realized that showing up here was a surefire way to out herself.

Or maybe she had and she was merely testing out the theory of hiding in plain sight.

Not that Wolfe should be interested in her secret or even her, for that matter. She seemed far too sweet and innocent for the likes of him. Yet that was exactly how he found himself.

There was something in Amy's eyes that intrigued him, made him want to know more.

"Here you go." Amy's melodic voice brushed every one of his senses, and he looked up as she delivered their breakfast.

"Thank you, sweetheart," Lynx rasped, grinning from ear to ear.

Lynx had been flirting with Amy since the first day they'd seen her in here about three months ago, yet she hadn't once returned his interest. Honestly, it irked the shit out of Wolfe that Lynx did it, but he didn't exactly know why. Since he couldn't explain it, he didn't bother telling Lynx to knock it off. That was the way Lynx was.

"We've got a truck comin' in at nine, Wolfe," Lynx noted.

Wolfe knew that was Lynx's way of telling him to hurry, but he didn't bother heeding his warning. The guy knew not to push him. When that happened, Wolfe tended to do the opposite.

As he ate, Wolfe felt eyes on him. He was used to that. People in this town were nosy as fuck. They didn't have a problem digging into other people's business, Wolfe's included. He was usually good at shrugging it off, but this time he looked up, his eyes scanning the well-lit room, trying to see who was so interested in how he took his eggs.

He met Amy's curious gaze from across the room.

A soft blush crept up her cheeks and she instantly looked away.

Damn, she was pretty. Big brown eyes, pouty pink lips. Her blond hair—darker at the roots—was always pulled back in a ponytail, making her look remarkably young, although he figured her somewhere in her mid-twenties.

He returned his attention to his food, then met Lynx's gaze briefly.

Lynx shook his head slightly, answering Wolfe's silent question. He had asked him to find out more information on Amy. Where she came from, how she ended up here. Basic questions that he wanted to know about anyone who lived here. That was how the Caines operated. They kept an eye on these people. That was the way it went and he couldn't explain why that was, either.

"What's up, sweetheart?" Lynx asked.

Wolfe looked up to see Lynx smirking at two women sitting at a table close to them. Both women were staring, batting their eyelashes. Relatively attractive, Wolfe guessed you could say. Granted, he wasn't all that impressed by the pearls with the tank top, but hey, what did he know about fashion?

Not that it mattered. Neither of them got his dick hard. Probably wouldn't even if they were naked and on their knees in front of him.

It had nothing to do with biology, either. He was capable of getting a hard-on, but the shallow women who solicited him just didn't do it for him anymore. At twenty, he'd been living high on life, fucking half the women over twenty-five in this town. Promiscuous had been his middle name. At one time, he'd ventured down an entirely different road, sharing women with his cousin on occasion, experimenting with men, sometimes hooking up with a man and woman at the same time. However, he'd kept that part of himself locked up tight for years. As he grew up, he'd started to have an issue with casual encounters.

Oh, that hadn't stopped him completely, of course. However, as he neared thirty, it took a little more than a smile and a wink to make his dick stand up and take notice.

That didn't necessarily explain why his body was on high alert when it came to the cute little waitress with the guarded brown eyes.

"Why don't you just offer her the job?" Lynx inquired between bites.

Wolfe snapped his eyes over to Lynx when he realized he'd been staring at Amy again. "Who?"

"Amy," he said softly. "Clearly she's a hard worker and you know we can pay her a hell of a lot more than she's makin' here. How many jobs does she have anyway?"

Only two that he knew of.

Wolfe glanced over to see Amy wiping down the counter for the tenth time.

"Plus, she's bored outta her mind," Lynx added. "We need an office manager."

They did. That was a fact.

"What makes you think she'd even consider it?" Wolfe knew Lynx well enough to know his interest in Amy wasn't merely as an employee. He'd made it abundantly clear that he was hot for her.

Hell, half the single guys in town had shown their interest.

His mind drifted to his conversation with Rhys. The sheriff seemed to have some interest in her as well. For whatever reason, Wolfe wasn't bothered by the idea. Not the way he'd claimed to be, anyway. Then again, Wolfe had some interest in the sheriff. More than he was ever willing to let on.

Lynx shrugged, then signaled Amy over.

Wolfe instantly put down his fork and picked up his coffee. God only knew what was going to come out of his cousin's mouth, and he'd rather not be chewing.

"Can I get you something else?" Amy pulled her pad from her apron pocket.

"Do you like workin' here?" Lynx asked, point-blank as always.

Wolfe peered up at Amy, noticing the way her brown eyes sparkled.

"Uh … yes?" A small frown line formed between her dark eyebrows. "Why?"

"See, we've got a spot open at the Cedar Door. It's an office manager position. Wondered if maybe you'd be interested."

Her confusion turned to wariness. "Why would you think I'm qualified?"

Lynx peered around, then met Amy's gaze head on. "I figure you run this place rather well, probably not a stretch to think you can manage an office."

"How much does it pay?"

Lynx's gaze slammed into Wolfe's. He shrugged. Wolfe would let his cousin figure this one out.

"That's negotiable," Lynx told her. "But if you'd like to stop by the shop, I'd be happy to talk to you more about it."

Amy placed the bill on the table. "I'll … uh … think about it."

That was a lie, Wolfe could tell. Since he was suddenly interested in finding out what this woman seemed to be running from, he decided to help Lynx out. “How about this afternoon? Three o’clock?” He grinned. “Lynx’s not pullin’ your leg, darlin’. We’re looking for someone to manage the office.” Wolfe waved his hand to encompass the diner. “I assure you, it pays a helluva lot better than this place.”

Amy’s eyes locked with his and Wolfe held her stare.

To hell with Lynx interviewing this woman.

Wolfe had every intention of handling Amy Smith himself.

RHYS WALKED INTO the diner as Lynx was walking out. He didn’t think he could’ve timed his arrival better if he’d tried.

When he stepped inside, he found Wolfe sitting at a table, two empty plates in front of him. He was staring at his cell phone with a frown on his face.

Figuring luck was on his side, Rhys nodded at Amy, then took one of the empty seats near Wolfe.

“Abandoned so early in the mornin’?” he said by way of greeting.

Wolfe spared him a brief look but then turned his attention back to his phone. “What do you want, Sheriff?”

You. Rhys refrained from admitting that though.

For the better part of the weekend, Rhys had given thought to Wolfe’s warning on Friday night. The man had referred to Rhys’s sexual proclivities as a game. He had to wonder just how much thought Wolfe had given to him previously. He’d wondered about it so much he found himself thinking about what it would take to seduce the sexy cowboy.

Having known Wolfe a long time, Rhys was convinced the man was as interested in men as he was in women. Sure, Wolfe had done a relatively decent job of keeping his preferences under wraps, but still, people talked. He'd heard a few things over the years that made him think there could be a chance to get the cowboy with the scarred knuckles and raspy voice right where he wanted him. Not to mention, Rhys had seen the way Wolfe looked at him. It was the same way Wolfe looked at pancakes and bacon.

Then, while Rhys had been fantasizing about Wolfe, his mind had conjured up some pretty hot images of a sweet little…

"Can I get you something, Sheriff?" Amy offered, her voice soft as she moved to stand beside him.

Yeah. *Her.*

Rhys's fantasies were never simple. They involved some smoking-hot interactions with the sexy cowboy and the cute little waitress. Of course, he hadn't even realized how interested he was until last Friday night, but hey, he wasn't going to fight it.

"The special would be great," he said, keeping his expression masked. "And a cup of coffee, if you don't mind."

Amy didn't meet his eyes, and a quick nod was all he received before she darted back behind the counter. Unable to help himself, Rhys stared after her. The way she filled out those jeans should've been a crime.

A rough growl drew his attention back to Wolfe. He turned his head and lifted his eyebrow, waiting for the man to offer up another warning. Instead, he found Wolfe staring back at him with what looked a hell of a lot like lust in his eyes.

Based on that look, Rhys didn't think he was the only one who'd imagined the three of them rolling around in Rhys's big bed.

For all the time he'd known Wolfe, he'd never witnessed anything to confirm that the man did swing both ways. Sure, there'd been some rumors over the years about the Caine cousins. They were known for their wild ways, which, if the stories were true, had included some rather interesting exploits.

Then again, most people didn't share those idiosyncrasies with the world. Especially not in a small town like theirs. A man could be persecuted for his desires in a town like Embers Ridge. Rhys knew firsthand. The fact that he was bisexual was something he had to keep on the down low. Not that he ignored his desires, but he was careful about who he was with.

Sure, the world was changing. People's acceptance was changing. Hell, not too long ago, the town had been overwhelmed by some untraditional relationships when some of Wolfe's family had opted to have a family reunion over at Dead Heat Ranch. From what Rhys had seen, there were some successful polyamorous relationships going on in that family. It gave a guy hope, sure.

Not that Rhys would ever be able to go public with a relationship of that nature. Nor did he expect to end up in one. However, there was one man he'd wanted for longer than he could remember. And he knew that Wolfe was into sharing. He wasn't entirely certain the man was as open to sharing the way Rhys had in mind, but hey, it was a nice fantasy.

And there was only one way to find out.

"Did you need somethin'? Or were you offerin' to pay for my breakfast?"

Rhys grinned. "I wanted to see if we could meet up later. I go on shift at three. Thought I'd stop by the shop once I head out for a bit."

Curiosity backlit Wolfe's emerald-green eyes. "What about?"

Giving a brief shake of his head, Rhys said, "Can't talk about it here."

He actually did have something he wanted to talk to Wolfe about. It concerned the woman he'd imagined walking naked across his bedroom toward him, in fact. Nevertheless, his interest in her wasn't limited to getting her naked and beneath him. That was something entirely separate. What he wanted to talk to Wolfe about was more along the lines of Amy Smith's history and her need to keep a safe distance between herself and everyone around her.

The truth was, Rhys was concerned for her well-being. He'd become rather adept at reading people. More importantly, helping people. If he was right, Amy Smith was in desperate need of some help. Maybe a friend or two.

However, Rhys wasn't about to tell Wolfe that he was looking into Amy Smith's history. Not here, anyway.

"You gonna be around?"

A short nod was Wolfe's answer as he pulled out two twenties and tossed them on the table alongside the other one lying there. "See you around, Sheriff."

Leaning back in his chair, Rhys watched Wolfe saunter out of the building. He didn't take his eyes off the man until he'd climbed into his big black Silverado, either.

One of these days…

3

AMY HAD ABSOLUTELY no idea why she'd come here in the first place. The second Lynx had made the job offer, she'd been suspicious.

That didn't mean she wasn't interested, just that she knew she needed to be cautious. Staying off the radar was important, and she'd be better off working at the diner and at Reagan's, even if she wasn't getting paid nearly enough. Being so visible wasn't exactly the best way to hide out, but so far, it seemed to be working. People saw her, which made them believe they knew her, which, in turn, had caused some of the curiosity to die down. Oh, sure, they were still asking questions, but people didn't seem to mind when she brushed them off with a smile. At least she didn't think they minded.

Unfortunately, the lure of more money was more than she could refuse. The house had drained every penny she had. The money she'd received when her parents died had been left alone in an account for the past nine years drawing a little bit of interest. It had been a whole lot more than she'd ever anticipated; still, she hadn't expected it to go far. Fortunately for her, the houses were relatively cheap out in this part of the country. After buying her used Nissan, a few pairs of clothes, and the house, Amy had no choice but to work in order to eat. Sadly, one job didn't cut it, though, so she was wearing herself thin at the bar and at the diner.

So, she'd spent the majority of her morning thinking about it, tossing around the idea of being an office manager. How hard could that be?

No, she didn't have any experience, but she hadn't had any experience waitressing when she applied for those jobs, either. She was confident that it was something she could learn over time.

"You gonna come in?"

Amy spun on her boot heel at the deep, rumbling voice. She found Wolfe leaning one shoulder against the doorjamb, his grin wide, straight white teeth flashing. He'd obviously been watching her pace the parking lot.

"I'm thinking about it," she admitted, a small smile tilting her lips.

She wasn't quite sure what it was about Wolfe, but Amy found herself relatively comfortable in his presence. He definitely was the type of guy you didn't want to mess with, but Amy didn't feel threatened by him. Perhaps it was his laid-back nature, or the protective gleam in his pretty green eyes. Whatever it was, she found she didn't fear him. Not physically anyway, even though by anyone's standards, he was the kind of man you would walk away from, not toward, if you encountered him in a dark alley. His sheer size alone overwhelmed everyone and everything else around.

Word around town was the Caines were a bunch of badasses. From what she could tell, people didn't mess with them unless they were drunk or stupid. She'd witnessed some of both working at Reagan's.

Wolfe gave her a quick nod. "Well, when you're ready…"

She watched as he disappeared back inside, his butt looking damn fine in those jeans.

Damn it.

She wasn't supposed to look at his butt.

Taking a deep breath, Amy debated on whether she should hop back in her car and go home or suck it up and go inside. Since her car didn't have any air conditioning and it was at least a hundred degrees in the shade, she figured the interior of the big warehouse was probably significantly cooler than the parking lot.

She hoped.

"How hard could it be?" she mumbled to herself as she made the trek to the door.

When she stepped inside, she was instantly assaulted by the sweet smell of sawdust. Not surprising, considering it was everywhere.

The metal building was even bigger than it looked from the outside. Probably a couple thousand square feet on the main floor with three-story-tall ceilings, at least. It would probably hold two of her houses inside just on the ground floor. Maybe three.

Laid out on the concrete slab before her were various pieces of furniture all in different stages of assembly. Tables of all shapes and sizes, various styles of chairs, dressers, media stands, even mirrors. The far end of the warehouse held planks of wood standing on their ends against the walls and shelves full of other items—paint cans, brushes, a wide assortment of tools. It was just as she'd expect a furniture warehouse to look. Not that she'd ever given it much thought, honestly.

"Can I get you somethin' to drink?" Wolfe offered.

Amy shook her head. "I'm good. Thank you."

He watched her for a second and she felt the urge to smooth down her dress. It was the only one she owned, but she'd figured she needed to wear something other than the jeans and T-shirts that had become her go-to wardrobe these days. This was, after all, a job interview.

At least she thought it was.

"Come on into the office." Wolfe nodded his head toward a metal staircase that led to the second floor.

Amy followed, taking it all in.

The second floor extended over one end of the warehouse with a metal railing that allowed one to see everything down below. Three doors lined the narrow walkway. Nothing fancy, but she doubted they needed to be. Since their main focus was building furniture, she didn't figure they had much need for office space.

Wolfe stopped at the door closest to them and pushed it open, then stepped back and waited for her to enter.

Keeping her eyes down, she quickly moved past him. His sheer size had her sucking in a breath, but she fought back the fear that tried to take hold. Wolfe Caine wasn't going to hurt her. She knew that much.

Then again, she'd thought the same thing about…

"So, what do you think?"

Amy lifted her gaze to his face. "About?"

"The warehouse?"

"It's ... uh ... big?"

Wolfe grinned and the smile changed his features from handsome to devastatingly attractive.

No wonder all the women in town talked about him.

Admittedly, Amy didn't have much interaction with him, but that was by choice. Although she saw him at the bar and at the diner, she'd done her best to keep her distance. Befriending people in this town would only cause more problems. Didn't matter that there were some days she'd give just about anything to have at least one friend.

Realizing she looked like an idiot staring back at him, Amy glanced around the room. "What does the job entail?"

Wolfe leaned back in his chair and the creak of the leather caused Amy to look at him again.

"A little this, a little that." He steepled his hands and set them on his flat stomach. "But mostly, it requires you to answer the phone, take orders, call the customers when there are questions. Maybe some light accounting work to start off. Every now and again, my old man might need help over at the store."

Amy nodded. That didn't sound too difficult. Well, except for the accounting part. She didn't have the first clue about that, but again, she was a quick learner.

"In the summer we work from six to three with an hour lunch. Monday through Friday."

That meant she would have to quit the job at the diner, but she could continue to work at Reagan's.

"Do you have any experience?"

She should've known he'd ask that question. Although Amy had considered lying to him, she knew he'd figure it out soon enough if he did hire her. "No, I don't." She bit her tongue to keep from telling him that the two jobs she now held were the first time she'd worked in her life.

Wolfe nodded but didn't say anything.

Amy had to chew on the inside of her cheek to keep from rambling. Wolfe made her nervous, but not the panicky kind. There was something in the way that he looked at her. Like a man who liked what he saw but wasn't exactly sure what to make of her yet. It made her want to tell him things, to assure him she was responsible and could be trusted.

When he leaned forward, Amy's gaze slammed into him. The sudden movement made her jump, and she realized there was no way to hide the reaction, so she kept watching him, praying he wouldn't ask her why she was so twitchy. It'd been a year since the attack that had nearly taken her life, but Amy still remembered it like it was yesterday.

Wolfe's tone was soothing when he spoke again, the deep rumble of his voice reassuring. "The job's yours if you want it. You can start whenever you're ready, but the sooner the better."

"And the pay?" That was what it would all boil down to.

"We'll start you out at twenty dollars an hour if that's good for you."

Twenty dollars an hour? Wow. She wasn't expecting more than thirteen or fourteen. And that had been more like wishful thinking on her part. She didn't even know what the going rate for an office manager was.

Nodding her head, she tried to calm the pounding of her heart. "I'll … uh … need to give notice at the diner."

Wolfe nodded, then pulled open a drawer.

Amy's eyes flew to his hand, watching intently.

He pulled out a packet of paper and slid it over.

"I'll need you to fill out the paperwork."

Amy's palms started to sweat. This was the part she was dreading. She'd managed to convince Reagan to pay her cash. She'd agreed since most of Amy's earnings were from tips, anyway. The diner had been a little more difficult, but they'd finally agreed, with the warning that if she stayed for more than a couple of months, she would have to go on the payroll. The day Amy had walked in, the place had been in chaos, their last waitress having bolted after a heated argument with the cook. Luck had been on her side that day.

It wasn't that she didn't have the necessary documents for employment. She had a birth certificate and a driver's license. The birth certificate had been in a safety deposit box, which had allowed her to get another driver's license *after*…

"That gonna be a problem?" Wolfe's tone didn't change.

"No," she lied, wringing her hands together in her lap. "Can I fill it out at home?"

"Of course."

When Wolfe didn't say anything more, Amy got to her feet, smoothing her dress down and picking up the papers.

Ever the gentleman, Wolfe moved to the door and opened it for her.

This time, when Amy passed him, she breathed in deeply. He smelled like sawdust and something spicy. It was a smell she could get used to.

Not that she would.

"Just let me know when you wanna start," Wolfe said as he followed her back down the stairs.

"I … uh … will." She didn't look back at him, instead keeping her attention on the door.

She thought she was home free when another looming presence filled the space.

Sheriff Trevino.

She fought the urge to look at Wolfe, to question whether this was a setup.

The sheriff's deep blue gaze swerved to her, following as she traipsed down the stairs. If she wasn't mistaken, he was checking out her legs.

She was okay with that.

Well, more okay than if he'd come here to corner her.

Deep breath.

Amy continued toward the door, half expecting the sheriff to lunge for her.

He didn't.

In fact, he didn't move, but he did remove his hat and offer a smile.

The relief that hit her was nearly enough to take her out at the knees.

Fortunately, she managed to keep the starch in her legs as she marched right for the door.

And out into the blistering Texas sunshine.

WOLFE WATCHED AS Amy slipped past Rhys. Her back ramrod straight, shoulders tensed, chin tilted in a slightly defiant manner. She seemed to keep as much space between her and the sheriff as the doorway would allow. All the while, Rhys kept his eyes on her. Wolfe saw the man's interest, knew what he was thinking.

It should've bothered him, but it didn't. He wasn't quite sure why that was, because his own interest in Amy had come to a head when he'd been sitting just a few feet away from her in his office. The dress she wore was sexier than should've been allowed. Cream-colored lace over a cream-colored fabric that hung a little loose on her thin body. It showed off her tanned legs and arms and had him wondering whether or not she had any tan lines. That combined with a pair of boots had damn near made his mouth water when he'd watched her pacing the parking lot earlier.

When she'd finally appeared inside the warehouse, Wolfe had seen the hesitation in her dark espresso eyes. The woman seemed to always be taking in her surroundings, scanning every corner of the room more than once. Even when they'd been in his office, her gaze never stayed put, straying to the door at least a dozen times.

And holy shit, had she smelled good. Something sweet had wafted by him when she stepped into the small office, and he had inhaled deeply—twice—trying to make out what it was. Honeysuckle had been his best guess, but what did he know?

Although mixing business with pleasure was never a good idea, Wolfe couldn't deny the way his body reacted to her. Hell, more than once while they'd been in that small office, he'd thought about sitting her atop his desk and sliding his hand beneath that short dress while his mouth followed close behind.

He was a dog, no doubt about it.

Not that he'd let her know that. He figured sharing with her all the dirty things he wanted to do to her was a surefire way to have her running for the hills. He'd deal with that when the time came. *If.* He meant *if*, not when. Damn.

But right now he had a different issue to deal with.

"Twice in one day," Wolfe grumbled. "Either you've developed a crush on me or whatever's on your mind must really be important."

Wolfe preferred the former.

Admittedly, he'd had a few fantasies that included the sexy sheriff and the sweet girl who'd just slipped out the door. They usually involved the three of them naked and his hands roaming all over both of them.

Rhys moved into the warehouse, his attention drifting out the door momentarily before he turned toward Wolfe. He raised his dark eyebrows in question and Wolfe knew what he was wondering. However, he'd never been the kind to give up information without a little interrogation.

So he waited.

And waited.

After several painfully tense seconds, Wolfe finally sighed and relented. "She's gonna work for us."

"Really?"

Wolfe nodded but didn't elaborate.

"New office manager?"

"Yep."

"She have experience with that?"

"Nope." Wolfe frowned. "You the office police now? What's with the twenty questions, Sheriff?"

Rhys moved closer, placing his hat back on his head, the move catching Wolfe's attention. He let his gaze stray over the man's lean form. Dark blue Wranglers encased his muscular thighs and a bright white button-down covered his well-built chest. The sleeves were rolled up to show off his tanned forearms.

Wolfe couldn't deny the attraction he felt for the man. He was solidly built and carried himself with an air of authority that should've irked the shit out of Wolfe, but it didn't. There was something about Rhys Trevino that made Wolfe want to strip him slowly and see how quickly he could get the man to unravel.

He got the feeling it wouldn't be all that easy.

Good thing Wolfe was up for a challenge.

"You get any information on her?" Rhys questioned.

Lifting his gaze higher, Wolfe studied the sheriff's face. He'd shaved that morning, obviously. His angular jaw was still smooth, his face expressionless.

"No," he said bluntly.

He wanted to know what the man's angle was. His curiosity wasn't completely out of character. Rhys Trevino was the sheriff of their small county. He'd been elected by an overwhelming majority and he was good at what he did. Mainly because he paid attention, so it only made sense that he was taking an interest in Amy. However, Wolfe wasn't entirely convinced that it was for the good of the community. It seemed more personal than that. Much more personal.

"She didn't fill out an application?"

Wolfe shook his head, continuing to watch Rhys. "Why so concerned?"

That question seemed to shock Rhys, but he merely shrugged as he glanced around the warehouse. It was obvious the man was trying to pretend he didn't really care when it was obvious he did.

"I'm not concerned. More like worried."

"And you're worried about her why?" Wolfe let his confusion ring in his tone.

"I think she's runnin' from somethin'."

The full impact of Rhys's midnight-blue stare hit Wolfe head on. He had to admit, the man could be intimidating when he wanted to be. Between the badge and gun and the intense look in his eyes, Rhys Trevino was a sight to take in. Wolfe would even go so far as to say that a lesser man would probably back away from the sheriff if he came up against him. Not that Wolfe was intimidated. He had at least two inches and a good thirty pounds of solid muscle on the guy.

Although Wolfe rarely entertained the idea of being with a man these days, he couldn't deny he'd had some lascivious thoughts where the sheriff was concerned. Wolfe had experimented in his youth. His sexual desires were intense, and he'd been curious, seeking whatever it took to sate his powerful urges. His penchant for the ladies wasn't due to some underlying denial though, so his interest in men confused him at times. At one point, he'd dubbed himself an equal opportunity lover. It suited him.

"Because I can," Rhys said and his tone resonated with truth. "She's new in town, keeps to herself more than most, and if I'm not mistaken, she's hidin' out here. Yet she's comfortable enough to work at the diner, where anyone and everyone can see her."

"Maybe she just needs money." Since she needed electricity and food, maybe it was the lesser of two evils.

"If she's runnin' from somethin', I'd like to know how to help her."

"Well, she ain't tellin' me nothin'."

"Not yet."

"Not ever," Wolfe countered. "A woman like that ain't gonna spill her guts unless she wants to." Hell, he figured it would be easier to wrestle a two-thousand-pound bull with his bare hands than to get that woman to talk.

Rhys moved over to the table Wolfe had just finished. He ran his hand over the smooth, varnished top, and an image of Rhys bent over that table while Wolfe fucked him from behind nearly blinded him.

Son of a bitch.

He was going to have to get laid soon. These damn fantasies were getting ridiculous.

"Why'd you offer her a job?"

Wolfe sighed. "No ulterior motive here, Sheriff. And technically, Lynx's the one who offered her a job. I just interviewed her."

"I talked to Donna," Rhys explained, referring to the diner's owner. "She said Amy didn't share a lot of information when she applied for the job there."

Wolfe didn't figure she had. "Maybe she's a private person."

"So private she insisted on being paid in cash?"

Okay, so maybe more like paranoid. Wolfe didn't know. "I'm sure she has her reasons."

"Or she's hidin'," Rhys reiterated.

Yeah. That, too. Wolfe put the lid on a can of stain. "Look, Trevino, I don't know what you want from me. I hired her."

"So you can keep an eye on her."

Wolfe's head snapped around and he glared at the sheriff.

"Don't bother denyin' it, Caine. I know you've got a protective streak."

Maybe that was true, but Wolfe wasn't going to let the sheriff rile him. "I'm not takin' in strays, Sheriff."

"No?"

Wolfe was tired of this conversation already. "I've got shit to do, Rhys. If you don't mind…"

Their eyes remained locked for a few seconds more than Wolfe was comfortable with, then Rhys turned and headed for the door.

Wolfe stared after him until he heard the man's truck leaving the parking lot. He'd just turned back to cleaning up his mess when Lynx stormed into the room.

"Son of a bitch!"

"What's the matter with you?"

"Tammy stole my goddamn truck."

Wolfe processed the words, and when they sank in, he roared a laugh. That woman was something else. Not only was she vindictive, she was also batshit crazy. Which made her double trouble. Oftentimes, Wolfe wondered what the hell Lynx had seen in her, anyway, never mind why the hell he'd been inclined to marry the looney bitch. Well, other than the fact the crazy woman had claimed to be pregnant. People could say whatever they wanted about Lynx, but he was a stand-up guy.

Granted, their marriage hadn't lasted the better part of a year, but according to his cousin, that was twice as long as it should've lasted.

"Rhys just left," Wolfe noted when he stopped laughing. "Want me to call him back here?"

Lynx shot a death glare his way, then stormed up the stairs, leaving Wolfe fighting the urge to laugh again.

When the office door slammed, Wolfe lost the battle.

RHYS PULLED OUT of the lot and onto the main road through town. Four minutes later, he took a left turn and headed to the oversized five-bedroom farmhouse he'd grown up in. It was Monday, which meant Rhys was going to check on his grandfather, make sure all was well. It was the only time Rhys could get alone with the man. If he stopped by on the weekend, there was generally tons of family hanging around. Aunts, uncles, cousins all there to spend time with the patriarch of the family.

The long dirt road leading up to the house had seen better days. He blamed his younger cousins for that. At sixteen, kids in this town seemed to think that driving through the mud was a rite of passage. Rhys merely wished they'd find somewhere other than Pawpaw's house to do their thing.

After parking his truck in the ruts in front of the house, Rhys climbed out, looked around. Someone needed to come out and mow the front yard. He'd have to remember to call the brats who'd made the mud hole, have them come over and put their restless energy to good use.

"Boy?"

"I'm here, Pawpaw," Rhys greeted, his boots echoing on the rotted wood porch.

Grabbing the screen door handle, he pulled it open. He found his grandfather sitting in his favorite chair—the one that Rhys's grandmother had sat in when she was alive—beside the picture window that overlooked the driveway and the big oak tree in front of the house. All the lights in the house were off, the sun shining through the window and highlighting the lingering smoke and dust motes. It seemed the air conditioner was working, despite the fact the old man kept the front door open.

Victor Trevino looked old, tired. Then again, he'd looked that way for the past two decades. He was a two-pack-a-day smoker who drank Schlitz from morning till night, and Rhys figured the old man's permanent scowl had something to do with too much nicotine and far too much beer.

"How're you doin'?" Rhys asked, leaning against the wall. He knew better than to make himself comfortable. These days, Vic preferred to be alone most of the time. He said it was enough that Rhys's mother still insisted on living with him despite the fact Rhys's old man had kicked the bucket.

Having raised three boys, Vic liked to say Cheryl Trevino was the daughter he'd never wanted. Although the old man tried to pretend he didn't like her, Rhys knew he appreciated her help. She'd put up with a lot of shit over the years, all in the name of family. Her own parents had disowned her when she up and married William Trevino, claiming the guy wasn't good enough for her. They'd probably been right, but she'd never strayed.

Although her life would be significantly less stressful if she lived on her own, she stayed with Vic to help out around the house, plus to keep the vultures that were his family from stealing every damn thing the man owned. Somehow, they managed to make it work between them. But when she was at work, Vic wanted a little peace and quiet, or so he said.

"I'm a grumpy old man. How d'you think I'm doin'?" The cough that followed was a testament to all those damn cigarettes.

"Ornery as ever," Rhys noted. "Good to see some things never change."

Vic spared him a quick glance, then looked out the window again. "You ain't found you some sweet girl who'll put up with that smart mouth yet?"

Rhys smirked. "Not yet, Pawpaw." *No sexy cowboy, either.*

Not that he'd mention that part. The one time his grandfather had heard that Rhys had been with a man, the guy had stopped talking to him for a month. Rhys was merely grateful the guy hadn't disowned him.

"Well, do us all a favor and find one, would ya? It ain't natural for a boy your age to be single."

He was thirty-four, but to hear his grandfather say it made Rhys feel a hell of a lot older than that.

"Probably not," Rhys said in an effort to appease the old man. "You or Momma need anything?"

"The dishwasher's actin' up again," Vic informed him, waving him off with gnarled fingers clutching the butt of a cigarette.

"Well, that's because it's twenty years old. You know, they make 'em real nice these days."

"Heh. Ain't forkin' out no more money for shit like that. Your momma's the only one who complains. Far as I'm concerned, God gave her hands. She can put 'em to good use."

Rhys glanced toward the kitchen, rolling his eyes as he did. Ornery was an understatement when it came to his grandfather. The man was downright mean.

Pushing off the wall, Rhys glanced back at Vic. "All right. I'll give it a look, then I'm headin' back to the office. Sure you don't need anything?"

Vic shook his head but didn't look at Rhys.

As much as Rhys loved the old fart, Monday afternoons certainly weren't the highlight of his week.

Two hours later, sitting at the desk in his office, Rhys propped his booted feet up on the desk and waited for the newest arrival to make his way down the hall. He'd heard Lynx Caine raising hell the second the man walked into the building five minutes ago.

Not that Rhys wondered what the man wanted. The grapevine had already delivered the news to every-damn-body that Lynx's crazy soon-to-be ex-wife had stolen his truck right out of his driveway.

"Whose dick do I have to suck to get shit done around here?" Lynx bellowed.

Dropping his feet to the floor, Rhys wiped the grin off his face and met the irate expression of their most recent crime victim. Not that Lynx Caine was a victim. The rumor was that he'd been banging some girl on his lunch break and Tammy—not-so-lovingly nicknamed Lynx's Stalker by the folks in town—had busted him.

Not that Rhys was defending the crazy bitch. The fact that Tammy had moved out of his county didn't hurt his feelings none.

"What the fuck, Trevino?" Lynx grumbled when he stepped into the small office.

"Nice to see you, too."

"I want my goddamn truck back."

"I'm sure you do. Kinda hard to take the girls home after you finish the job without it."

Lynx glared at him, a look that Rhys was all too familiar with.

"The papers are filed," Lynx countered defensively. "I wasn't cheatin'."

"Don't need to explain it to me. I don't care who you're bangin'. Or where. But I think you've learned your lesson about leavin' your keys in your truck."

Lynx flipped him off.

"Your truck's out back," Rhys informed him.

Lynx's dark eyebrows shot up into his hairline. "What?"

Chuckling, Rhys opened his top desk drawer and retrieved the set of keys he'd stashed there. He tossed them over to Lynx. "We pulled Tammy over just south of the county line for speedin'. She admitted to bein' pissed when she saw your bare ass and some redhead beneath you on your couch. We told her we'd talk you outta pressin' charges if she gave it back without a fight."

Lynx dropped into the chair. "Goddamn. I'm so fuckin' sick of this shit."

Rhys felt sorry for the man. Sort of. The Caine cousins were a wild bunch, always had been. However, underneath the wild exterior, they weren't bad guys. Hell, Rhys had been pretty damned impressed when Lynx married the girl in the first place and put forth the effort to be a good husband. Turned out, Tammy had faked being knocked up in order to land one of the Caine cousins. Lynx had been the unfortunate one who'd banged her in the first place.

From the second the news hit town that Lynx had gotten hitched, there'd been a few bets that Lynx would be the one to stray. To everyone's shock, Tammy had hooked up with one of the wranglers over at Dead Heat Ranch. Lynx had caught the two of them buck-ass naked in the bed of his truck, in fact.

Guy deserved a break.

"Thanks," Lynx offered, getting to his feet.

"Keep your damn truck locked," Rhys ordered.

"Right." Lynx waved over his head as he disappeared down the hall.

Some days Rhys loved his job.

With the office once again quiet, Rhys pulled out his keyboard drawer and brought his computer to life. He typed in his password, then brought up his Internet browser.

Amy Smith. Texas.

He typed in the words and waited to see what the search would reveal. Just as he'd suspected, the list of people was vast.

Leaning back in his chair, he stared at the screen.

No one knew one single thing about the woman, which meant his search was pointless. He didn't even know where she came from. If he had the name of a city, he would have a place to start. Unfortunately, the little bit of asking around he'd done today had resulted in zilch. The woman had managed to be in Embers Ridge for three months and keep every detail about herself under wraps.

He had an overwhelming desire to find out what the woman was running from. Maybe it was his protective nature that had piqued his curiosity, or possibly something else entirely. Whatever it was, he hated the fear he saw in her eyes, hated knowing that someone had put it there.

Shit, even the fact that she would be working for Wolfe made him feel significantly better. At least that way, he knew someone would be able to watch over her, keep her safe from whatever demons were haunting her.

"Hey, Sheriff? We've got a loose cow out on No Name Road."

Locking his computer, Rhys got to his feet and grabbed his hat and his keys.

Time to do some real work.

4

Three days later

PAIN.

It was all-consuming, taking over her entire body. She couldn't pinpoint exactly where it was coming from. If she had to guess, she'd say everywhere.

God, please make it go away.

"Jane? Talk to me, hun. I need you to keep your eyes open."

Jane? *Who was Jane? Was that her?*

She felt the lightest of touches against her hand, but even that hurt. She tried to flinch, but nothing happened. She couldn't move.

"No, Jane. Don't close your eyes. I need you to stay with me. You're safe here."

Safe?

Was there any such thing as safe? Did this woman honestly believe that?

"Jane, how old are you?"

Since the woman seemed to be talking to her, she assumed she was Jane.

How old was *she? She didn't even know. Nothing made sense.*

She had no idea why her brain wasn't connecting the words with her mouth. She was trying, but no matter how much effort she put into it, nothing was coming out.

"Jane, this is important. Tell me how old you are."

Why wouldn't her mouth work? She didn't understand it. She tried to lift her arm, wanting to tell the nurse that she couldn't talk, but nothing happened.

She could feel the panic setting in, a bubble of anxiety building in her chest. What was happening to her?

"Jane? Honey, I need you to relax. It's going to be fine. Jane? Jane? Doctor, she's losing consciousness."

Amy bolted upright in bed.

She was soaked in sweat, her heart beating like a bass drum at a rock concert, breaths labored, hands trembling.

"Only a dream," she whispered into the dark room, her voice shaky, a chill racing over her clammy skin.

Technically, it was a memory, but the good news was, she wasn't having to relive it. Not the excruciating pain she'd endured, anyway. She wasn't battered and broken, barely clinging to life.

Not anymore.

Willing her heart to stop pounding, Amy slipped her feet over the edge of the bed and onto the hardwood floor. It took a second before her legs were steady enough to hold her up. When they were, she went through the house and turned on every light, punching the air conditioner down a couple of notches to cool her off. The clock on the microwave told her it was 4:47 a.m.

"Looks like it's time to get up," she muttered to herself, one arm snuggly wrapped around her middle as she sipped water from the glass she'd left on the counter when she went to bed five hours ago.

Her stomach grumbled a warning and she remembered she hadn't bothered to eat the night before. Ever since she'd received a hang-up call two nights ago, Amy hadn't been able to stomach much of anything. She had a pay-as-you-go phone, so no one knew the number. Well, no one other than Reagan and Donna because she had put the number on her job applications.

Surely they wouldn't call and hang up. Would they?

No. Of course not.

Her anxiety was at an all-time high. Didn't matter that the call was probably just someone who realized they'd gotten the wrong number. Amy's imagination had turned it into a dozen worst-case scenarios.

The dream certainly hadn't helped. It brought the memories of that long-ago night to the forefront of her mind. Not that they were ever far away. She remembered it like it was yesterday. Sometimes her bones even ached. Her jaw, both wrists, all the bones in her left hand, her left clavicle, both bones in her lower right leg, three ribs...all had been broken and then repaired but still had the ghost ache from time to time.

The beating she'd taken that night should've killed her. She figured that was the reason he had dumped her body in the ditch. Fortunately, a flat tire had caused an old man and his wife to pull over to the side of the road, just a short distance from where she'd lain broken and barely clinging to life. Had the wife not gotten out of the car to help, had she not seen Amy lying there, had they not called an ambulance, Amy wouldn't be here today. She would've died in that muddy drainage ditch just fifteen feet from the highway.

Dropping onto the couch, Amy put her head in her hands. The tears had long ago dried up, but the fear was rooted deep in her soul. If he ever found her, Amy knew he would kill her without hesitating. He'd tried it once. Although she had kept her mouth shut and never told the authorities who had come close to beating her to death, Amy knew he would want to silence her forever. If the news of what he'd done, what he was capable of ever got out...

"No more." She shot to her feet and stomped to the kitchen.

Thinking about it only made it worse.

She needed something to do. Something to keep her busy. She'd given her notice at the diner, and they said she was free and clear to go, that Donna would fill in temporarily.

Her gaze landed on the paperwork she'd brought home from her interview with Wolfe. She skimmed it over for the hundredth time in the past three days. She'd gone so far as to put her first name and her address, her cell phone number. However, the lines for her last name, social security number, and date of birth were still blank.

She needed to take the job. No way could she turn down that kind of money. For one, it would give her something to do. Plus, she wouldn't be out in the open; she'd be safely hidden inside a building, not dealing directly with customers all the time. And, as a side bonus, she didn't see how it could hurt to surround herself by men who didn't take shit from anyone. If she was lucky, maybe they'd befriend her, and should he come for her…

"Shower," she said to the empty house, her gaze darting to the locks on the door, ensuring they were engaged. "Then I'll go in."

She could only hope Wolfe was still willing to hire her.

If not…

Well, she'd deal with that when the time came.

WOLFE HAD JUST plugged in the power sander when he heard tires crunching on gravel out front. He glanced over at the coffeepot, realizing he hadn't bothered to start it yet. God help him if Lynx had showed up early. It was anyone's guess when the guy would show up for work. He rarely came in at six, other times closer to seven. But generally, Lynx strolled in at eight. He wasn't known for punctuality, that was for sure.

Before he could get the coffee can off the shelf, the door opened.

"I'm makin' it," he hollered, not bothering to turn around. Time was of the essence here.

"Making what?"

The sound of her voice went straight through him. He took a breath, then peered over his shoulder to see Amy standing in the doorway. She was wearing jeans and boots and a formfitting black T-shirt, hair pulled back in a ponytail, her bangs sweeping across her forehead. She was the most beautiful woman he'd ever seen.

"Mornin'," he greeted. "Thought you were Lynx. Figured he was gonna rip me a new one if I didn't have coffee ready."

She smiled, but it didn't quite reach her eyes. He noticed there were dark circles beneath the long fringe of her lashes. The woman looked tired and a little thin. Too thin.

"I can make that," she offered, coming to stand beside him. She peered down at her clothes. "And I didn't really know what the dress code was. I hope this is okay."

"Perfect." Literally.

Granted, he'd have to pay attention in the event she walked across the room while he was working. One look at her ass in those jeans and it was likely he'd cut his damn finger off.

"So, does he like it strong? The way he drinks it at the diner?"

Wolfe paused, staring down at Amy as he tried to understand what she was talking about.

She nodded toward the coffee. "Lynx. Strong coffee?"

He grinned. "Yeah. Stronger the better."

When Amy reached for the coffee can, Wolfe released it, his fingers brushing hers in the process. The slight touch had his breath shuddering in his chest. Her eyes flew up to meet his briefly, but then she looked away quickly. This time he didn't see fear, he noticed something else burning brightly in her espresso-brown eyes. Interest, maybe?

"I filled out the paperwork, too. It's in the car. I'll … uh … I'll get it to you in a bit?"

"Perfect."

Looked as though his vocabulary had been reduced to few words.

While Amy prepared the coffee, Wolfe unplugged the power sander—a safety precaution—then grabbed a few other things he'd need, set them out for when he returned. When she was finished and the pot was brewing, he nodded toward the stairs. "Come on. I'll show you around."

Amy's eyes made a quick sweep of the room before she followed. "You're the only one here?"

"Right now, yeah. My old man usually stops by on his way to the shop, but not quite this early. Who knows when Lynx'll get his lazy ass outta bed. Some days he goes right to the store to check on things before bringing his happy ass on this way."

It was clear the woman was on edge. Every minute of every day if he had to guess. Whatever it was she was running from, Wolfe wanted to eliminate it for her. Rhys had been right when he'd accused Wolfe of being protective. He wasn't sure what it was about this one tiny woman, but he vowed right then and there that he'd keep her safe from harm.

As for keeping her safe from *him* ... well, that was still to be determined.

Wolfe opened the first door they came to. "You remember this room. This is our office. No one's usually in here, and if you're lookin' for anything, chances are you won't find it." He smiled sheepishly. "We're not the most organized bunch."

"I can fix that."

He nodded, then closed the door and moved to the next one. "This is a makeshift break room." He pointed to the far wall. "There's a love seat, recliner, and a television. Refrigerator's over there. No sink though. But if you ever wanna take a break, you can hide out in here." He smiled down at her. "That is if Lynx ain't asleep in the chair."

Amy smiled.

Wolfe closed the door and moved to the next one.

"This is your office."

"I have my own office?"

"Trust me, you'll want one. It gets kinda loud out there when we're workin'. Plus, you'll need the computer and the phone."

Amy stepped inside the small eight-by-eight room, and Wolfe did his damnedest not to stare at her. It was difficult, considering. The woman stoked a fire in his blood that hadn't been kindled in a long damn time. He knew absolutely nothing about her, but he found he wanted to know every damn thing.

"The restrooms're downstairs," he informed her. "Back wall. Men and women's. Patty, our previous office manager, insisted we have a women's restroom," he rambled. "You know, because we're guys."

Amy smiled, a real one this time, and the move made her prettier than she already was.

"There's also a phone on the wall down by the coffeepot in case you're not in your office when it rings."

"Does it ring a lot?" She seemed genuinely curious.

"It does. We mostly make custom furniture. There're some standard pieces we'll put in the store, but most of what we work on are customer-specific pieces. We ship all over the country, but the store does a steady business."

"Who runs the store?"

"My old man. I tend to steer clear of it if at all possible, but you're welcome to go over there if you'd like. I'll introduce you to Calvin."

Amy nodded.

"Well, why don't you get familiar with it all. When Lynx gets here, I'll have him run down the accounting software with you."

"Lynx? Really?" Amy blushed. "I mean … uh … you don't handle that?"

Wolfe smirked. "Not on your life, darlin'. You don't want me anywhere near it. I'm an IRS audit waitin' to happen. And don't let all those tats fool you. Lynx is pretty damn smart for a dumb ass."

Amy laughed, exactly what he was hoping for.

Turning, Wolfe prepared to leave her to it, but Amy stopped him with a hand on his arm. He felt the jarring impact from his arm straight to his dick.

He looked at her pale fingers against his much darker skin. Her hands were covered in thin scars, and his gut tightened, anger simmering at the thought of someone—*anyone*—hurting this woman.

"Wolfe … I … uh … I just want to say thank you."

He peered down at her, his eyes raking over her face. "You're welcome. I'm glad you're here."

With that, he turned and left the office, doing everything in his power not to run.

FIGURING HE WAS probably crossing a line by stopping by twice in one week, Rhys decided to run over to Wolfe's shop after he left the diner. If Wolfe wanted to call him on it, he'd deal with it. His curiosity was what was driving the social visit this morning though. Not official business.

He hadn't been surprised to find out that Amy wasn't at the diner this morning considering Donna had mentioned she'd turned in her notice a few days ago. However, he had been shocked when he realized the Caine cousins hadn't come in for their morning breakfast. Wolfe and Lynx were creatures of habit, and there was hardly a day that went by when they didn't go into the diner for breakfast. Hell, they were there so much, everyone knew to steer clear of the table they'd claimed as their own.

When Rhys arrived at the shop, he found the cousins' trucks parked in the lot—Wolfe's black four-door Silverado and Lynx's new shiny blue Ford F-350—and Amy's little silver Nissan beside them. That explained why she wasn't at the diner.

The door was open, so he stepped inside and quickly took stock of the room.

Lynx was at the far end, digging something out of a box, and Wolfe had the power sander going as he bent over what appeared to be a nightstand. Amy was nowhere in sight. He quickly glanced up at the second floor. The third door was open and he caught a glimpse of Amy on the phone, talking to someone.

The power sander quickly shut off and the silence was jarring.

"Ah, hell," Lynx grumbled, carrying a handful of bronze hardware toward Wolfe. "What'd you do this time, Wolfe?"

Everyone knew that Lynx would be the first person Rhys would be seeking out if it came to trouble.

Wolfe briefly glanced at Rhys before he stood to his full height, stretching his back as he did. The move caused his T-shirt to lift, offering a quick glimpse of the muscular V that disappeared into his jeans. Rhys tried not to look but couldn't help himself.

When he met Wolfe's eyes again, there was something akin to amusement in the emerald depths.

Yeah, the guy was fucking with him.

"Should I be worried that you're makin' another house call?" Wolfe questioned, moving toward him.

Rhys nodded toward the parking lot and then stepped outside. The temperatures were going to be record-breaking today.

Wolfe stepped outside, keeping to the edge of the building, where there was some shade. "What's up, Sheriff? You know I run a business here. I don't have time for this shit."

His tone belied his words. Wolfe sounded more amused than put out.

"Just thought I'd stop by. See how things're goin'," Rhys admitted, moving around to the side of the building. The sound of boots crunching on gravel told him that Wolfe was following.

"Not to check up on me?"

Rhys turned to face the taller man.

And Wolfe Caine was a big man. A couple of inches taller and a good twenty-five, maybe thirty pounds of solid muscle more than Rhys, the guy made Rhys feel small almost. Not that he was a little guy, but next to Wolfe…

Wolfe seemed to be closing the distance between them, and Rhys had to keep his boots firmly planted to keep from taking a step back. He wasn't intimidated by Wolfe, and he damn sure wasn't going to pretend he was.

When they were nearly toe to toe, Wolfe stared down at him and Rhys held his gaze.

"What do you want from me, Sheriff?"

Well, hell. That was a loaded question if he'd ever heard one. He had a million answers on the tip of his tongue, but he wasn't about to admit his interest.

Not yet.

Wolfe moved closer, but Rhys held his ground even when the warmth of Wolfe's body surrounded him.

"Is it information on Amy you want?"

"Yes and no," he confessed. "Not for reasons you might think."

"No?" Another inch disappeared between them. "You're not seekin' information so you can *protect* her? Or maybe that's just bullshit and you're sniffin' around 'cause you're interested." His dark eyebrows lifted.

Rhys didn't respond. Hell, he could hardly breathe.

"Or is it me you want?" Wolfe's tone dropped an octave, lower than Rhys had ever heard it. The growl that accompanied the words suited his name.

Rhys knew Wolfe was baiting him, but he couldn't deny his attraction.

"Right here? Right now?" Wolfe continued, his voice dropping lower.

When Wolfe leaned in closer, his breath fanning Rhys's ear, it took every ounce of willpower he possessed to not shift closer.

"Is this what you're comin' 'round for? Tauntin' me? Teasin' me? You tryin' to see if I'm interested?"

Rhys swallowed hard.

Wolfe's voice was hardly a whisper when he added, "Because I might be."

Rhys was trying to catch his breath when Wolfe pulled back and stared at him.

Without another word, the big guy smirked, then turned and headed back inside, leaving Rhys standing there, staring after him.

Even if he'd had a reason for coming to the shop, Rhys would be damned if he'd be able to remember what it was.

Not after that.

LYNX CAINE SMIRKED to himself when Wolfe followed the sheriff out the door.

He wasn't the most perceptive person on the planet—by choice—but even he noticed the sheriff had taken a special interest in Lynx's cousin in the past week. Whatever it was, Wolfe was taking the bait. Hook, line, and sinker. And perhaps that was what was most surprising. Lynx couldn't even remember the last time Wolfe had shown genuine interest in anyone.

Well, anyone other than Amy Smith. He did seem to have a hard-on for the girl, although Lynx had to give the guy props. He was doing a damn good job of pretending otherwise.

Lynx glanced around. Damn, he missed his dog. He understood Wolfe's request for Lynx to keep Copenhagen out of the shop for a bit, but that didn't mean he liked it. His three-year-old German shepherd was his buddy and they spent all their time together. However, he knew Cope enjoyed hanging out at the store, and more importantly, his uncle enjoyed the hell out of having him there.

Glancing up at the second floor, Lynx considered going up to talk to Amy but decided against it. The girl was a nervous wreck. Seemed every time he got near her, she shrank in on herself. He didn't think she was scared of him, but she was damn sure scared of something. He figured it was best to talk to her when Wolfe was around. Put her at ease a little. He wasn't an asshole, after all.

Plus, he didn't want to make Wolfe think he was sweet on the girl. Sure, she was cute, but no way could that girl handle him. Not even at her absolute wildest.

But there was one girl who could. A fucking spitfire of a woman who'd held his damn interest since he was eighteen fucking years old. Unfortunately, that girl was completely off-limits. Hell, if she didn't have a fuckup for a boyfriend, Lynx would still keep his distance.

A woman like Reagan Trevino could break a man. And Lynx had absolutely no intention of being broken. Not in this lifetime, anyway.

5

One week later

BY THE FOLLOWING Friday afternoon, Amy had gotten the hang of her new job.

Well, the parts they'd told her about anyway.

It had taken a full week to get comfortable, though. She wasn't sure if that was normal or not, but she felt good about it.

Answering the phones was simple; taking the information to pass along to Wolfe or Lynx wasn't hard most of the time. When someone wanted to go into detail about a design, Amy had a little difficulty. She wasn't artistic by any means, but she'd learned that having Lynx take those calls worked well. He could draw something up in a few strokes of the pencil, then he'd pass it along to Wolfe for more detail if needed.

The quick tutorial she'd received from Lynx in regard to the accounting software had been the hardest part. He promised he'd only show her the things she would need to do when the time came so she'd get plenty of practice.

Other than that, Amy had spent the past week organizing things on the second floor. She'd quickly learned that the Caines didn't utilize an alphabetized filing system, so she'd implemented one and gotten to work.

Which was what she was still doing now when she heard the sound of footsteps outside the door.

"It's about quittin' time," Wolfe informed her.

Sitting up straight, Amy stretched her neck. She had actually been dreading this part. She didn't want the day to end, preferring to do the mindless task of alphabetizing paperwork instead of going home and pacing the floor. Every day this week, she had bolted out of bed before her alarm, eager and excited to spend the day at the shop. With something constructive to do, she found she spent far less time worrying.

"Okay," she finally said, pushing to her feet. "I'll finish this up on Monday?"

"It'll be here waitin' for ya," he said, grinning.

Smiling, Amy moved past Wolfe, knowing he was waiting so he could close the door behind her. She'd gotten used to his gentlemanly gestures. Opening doors, walking her to her car, bringing her coffee or water during the day. One day he'd picked up lunch and brought her a hamburger without even asking. He made being around him comfortable. So much so, Amy wasn't looking forward to going home to an empty house. Granted, she did have to work at Reagan's tonight, but she didn't have to be there until seven, which meant she had about four hours to kill.

"You ever shoot a gun?"

Jerking around to face him, Amy stared at Wolfe, shocked by his question. "I … uh … no."

"You wanna learn?"

Swallowing, she found herself nodding. She wasn't sure if Wolfe was offering because he could sense the terror that lurked just beneath the surface or if that was simply something they did here in Embers Ridge during their downtime. She knew the cousins were comfortable with firearms. Namely shotguns. It seemed they had one everywhere she turned.

"You got any plans *now*?"

She shook her head.

Wolfe jerked his chin in the direction of the stairs. "Come on. I'll drive."

Amy had to hold back the words that hung on the tip of her tongue. She was going to say that she could drive herself, but she didn't want to. She needed to prove to herself that she really could trust this man. He'd given her a job and hadn't questioned her about anything. Even when she'd turned in her paperwork, although some of the information was missing, he hadn't asked about it.

Oh, she knew she would have to provide her social security number, birthdate, and all that crap in order to receive a paycheck, but she was hesitant. Being paid biweekly meant she had a little time. If it meant she worked for two weeks for free, so be it. At the end of next week, if she felt comfortable enough, she'd give it to him.

If not, then she'd walk away. It was that simple.

"Okay," she agreed, turning toward the stairs.

Amy waited while Wolfe closed up the shop, setting the alarm and locking the doors before he made his way to his truck. He walked her around to the passenger door and opened it, lingering there while she climbed inside.

The truck was a beast. Thank goodness for step bars or she never would've managed to get inside without help.

"Buckle up," he said, closing the door and then moving around to the driver's side.

When he joined her, Amy had the seat belt locked into place. She scanned the interior of the truck, not at all surprised to see it was clean. Wolfe's office was unorganized, but she had to say, everything was always spotless. That characteristic carried over to his vehicle as well. It made her wonder what his house looked like.

As Wolfe steered the truck out of the lot, he picked up his phone and hit a button.

"Hey, Sheriff. Thought I'd let you know that I'm takin' Amy out to the range behind my house. Gonna teach her how to shoot a gun."

There was a brief pause. Wolfe glanced both ways at a stop sign, his expression unchanged.

"Yep. Just thought you should know. Later."

Amy got the feeling that it wasn't customary for residents to inform the sheriff when they were going to be shooting on their own land. She was pretty sure Wolfe had done it for her benefit. It did make her feel better knowing that someone was aware of where she was going, although, if she was completely honest, she wasn't worried that Wolfe would hurt her. In fact, she felt safe with him.

Safer than she had in a long, long time.

And she wasn't sure what to think about that yet.

WOLFE DISCONNECTED THE call and tossed his phone into the center console.

He could feel Amy's eyes on him.

"Do you always call the sheriff when you're gonna be shooting?"

The doubt in her tone told him she knew better.

He smirked, cutting his eyes to her briefly. "Not usually, no."

A smile formed on her face and he could see that she had relaxed somewhat.

His reasons for calling Rhys had been twofold. Mainly to put Amy at ease. He figured she'd be more comfortable knowing that the sheriff was aware of where she was and who she was with. And two, because he'd wanted to entice the sheriff to show up. He didn't bother to mention to Amy that Rhys wasn't on duty at the moment. Nor did he share with her what Rhys had said.

"You callin' to brag? Or is that an invitation?"

"Yep. Just thought you should know. Later."

Wolfe would let Rhys figure out which question he'd been answering. Either the sheriff would show up or he wouldn't. Knowing Rhys, he'd be there. Since Rhys had avoided Wolfe since the day he'd confronted him outside the shop, Wolfe figured it was time for him to make a move. It wasn't like him not to go after what he wanted, and since he had half of what he wanted right there in the truck with him, he simply needed to get Rhys on board for everything to fall into place. Wolfe had waited long enough.

"Where do you live?" Amy asked, her attention fixed on the scenery passing by the truck.

"My family's got about two hundred acres out on the edge of town."

"Two *hundred*?" Her eyes were wide when she looked over at him.

"Yeah. We lease about half of it out for cattle. Another portion is used for hay. The rest we live on."

"And play on?"

Was she teasing him?

Smiling, he nodded. "And play on."

"My aunt and uncle had some land." She didn't look at him as she spoke. "I lived with them for a brief amount of time. They didn't have a lot, only eight acres, but it was wooded and I spent some time wandering."

Wolfe could've sat right there in his truck all damn day if she would simply talk about herself more. He was still amazed that she'd agreed to come with him. And he had more than one reason for inviting her. Sure, he wanted to spend some time with her, get to know her. Not only because he was curious about what she was running from, either. He'd come to like the woman. A lot. But Wolfe figured if she wanted him to know about her past, she'd tell him. In the meantime, he could be her friend, teach her how to defend herself if it was necessary.

"In case you couldn't tell, I'm close to my family," Wolfe told her. "The Caines have lived on that land for generations. My grandparents' house sits empty since they passed, but Lynx usually takes care of it. I'm still out there, though. In my own house. I built it out on the northeast corner a few years ago. It keeps me out of sight of everyone. Lynx's dad's got a place, too, but he's a shut-in now. Never leaves."

"And *your* dad? Does he live out there?"

Wolfe shook his head. "Nah. After my mother died two years ago, he moved into the apartment above the store. He said he didn't need much space, was tired of having to deal with upkeep around his house."

"I'm sorry about your mom." Amy continued to stare out the window.

"Thanks."

"Did he sell his house?"

"Nope. Lynx decided to move in there. He'd been rentin' a house in town when he was with his … ex-wife. He hauled ass back as fast as he could."

"Do you have horses?"

Wolfe shook his head. "Nope. Not enough time to take care of 'em. Cooter had some at one point. Ended up sellin' 'em about six years ago. Couldn't handle all the work on his own."

When Amy didn't shoot off another question, Wolfe thought of the million he had spinning around in his head, but he held them all back. If Amy wanted to ask him about his family, he was more than willing to share the details. He loved his family. Didn't matter how fucking crazy they were. And he hoped one day she'd feel comfortable enough to share a bit of herself with him.

When they reached the Circle C Ranch, Wolfe pulled up to the gate and hit the button in his truck that would open it electronically.

"It's solar-powered," Amy said softly. "That seems to be a thing now."

Wolfe didn't respond, figuring it didn't require him to.

Assuming Rhys wouldn't be far behind him, Wolfe left the gate open as he headed down the long dirt road that forked off to his house. The other direction headed out to his uncle's place.

Not wanting to make her uncomfortable, Wolfe opted not to stop by his house. He had the guns he needed with him, enough to help her get started, anyway. However, he did have to pass by the place.

"Is that your house?" Amy leaned forward and stared out her window as they passed.

"Yeah."

"Wow." Her head jerked around, her eyes stopping on him. "It's beautiful, Wolfe."

"Thanks."

"You said you built it?"

He was a little surprised that she'd caught that part. "Yeah."

"With your own two hands?"

Wolfe chuckled. "Yeah. Well, I had some help. My dad's pretty handy with a hammer and Lynx's good with tile."

"How long did it take?"

"About a year."

"That's impressive. More so that you had family to help you."

"Yeah, well, in return, I helped my dad upgrade the kitchen in the apartment." Wolfe smirked. "And Lynx … well, because he helped, I don't stomp his ass when he makes a fool outta himself."

He pulled the truck to a stop out near the makeshift range he and Lynx had put up. It wasn't much more than a tin roof awning with a railing and a few barrels set up about thirty yards from two bales of hay along the fence line.

"This is it?" Amy glanced around, her eyes wide as she took it all in.

Wolfe had no idea what she was thinking.

"This is it," he confirmed. "I've got a couple shotguns in the back. Figured we'd start with that."

"Okay."

Opening his door, he glanced over at her. "Stay there. I'll open the door for you."

Not waiting for a response, he hopped out of his truck.

As he headed over to help Amy out, he hoped like hell he could make it through the next hour without making a complete fool of himself. Whatever it was about this girl, he felt like a gangly teenage boy all over again. His hormones were on the fritz.

God only knew how bad it would get when Rhys showed up.

RHYS PULLED UP in time to see Wolfe getting Amy situated with a shotgun. He was helping her with her stance, and Rhys had to sit in his truck for a second longer than he should have.

His dick was being a nuisance as he took in the sight of Wolfe touching Amy. It was a sight most people wouldn't have thought twice about, but since Rhys's most recent fantasies involved the two of them in a similar position, only naked, horizontal, and without the shotgun, Rhys was having to count backwards from one hundred. If he got out now, there'd be absolutely no way to disguise the hard-on threatening to break his damn zipper.

It wasn't that he cared that Wolfe saw it, but Rhys knew for damn sure that Amy wasn't ready for him to declare his craving to strip her naked and feast on her for a while. Hell, Rhys wasn't sure she'd ever be ready for that. Certainly not ready to be the filling in a sandwich that had Wolfe on one side and Rhys on the other.

Wolfe peered over his shoulder at Rhys's truck but then turned back to the task at hand.

One hundred.

Ninety-nine.

Ninety-eight.

Wolfe said something to Amy. She adjusted the protective glasses on her face, then loosened her stance. Wolfe helped her position her hands around the gun, then pointed out toward the target. He took a step back and then they were both watching her.

After a few seconds of hesitation, Amy pulled the trigger, the recoil knocking her back, but Wolfe was there to steady her. She looked up at him over her shoulder, shifting the ear protection off one ear, and Rhys was surprised to see she was smiling. A grin that held a million megawatts and transformed her from cute to downright beautiful. He had no idea what Wolfe said to her, but she nodded and they went through the motions once more.

Eighty-nine.

Eighty-eight.

Eighty-seven.

Yeah. This was bullshit.

He was a grown man, not some horny fucking teenager. Surely he could get out of his truck, walk over to them, and not slobber all over himself in an effort to stave off the lust. It had been a difficult week. He'd done his best to stay away from the pair of them, wanting to play it cool. As much as he wanted to kick this into high gear, to make his move and see what their reactions were, Rhys knew he couldn't. He needed to lie low for a while. There were too many prying eyes on Wolfe and Amy right now. Ever since she'd started working at the Cedar Door, rumors had started. There were some doozies, too.

Amy was Lynx's long-lost sister.

That was an interesting one. Rhys had no idea who would've thought that one up, but hey. Gossip had no rhyme or reason.

Amy was Lynx's new wife.

Considering the first one, that one kind of creeped him out. But still, it wasn't as hard to understand. Since Lynx's impromptu nuptials, no one knew what to expect from the guy. But seriously, the ink wasn't even dry on the divorce papers.

Amy and Wolfe were undercover, working with Rhys.

How he'd been dragged into that one, Rhys wasn't sure. It could've had something to do with his repeat visits to Wolfe. Hence the very reason Rhys had been playing it cool. The last thing he wanted was to be caught up in the rumor mill.

Rhys opened the truck door and climbed down. He adjusted himself, his jeans damned uncomfortable, but he sure as shit wasn't about to miss this opportunity.

"Hey, Sheriff," Wolfe greeted.

Amy glanced back, her eyes rounding slightly before darting over to Wolfe.

"It's cool," Wolfe assured her. "He's off duty."

"Oh."

That seemed to appease her somewhat. Rhys wasn't sure what she'd been expecting. Maybe she thought he was there to stop them?

This was the country. Rhys couldn't stop the Caines from taking up target practice on their own land. They were secluded, and with all the animals on the far side of the ranch, not even they would get in the way.

"Go ahead, try again when you're ready." Wolfe stepped back.

Amy held the shotgun steady, her eyes trained on the bale of hay at least thirty yards out.

Rhys refrained from talking, not wanting to startle her while she was getting ready. She pulled the trigger and this time her shot went way left.

"You're jumpin' before you get the shot off," Wolfe informed her.

"But I didn't do that the first time," she countered.

"Because you hadn't felt the recoil. Now you're expectin' it."

"Oh."

"Remember how to load it?"

Amy nodded.

"I want you to do it yourself this time. It'll hold five in the barrel and one in the chamber."

Rhys leaned against the wooden rail and watched. Amy caught on quickly. She loaded the shotgun in no time and had it up and aimed before Wolfe said anything more. When she fired the shot, her aim was significantly better, although she missed the target by at least three feet.

"I'm gonna step back here. You've got plenty of ammo. Shoot until your heart's content. Remember, five in the barrel, one in the chamber. And when you're not using it, keep the barrel aimed at the ground."

Amy smiled up at Wolfe, and that lightning bolt of lust shot through Rhys once again. There was something seriously hot about a pretty woman with a pump-action shotgun. Provided the shotgun wasn't aimed at him, of course.

Wolfe joined him, hefting his big body up on the railing beside Rhys. They weren't quite close enough to touch. Rhys was tempted to remedy that, but he kept his cool. He had all the time in the world when it came to moving this forward. He'd waited years for an opportunity at something that wasn't casual. Which meant he couldn't treat it as such.

No reason to push when the timing wasn't right.

With every shot, Amy's aim was better, the slug moving closer and closer to the target.

"She's good with the twenty gauge," Rhys said, keeping his voice low.

"She is."

Rhys didn't have to ask why Wolfe had made the offer to teach her to shoot. That was pretty damn obvious. The woman was running from something. It only made sense that she knew how to take care of herself.

"You have a .22 in your truck?" Wolfe asked.

"No. Got a .45 though. Plus, a twelve gauge and a thirty ought six."

Wolfe shook his head. "Nah. I want her to focus on aim this go 'round."

"Next time you invite me, I'll bring one." Rhys peered up at Wolfe.

"You do that."

They sat in silence for a few minutes while Amy continued to load and shoot, load and shoot. She was getting better, the target taking a few slaps from the slug with the last shots.

When she turned around to face them, she was sweating, but she was smiling. "I never thought shooting a gun would be fun."

Rhys smiled, then looked at Wolfe. "You up for a little friendly competition?"

"Always." Wolfe hopped down from the wooden rail. "Mind if I borrow that, darlin'?"

Amy handed over the shotgun, and Rhys grabbed the other that was lying across one of the barrels.

Rhys smiled at Amy as he passed her, and his breath slammed to a halt in his lungs when she smiled back at him. It was a feeling he knew he would never forget for as long as he lived. Why it meant so much that she'd smiled at him the same way she'd smiled at Wolfe, he wasn't sure, but it was something, all right.

"You ready, farm boy?" Rhys taunted, then hopped the railing to the side closest to the targets.

Wolfe hopped over, then reached back and grabbed several shells. Rhys did the same. Once loaded, he turned to his friend, nodded, then faced the targets.

There was no doubt who would win, but Rhys was all for giving it his best shot.

6

AMY HAD NEVER in her life felt the sort of exhilaration she felt when she'd fired Wolfe's shotgun. She wanted to continue, but her shoulder was already sore, her arms like cooked spaghetti noodles, loose and limp. So, she stood back and watched as Wolfe and Rhys hopped the small wooden fence and moved toward the target.

Another shot of adrenaline flooded her veins as she watched the two men. Sexy men wearing boots, jeans, and T-shirts and wielding shotguns. She wasn't sure she was supposed to be turned on by the sight of them, but she was.

They both exuded some serious sex appeal. Tall, lean, muscular… And their butts. Yum. Encased in Wrangler jeans, these two were the reason for the saying "Wrangler butts drive me nuts." Or at least Amy thought that was a saying. If not, it was still true.

Did all women find this hot? Or was it just her?

They pulled the shotguns up to their shoulders, aimed.

Wolfe's deep voice rumbled something Amy couldn't make out and then…

Click-click. Boom!

Amy jumped when they fired their first shots, the sound reverberating off the trees in the distance.

Click-click. Boom!

Both men continued, rapid-firing the full six shots as they moved one step closer to the target each time. Wolfe got all six of his shots off first, but Rhys wasn't far behind.

Both men looked at one another and grinned.

From this distance, Amy had no idea who had hit the most targets.

While her stomach churned with excitement, she waited for them to join her.

"Who won?" she asked, glancing between the two of them.

"I did," Wolfe noted.

"How do you know?"

"Because I got the shots off first."

"Oh." Amy frowned. "I thought it would depend on who hit the target the most."

"We both hit dead center every time," Rhys noted and Wolfe grinned.

Wow. That was … impressive.

They'd obviously done this before.

"You workin' tonight?" Wolfe asked and Amy realized the question was directed at her.

"Yeah."

"You still workin' for my sister?"

Amy's eyebrows rose as she stared at the handsome sheriff. "Reagan's your sister?"

Rhys glanced over at Wolfe, then back at her. "She'll deny it if you ask her, but yeah." He chuckled. "She's my baby sister."

Huh. She'd never thought to get Reagan's last name.

Now that Amy thought about it, she did notice the resemblance. They had the same straight nose, the same dimpled chin. However, there were a few differences. Like their heights. Plus, Reagan had brown eyes while Rhys's were a deep, dark blue.

"What time do you go on duty?" Wolfe asked Rhys.

"Six." He glanced at his watch. "Which means I need to get goin'." Rhys met her eyes. "Thanks for lettin' me tag along."

"Anytime," she answered before thinking. Oddly enough, she meant that. She liked Rhys. He wasn't as intimidating as she'd once thought. She had no idea when she'd changed her perception of him, but now that she knew he was Reagan's brother, he seemed more approachable.

"I'll catch y'all later." Rhys smiled at her, and Amy once again found herself smiling back at him. "Try to keep our boy here outta trouble tonight."

Looking over at Wolfe, she noticed he was grinning. A sexy, mischievous smile that said that wasn't likely.

Amy smiled, too, the movement natural. “I’ll do my best.”

Wolfe nodded toward his truck as he double-checked his shotgun, likely ensuring it wasn’t loaded. Rhys checked his, then handed it over to Wolfe. “Come on. I’ll drive you back to your car.”

“I’m goin’ right by there,” Rhys noted, his tone soft, non-threatening. “If you’d like, I can drive you.”

Amy looked to Wolfe. She wasn’t sure what she should say. She didn’t mind the idea of Rhys taking her back to town, even if she didn’t like the idea of leaving Wolfe. Since Wolfe was already at home, it seemed like a waste of time and gas for him to drive all the way back though.

“Up to you, darlin’,” Wolfe said, making his way to the truck.

“I’ll … uh…” She glanced over at Rhys. “I’ll ride with you. If you really don’t mind.”

“Not at all.” Rhys walked over to his truck, opening the passenger door.

Amy stopped beside Wolfe. “Thank you. For this.” She glanced down at the ground. “Do you … uh … think we could do it again?”

Wolfe’s finger curled beneath her chin, gentle and warm. He lifted her face so she had to look at him. “Anytime you want. Just say the word. And next time I’m in town, I’ll see what the pawn shop has. It’d be good for you to have a shotgun, at the very least. But I want you comfortable with it first.”

Amy found another smile slipping free. When Wolfe’s finger dropped, she immediately missed his touch. She was sure he was just being friendly. The last thing she needed was for him to see how his touch had affected her. She liked it. A lot. For whatever reason, his touch was reassuring. It made her feel safe. Safer than she had in a very long time.

With an awkward wave, she hurried over to Rhys’s truck.

“Here’s the keys if you wanna start it. I need to talk to Wolfe for a second.”

Amy nodded and took the keys from his hand.

Once she was inside, the door closing behind her, she noticed Wolfe was watching her. A thrill shot through her, but she managed to ignore it. Mostly.

The temperature in the truck was scorching, so she shoved the key in the ignition and started it, her attention lingering on the two men.

Rhys walked over to Wolfe, stepping right into his personal space.

Amy couldn't read their lips, but based on their body language, they weren't talking about anything serious. Wolfe's smirk was one she'd seen before, one he'd given her. And the way Rhys was looking at Wolfe…

Damn.

Maybe she'd misjudged Wolfe altogether. Maybe he wasn't interested in women the way she thought. It was almost as though Rhys and Wolfe were engulfed in some powerful sexual tension. Again, Amy found it incredibly hot to watch, although a little disappointing at the same time.

"Probably for the best," she mumbled to herself, turning away when both men glanced over at her.

And it was. For the best.

The absolute last thing Amy needed right now was to let her guard down. It was one thing to hang around a few men who could provide a measure of protection, but it was something else entirely for her to let her guard down.

She'd done that once.

She would never do it again.

Ten minutes later, they were heading past the solar-powered gate at the entrance to Wolfe's ranch. The truck was silent except for the steady hum of the air conditioner blasting cold air that did little to fight off the suffocating heat.

Amy did her best not to fidget, but it wasn't easy.

"Can I … uh … ask you a question?" she blurted, realizing that the silence was making her far more nervous than talking would.

"Anything," he answered, his tone soft.

"What made you wanna be a sheriff?"

His smile was warm as he stared out the windshield, his eyes darting toward the rearview mirror every so often.

"I don't think that was ever my intention."

"No?"

"Nah. Deputy, yeah. Since I was a kid, I knew I'd be a police officer."

"Did somethin' happen to make you decide that?"

Rhys sighed, his gaze swerving toward her briefly, then back to the road.

"When I was a kid, the cops were constantly bein' called out to my grandfather's place. I grew up there. I've got a big family and they were always hangin' around, too. Probably got a little rowdy from time to time."

"*Probably*?" she teased, her mouth clamping shut as soon as the word came out.

Rhys chuckled. "Okay, definitely."

He pulled up to a stop sign, glanced both ways. "Anyway. They were always comin' out for one reason or another. The old couple livin' next door liked to bitch and moan, although there were about fifteen acres between the two houses." He sighed. "There was this one hard-ass deputy who'd gotten caught up in his power trip. Pissed me off the way he treated everyone. Lookin' down his nose like he was better than us.

"One day, my aunt's smart mouth got the best of her and she said somethin' she shouldn't have. He got rough with her. My cousin stepped in, ended up goin' to jail for protectin' his momma." Rhys glanced over at her. "I didn't assume all cops were assholes. I knew better. But I also knew there were some out there. Told myself that day that I would become a deputy in this county and I wouldn't put up with shit like that. The people livin' here don't need to be hassled by the cops. No reason for all that nonsense."

Amy nodded but kept her eyes trained out the window, even as they pulled into the parking lot behind her car. She knew all about how power trips affected people. They could make them mean. Or worse. It could turn them into monsters.

Clearing her throat, Amy forced her eyes over to him. "Well, I think this town's lucky to have you."

His smile was so warm it did something funny to Amy's insides. It was obvious he didn't get compliments like that often.

"Thanks."

With a deep breath, she forced a smile and unbuckled her seat belt. "I … uh … had fun. Thanks for … uh … coming out there with us."

"Anytime," he said, tossing her response from earlier back at her.

That drained some of the tension coiling inside her and Amy smiled for real. She really did like this man. And so far, she got the impression he was one of the good guys.

Not that she was the greatest judge of character, but still.

"Hang tight," he said before hopping out of the truck and walking around to her side.

The men in this town were so chivalrous. Amy wondered if that was a small-town thing. She hadn't encountered the same in Houston.

Rhys helped her out, then walked her to her car, opening the door for her there, too.

"If you need anything," he said, his hands on her door, "holler."

She smiled up at him. "Thanks."

Amy got a wink that made her insides go haywire and then the door closed.

It took two tries to get her car started, but once it screeched to life, she took a deep breath. She had just enough time to run home, change clothes, and make it back to Reagan's.

Or … in an effort to save money on gas, she could just wear what she had on and drive straight to Reagan's. Not only would it be kinder to her pocketbook, she also wouldn't have to go home to an empty house.

Yeah. She liked that plan much better.

THE COLD SHOWER felt incredible.

But not nearly as good as his hand on his dick.

Wolfe stood beneath the chilly spray with his cock firmly gripped in his fist. With his eyes closed, he leaned against the slate-tiled wall and gave in to his fantasies, to the overwhelming lust surging in his bloodstream. The image of Amy, all sweaty and naked, laid out beside Rhys on Wolfe's bed…

Yeah, it was a fantasy that would likely never become a reality, but *holy fuck*. His dick throbbed in his grip, and he squeezed more firmly, sliding his soapy hand up and down his length. His breaths were coming rapidly, his body coiling tighter with every passing second. Wolfe wasn't sure he'd ever found a mental image to be quite as hot as the idea of the three of them together. All the things he wanted to do to *both* of them…

"Fuck," he groaned, jerking himself harder, faster.

He imagined Amy and Rhys on their knees before him, their tongues sliding over his shaft, licking, sucking, alternating between the warm rasps of their mouths.

"Son of a bitch!" His body jerked, his thigh muscles locking as he came hard, his head falling back against the tile with a thud.

Lord Almighty.

Wolfe sucked in air and turned his face to the spray.

And to think, he'd spent just a short time in their presence and now he was thinking about fucking them both into oblivion.

Oddly enough, Wolfe wasn't even trying to deny his attraction to Rhys. He actually felt relief to acknowledge it. As for Amy… Yeah, Wolfe had known he'd been attracted to her from the first second he laid eyes on her. As to whether he'd ever be able to act on that attraction… He wasn't sure it would be possible. As skittish as she was, Wolfe knew he would have to allow her to make the first move. Until then, he'd have to get reacquainted with his hand.

After soaping up and rinsing off, Wolfe shut off the water and grabbed a towel. He was going to meet his cousin at Reagan's, but for the first time in a damn long time, he was looking forward to going for a reason other than to hang out with Lynx. He would get to see Amy again. Although she and Rhys had left only half an hour ago, Wolfe couldn't wait to see her, to simply be in her presence.

He couldn't help but think they'd made some progress this afternoon, spending time together on the range. Wolfe had been paying attention to how she reacted to Rhys. Even he had noticed the moment she had relaxed her guard with him.

After rubbing the towel over his hair, he tossed it over the shower door and went to his bedroom to get dressed.

"What's up, old man?" Wolfe called out to his father when he walked into the small one-bedroom, one-bathroom apartment above the Cedar Door store an hour later.

"Hey, kid," his father greeted from his recliner in front of the television. "What're you doin' over here tonight? Shouldn't you be out startin' shit at Reagan's?"

"Lynx is the one who starts shit," he told his father as he did every time he came over.

"That's what they all say."

"'Cause it's true."

"Seriously, what brings you by?" Calvin asked, peering over at Wolfe.

"Just wanted to check in. See if you needed anything?"

"Got some iced tea, popcorn, and a baseball game. I'd say I'm all set."

"You wanna come down to the bar? I'll buy you a beer."

His father chuckled. "These old bones are gonna sit right here for the rest of the night. That is, till I drag my old ass right to that bedroom in there."

Old bones, his ass. At fifty-two, Calvin Caine was in as good of shape as he'd been all his life.

"You sure?"

Calvin nodded.

"All right. Don't say I didn't ask."

Another chuckle came from the old man. "How's that little gal workin' out? Amy, right?"

"Yep. She's doin' good. Catchin' on quick and she's cleanin' shit up."

"Really?" His father seemed more interested. "Think maybe she can come by the store? Try to get the office organized?"

Wolfe figured Amy would love that. Plus, he wanted the old man and Amy to get along. Aside from Lynx, his father was the closest person in his life, and he enjoyed every minute he got to spend with him. These days, they didn't do much more than chat for a few minutes here and there.

"If you ask her nicely," Wolfe told him, "I'm sure she'd be happy to."

"Heard the sheriff's been stoppin' in." Calvin's gray eyebrows rose. "Things good?"

"Yeah. He's just checkin' in."

Emerald-green eyes so like his own stared back at him. Wolfe knew his father was a smart man. He'd heard the rumors, knew what Wolfe and his cousin had been up to all these years. If Wolfe had to guess, the man probably even knew about Wolfe's preference for men and women. Not that they'd ever talked about it. His father tended to stay out of his business when it came to shit like that.

"Heard you had 'em both out at the house this afternoon."

Well, no one said anything was sacred in a small town. Wolfe had no idea how word had traveled that fast, but it didn't surprise him.

"Teachin' Amy to shoot."

"Good idea."

Wolfe was tempted to ask him what he'd heard but decided against it. Until he figured out what was going on with Amy, he didn't want any speculation to cloud his thoughts or anyone else's.

"All right. I'm meetin' up with Lynx at Reagan's. Talk to you later."

Calvin lifted a hand in a short wave. "Love ya, kid. Y'all be good."

"Love you, too, Dad."

With that, Wolfe headed out the same way he'd come.

The drive to Reagan's took all of five minutes. Getting into the bar took another two after stopping to chat with one of the cowboys hanging in the parking lot, and then Wolfe was finally perched on a barstool with a cold beer in front of him. His cousin hadn't arrived yet, but Wolfe was already anticipating the knock-down drag-out that was coming. In fact, it was likely going to happen before Lynx even arrived. If the obnoxious cowboys in the back didn't cool their jets and leave Amy alone, Wolfe was going to rearrange their priorities right quick.

"Oh, come on, honey. I'm sure Reagan won't mind if you have a beer with us. We'll even let you break if you want."

One guy leaned on his pool stick while the other moved closer to Amy.

Amy sidestepped a hand that reached for her and Wolfe inadvertently growled.

"What's the matter, doll face? Shy? Don't worry, we'll be easy on you."

Wolfe looked up and met Reagan's concerned gaze. He nodded, taking a long pull on his beer as he got to his feet. "Might as well call the sheriff now," he told her, then set the bottle down with a little more force than necessary.

"We'll be happy to show you around town, sugar," the younger one said. "You're new here, right? Probably don't know a lot of people? We can fix that for ya. And we'll even end the outing with a personal tour of my bedroom." The guy chuckled.

Wow. What a fuckup.

Shaking his head in disbelief, Wolfe stepped up behind Amy, careful not to touch her.

"I doubt she'd be impressed by your momma's house," Wolfe told the younger one.

That earned him a glare from both men. Wolfe recognized them. They were wranglers over at the Double D.

"Fuck you, Caine. Why don't you mind your own damn business," the older one spat.

Amy inadvertently stepped back, her body coming up against Wolfe's. He didn't know if she was even aware how close she was, but he damn sure wasn't about to say anything. Placing his hands on her shoulders, he steered her around and turned her toward the bar. "I got this."

Her big brown eyes flew up to meet his and he forced a smile.

"Who the fuck do you think you are?" the young dumb ass questioned. "We were talkin' to her."

"You were actin' a fool," Wolfe informed him, turning back slowly.

It was too damn early for these idiots to be acting like … well, like idiots. No way had a couple of beers pushed them to the limit and made their inner jackasses take over. They simply lacked any fucking manners.

When the older one took a step closer, Wolfe noticed the instant he realized their true size differences.

"Look. We don't want no trouble." Holding his hands up in surrender, the guy kept his eyes locked with Wolfe's.

"Don't let me hear you disrespectin' her again."

"Of course not."

Wolfe pointed at the younger one. "And if you touch her, I'll break your fucking hand."

Knowing it was a gamble, Wolfe gave the two men his back. Even as he did, he knew what was coming. The pool stick cracked right across his shoulder blades. The force of the blow would've sent him sprawling across the floor if he hadn't braced for it. The second strike across his kidney made him wince, but he managed to turn and block the next one.

"Fight!" someone hollered.

Wolfe grabbed the fist flying toward him and stilled it. He squeezed until the guy grimaced.

"You wanna do this? Let's take it outside." No way would Wolfe disrespect Reagan and let this go on inside her bar.

"Come on, then!" the younger guy blustered. "I ain't scared'a you."

"Let's do this." Lynx's voice boomed, echoing off the walls of the bar. "Right fucking now."

Wolfe peered over his shoulder to see his cousin standing there. Lynx looked fit to be tied; the dark scowl on his face accentuated the danger that often surrounded him. Clearly, he had walked in on the action.

"What the fuck, man?" the older guy said. "This ain't got nothin' to do with you."

"The hell it don't," Lynx growled, then spun on his heel and waved his hand in the air. "Let's take this shit outside. Reagan, round 'em up."

Wolfe gave a firm push on the fist he was still holding, sending the guy onto his ass. The distinct sound of a shotgun being cocked had the two fools glancing over at the bar.

Figuring this was going to happen one way or another, Wolfe turned toward the door, but not before searching out Amy. He wanted to ensure she was okay.

Her pretty brown eyes looked wary but not fearful.

"Son of a bitch!" Reagan grumbled as she pointed her shotgun toward the ceiling. "Just one Friday night. That's all I want. One fucking Friday where I don't have to deal with a bunch of dumb asses."

With that parting shot, they all headed out to the parking lot.

THE CALL CAME in earlier than he'd expected, but Rhys had been waiting for it. In fact, he'd been just a block from Reagan's when he got the call, so he arrived at the bar before the fight spilled out into the parking lot.

Climbing out of his truck, Rhys made his way toward the idiots getting ready to throw down.

"Lynx Caine," Rhys bellowed. "Stand down, boy."

Lynx flipped him off.

Rhys sighed.

"Fucker took a cheap shot at Wolfe." Lynx glared at the man he was toe to toe with. "I think I'm entitled to beat his ass."

Rhys's gaze swung to Wolfe. The man looked to be in one piece, but that didn't mean there wasn't some damage. He'd have to get the story in a minute though. Right now, he needed to keep Lynx from killing these boys. The guy was coiled tight, and he figured the shit going down with his soon-to-be ex-wife wasn't helping his mood.

"Party's over," Rhys informed the crowd that was gathering. "Take your asses back inside or move out."

With a disappointed grumble, the handful of people who'd come outside turned to go back.

"Not you," Rhys called out to the two guys who'd obviously started this.

"We didn't do shit."

"Sean, don't be a dumb ass," his friend said, although that warning was clearly coming a little late. "We don't want no shit, Sheriff. We'll head out."

Rhys glanced at Wolfe once more. When the big guy nodded his consent to let the idiots go, Rhys turned back. "Don't come back here tonight."

"No fuckin' woman's worth this shit," the younger guy grumbled.

Rhys frowned, trying to catch up.

"Especially no two-bit trashy waitress."

"Fuck," Lynx groaned seconds before he stepped directly in front of Wolfe, holding him back with a hand on the man's chest.

The fury etched on Wolfe's face was something Rhys had rarely seen. The guy was a good ol' boy by nature. He didn't *seek* trouble, but the opposite couldn't be said.

"I'm sure she's banged half the boys in this town already," the younger one threw in for good measure.

Wolfe growled.

It was a damn good thing Rhys was on duty. Otherwise, he would've taken the little asshole down himself. As it was, he was tempted to pull out his gun and fire a warning shot just to make the asshole dance.

He wouldn't, but he wanted to.

"You've got three seconds to get off the property," Rhys declared. "Otherwise, you'll be spendin' the night in jail."

"What for?" the younger one hissed. "We didn't—"

"One," Rhys began. "Two…"

His friend was clearly smarter, grabbing the smartass's shirt and jerking him backwards. "Shut the hell up, Sean."

Rhys waited for Sean and his smarter friend to leave. When he was left with only Lynx and Wolfe, he turned to the Caine cousins. "What the hell happened?"

Lynx shrugged. "No fuckin' clue. Got here just in time to see the bastard—"

Wolfe held up a hand to stop Lynx mid-sentence. "I got this."

With a curt glance between the two men, Lynx shrugged again, then sauntered toward the door.

Wolfe was still staring after the two men who'd started walking.

"You wanna tell me what happened?"

It took a few seconds, but Wolfe finally looked his way. "No."

"Should I ask Amy?"

Wolfe frowned. "Be my guest, but I think she'll tell you the same thing."

Rhys sighed.

These boys knew exactly how to wear down his last nerve.

Before he could decide how to handle it, his radio chirped, the signal for another call.

"You think you can behave?" Rhys asked Wolfe directly.

The big man glared at him, but there wasn't any heat in his scowl. Not from anger anyway.

"I'll catch up with you later," Rhys told him, then headed for his truck.

The night had been unbearably busy. One call after another had kept him running from one side of the county to the other. He'd wondered if there was a damn full moon, but the cloud cover had made it impossible to tell.

By the time he was ready to call it a night, Rhys drove by Reagan's to ensure the place had closed down. All was quiet on that front, so he went over to Marla's Bar. Normally, he would stop in and check on things, but he had something more pressing to do tonight. Seeing that Wolfe wasn't over at Marla's, he could only assume the man was at home.

Rhys fully intended to find out and to pay him a little visit. It had taken some time, but he'd finally gotten the details of what went down. The altercation between the two men and Amy, Wolfe stepping in and taking a pool stick across the back. Twice. It was a damn wonder those boys were still walking. It didn't happen often, but Rhys had seen Wolfe lose his shit a time or two. No one wanted to be on the receiving end of that man's anger. No one.

When Rhys was a mile out, he called Wolfe.

Wolfe answered on the second ring. "'Yello."

"Open the damn gate," Rhys demanded. "I'll be there in five."

The call disconnected without a response.

Eight minutes later, Rhys was pulling up in front of Wolfe's house. It was pitch-black outside and in, but he knew Wolfe was home.

Rhys knocked on the front door.

A second later it opened, and a shirtless Wolfe stood before him, taking up a spot against the doorjamb. The only light came from a lamp inside that offered a pale yellow glow silhouetting Wolfe from behind.

"What can I do you for, Sheriff?"

Rhys didn't even pretend not to eye every mouthwatering inch of the man that was visible. The various tattoos that decorated Wolfe's body did nothing to hide the sinful musculature. In fact, the ink enhanced his physique, enough that Rhys's mouth suddenly watered with the need to taste him.

But he wasn't here for that.

Not entirely, anyway.

"You cool?" Rhys asked, meeting Wolfe's eyes.

One dark eyebrow lifted as Wolfe stared back at him. "You came all the way out here to ask me that?"

Wolfe pushed off the wall and moved closer.

Once again, Rhys found himself standing his ground.

"Or was there somethin' else you had in mind, Sheriff?"

Rhys kept his eyes locked on Wolfe's rugged features.

Wolfe grabbed Rhys's wrist roughly. "Maybe you wanted to feel for yourself?"

"This a game to you?" Rhys asked. He needed to know for sure that Wolfe wasn't fucking with him.

Wolfe pressed Rhys's hand to the hard ridge behind his zipper. When Wolfe hissed in a breath, that was the only response Rhys needed, but Wolfe added, "What do you think?"

Rhys kept his hand pressed against Wolfe's rock-hard dick, adding a small amount of friction, wishing like hell those unbuttoned jeans weren't in the way. He didn't intend to take this any further, but he couldn't stop the need to touch Wolfe.

"Is that what you want?" Wolfe asked, his voice pitched low and laced with gravel. "My dick?"

"I want more than that," Rhys admitted. "The same as you."

"How the fuck do you know what I want?"

Rhys stepped forward, and to his surprise, Wolfe took a step back. He continued to crowd the bigger man until Wolfe was up against the stone wall of the house. Grinding his palm against Wolfe's erection, Rhys held his gaze. "Trust me. I know exactly what you want. You want to know what it'll feel like with my mouth wrapped around your dick."

Wolfe's expression didn't change.

"You wanna know how fucking hot it'll be when the two of us are makin' Amy burn hotter and hotter until she can't contain it anymore. Then you want to slide your dick inside her sweet body while I take her ass." Rhys waited to see if Wolfe would deny it. He didn't. "It's drivin' you fuckin' crazy, ain't it?"

Wolfe didn't respond with words, but he reached down and pushed his jeans off his hips, freeing his cock. "Put your mouth on me."

The rough growl was almost impossible to resist. However, Rhys still wasn't sure Wolfe wasn't fucking with him. Rather than give in to the temptation only to be disappointed later, he shook his head.

"Not yet." Instead, Rhys wrapped his hand around Wolfe's cock, fisting him tightly. Wolfe's dick was long and thick. Fucking huge, just like the man. "You'll have to be patient."

Wolfe hissed in a breath when Rhys began jerking him off, stroking roughly.

"Son of a bitch. Rhys … goddamn … fuck…"

Wolfe's hips thrust forward, fucking Rhys's hand.

Rhys's dick twitched against his zipper. He would've given any damn thing for Wolfe to touch him, but he couldn't allow it. Not yet. Not until he knew how this would play out. As much as he wanted Wolfe, he wanted Amy just as much. He knew Wolfe felt the same, but the man was in desperate need of relief. Rhys understood that. Shit, for the past week he'd jacked off morning and night just to take the edge off.

Wolfe's hand wrapped around Rhys's, and they stroked the length of Wolfe's cock together right there on Wolfe's front porch, the warm night breeze blowing over them.

"Imagine if Amy was here," Rhys said, his voice low. "If she was watchin'. You think she'd get off on it? You think she'd wanna join in?" That was a question Rhys knew no one had the answer to, but it was a fantasy they could live out right here and now. "Think about it, Wolfe. That sexy woman ridin' your face, her tight little pussy grindin' against your mouth while you drive her fuckin' crazy. And while you're doing that, I'll be suckin' your cock, takin' all of you in my mouth…"

Rhys knew the moment Wolfe lost control. He felt the big man's body tighten, his hand gripping Rhys's painfully hard as he erupted, cum splashing on Wolfe's bare stomach.

When Wolfe finally opened his eyes, Rhys stared at him.

Rhys could see the need in Wolfe's eyes. Hell, Rhys felt it.

Rather than give in, though, Rhys knew he had to hold out. And if he did, so did Wolfe.

"Be patient." Rhys wasn't sure who he was talking to, himself or Wolfe. Probably both.

It took more willpower than he thought he possessed to turn and walk away from Wolfe Caine when he had him right where he wanted him, but Rhys managed.

He would likely regret it later, but he still put one foot in front of the other and climbed back into his truck.

7

AMY WOKE UP Saturday morning to the sun shining in through her bedroom window. Her eyes opened and she lay there, staring at the ceiling. She felt different. At first, she didn't know why, then she realized…

No nightmare.

She wasn't sure when the last time was that she hadn't had the same terrifying dream, but last night she'd slept soundly. Well, sort of. She'd had a dream of a different kind, one she'd never had before. This one involved a sexy black-haired, green-eyed cowboy and a handsome brown-haired, blue-eyed sheriff. Both of them were touching her, kissing her, driving her absolutely crazy.

She realized she was sweating, but it wasn't from terror. It was from…

Oh, man. That had been *some* dream.

"You're crazy," she whispered to herself, unable to keep from smiling.

She seriously doubted either man was even half-interested in her. Sure, she'd seen them give her a couple of what she'd thought had been *I'm interested in you* looks, but she'd obviously misinterpreted them. Amy was almost positive the two men were into each other, which meant they were definitely *not* into her.

Her cell phone buzzed and she jumped, knocking her alarm clock onto the floor when she reached for it. Her throat felt thick as she stared at the screen.

So much for thinking the fear had abated.

The alert showed it was a text from a number she didn't recognize. Clicking on the text app, she stared at the screen.

Do you like to swim? If not, we could go to the range again. You know, if you're up to it.

Amy's heart did a double tap in her chest. The good kind.

Oh, and if you don't recognize the number, this is Wolfe.

She laughed. As if she thought it was anyone else.

With trembling fingers, she tapped out a response: *I like to swim.*

And she did. Although she couldn't remember the last time she'd been swimming. Would've been sometime in high school, she figured.

The reply came almost instantly. *Good. I'll pick you up in twenty minutes. We'll grab breakfast on the way out to the lake. It's a private lake, so you don't have to worry about an audience.*

Amy could think of nothing to say except: *Okay.*

As soon as those four letters were out there, Amy launched herself out of bed.

Twenty minutes later, there was a knock on her door. Her heart was once again in her throat, but it wasn't from fear. This was something else. Anticipation, maybe?

Yeah. That had to be it.

Smoothing her hands down her shirt, she walked to the front door. With a firm grip on the knob, she turned it, pulled back, and grinned.

"Mornin'," Wolfe greeted.

He looked good.

Really good.

He was wearing jeans—not a surprise—and a black T-shirt with the Cedar Door logo on it. He had a ball cap on. The brim had been arched, which did little to shield his eyes but a whole heck of a lot for his sex appeal.

"You ready?"

Amy nodded, feeling somewhat light-headed.

Since she didn't carry a purse—she purposely kept all identification hidden in a safe in her house—she had nothing to get except her house key. After locking up, she followed Wolfe out to his truck. Once again, he opened her door for her, allowed her to get in, then shut it gently behind her.

A second later, he was in the truck.

Amy noticed a box on the center console. A rectangular white box. "Are those...?"

"Donuts?" he supplied.

Her eyes widened as she looked up at his face. "You bought donuts?"

He nodded.

One day last week, Lynx had brought donuts to the shop. Amy hadn't meant to show her excitement, but she had. And now Wolfe had gotten more. She was tempted to throw her arms around him.

She wouldn't, but the idea was appealing.

Amy smiled at him. "Lynx said the nearest donut store is twenty minutes away."

One dark eyebrow lifted as though he was waiting for the punchline.

"You were at the donut store when you texted me."

"I was."

"So, how'd you know I'd go with you?"

Wolfe chuckled, putting the truck in gear. "Didn't. Figured if you shot me down, Lynx would've finished off the donuts."

Amy couldn't keep the smile off her face. "Is he gonna be disappointed?"

Wolfe's sideways glance sent warm fuzzies through her. "What he doesn't know won't hurt him." He nodded toward her. "You did bring a swimsuit, right?"

"I did." As soon as she'd brushed her teeth and pulled her hair back into a ponytail, Amy had gone in search of a swimsuit. She'd bought one when she went to Walmart right before she moved into her house. She hadn't figured she'd ever wear it, but every woman needed to have a swimsuit, just in case.

This was that *just in case* moment.

Granted, it wasn't anything fancy, but it was a two-piece. She hadn't considered how revealing that would be until she'd put it on. Hence the reason she had on a T-shirt she intended to keep on.

"Is Rhys going with us?" She wasn't sure why she asked that, but the words had stumbled right out of her mouth before she could think about it.

"Do you want him to?"

If Amy wasn't mistaken, there was some serious interest in Wolfe's eyes. "Sure. Why not? He's your friend, right?"

"He's my friend."

"Then invite him. It'll be three friends going for a swim."

If Amy wasn't mistaken, Wolfe's heavy sigh wasn't exactly laced with disappointment.

WOLFE KNEW HE was reading too much into it when Amy asked about Rhys. Taking her at face value was the smartest thing to do, but there was a deep, dark, underlying desire that had Wolfe holding out hope for something he knew would never happen.

Still, he called Rhys.

"'Sup?" the sheriff greeted, his voice a rough rasp in Wolfe's ear.

"Amy and I are headin' to the lake." Wolfe glanced over at Amy. "She wants to know if you wanna join us."

She smiled back at him.

"*She* wants to know?" Rhys sounded skeptical.

"Actually, yes," Wolfe assured him.

"When?"

"Right now."

Rhys yawned. Apparently, Wolfe had woken him up.

"Yeah. I'll meet y'all there. I assume you're takin' her to *your* lake?"

"Yep."

"Cool." Another yawn. "See you in an hour."

"We won't wait on you." Wolfe chuckled. "And we've got donuts. You'll be lucky if there're any left. Amy's eyein' them right this minute. Later." Wolfe hung up and set his phone in the center console. "He'll meet us in an hour."

"How long have you known Rhys?" Amy asked, pulling one of the glazed donuts from the box.

"Since elementary school. Maybe before that." He cut a quick glance her way. "We're both from Embers Ridge."

"Are y'all … close?"

Wolfe chuckled, his thoughts drifting back to last night on his front porch when Rhys had jacked him off. Couldn't get much closer than that, but still, Wolfe said, "Not really, no. He's five years older than I am. Our families aren't exactly on good terms."

"No?"

"No." He laughed. "It's a redneck thing, I guess. A lot of glares and grumbles. Although it's calmed significantly over the past few decades." Even more so since Rhys's old man died. People said Rhys's grandfather was an ornery old shit. Rhys's old man had made the guy look like a fucking teddy bear.

"Is there a reason for it?"

Wolfe shrugged and turned off the main road. "Probably. If I had to guess, someone stole someone's girl or gun or land. That's the way it usually goes."

Amy laughed softly. "It must've been fun growing up in a small town."

"I wouldn't trade it," Wolfe admitted. "No small-town livin' for you?"

Amy shook her head. "Not unless Houston counts as small."

Wolfe didn't say anything immediately. He didn't know if Amy had meant to tell him something so personal. She'd been careful not to talk about herself and he'd been careful not to pry.

"Well, I'd say Embers Ridge is much smaller than Houston."

"I like it here," Amy told him.

"What do you like most?"

"I don't know."

"The people? The pace? The eggs at the diner? Or maybe seein' the cattle graze alongside every road that goes through town?" He smiled at her, then cocked an eyebrow. "It's the donuts, right?"

Honest to God, Wolfe had never seen someone react to donuts the way Amy had the day Lynx brought them into the shop. It was as though she'd been deprived of them her entire life. And that beaming smile was the very reason Wolfe had gone forty minutes out of his way to get donuts this morning.

Another laugh from Amy and Wolfe felt the tension in his spine ease. Being around her felt right, but every time he was, he was apprehensive. Not necessarily because of any tension between them, either. His problem came more from the fact that he didn't want to intrude on her. He liked that Amy was opening up to him slowly. They were becoming friends, as she'd said. And yes, he wanted to get his hands on her, but that was something he could wait for.

"You," she said softly.

Wolfe's head jerked toward her. "What about me?"

He noticed the blush that colored her cheeks. "That's what I like most about this town."

"Is that right?" He couldn't deny his ego swelled from that knowledge.

"And Rhys." She grinned. "And maybe Reagan and Lynx, too."

Laughing, Wolfe turned the truck down the dirt road that led to the lake. "Aww, come on now, girl. Why you wanna wound my pride like that?"

"I seriously doubt anyone could wound your pride."

"Why do you think that?" It was probably true, but he still wanted to hear her take on it.

"I've seen you, Wolfe. The way all those cowboys look at you. They're intimidated, but it's like they can't let anyone know it."

"Naw. They're intimidated by Lynx."

Amy giggled. "Yes, I'd say they are. But also by you."

Silence descended as Wolfe steered the truck down to the edge of the water. He parked beneath a tree. Although it was only nine in the morning, it was already ninety degrees.

"You ready to do this?" he asked, noticing Amy was wringing her hands in her lap.

She peered over at him from beneath her lashes, a small smile forming on her lips as she reached over and unbuckled her seat belt.

Her smile widened. "Last one in's a rotten egg!"

Wolfe roared a laugh as Amy launched herself out of the truck, running full out toward the lake.

It took a second for him to toe off his boots, but Wolfe was right behind her.

Jeans and all.

WHEN RHYS ARRIVED at the lake, he found Wolfe and Amy already in the water. She was splashing him and attempting to get away while Wolfe was laughing and swimming circles around her.

Rhys found himself transfixed by the sight of Amy above all else.

The woman was so damn pretty when she smiled. With her hair slicked back, shirt plastered to her body, showcasing her perky tits, she looked like an angel sent down to wreak havoc on Rhys's good sense.

But still, that smile. It did something for him in a big way.

Considering he hadn't seen her do it that often, perhaps that was why he was so taken with her. He still didn't know the first thing about her—not where she was from, who her parents were, if she'd gone to college or simply decided to work for a living, who she was running from—but he found he didn't care. Whatever her demons were, they didn't matter. Not while she was here and certainly not when she was laughing like that.

"'Bout time, Sheriff," Amy taunted, her arms moving to keep her afloat.

They weren't far from the water's edge, but obviously far enough Amy couldn't touch the sandy bottom. Wolfe didn't seem to be having the same problem.

"I brought coffee," Rhys announced.

"Wolfe brought donuts!" Amy informed him.

"I heard. Did you eat 'em all?" Rhys lowered the tailgate on his truck and set the coffee cups in the back before heading over and retrieving the donut box from Wolfe's truck. He peeked inside and noticed there was only one missing.

"Not yet," Amy answered, her response delayed when Wolfe tried to grab for her.

After depositing the donuts on the tailgate, Rhys turned to find Wolfe walking out of the water with Amy on his back. She had one arm curled around his neck, holding on tight, while she giggled. Wolfe still donned his jeans but lacked a shirt. To his dismay, it looked as though Amy was wearing her shorts along with her T-shirt.

Wolfe set Amy down on the tailgate, then shook his head, spraying water over Rhys.

"I think you should get wet," Amy teased, her eyes locked on Rhys.

"Yeah?"

She nodded.

"If I go in, I'm takin' you with me."

Amy hopped off the tailgate. "You'll have to catch me first!"

She took off and Rhys looked at Wolfe, shocked by the complete one-eighty this woman had done in the past week. He briefly wondered if working for the Caine cousins had brought her out of her shell. If so, he hoped she continued doing it.

Wolfe shrugged and Rhys toed off his boots and ripped his shirt off over his head, then took off after her. She was already in the water by the time he caught up, so he dove in, coming up beside her. He pretended to grab for her, gauging her reaction. Surprising him even more, Amy belted out a laugh, then dunked him with her hand on his head.

Rhys came up for air and put his arms around her. He didn't try to hold her tight, but that didn't matter because she clung to him, hopping on his back, her legs coming around his waist.

Sucking in a breath because the feel of her body against his was damn near enough to take him out at the knees, Rhys steadied himself.

"I need a donut, Sheriff," she whispered against his ear.

"Your wish is my command." Without hesitating, he carried her out of the water and back over to the truck.

Rhys knew he looked bewildered, which he was. This side of Amy was something he hadn't expected. Oh, he liked it, all right. More than he could say. He liked seeing the light in her eyes and a smile on her face, the carefree, almost naïve attitude she seemed to have. Hell, he'd go so far as to say he loved to hear her laugh.

He caught Wolfe watching them, a heated look in his emerald eyes.

"Best idea you've had all year, Caine," Rhys muttered as he set Amy on the tailgate.

She grabbed for a donut, kicking her legs.

He wasn't sure what had caused her to be this relaxed, but whatever it was, Rhys wanted to bottle it and use it all the damn time.

"So…" Amy chewed, glancing between the two of them. "Do y'all come here often?"

Rhys laughed. "That's a serious line there, girl."

Amy grinned. "You know what I mean."

Rhys looked at Wolfe.

"I come here with Lynx most of the time. My dad'll sometimes wander out here, too."

"What he's not sayin' is that they've had some serious parties down by this lake."

Amy canted her head to the side. "Is it true what they say about you and Lynx? Were y'all really that wild?"

Wolfe grinned. "Probably."

"No probably about it," Rhys countered. "And they haven't grown out of it, either."

Amy smiled, taking another bite of her donut. "What about you, Sheriff? I'm sure you weren't all sweet and innocent."

"Oh, he was a good little church boy," Wolfe said, his voice gruff, teasing.

"Yep. I was."

"Really?" Amy didn't look convinced.

"No." Rhys hadn't been nearly as wild as the Caine cousins, but he'd started enough shit back in the day.

"Do you go to church?" Amy looked from one to the other. "Either of you?"

"Yep," Wolfe admitted. "We do."

"Does Lynx?" she asked, grinning.

"He does." Wolfe laughed. "Why? You think he needs to find God?"

Amy laughed. "I didn't say that." She took another bite. "How old are you?"

She was looking at him, so Rhys answered. "Thirty-four."

Amy nodded, then looked at Wolfe, lifting an eyebrow.

"I'll be thirty in August."

"Hmm." She tore a piece of her donut off. "Y'all are old." Her eyes lifted to theirs and she laughed.

"Watch it, little girl, or I'll toss your ass back in that water," Wolfe told her as he reached out and flipped her hair.

Amy grinned. "I really like it here."

"Here?" Rhys took a sip of his coffee. "Like *right* here?"

"Yes. Right here." Her face sobered somewhat. "With the two of you."

There was a strange warmth that filled his chest at her admission. Amy Smith—or whatever her name really was—was going to have him wrapped around her little finger if she wasn't careful.

Oh, hell, who was he kidding?

He was over halfway there.

8

"I'M JUST GLAD you had the sense to make me wear sunscreen," Amy told Wolfe as he drove down her street.

"You didn't put it on your nose," Wolfe teased.

Amy pulled down the visor to look in the mirror. When she saw how red her nose was, she laughed.

Seemed she'd been doing that all day. Laughing. It felt good. Strange, almost. But definitely good.

Now that she was going home to an empty house, the familiar trepidation was coming back and she was dreading it. They'd spent the better part of the day at the lake, the three of them laughing and joking and enjoying the sunshine. To her surprise, both men had kept things relatively impersonal. They'd answered her questions when she rapid fired them, telling her about growing up in a small town, about Friday night football at the high school, bonfires and all-night parties, but not once had they turned the questions on her.

Halfway through the day, Amy realized they'd done it on purpose. They were respecting her space, and she appreciated them for it, even if she did want to share a little bit about herself with them. She hadn't had real friends in … well, not since high school. Before her parents died, before…

Wolfe pulled up in front of her house.

Shaking off the revelry, she took a deep breath. "I had fun today," she told him, closing the visor and looking directly at him.

Of course, *his* nose wasn't red. In fact, his skin had bronzed more than it had been already, and he really was too handsome for words.

"Me, too." Wolfe turned and looked out the front windshield. "Do you work tonight?"

"Yeah." Amy peered up at the empty house. "But I could make dinner if you … uh … want to come inside."

She noticed Wolfe's hands gripping the steering wheel until his knuckles were white. He obviously had something on his mind, something she probably wouldn't like.

"Sorry. I didn't mean to be forward. I … uh…"

Wolfe's warm gaze traveled over to her and Amy sat still, waiting for him to say something. Anything.

"I'd like to go inside your house. And I'd love for you to cook for me," he said, his voice soft, deep. "But I'm not sure that's a good idea right now."

"Oh."

Oh. Right.

Rhys.

Amy shook her head. "I didn't mean… I…" She swallowed hard. "I know about you and Rhys."

Wolfe cleared his throat.

"I mean, I don't *know* about you. It's not like anyone has said anything, but it seems to me that you like each other."

"Like each other?" Wolfe's words echoed with amusement.

Amy squared her shoulders and looked directly at him, her face flaming. "It's okay. I get it. I didn't expect … anything. I mean, I like you as a friend and all. If you and Rhys are in a relationship, that's cool."

Wolfe laughed, the sound booming inside the truck.

"What?" Amy's face heated more. "What are you laughing at?"

"Is that what you think?" He grinned and Amy couldn't look away. The man was so incredibly good-looking. "That Rhys and I are…"

Amy swallowed hard.

"Darlin', there's a lot you don't know."

"Then tell me." She wasn't sure she wanted to know, but she could handle the truth. She'd accepted the fact that whatever was going on between her and Wolfe and Rhys was friendship. She liked both men immensely, and she was sort of happy that they liked each other. It meant she would never have to choose between them, because honestly, she wasn't sure she could at this point.

"It's … complicated."

Amy nodded, understanding. "I get it. I promise I won't say anything to anyone. It's really not my business."

Wolfe turned to face her, his arm sliding behind her head, over the seat back, his hand brushing her neck. He tilted his head forward, holding her gaze with such intensity it stole her breath.

"I guarantee, darlin', it's not what you think."

Amy held her breath, silently willing him to tell her. There was a tiny ray of hope lingering deep inside, although she had no idea where it had come from or why it was there.

His touch, his mere presence was so comforting Amy wished it could be different. She'd never thought she'd want anything to do with another man after the hell she'd been through, but when she was with Wolfe and Rhys, she felt safe, cared for.

Then again, Wolfe was her boss. Her friend.

And here she was pushing for something that she couldn't have no matter what she wished for. She wasn't at a place in her life where she could share anything about herself, and Wolfe deserved to have someone who could be honest with him. He'd been nothing but honest with her, and she couldn't return it.

On top of that, Amy wasn't sure she was ready for anything as serious as a relationship. It seemed she'd been under someone's thumb her entire life, and she wasn't interested in doing that again. Wasn't sure she ever would be.

"It's okay," she told him, leaning into his touch slightly as she reached for the door handle. "Thanks for today. I hope we can do it again."

Wolfe nodded, but he didn't say anything. She noticed how his eyes dropped to her mouth, and for a second, Amy thought he might kiss her. Instead, he pulled back, put both hands on the steering wheel again.

"I'll see you at Reagan's tonight."

"Okay." Not wanting to make things any more uncomfortable than she already had, Amy hopped out of the truck and shut the door quickly.

The hair on the back of her neck prickled as she walked to her front porch. Rather than look around like a scaredy-cat, she shored up her nerve and went right for the door. If Wolfe hadn't been there, she probably would've walked around the house a few times, peered in the windows to ensure nothing had been tampered with. She didn't think he'd found her yet, but Amy knew he would eventually. If he'd figured out that she wasn't dead, he would try to find her.

Swallowing against the lump of fear in her throat, she inserted the key into the lock and twisted. Forcing a smile, she turned to look back at Wolfe. He was watching her. Amy offered a quick wave and then slipped inside, her heart thumping painfully in her chest. Closing the door, she leaned up against it and strained to listen for any unusual noises. Her eyes darted around the room, taking it all in. She didn't notice anything out of place. The throw pillows were still in the same position on her couch, the coaster holding last night's glass of water still on the coffee table, her sandals still tucked underneath.

With the air conditioner on and her clothes still damp, a chill ran through her.

She needed to take a shower. Not only to warm up but also because she had to be at work in a couple of hours.

Surely she could get through a couple of hours alone without having another panic attack. It shouldn't be too hard considering she could relive today over and over again. Hands down, today had been the best day she'd had in years.

Granted, she was going to have to tamp down the anticipation of seeing Wolfe or Rhys again. It wasn't going to do her any good, and if this crush she had on the two men turned into something more, she was in for some serious heartache.

Amy had been through enough.

That was the last damn thing she needed.

WOLFE WATCHED AS Amy disappeared inside her house. He should've put the truck in gear and pulled back down the gravel driveway, but he couldn't seem to do it.

He'd hated seeing the disappointment in her eyes when he turned her down. Hell, he would've given his left nut to go inside that house, but he honestly didn't trust himself. It'd been a hell of a day, one that had tested his patience. Spending the better part of it with Amy and Rhys had been more than he could stand. Not in a bad way, of course. But Wolfe wasn't a damn saint. He could only handle so much. And the temptation they presented was too much. It made him want things, crave things. *Need* things. Truth was, he had no business going down that road. Not yet.

"Fuck." He twisted his hands on the steering wheel, staring out the front windshield. "Go home, Caine. You'll see her tonight. Go. The fuck. Home."

Wolfe turned off the truck.

He got out.

He walked right up to Amy's front door.

He knocked.

And when she opened the door, he nearly fell to his knees at her feet.

Her big brown eyes stared back at him, confusion etched on her pretty features.

Wolfe put his hands on the doorjamb and leaned forward. He refused to touch her, afraid if he did, he'd never let her go.

Locking his eyes with hers, he decided to give it to her straight.

"I want to come inside."

Her eyes widened, but she didn't say anything.

"But I'm fucking scared, Amy. I'm scared that I'm gonna do somethin' to scare you, and that's the last goddamn thing I wanna do."

"You won't," she said softly.

"I will." He made sure there was a ton of confidence in his tone. "I can only take so much, and the more time I spend with you, the more I want to touch you, to kiss you." *To lay you down and bury myself inside your body.* He kept that part to himself though. "And if you let me in your house, if you sit down to dinner with me, if you smile at me the way you did today … I'm scared I won't be able to stop myself."

He saw the way she swallowed hard.

"Do you understand what I'm tellin' you?"

She nodded.

"That's why I can't come inside. It has nothin' to do with Rhys." He shook his head. "Well, maybe a little, but like I said, that's complicated."

He got another nod.

Wolfe pushed off the wall and stood to his full height. "I'll see you at Reagan's."

Turning away from her was the hardest damn thing he'd ever done, but Wolfe knew he had to. It was the right thing to do.

"Wolfe."

He heard her feet on the wooden porch behind him.

"I want you to come inside."

Dropping his head, Wolfe closed his eyes. "I don't wanna fuck this up with you, Amy."

"You won't."

"You don't know that."

"I do."

Wolfe turned to face her. Only then did he realize how close she was standing. He had to stare down at her, holding his breath when her arms moved toward him, her hands sliding up to his neck, pulling him down.

His entire world collapsed into that one single moment when her mouth touched his. He didn't kiss her back. Not at first. But when her fingers slid into the hair at his nape, Wolfe lost control.

Cupping the back of her head as gently as he could, he tilted her head and pressed his lips to hers. When she drew in a deep breath, he slid his tongue over her lower lip, then dipped into her mouth. Amy kissed him back, her tongue gliding against his hesitantly at first, then more confidently.

Jesus.

How could one kiss be so fucking hot?

He was lost to it. Lost to the sensation, the overwhelming desire that crashed in his veins. His body tightened, but he remained as still as he could, afraid to move closer, afraid to do anything that would cause her to pull away from him.

Wolfe allowed the kiss to go on for a minute, but then he pulled back, his entire body aching for her. Keeping her head cradled in his hand, he pulled her against his chest and sighed when she wrapped her arms around his waist.

He held her, his muscles vibrating with need, but sated by the fact she was in his arms, touching him even if they were still outside, still standing on her porch. Even if he still wasn't going to go inside.

This woman … this one sweet, far-too-innocent woman was going to be the one to bring him to his knees.

He knew it.

And the worst part was that he didn't even care.

Not one fucking bit.

SATURDAY NIGHTS IN Embers Ridge were much like Friday nights. Mostly disturbances of the inebriated variety, some domestic disputes, usually a riled-up cowboy who hadn't figured out the best way to wind down after a long, hot week. And of course, the animals that tended to wander away from where they belonged.

Fortunately, tonight had been slow. With two of his deputies out on patrol, Rhys spent the majority of the evening in his office doing his damnedest not to do another search on Amy Smith.

The buzzer sounded on the main door and Rhys got up to go see who it was. Generally, the public only stopped by during weekday hours, but from time to time, someone showed up to bitch about whatever it was they had on their mind.

The buzzer sounded again just as he was about to turn the corner. Rhys was gearing up to tell whoever it was to chill, but then he saw Wolfe standing there, glaring at the glass.

Rhys fought the urge to grin. The man looked worse for wear, but he couldn't imagine why. After the day they'd had…

"What's your problem?" Rhys asked as he opened the door.

Without a response, Wolfe walked right past him and down the hall.

Rhys flipped the lock on the door, then followed, trying to figure out what could've possibly pissed Wolfe off to the point he'd show up at the sheriff's office on a Saturday night.

He found Wolfe in his office, pacing the three feet in front of his desk. The man's long legs didn't allow him to take too many steps.

"Who else is here?" Wolfe asked, his tone rough.

"No one. They're out on patrol. Why? What's wrong?"

As soon as Rhys cleared the doorway, Wolfe closed the door behind him. The next thing Rhys knew, he was up against the wall, Wolfe's solid body pressing into him, his lips crushed beneath Wolfe's firm, warm mouth.

Son of a bitch.

Unable to help himself, Rhys grabbed Wolfe and jerked him closer, kissing him back with every ounce of the pent-up lust that had been coursing through him for days now.

His brain fought to keep up, to process all that was happening.

Wolfe's soft, warm lips.

His scratchy jaw.

Strong fingers digging into his flesh.

The confident, eager thrust of Wolfe's tongue.

The kiss was overloading his circuits and Rhys didn't even fucking care.

Wolfe growled, grinding against him, his rough hands cupping Rhys's head, his tongue roughly searching Rhys's mouth. Although Rhys fought to take control, it didn't happen. Wolfe was having none of that, so he gave in and let the man devour him.

When they eventually pulled apart, Rhys was breathing hard, but so was Wolfe.

"What the fuck?" Rhys's voice was hoarse.

"I kissed her."

"What?" Clearly his brain had been rattled a little from that.

"I kissed Amy. I told her I shouldn't, but ... well, technically she kissed me, but fuck if I didn't kiss her back."

Rhys righted his clothes. "And that's a bad thing why?"

"It's not a bad thing." Wolfe pulled off his ball cap and thrust his hands through his hair. "Well, not entirely. She seems to think you and I are... Fuck. I don't even know what she thinks, but she doesn't seem to mind it. And then she asked me to come inside her house, said she'd make me dinner. I refused because I fucking knew I would kiss her." Wolfe frowned. "She looked so goddamn disappointed. Dumb ass that I am, I went to her door." Wolfe looked at him for the first time. "I told her why I couldn't come in. And I didn't, but she kissed me anyway."

"Take a breath. Shit." Rhys understood everything except... "So why are you *here*?"

Wolfe's face was hard. "Because when she kissed me and I kissed her, I realized I wanted to fucking kiss you, too."

Well. Okay then.

Wolfe seemed to be waiting for Rhys to say something, so he said, "I don't see a problem with that."

The big man eased down into a chair, dropping his head into his hands. "I don't want to scare her."

"If she kissed you, I'd say you accomplished that goal."

Wolfe looked up. "I left after that. I couldn't go inside. Not after that kiss. Fuck. She's driving me goddamn crazy."

Rhys knew the feeling.

"I don't know what to do now," Wolfe admitted. If Rhys wasn't mistaken, there was a significant amount of confusion in the big man's tone. That was unusual for the normally confident cowboy.

Moving over to his desk, Rhys perched on the edge.

"Take it one day at a time."

Wolfe stood, taking one step and clearing the distance between them. Rhys looked up at him, waiting, wanting.

"Yeah?" Wolfe didn't sound convinced that was a good plan.

"Sure." Rhys's voice was rough. "Why not?"

Wolfe cupped his face and once again lowered his mouth to Rhys's. Without thinking, Rhys gripped Wolfe's shirt in his fist, kissing him back. This time, Wolfe's lips weren't quite as rough, not nearly as demanding. It was an exploratory kiss, one to confirm that this thing between them was real and it was explosive, regardless.

The kiss didn't last nearly long enough, but Rhys swallowed the groan of disappointment.

"She has to know about this," Wolfe said. "I need her to understand what's goin' on."

Rhys nodded. He got that. Of course, he had no idea how Amy would react, but he understood.

"What time do you get outta here?" Wolfe asked.

"Midnight."

The big man moved back, causing Rhys to release his shirt.

"Meet me and Amy at Reagan's when you're done. I wanna show her the lake at night."

Rhys nodded. "I'll be there."

Some of the warmth in Wolfe's eyes dimmed. "I don't know how this'll play out, but she has to know what we want."

"She does."

That didn't seem to ease the battle going on inside Wolfe's head, but neither of them could prepare for this. Whatever happened between the three of them—or *didn't* happen, for that matter—was all up to Amy.

Rhys hoped to God she was willing to explore.

It was all he could ask for.

9

FROM WHAT AMY could tell, the rough crowd had stayed at home tonight. It was already closing in on midnight and not one single fight had broken out.

Then again, that could've been due to the fact Lynx Caine was itching to take someone down and not a single person was man enough to go up against him. She had no idea what was bothering Wolfe's cousin, but he was practically vibrating with anger. And every now and then, she would catch him glancing over at Reagan as though he wanted to have the woman for dessert.

Amy had no idea what was up with that, but she was not going to stick her nose where it didn't belong.

Reagan had already called last call since she consistently closed the bar down at midnight. If these cowboys and cowgirls wanted to continue the party, they could head over to Marla's Bar, where the drinks were stronger.

As for Amy, she was doing her best not to stumble around. She still couldn't get that kiss off her mind, and having spent the better part of the evening watching Wolfe hadn't made her job any easier. He looked as though he had something on his mind, but that hadn't stopped him from smiling every time he caught her looking.

The door opened and Amy glanced up from the table she was clearing to see Rhys walk in. Their eyes immediately met and she found herself grinning like a fool although she didn't know why. Her gaze quickly strayed over to Wolfe. He was watching her, his face shadowed by his hat, but she could see his eyes were definitely on her.

"Don't worry, we're closin' it down, Sheriff," Reagan called out.

Rhys waved her off, moving over to stand beside Wolfe. He leaned against the bar, one elbow propped on the wooden top as he scanned the room.

The two empty bottles on the table clanked together when Amy went to pick them up.

"Get it together," she whispered to herself as she carried the bottles to the trash can.

"Hey, girl," Reagan called out to her. "Why don't you head on out. I've got it from here."

"You sure?" Amy wasn't particularly looking forward to going home, but her legs were about to give out on her. All day in the sun and all night on her feet had taken its toll. She was exhausted.

"Yep. See you next week."

Amy nodded, then removed her apron and tucked it beneath the bar before grabbing her car keys. She wasn't sure if she was supposed to talk to Wolfe or Rhys or if she was supposed to go straight to her car and go home. This was new for her.

Really new.

For one, Amy had never dated anyone. Kind of sad to think since she was twenty-six years old. But it was true. Amy had gone from her aunt and uncle's house at nineteen years old to … *his*. There had been a very brief courtship, but since Amy had nothing to compare it to, she wasn't sure she could consider it dating. It felt more like … ownership.

Not that she and Wolfe were dating. She didn't think that. Really.

"Hey."

Amy looked up to see Rhys standing before her, his beautiful blue eyes sparkling. "Hi."

His concerned look faded, replaced by a smile, and Amy relaxed.

When Wolfe came over, she felt heat swamp her, the memory of that kiss coming to the forefront of her mind.

"You headin' out?"

Amy nodded.

"Thought maybe you'd like to go out to the lake," Wolfe offered, sounding oddly nervous.

"The lake?" Amy watched the two men. "At night?"

"The moon's out," Rhys added. "We can chill. Talk."

"Or not," Wolfe added, his eyes skimming her face.

Amy did not want to go home to her empty house, so she quickly nodded. "I'd like that."

The tension lines around Wolfe's eyes seemed to fade away with her answer.

"Why don't we follow you home so you can drop your car off," Rhys said. "Don't want you out drivin' too late by yourself. Then, when you're ready to go home, we can drop you off."

That sounded like a smart idea. Plus, it would give Amy a chance to change clothes. "Okay."

She glanced between the two men. The three of them hadn't moved from their original spot by the bar, and now they were still standing there. There was some sort of tension surrounding them, but Amy had no idea what it was from. After the day they'd had at the lake, she couldn't imagine this would be awkward.

Unless…

She looked at Wolfe.

Had he told Rhys about the kiss?

Were they going to break the news to her that they were really into each other and that kiss had been a mistake?

Before she could come up with a dozen more questions that she would never voice, Rhys put his hand at the small of her back and urged her toward the door.

Amy pushed all the questions back, deciding that she couldn't change the outcome one way or another. She would have to wait until they decided to broach the subject.

Until then, she would proceed as they had been.

As friends.

Nothing more.

WOLFE FOLLOWED AMY in his truck while Rhys pulled up the rear. The fifteen-minute drive out to her place did absolutely nothing to ease the tension in his shoulders. He had no idea why he was sweating this so damn much.

Okay, that wasn't necessarily true. He did know.

And it all boiled down to the fact that he was twisted up in a knot when it came to what he wanted.

In the past forty-eight hours, everything he thought he knew about himself had been chucked right out the window. If he had to choose between Amy or Rhys right now, he didn't think he'd be able to do it. Last week, he would've easily said Amy.

However, kissing Rhys…

"Fuck," he grumbled to himself as he pulled in behind Amy's car.

After getting out, Wolfe walked over and opened her car door, then stepped aside so she could get out. The smile she gifted him with made his chest ache.

"Do you mind if I change?"

"Not at all."

Rhys joined them as Amy was turning toward the house.

Wolfe noticed her hesitation, the way she stopped and stared at the front door.

"Somethin' wrong?" Rhys asked, his eyes darting from Amy to Wolfe.

She shook her head.

Still, she didn't move.

"Gimme your key," Rhys insisted, stepping around her and holding out his hand.

Amy looked up into his face, her eyes wide, that same terror Wolfe had seen before present and accounted for.

Wolfe watched as Rhys took the key from her hand and then turned toward the door. The man still had his gun holstered on his hip, his badge clipped on his waistband. At this point, they were probably extensions of his body.

Putting his arm around Amy's shoulders, Wolfe started walking, urging her to the porch behind Rhys. Although he tried to hide it, the tension in his body was coiling tighter, only this time it had nothing to do with the kiss and everything to do with whatever was terrifying her. He'd noticed her hesitance to go inside earlier when he'd dropped her off, but he hadn't thought much of it when it was broad daylight.

Rhys disappeared inside the house, and the lights clicked on one at a time as he moved through it.

"I'm sorry," Amy whispered.

"Don't be," Wolfe told her. He wanted to know what or who she was scared of, but he couldn't bring himself to ask. He needed her to tell him when she was ready.

"All clear," Rhys informed them when they stepped into the house.

"We'll wait on the porch," Wolfe said, turning and stepping back outside.

Rhys joined him, closing the front door behind him.

Their eyes met in the darkness, the only light coming from the full moon.

"What the fuck was that about?" Rhys whispered, his eyes searching Wolfe's face.

"No fucking idea."

"She was scared to go in her own damn house."

Wolfe nodded. He'd seen it with his own two eyes.

Rhys turned and leaned against the porch railing, crossing his arms over his chest. "No wonder she always looks so damn tired. Hell, I'd be shocked if she sleeps a few hours a night."

Wolfe was thinking the same thing as he stared out at the surrounding area. The land adjacent to the small farmhouse was mostly flat, very little to conceal anything. Only a few trees stood off in the distance. If anyone came up on the house, Amy would be able to see them.

"She's from Houston," Wolfe told him, keeping his voice low.

"Houston?"

"Yeah. That's all she told me and I don't think she meant to tell me that much."

"Well, it's a start."

Wolfe turned and stared at Rhys. "I don't want you lookin' into her."

Shaking his head, Rhys looked away. "I won't." He met Wolfe's gaze again. "But that doesn't mean I won't look into what might've happened to her."

Wolfe got that. He hoped Rhys didn't have to do any digging. He wanted Amy to tell them her story herself. She was opening up. Slowly but surely. Wolfe figured it was only a matter of time.

The door opened behind them.

Rhys stood tall, his arms falling to his sides, a smile replacing his frown. "Ready?"

Wolfe turned around as Amy stepped out of the house. She was wearing a pair of short denim shorts, a tank top with a thin plaid shirt over it, and a pair of boots on her feet.

Lord have mercy.

Was the woman trying to kill him?

"Yeah," she said sweetly, locking the door behind her and tucking the key into her pocket.

"We'll take my truck," Wolfe informed them, waiting for Amy to move in front of him.

When they reached the truck, Amy stepped up to the back passenger door.

"No you don't," Wolfe said, chuckling. "Lift the console. You get to ride in the middle."

Amy peered up at him, and the look she gave him was more amused than anything. He opened the door and waited for her to hop in. When Rhys moved closer, Wolfe walked around to the driver's side.

A few minutes later, Wolfe had the truck out on the main road heading toward his house. Or rather, toward the lake.

"Is this what you do out here in the country to pass the time?" Amy asked, her sweet voice a welcome sound in the silence.

Rhys shifted, resting his arm on the window. "Depends. When we were kids, we did all sorts of shit."

"Is cow tipping a real thing?" Amy questioned, her attention divided between them.

Wolfe could hardly focus on driving with Amy's thigh up against his, so he didn't answer.

"It's a thing," Rhys confirmed, chuckling. "So is paintin' the water tower."

"Did y'all ever do that? Cow tipping or painting the water tower?"

"Of course not," Wolfe said, deadpan.

Rhys laughed.

"Shit. Wolfe and Lynx got a spur up their ass… What was it? Two years ago? They climbed up the water tower and would've started painting if they hadn't dropped the damn spray paint off the side."

"Two years ago?" Amy giggled. "Aren't you a little old to be raisin' that kind of hell?"

"Never too old, darlin'," Wolfe said softly. "Never too old."

THE SILENCE THAT descended in the truck was almost deafening. If it weren't for the rumble of the engine, Rhys figured you could've heard the crickets out in the fields and the cicadas in the trees.

"Okay." Amy glanced over at him, then back to Wolfe. "What gives?"

"Huh?" The confused look on Wolfe's face mirrored Rhys's.

"Why are y'all acting weird?"

"Weird how?" Rhys knew playing dumb probably wouldn't work, but he was going to give it a shot.

Wolfe pulled the truck down by the lake, then turned it around so the bed faced the water.

Rhys opened his door first, then helped Amy down to the ground. She was still staring at him, obviously waiting for him to do something more than answer a question with a question. He wasn't sure what the hell he was supposed to say, so he was really buying time.

When Wolfe opened the tailgate, Rhys picked Amy up and set her on it, not even thinking about what he was doing. Being that they were on a decline, it would've been difficult for her to do on her own.

When her hands wrapped around his biceps, Rhys froze, standing directly in front of her, his hips between her thighs. She sucked in a breath at the same time Rhys did.

"Is this weird? Or is it just me?" she whispered, her eyes wide.

Rhys waited to see if Wolfe would say anything, but the man kept his mouth sealed shut as he leaned against the tailgate and crossed his arms over his chest, his gaze fixed out over the water. It was clear he was conflicted about what was going on.

Rhys placed his hand on Amy's thigh. Just set it there, his thumb brushing over her smooth skin. She continued to stare at him, her fingers still curled around his biceps. She hadn't let go and he hadn't moved. Not an inch.

Her eyes were locked with his and Rhys was waiting. For what, he had no fucking idea, but he wanted her to make a move.

"I don't understand what's going on here," she finally said, her gaze leaving his to move over to Wolfe. "Someone's gonna have to tell me something." She looked back at Rhys. "I thought…"

"What?" Rhys knew she was putting all the pieces of the puzzle together. As for how she was going to handle it once she saw the big picture, that was still to be seen.

"I thought you and Wolfe were…" Her eyes dropped to his chest. "I thought y'all liked each other."

"We do," Rhys admitted, still brushing his thumb over her skin. Although *like* was a somewhat elementary term that Rhys probably wouldn't use to describe what he was feeling for Wolfe.

Her eyes darted back up to meet his, then shot quickly over to Wolfe, who was still standing like a statue, staring out at the lake.

"But..."

Rhys cocked one eyebrow when she turned back to him.

"Is this...?"

He continued to wait.

Amy's eyes widened. "Is this like one of those situations in those Nicole Edwards books?"

Rhys frowned. Who the hell was Nicole Edwards?

"What the hell kinda books are you readin'?" Wolfe asked, turning toward them.

Amy peered up at him, ignoring his question. "You kissed me earlier."

"I did." His admission was absolute, his voice softening when he added, "And I wanna do it again."

Amy looked down at Rhys's hand on her leg, then slowly lifted her head until their eyes met again.

He saw the moment she accepted what this was. Whether or not she would move forward, he couldn't tell, but she'd figured them out.

She shook her head, dropping her gaze once again. "I'm so confused. This doesn't happen in real life. I mean ... I've never met anyone who..."

"It happens," Wolfe stated. "And now the question is, do you want it to happen?"

Rhys glanced heavenward.

Please, God, let her say yes.

10

AND WASN'T THAT a good question.

Amy had no freaking idea what she wanted. This was too weird.

And yes, she'd stumbled across some books that depicted situations like this, but she honestly never thought it really happened. She'd been so disbelieving that she hadn't even given it a thought when it came to Rhys and Wolfe. *And her.*

Here she'd thought she was the odd woman out.

Turned out they wanted to include her.

The idea was hot.

However, it was still weird.

Could she really kiss Rhys after having kissed Wolfe just a few hours ago?

His hand did feel good touching her leg, and for a brief second, she'd felt like she was cheating on Wolfe, although Wolfe was standing right there and clearly saw it.

Not that she and Wolfe were together or anything, but he had kissed her. Well, he'd kissed her *back*. She'd been the one initiating the kissing, but she couldn't help it. The man made her want things she'd never thought she would want again.

"We're not tryin' to rush anything," Rhys said, drawing her attention to him once more.

She stared into his dark blue eyes, trying to figure out what he was thinking. What he *really* wanted.

When he'd first picked her up, helping her onto the tailgate, her body had caught fire from his simple touch. It had taken her breath away, even if she'd felt guilty because Wolfe was right there.

"Amy?"

Wolfe's deep voice drew her out of her thoughts and she peered over at him. He looked worried.

"I'm not saying no," she admitted, although the words made her blush. "I'm just… I need some time to understand what this is."

Rhys pulled back, his hand leaving her leg, but Amy clamped her fingers into his biceps. "No. Don't move."

His dark eyebrows lifted.

She looked over at Wolfe. "And you sit."

He was making her nervous the way his body vibrated with tension.

Wolfe hefted himself up onto the tailgate, the weight of his body causing the truck to dip.

Sliding her hands down Rhys's arms, she took his palms and once more placed them on her thighs, staring down at them. Even in the moonlight, his sun-bronzed skin was significantly darker than her pale legs. She covered his hands with hers as they rested on her leg, his warmth seeping into her.

She watched as his thumbs slid across the insides of her thighs, gently, softly. He wasn't making a move, but the simple touch had fire streaking through her.

Pulling her attention away from the sight, Amy reached for Wolfe's hand, placing it on top of Rhys's hand, on top of her thigh. She covered his hand with hers, mesmerized by his long fingers as they closed over Rhys's, his thumb brushing the outside edge of Rhys's wrist.

Amy swallowed hard. Even the sight of something so innocent was highly erotic. She briefly wondered how Nicole Edwards wrote those books. Seriously.

"Amy…"

She jerked her attention to Rhys, his voice sounding strained as he stood between her thighs. With his hand trapped beneath Wolfe's, Amy kept her other hand on his free one and then cupped his face, scooting closer to him, her legs dangling off the tailgate.

When they were close enough she could feel his breath on her face, she leaned forward, pressing her lips to his. A rough growl sounded, but it didn't come from Rhys. Wolfe's hand pressed down on her thigh, his fingers wrapping around, pressing into her flesh. He clearly wasn't objecting.

Heat consumed her as she explored Rhys's mouth with her tongue. He was kissing her back but letting her lead. She'd noticed the same thing with Wolfe earlier. These men were hesitant when it came to her. They'd obviously caught on to her twitchiness. Although she appreciated them being gentle with her, Amy wanted more. Even just a little more.

She moaned and Rhys must've read her mind because his hands came up to cradle her face, tilting her head, which allowed him to take full control of the kiss, his tongue darting inside. He wasn't rough, more like commanding, dominant. She'd never felt anything like it before and she didn't want him to stop.

When she pulled back, they were both breathing hard, their eyes locked together. For a brief second, she forgot Wolfe was sitting there, although his big hand was still resting on her thigh, warm and secure. She shifted toward him, confusion warring with the urge to kiss him, to let him know that she felt the same thing for him that she felt for Rhys.

His gaze was smoldering hot, boring into her. When she leaned toward him, his hand moved beneath her hair, cupping the back of her head and pulling her close.

The kiss detonated upon impact and Amy was almost desperate to get closer to him, but she held back. This was moving too fast. She wasn't sure how this worked, what the rules were, or even if she was ready for something like this.

But that didn't stop her from kissing Wolfe for all she was worth.

NO DOUBT ABOUT it, Wolfe had been wild in his younger days. He'd shared plenty of women, oftentimes with his cousin, a couple of times with a buddy he went to school with, but that was significantly different than this thing between him and Amy and Rhys. Wolfe had never shared a woman with a man he was attracted to. It had always been about the woman.

And this was just kissing out under the stars by the lake, yet it surpassed any and every single one of his previous encounters by miles.

Wolfe knew they wouldn't go any further than this. As much as he wanted to, he would take things slow with Amy. He wanted her too damn much to fuck things up between them. Hell, he was surprised she was still there, her lips melding to his, her hands roaming over his upper body. She was fire in his arms, but she was still hesitant, he could tell.

The only thing Wolfe worried about was how to make it through the night without making a complete fool of himself. He'd never been so close to coming in his jeans as he was right then, and that was from Amy's kiss and Rhys's hand on his leg.

He managed to break the kiss before he lost all good sense.

"Come here," he told Amy as he shifted back, leaving room for her to sit on the tailgate between his legs.

When she got situated, her back to his chest, Wolfe grinned to himself as she pulled Rhys in front of her, his ass resting against the metal, positioned between their legs.

No one said anything for several minutes as they stared up at the stars and out at the lake. The moon was bright, bouncing off the water and highlighting the tree line in the distance. It was peaceful.

Wolfe wasn't sure there'd ever been a more perfect place than here. Right now.

Amy relaxed into him, her breathing returning to normal. When she reached for his hand, linking her fingers with his, Wolfe allowed her to position it on her leg. He breathed easier, more comfortable like this than he could remember being in his life.

"Have y'all done this before?" she asked.

"No," Wolfe answered easily. "Not like this."

Amy cocked her head to look up at him. He peered down his nose at her.

"Like this? What does that mean?"

Wolfe sighed. He really didn't want to get into this with her. Even thinking about his previous sexual encounters tainted this moment and he didn't want that.

"Have you shared a woman before?" She didn't sound judgmental. "Rumors go around, Wolfe. It isn't like I haven't heard a few things about you and your cousin."

"Yeah. I've shared a woman with my cousin."

"What about you?" Amy tapped Rhys on the back, her fingers lingering.

"I've never shared a woman with Wolfe or his cousin."

Amy laughed. Wolfe did, too.

She shifted in his lap, making Wolfe's cock twitch. He was hard as steel and there was no way to hide it from her, but he was ignoring it, hoping she would, too.

"Now, I'm no expert on it, but I do know what it means to be bisexual. I mean, come on, I do read books. I take it you are? Both of you?"

"Yes," Rhys answered instantly, turning so that he was facing them. "But it's not somethin' I broadcast." His gaze met Wolfe's.

"And you?" Amy peered up at him again.

"I've experimented," Wolfe said, his eyes locked with Rhys's, speaking more to him than anyone. "But it's never felt like this before."

Wolfe could feel Amy watching them, studying them. Wolfe couldn't look away from Rhys for whatever reason.

"Have you kissed him?"

Okay, now he could look away. Was she serious?

Wolfe looked down, trying to see who she was asking. Her smile was wicked, and it did something to his insides, made him want to do wicked, dirty things to her.

"Yes," Wolfe told her.

"Do you want to kiss him again?" She giggled. "I sound like I'm in sixth grade, trying to get the cute boy to kiss my best friend. But do you?"

Wolfe smiled. "Yeah."

"What's stopping you?"

Amy shifted, pulling Rhys forward at the same time, which brought Wolfe's mouth dangerously close to the man's. He didn't move, figuring Rhys could do as he wished. Wolfe had been the one to initiate their first kiss, so turnabout was fair play.

"Don't mind me," Amy said with a chuckle. "I'm just a girl watching two smoking-hot cowboys make out."

Wolfe grinned as Rhys leaned in and kissed him. The groan that came up from his chest was rough and laced with a need he was doing his best to fight. Unlike kissing Amy, Wolfe didn't have to control himself with Rhys. He knew the man could handle any damn thing he could dish out.

"Oh, my." Amy's words were accompanied by a gasp. "That really is hot."

Unable to keep from laughing, Wolfe pulled back and they both stared down at her. The innocent expression she shot back was feigned, he knew it.

"What? Did I say something wrong?" She laughed when Rhys tickled her thigh, her butt rubbing up against Wolfe's now throbbing erection.

Not helping.

Not at all.

RHYS DIDN'T WANT to call it a night, but he knew it was time. With Amy unknowingly teasing them, there was no telling where this night would lead. As far as his willpower was concerned, Rhys was all tapped out. When he mentioned they should head back, Amy seemed disappointed, but Wolfe looked almost relieved. He probably felt the same as Rhys—too damn close to the edge.

"Fine," Amy said with a dramatic huff, but she was smiling.

Rhys helped her down from the tailgate and into the cab of the truck. When she linked her fingers with his, he once again had to focus on keeping his heart from pounding out of his chest. The move was innocent yet so seductive at the same time. He honestly couldn't remember a time when he'd held hands with a woman.

It wasn't until Wolfe was pulling out onto the main road that Amy spoke again.

"Now that the making out portion of the evening is over, I guess it's time to go home and go to bed." She stretched and Rhys suspected it was her way of continuing to touch them both.

He liked that she wanted to.

"I'm on board with the goin' to bed part," Wolfe noted.

Rhys could see Amy's cheeks darken. "By bed, I mean to sleep."

"Oh. Well." Wolfe grinned over at her. "Another time then."

Amy chuckled and Rhys's dick stirred to life. All this talk of beds was making him hurt.

"Do you boys have to get up for church?" Amy looked back and forth between them.

The quick change of subject was just what his dick needed to control itself.

"Yep," Wolfe grumbled. "Not somethin' you miss if you're a Caine. Unless you're Lynx's old man. Since he doesn't leave the house…"

"He really doesn't leave the house?"

"Not in ten years."

"And you?" Amy asked Rhys directly. "Do you have to get up?"

"Yeah, but my family goes to the later service." He grinned. "Heaven forbid the Caines and the Trevinos go to church at the same time."

"So, that's still a thing? The... What do you even call it? A falling-out? A war, maybe? Between your families?" She looked genuinely curious. "What happens if ... you know... What happens if things work out for the two of you? What will that do to the ... war?"

That wasn't something Rhys wanted to think about. He loved his family and he knew they loved him. Since his old man was no longer with them, he didn't have to worry about his reaction; however, his grandfather was still kicking and he'd probably have a coronary. More so about the fact that Rhys would be with a man than necessarily Wolfe Caine.

"We'll deal with that when the time comes," Wolfe noted.

Rhys stared at him, stuck on the fact that Wolfe said *when,* not *if.*

Amy was yawning for probably the twentieth time by the time they pulled down her driveway. For a minute there, Rhys thought she was going to fall asleep. However, as soon as they pulled up to the house, she was wide awake, her eyes huge in her face as she stared at the dark house.

"Give me your key," he instructed, holding his hand out as he opened the truck door and climbed out.

"You don't have to do that," she said, but her voice was shaky.

Rhys pulled her to the edge of the seat so he was standing directly in front of her. He lowered his voice, keeping his tone even. "I don't know what you're scared of or what you're runnin' from, but I'm not gonna let anything happen to you. You should know that by now."

He folded his hand and opened it again, signaling for her to place the key in it. Amy reluctantly passed it over, and Rhys passed Wolfe on the way to the door. He didn't see anything amiss out front, but he looked it over, making sure her front windows were still intact.

Once inside, Rhys did the same thing he'd done earlier. He walked into every room, flipping on the lights as he went. This time he went so far as to check that all the windows were locked, looked in her closets and even under the full-size bed in her bedroom. No way were the three of them fitting on that thing.

The thought made him laugh.

He returned to the living room to find Wolfe and Amy standing in the doorway.

"I'm sorry," she said softly. "I don't want you to think you have to protect me. That's not why I like hanging out with you." She looked up at Wolfe. "Both of you."

Wolfe cupped her face and stared down at her. "No one's gonna hurt you, Amy. You've got my word on that. And when you're ready to tell us what's goin' on, we're here to listen."

She nodded and Wolfe released her face, but not before pressing a kiss to her forehead.

"Good night," Rhys said, pausing in front of her and pressing a kiss to her lips.

Her hand brushed over his chest and he wished like hell he wasn't leaving her alone tonight. However, Rhys couldn't impose on her. The woman had to come out of her shell sometime, and Wolfe was right, whenever she was ready to talk about it, they'd both be there.

In the meantime, Rhys was going to do a little digging. Now that he had more information, he wouldn't be able to help himself.

Because if someone was out to hurt Amy, he damn sure wasn't going to sit back and wait for it to happen.

11

AMY WAS UP before the sun on Monday morning.

That wasn't surprising since she'd gone to bed at eight o'clock last night. She'd spent her entire Sunday alternating between reading and watching movies. Oh, and she'd spent about two hours total texting back and forth with Wolfe and Rhys.

Although she had hoped to see them, she knew that it was for the best that she hadn't. They'd already been moving too fast, and Amy wanted time to let it all sink in. To *really* sink in. The whole thing was surreal, and she still wasn't sure how she felt about it. Not only because there were three of them in this erotic triangle, either.

No, that wasn't too difficult to handle. It felt right, for whatever reason.

Amy's reluctance had more to do with the fact that she'd spent five years of her life under the thumb of a man who wanted to own her. Before him, she'd lived by her parents' rules, as well as her aunt and uncle's. Making decisions for herself wasn't something she'd had to do, and the truth was, despite her fear of coming face-to-face with a monster, Amy did like being on her own. She wasn't sure she was ready to be at someone's beck and call ever again.

But it was Monday and she had a job to do. No time to think about any of that.

When she arrived at the shop, Wolfe was already there, but no one else was.

"Mornin'," he greeted from his position near a long, narrow table that looked to be almost completed. He appeared to be setting up the stain and varnish nearby.

"Morning," she replied. "Do you always get here first?"

"Most of the time, yeah. Lynx doesn't like to get out of bed. He says I'm lucky that he's usually here by eight."

"Should I make coffee yet? Do you drink it?"

"Most days, no. However, I slept for shit last night. I could use some, but you don't have to make it. I can handle it."

"I don't mind." Amy went to the coffee machine and got it all set up and brewing. As she wiped down the counter, she turned to look at him. She wasn't sure how she was supposed to respond to him at work. She didn't think waltzing up to him and kissing him would be appropriate; however, she didn't want to appear as though she was brushing him off, either.

Truth was, she wanted to kiss him. In fact, she wanted to spend all day and night kissing him *and* Rhys. Maybe it made her a hussy to want two men, but there it was. The situation was beyond confusing, but it felt right. She wasn't sure how she'd come to a point in her life when having two men want her and each other at the same time was even a thing, but that did seem to be the case, strange as it was.

Tucking her cell phone into her back pocket, Amy decided she would address the work situation now. That way she wouldn't spend the rest of the day trying to figure it out.

Wolfe's eyes trailed her as she moved toward him. It was almost as though she made him nervous. Big, badass Wolfe Caine. If that wasn't an empowering feeling, she didn't know what was.

"Is … uh … everything okay?" God, she hated the way her voice wobbled and her brain couldn't connect the words together.

His dark eyebrows lowered. "What do you mean?"

"I … uh…" Amy tucked a stray strand of hair behind her ear before slipping her hands into her pockets. *Suck it up and spit it out.* "I'm … uh … not sure how I'm supposed to react around you. You know … here. At work. I mean, you are my boss." She looked up at him. "But you also kissed me."

He smiled, his green eyes glittering. Clearly he remembered the kiss as well as she did.

"So, I just don't want you to think I'm being weird. I don't know how to act, and I'm here to do a job, so…"

Wolfe took a step closer. Then another.

Amy didn't look away, craning her neck to look up at him the closer he got.

His palm grazed her cheek, his eyes scanning her face briefly. "I don't know how to act, either, but I do know that I wanna kiss you again."

"You do?" She wasn't sure why she sounded so surprised.

Wolfe chuckled, the deep rumble of his voice making her insides vibrate.

"I definitely do."

"Okay." She continued to stare at him, waiting.

When his mouth met hers, Amy sighed. Her hands instantly came out of her pockets, sliding to his hips as the kiss heated a degree or two, his tongue swiping into her mouth. He tasted like toothpaste, smelled like sin. Considering she wasn't much of a morning person, Amy realized if she woke up to this every day, she'd start looking forward to dawn.

Unfortunately, the kiss didn't last nearly long enough, but probably twice as long as it should have considering where they were.

Wolfe pressed his forehead to hers, his hand still cupping her neck, his thumb grazing her jaw. "I slept for shit because I couldn't stop thinkin' about you." He sighed. "I missed you."

Hearing those words coming from such a rough, tough … well, for lack of a better word … *badass* nearly melted her. Amy was pretty sure her heart did a triple Lutz in her chest from those three words. It had been so long since she'd been around someone who showed any sort of affection for her. Not since her aunt and uncle had anyone made her feel as though she mattered, as though she was worth caring about. As though she was wanted.

"I missed you, too," she admitted.

The rough sound of someone clearing their throat resonated from behind her.

Amy jerked back from Wolfe, spinning to find Lynx standing just inside the doorway, a giant black-and-tan German shepherd sitting at his feet, tail thumping on the floor. Unlike Saturday night, Lynx didn't look grumpy. Which was interesting considering Wolfe basically said Lynx wasn't a morning person.

"Mornin'," Wolfe greeted. "Don't say a damn word."

Lynx's grin widened as though he were holding the words back with his smile alone.

"Come here, Copenhagen," Wolfe called out.

Amy assumed he was talking to the dog, and sure enough, the beautiful animal peered up at Lynx, obviously for permission. Lynx used a finger to signal, and the dog trotted over to Wolfe, tail going ninety miles an hour.

"Amy, meet Cope. Cope, this is Amy."

"He's beautiful," Amy mumbled, not meaning to say the words out loud.

"He's too sweet for the likes of Lynx."

Amy leaned down and stroked the dog's big head. Copenhagen's tongue darted out, but he didn't lick her. He just looked like he wanted to.

"I'd say I'm the luckiest bastard on the face of the planet," Lynx said from across the room. "But I'm thinkin' Wolfe's got me beat in that department."

"Shut it," Wolfe growled, standing to his full height once again.

Lynx's shit-eating grin said more than any words could have. Amy's face flamed from embarrassment, but she did her best not to acknowledge it.

"I smell coffee," Lynx said, his eyes darting over to the coffeepot. It had just finished. "Hot damn. Amy, if I haven't said it before, I fuckin' love you, girl."

"Okay, then," she squeaked out. "I'll … uh … just go upstairs and … uh … get to work."

It took everything she had not to run.

BY THE TIME Wolfe had finished the table for one of their out-of-town customers and he was cleaning up, Lynx was already showing signs of unraveling for the day. After Lynx had waltzed in, downed two cups of coffee, and spewed a random bunch of nonsense, he and Copenhagen had started pacing the floor, which wasn't uncommon. The man's restless energy was unprecedented.

Wolfe's stomach rumbled, as though reminding him it was time to eat.

"We headin' to the diner?" Lynx asked, his eyes straying up to the second floor, where Amy was tucked away in one of the offices.

"Yeah." He wiped his hands on a rag. "Lemme get Amy and we'll meet you over there."

Lynx's expression didn't change, but there was something akin to understanding in his gaze. Wolfe hadn't made a public claim on the woman yet, but he would if it came down to it. No matter what happened, she was off-limits to every damn person in this town. Except for him. And Rhys.

And okay, fine, maybe he couldn't decide that for her, but if Wolfe had anything to say about it, she was theirs. It was a decision he'd come to on Sunday, when he'd spent the entire day wishing like hell he was with the two of them. He would've been content to sit on his ass at his house if they'd been there. With that acknowledgment, Wolfe had come to the decision that he was playing for keeps with these two. No holds barred.

After a brief detour to wash his hands, Wolfe ventured upstairs and found Amy in their office, still slipping papers into file folders inside the cabinets that they'd bought for that reason. Not a single thing had been filed since their previous office manager left, but now he could actually see the top of the oak desk. Huh. So that was how that worked.

He rapped his knuckles on the open door, then leaned his shoulder against the jamb. "You hungry? We're headin' over to the diner if you wanna join us."

"Oh … uh…" She sat up straight. "I'm not sure that's a good idea."

"Lynx doesn't bite," Wolfe assured her. When she frowned, he continued, "And if he does, it's not hard enough to leave a mark."

That made her laugh, something Wolfe fucking loved to hear.

"Come on. Take a break. We'll grab a bite, then come right back. All that shit'll be here waitin' for you."

Amy seemed to contemplate her decision, then nodded. Wolfe immediately moved toward her to help her to her feet. Once she was standing, he found he couldn't release her. Didn't want to.

He slid one hand over her hair, which was pulled back in a ponytail—her signature style, obviously—then grazed the side of her face, still looking into her eyes.

"Why do you look at me like that?" she asked, her voice soft.

"Like what?"

"Like I mean something to you."

Wolfe frowned. "Because you do."

"You don't even know me."

No, he didn't. "But I want to."

And he would know her. Eventually. When she was ready.

Wolfe wasn't known for his patience, but he could wait as long as this woman needed him to. He wasn't going anywhere.

"Come on," he said, grabbing her hand and tugging her toward the door. "Let's eat."

By the time Wolfe and Amy arrived at the diner, the parking lot was full. Lynx hadn't arrived, but Wolfe knew he would be along shortly. Knowing Lynx, he'd gone over to the Cedar Door to drop Copenhagen off with Calvin for the day. Wolfe's old man loved that dog, as did anyone who met him.

"Mornin', Wolfe, Amy."

Glancing over, Wolfe smiled at Reagan, sitting at a table with her loser of a boyfriend, Billy.

Wolfe tipped his hat while Amy gave her a warm, "Good morning."

"What brings you kids into this fine establishment?"

Kids. Right. Wolfe hadn't been a damn kid in a long-ass time.

However, it was amusing coming from a woman who was four years younger than he was. Now that he thought about it, that made Reagan and Amy about the same age.

"Breakfast," Wolfe said, his eyes sliding over to Billy, who was shoveling food into his mouth as though he hadn't eaten in a year.

"Quit yappin'," Billy grumbled to Reagan. "I got shit to do."

Every single time Wolfe laid eyes on Billy Watson, he wanted to punch the fucker in the face. He had absolutely no idea what Reagan saw in the guy. He was a two-bit mooch who cheated on Reagan more often than not. Yet for whatever insane fucking reason, she kept him around.

"We'll talk to y'all later," Wolfe told Reagan as he slid his hand behind Amy's back and urged her toward their table. He threw one last disdainful glare at Billy for good measure. One day somebody was going to steal that girl away, and he hoped like hell he was there to see it. Clearly the fucker didn't know a good thing when he had it.

Wolfe pulled Amy's chair out for her. Once she was seated, he took his. The bells jingled over the door, and all heads turned toward it as Lynx made his way inside. The place was relatively packed this morning, so it was interesting to see the way Lynx's eyes instantly zoned in on Reagan and Billy. That good ol' boy grin disappeared instantly.

"Son of a bitch," Billy groaned, his voice louder than it should've been. "Can't we fuckin' go anywhere in this stupid fuckin' town without your sorry ass showin' up?"

What the fuck?

Wolfe glanced over at Amy, then around the room, wishing like hell someone could fill him in on what was going on. Everyone who knew them looked as surprised as Wolfe.

"Watch your goddamn mouth," Lynx snarled.

Amy chuckled beside him. That was Lynx for you. Cursing while telling someone else not to.

"Fuck off, Caine," Billy growled.

"Billy, stop," Reagan said, placing her hand on his arm.

Billy shrugged her off. "Always defendin' that asshole. If I didn't know better, I'd think you were suckin' his dick instead of mine."

The room went deafeningly silent. No chatter, no clank of silverware, no hiss from the griddle in the kitchen. Absolutely nothing except for the warning growl that emanated from Lynx seconds before he reached over and ripped Billy right up out of his chair.

"Lynx, don't!" Reagan yelled, jumping up and sending her chair over backwards.

"Stay here," Wolfe instructed Amy, getting to his feet at the same time two more cowboys in the back stood.

No one took kindly to men treating women the way Billy did.

Wolfe held up a hand to halt the two cowboys, letting them know he'd handle it. Wolfe shoved the door open harder than necessary, watching as Lynx dragged Billy halfway across the parking lot.

"Lynx, let him go," Reagan hollered, moving in close.

Wolfe got to her in seconds, picking Reagan up off her feet and pulling her back.

"Put me down, you asshole!"

"Chill, darlin'," Wolfe crooned. "He ain't gonna kill him. Although he probably deserves it."

"If I ever fuckin' hear you say some shit like that again," Lynx hissed, his hand fisted in Billy's shirt as he held the man in place, "I will beat you so fuckin' bad your momma won't recognize you no more."

The sound of tires on gravel had Wolfe looking over. The familiar dark brown truck pulled to a stop right beside Lynx and Billy. Rhys climbed out, shoving his hat on his head. The man was wearing his signature Wranglers and white button-down shirt, badge clipped to his hip, gun holstered there, too.

"Let him go, Lynx." Rhys's deep voice rang with a command most men wouldn't ignore.

Wolfe set Reagan on her feet with a soft warning for her to stay put.

Lynx released Billy with a shove that sent the other man sprawling in the dust and rock.

"I wanna press charges!" Billy yelled. "This asshole hit me."

"Shut the fuck up, Billy," Wolfe warned. "Provoke him a little more and he will fuckin' hit you. And if he doesn't, I will."

To Wolfe's surprise, Reagan didn't run over to Billy. Again, he had no fucking clue what she saw in that asshole.

Lynx turned, his hard gaze slamming into Reagan. "He's a fuckin' loser, Reagan. You can do a helluva lot better than that."

With that, Lynx turned and walked inside.

Wolfe decided to join him.

After all, the show was over. The sheriff was there.

RHYS STOOD IN front of his truck, watching as the Caine cousins went inside, leaving Billy Watson's ass sitting on the ground.

Had he known what he would find when he got here, Rhys would've ignored the call and let Lynx take care of Billy.

Never having been one to hate anyone, Rhys fucking hated Billy. Hated him with a passion. He wanted to kill the fucker for the way he treated Rhys's sister. The only thing stopping him was the fact that Billy wasn't worth the prison sentence Rhys would get.

Choosing to ignore Billy, Rhys turned to his sister. "What the hell's goin' on, Reagan?"

"Nothin'," she snapped, not looking at him.

"You better fuckin' tell him that Lynx hit me, goddammit. I'm so fuckin' tired of you defendin' his ass."

"Fuck you," Reagan hissed, the words so soft Rhys hardly heard her and he was standing right beside her.

"What did you say?" Billy launched to his feet.

Right before his eyes, something inside his sister snapped. Reagan's back straightened as she watched Billy right his shirt before dusting his jeans off. "I said fuck you."

"You're fuckin' him, aren't you?" Billy accused, grabbing his ball cap from the ground. "I always knew you were whorin' around on me. And you wonder why I get pussy on the side. It's because of this shit right here."

Reagan's face hardened, her brown eyes practically burning with fury. "I've never stepped out on you, Billy Watson. But I'm done. I'm so fucking done."

Reagan spun around on her boot heel and headed over to her truck. When Billy started to follow, Rhys grabbed him by the back of the shirt and yanked him back. "No you don't."

Billy jerked out of his grip. "Get your fuckin' hands off me."

Rhys straightened as he looked the other man square in the eye. "Look here, you little piece of shit. I've tolerated you because, for whatever fuckin' reason, my sister has put up with your shit. But don't think I won't haul your ass in."

"For what?"

Unfortunately, Rhys didn't have a good reason. He couldn't arrest the guy for being an asshole. If he could, Billy Watson would've been behind bars a long-ass time ago.

"Go home, Billy. And stay the fuck away from my sister."

Billy's chest puffed out, a sardonic smile tilting his mouth. "She'll be back. She always comes back. She can't live without me."

Yeah, unfortunately, Rhys figured that was true. Reagan did always go back to Billy no matter what the damned fool did or said. The only reason Rhys didn't interfere was because up to this point, Billy had never laid a hand on her. Then again, he didn't have to in order to inflict pain. His verbal assault was just as bad. Which, Rhys figured, was the very reason Lynx had interfered this morning. God only knew what the little shithead had said.

"Stay the fuck away from her," Rhys warned. "Or I will sic Lynx on you, you dumb fuck."

Stepping back, Rhys nodded in the direction of Billy's piece-of-shit Dodge.

When the parking lot cleared, Rhys turned toward the diner. He noticed Lynx standing at the window, watching him, his beefy arms crossed over his chest. The guy looked pissed, and Rhys couldn't blame him.

He wasn't privy to what had ever transpired between Reagan and Lynx, but Rhys had always suspected there was something there. They both made stupid decisions day in and day out, and Rhys had the feeling it was because they were avoiding the real issue at hand. Whatever that might be.

Figuring it would only cause a scene, Rhys decided to bypass going inside. He'd catch up with Wolfe and Amy later.

In the meantime, he was going to head to the office. There was some information he was eager to dive into.

LYNX WASN'T PRONE to regret. However, as he stood at the window and stared out at the little fucker getting into his POS, he regretted that he hadn't pounded his fist into that shithead's face.

What the fuck Reagan saw in Billy, Lynx didn't know. He would never know. Every damn time he thought she was going to walk away from the little shit, she ended up taking his sorry ass back.

And it pissed Lynx off to no end.

There was a cowboy code that Lynx lived by. You didn't touch another man's girl. No matter what.

For years he'd wanted to get his hands on Reagan. Unfortunately, she'd been with Billy, which meant she was off-limits. And every damn time he saw the two of them together, Lynx wanted to strangle the fucker.

A man did not treat a woman the way Billy Watson treated Reagan. A woman should be worshipped, loved. Not treated like the dirt beneath his feet.

His eyes strayed to Reagan's truck as she peeled out of the parking lot. He was tempted to go after her, to insist that she break up with Billy for good, that she give him a fucking chance to show her just how damn good the two of them would be together. Hell, that kiss they'd shared all those years ago should've been enough to convince her.

But Lynx couldn't do that.

If Reagan was meant to be his—and he suspected that was what fate had in store for him—then she would come to him.

Until then, he'd just go on living his life one day at a time.

Waiting.

Always fucking waiting.

12

AMY WAS QUICKLY starting to think that trouble followed the Caine cousins like a hungry puppy looking for scraps. Or perhaps they were the magnet for it. She hadn't been sure what to expect when Wolfe invited her to breakfast, but watching a near-brawl in the parking lot hadn't been anywhere on the list.

Of course, Amy had met Reagan's boyfriend, Billy, but only once, and that had been one night at the bar. He'd come in to play pool with a couple of his buddies, and right there in the back of the room, he'd blatantly flirted with some blonde, not to mention Amy. His slimy smile had put her on edge, though, and Amy had stayed as far from him as she could manage.

Amy had suspected there was trouble in paradise, but she hadn't realized it was quite that bad. Having watched that asshole talk to Reagan like that made Amy want to go find Reagan to see if she was all right. Since Amy didn't have to work tonight, she wouldn't have a chance to talk to Reagan then. Or maybe she could. She'd just stop by the bar for a minute.

Yep. That was what she would do.

But right now, she had to get back to work. The rest of their breakfast had gone smoothly, although Lynx hadn't stuck around. As soon as Rhys left, Lynx was out the door without a word to anyone. She'd half expected Wolfe to say something about it, but he never did, and Amy wasn't the type to bring it up, so they'd shared minimal small talk.

And now she was once again tucked away in the office, finishing up her filing. She didn't have but a few more to go, and she knew she couldn't pretend to do it for long. For one, she would get bored if she didn't have something to do. So, after tucking away the last invoices where they belonged, she got to her feet and decided she'd go back to her own office and wait for the phone to ring.

When she stepped out, she heard voices downstairs, so she peeked over the rail and noticed a tall brunette standing close to Wolfe, the two of them looking at a table.

Amy gave the woman a quick once-over, starting with the four-inch black pumps, the A-line skirt that molded to her curvy body, and the white silk shirt that showed off her generous breasts.

She noticed how Wolfe took a step to the side, putting some space between them as he pointed out something on the table. The woman quickly closed the distance between them, her hand coming to rest on Wolfe's arm.

Nope.

Uh-uh.

A foreign possessiveness flooded Amy, and the next thing she knew, she was walking down the stairs, her boots clanging on the metal. Wolfe's eyes quickly shot to her, and Amy saw relief, as though her coming down was going to possibly save him from the woman with the red talons practically digging into his forearm.

"Hey," she greeted, walking right up to the two of them. "I didn't realize we had someone coming to pick up a piece today."

Wolfe glanced at the brunette, then at Amy. "Amy, this is Melissa Stephenson. Mrs. Stephenson, this is Amy Smith. She's our new office manager."

Mrs. Stephenson.

No doubt, Wolfe had tacked that on to remind the woman that she was married.

Not that it seemed to faze her. She didn't take her hand off Wolfe's arm.

Amy gave her another once-over, starting with her professionally highlighted brown hair, her painted-on eyebrows, the fancy shimmering eye shadow, dark liner around her eyes, and the shiny gloss on her red lips. All the way down to her perfectly painted toes peeking out of her impractical shoes.

"Nice to meet you, Amy." The woman said her name like it gave her a bad taste in her mouth.

"You, too," Amy said. "Is this your dining table?"

When the two of them turned toward the table, Amy purposely inserted herself between them. It was almost funny considering Amy looked like a child standing between her parents.

"It is. Wolfe was just explaining the process to me."

The process? Really?

How freaking hard could it be? The woman surely knew what it took to build a table, slap some stain and sealant on it.

Okay, so maybe it wasn't *that* easy, but it shouldn't require an educational course.

"It'll be delivered on Friday," Wolfe informed her, his hand sliding down Amy's back, his finger hooking into the belt loop on the back of her jeans. Anyone looking at them would likely miss the movement, but his simple touch stole the air from Amy's lungs momentarily.

"I'd like for you to personally deliver it," Mrs. Stephenson said, turning to face Wolfe. "I'll pay extra."

Wolfe was shaking his head.

"I'm sorry," Amy inserted. "That won't be possible. Wolfe has another project he has to have completed by then." She didn't know that for sure, but hey, it sounded good.

Wolfe tugged at her belt loop and Amy had to bite back a smile.

"Then I can wait for it," Mrs. Stephenson said. "Just pencil me in for the next available day that you can deliver it. I'm not trusting it in anyone else's hands."

Wolfe sighed.

"I'll check the calendar," Amy told her. "And I'll call you to let you know."

"That'll be perfect." The woman's eyes never left Wolfe's face.

It wasn't enough that the woman was married. Based on the crow's feet around her eyes and the permanent wrinkle in her forehead, Amy would guess the woman was over fifty. At least two decades older than Wolfe.

A cougar after a Wolfe.

Amy laughed but managed to cover it up with a cough. Sort of.

She turned to Wolfe. "I actually need your help with something upstairs, if you don't mind."

"Sure." His eyes said he knew she was full of shit.

Ignoring him, she turned to Mrs. Stephenson. "I'll call you this afternoon with a new appointment."

The woman turned to Wolfe. "Walk me to my car?"

"Yeah. Sure."

Well, it looked as though she hadn't been able to save the day after all.

Amy watched as Wolfe walked the well-dressed woman out the door and into the blistering Texas sun. Not knowing whether she should wait for Wolfe to return, Amy decided she would get back to work. Something told her he would come find her when he was ready.

"A cougar after a Wolfe," she muttered to herself, giggling as she bounced up the stairs. "Now that's funny."

LOOKED AS THOUGH Amy Smith was a bit of a spitfire.

Wolfe thought about how she'd discreetly come between him and Mrs. Stephenson, obviously in an attempt to protect him from the viperous woman. He liked that she had.

"I really appreciate your little helper making this happen," Mrs. Stephenson said as Wolfe opened the door of her Lexus for her. It wasn't that he was being overly gentlemanly, but his upbringing wouldn't allow him to be rude. Not to a lady. Not even a man-hungry one like Mrs. Stephenson.

She rubbed up against him, the scent of her perfume assaulting his nose. He was pretty sure the woman had bathed in that shit.

"Hopefully she's competent enough to get it taken care of correctly."

How fucking hard could it be to schedule an appointment? Jesus. The woman made it sound like rocket science.

"She will," he assured her, waiting as she got situated in her car.

After pushing her sunglasses on her face, the woman stared up at him. "I look forward to seeing you again."

He nodded, then shut the door, turning to walk away before the engine started.

Thankfully, he remembered they had a box of Cedar Door T-shirts stashed on one of the shelves. He quickly made his way over and snatched one. He traded it for the one that had the stench of overpriced perfume and then headed up the stairs. Wolfe found Amy in the break room, retrieving a bottle of water from the refrigerator.

He stepped inside, shut the door, then leaned against it, keeping his eyes on her. On her ass, specifically, because Lord have mercy, her ass was so damn sweet in those jeans.

Wolfe was still staring as she turned to face him. He slowly lifted his gaze to her face.

She was smiling.

He lowered an eyebrow and pinned her with a glare. "What was that?"

He saw right through the innocent countenance that washed over her features.

"What was *what*?" Her sweet tone didn't fool him, either.

The corner of his mouth tipped up. The woman was something else. The more he was around her, the more he got to know her, the more he liked her. No, he didn't know the first damn thing about her past, but he knew what he needed to in order to form an opinion. The fact of the matter was, Wolfe liked Amy Smith.

A lot.

"Come here." Wolfe pointed to the spot directly in front of him.

Amy set the water down, then moved to the spot he'd pointed at.

Her smile was still in place. "Yes?"

Wolfe tilted his head, studying her face. "You're so damn pretty," he found himself saying.

That seemed to surprise her, but her smile didn't falter. "Uh … thank you?"

"I think you've got a devious side," he teased. "One I'd like to get to know better."

"Me?" Her wide brown eyes were full of feigned innocence. "Whatever do you mean?"

"You came all the way down those stairs to protect me from that viper."

Amy giggled. "I was thinking she was more like a cougar, but that works, too."

Unable to resist touching her, Wolfe put his hands on her hips and pulled her against him. She placed her palms flat on his chest, slowly sliding them north toward his neck.

"I like when you touch me," he admitted.

"I like when you touch me, too," she said softly.

"All the things I wanna do to you…"

He hadn't meant to say the words out loud, but rather than apologize for them, Wolfe leaned down and kissed her. Softly at first, letting her lead as he had the first time. That lasted for at least a solid minute before Amy pulled back, her eyes locking with his.

"Why do you do that?"

"Do what?"

"Act like I might break."

"I..." Hell, he couldn't answer that because it was true.

"Is Rhys the dominant one in this relationship?" she asked, her tone sassy.

"How's that again?" he asked, grinning.

"Well, he kissed me like he was trying to possess me. I just thought..."

He lowered his voice, leaned in close. "Is that what you want? Me to possess you?"

"I want you to kiss me like you mean it."

Pulling back a little, Wolfe studied her face, trying to read her. He heard what she was saying, and he was so damn tempted to do just as she'd requested, but he'd seen the fear in her eyes too many times. He had no idea who had put it there, but he damn sure didn't want to be another one to do so.

"Wolfe, you won't hurt me." She said the words with such conviction he couldn't help but believe her.

Sliding his hands down to her ass, Wolfe hefted her off her feet in one quick move, spinning them around so her back was to the wall. When she inhaled sharply, Wolfe crushed his mouth to hers.

Amy knocked his ball cap off as her hands gripped his head, holding him to her. Her soft mewls and sweet moans had his dick roaring to life. What he wouldn't give to strip her naked and sink deep inside her right this fucking minute. He felt like he'd been waiting a lifetime for her.

Wolfe finally pulled back for air, but Amy's mouth trailed over his jaw, down to his neck, and he groaned. "Darlin', you're temptin' a very hungry man right now."

"Mmm-hmm."

No, she clearly didn't understand. Wolfe was nearing his breaking point. One of these days, he wasn't going to be able to stop. And he had to stop. Seriously. They were at the shop, and the first time he was inside this woman damn sure wouldn't be here.

She licked him and his breath locked up. "Amy... Darlin'..."

When she lifted her head, their eyes met and he saw her desire reflecting back. She wanted this as much as he did.

"I've never felt anything like this," she whispered. "Never."

Yeah, that made two of them.

"Yo! Where the hell you at, Wolfe?"

Shit.

Wolfe lowered Amy to her feet knowing Lynx would come directly upstairs looking for him. The last thing he wanted was for the man to find them like this. Not that he really gave a shit, but Wolfe wasn't interested in Lynx giving him shit for the rest of his life. Which he would.

"I should get back to work." Amy glanced around the room as though looking for something to do. "Crap."

"What?"

"No way he's gonna think we were working."

Nope, he wouldn't.

Amy's head snapped up, her eyes meeting his. "Next time you wanna make out like teenagers, let's make sure to do it in my office. That way I can at least *pretend* to be doing something productive when we get caught."

Wolfe laughed. "Yes, ma'am."

He would definitely remember for next time.

RHYS HADN'T HEARD from his sister all damn day although he'd texted her twice and tried to call her once. On his way home, he decided to stop by the bar to check on her, but he found it closed up tight.

As he was sitting in the parking lot, another car pulled in. He glanced in his side-view mirror to see Amy pulling up beside him. She got out of the car and walked around to his side of the truck after looking at the door and seeing the same CLOSED sign Rhys saw.

He rolled down his window when she walked over. "Hey."

"Hi." She smiled, her eyes softening as she looked at him. She rested her hands on the door. "I came to check on her. I've been worrying about her all day."

"Yeah. Me, too."

"Where do you think she is?"

He shrugged, glancing back up at the door. "At home, most likely. She's done this before when she and Billy get into it."

"He's an asshole."

Rhys's eyes slammed into her face, his laugh rumbling out of him. He hadn't expected that to come out of Amy's sweet mouth. "That he is."

She leaned back, her fingers still curled over the door. "Well, I don't know where she lives, so I can't very well go check on her. But if you are, I guess—"

"Hop in," he said, nodding toward the passenger door. "We can go together. Maybe she won't kick my ass if you're there."

Amy's face lit up. She released the truck and hurried around to the passenger side. When she was in and buckled, Rhys pulled out of the parking lot and headed south on the main road through town.

"I know it's none of my business, but…" Amy fidgeted with her hands in her lap.

"What?" He glanced over at her briefly, then turned his gaze back to the road.

"Have they been together long?"

He nodded. "Eight years or so, I guess."

"They're not married, right?"

"Nope." That was the only good thing about their relationship.

"Does he hit her?"

"No."

"How do you know that for sure?" Her eyes were wide, as though she didn't believe him.

"I know Reagan. She puts up with a lot of shit, but she would never tolerate him laying a hand on her."

"Oh. Okay."

The way she said it made him think she felt as though he was judging her. Was that what she was running from? An abusive ex-boyfriend?

"I don't mean it like—"

"No. I get it. Reagan's tough, anyway. I'm sure she could kick his butt."

Reagan was feisty, there was no doubt about that.

"I honestly don't know why she's with him," he told her, wanting to explain. "They've been together on and off since high school. I always thought…"

"What?" Amy was watching him intently.

Rhys pulled off the main road toward Reagan's house. "I always thought she had a crush on someone else."

"Who?"

He shrugged. "No clue. But it never seemed like she was really into Billy. He was just a way to pass the time."

"Good grief. I'm sure there are two dozen other men in this town who'd be better to pass time with than him." It was clear Amy wasn't fond of the guy.

"Yeah. There are."

When they pulled up to Reagan's little two-bedroom rental, Rhys noticed her truck was outside.

So was Billy's.

"Do they live together?"

"Yeah. But he's gone a lot. He installs fiber optic lines throughout the state. And when he's not workin', he's usually out partyin'. Stay there. I'll get your door."

Rhys shut off the engine, then made his way around to her side of the truck. When he heard the yelling coming from inside, he was tempted to tell Amy to stay put. He doubted that would go over well. After all, Amy had gone to the bar specifically wanting to check on Reagan.

Opening the door, he paused, his attention turning toward the house. He checked for his gun although he knew it was there.

"You think we should interrupt?" she asked, her eyes wide as she watched the house.

"Someone has to."

Amy linked her fingers with his and Rhys paused to stare down at their hands for a moment. It hit him then that he was here with Amy and he hadn't seen her since Saturday night. Although he knew there was an incident inside that had to be dealt with, there was suddenly something more pressing.

Turning to face her, he tilted her head back with his finger and leaned down.

She met him halfway and Rhys felt some of the pressure on his chest dissipate. He hadn't realized he'd been holding his breath until then.

Her free hand clutched his waist as he deepened the kiss. As much as he wanted to linger, Rhys knew they needed to get this over with. Maybe then he could spend a couple of hours with her. Alone.

"Come on," he said, kissing her nose before pulling her to his side. "Let's see what's goin' on."

Rhys didn't bother knocking. It wouldn't have been heard over the angry voices coming from inside.

"I fucking hate you!" Reagan screamed. "Hate. You."

"Yeah, well, I fuckin' hate you, too."

"Then let me leave!"

"Hell no. And what? Have you go fuck Lynx Caine? Ain't happenin', sweet thang. No way am I lettin' that bastard get his hands on you."

"Give me my truck keys!" Reagan yelled.

Rhys stepped inside, quickly scanning the room for a threat. Reagan was standing just a few feet from the door with a suitcase at her feet. Her hands were on her hips as she stared back at Billy, who was lounging in a ratty recliner.

"Get the fuck outta my house!" Billy hollered, shooting to his feet as soon as he noticed Rhys and Amy.

"What's goin' on?" he asked, looking at his sister.

"He stole my truck keys. I'm tryin' to leave."

"And go where?" Billy taunted. "You ain't got nowhere to go. I'm the only one dumb enough to put up with your shit."

Same fight, different day.

Rhys released Amy's hand and stepped back, motioning toward the door. "Y'all go outside and I'll get your keys."

In the past, Reagan would've told Rhys to mind his own business. He'd figured the fighting was as much her fault as Billy's and she did it to piss the man off. He'd intervened before only to be kicked out of her house with her insisting that they would work through it; they always did.

This time, Reagan nodded her head, snatched up her suitcase, and barreled through the screen door with Amy just a couple of steps behind her.

Looked as though his sister really was done with this asshole.

Thank God for small miracles.

Rhys held out his hand. "Pass 'em over."

"Fuck you."

Rhys sighed. "Don't you think it's time you grew the fuck up?"

"Oh, don't go gettin' high on your horse, Sheriff."

"I'm not here in an official capacity, Billy. That's my sister you're stringin' along. What I don't get is why she hasn't left your sorry ass long before now. Just give me the damn keys and you can move on with your life."

"She ain't gettin' the rest of her shit."

Rhys cocked one eyebrow. If Reagan wanted anything else in the house, he'd make sure she got it, but he wasn't interested in playing this game with Billy right now.

"Keys, Billy."

Billy tossed them over, glaring at him. "I ain't takin' her back this time. She just lost the best damn thing she ever had."

He choked on a laugh. If Billy Watson was the best damn thing in her life, Reagan had nowhere to go but up.

With that, Rhys walked out the front door, gently pulling it shut behind him.

13

"GOD, I HATE him!" Reagan snapped, standing beside her truck while they waited for Rhys to come outside.

When Amy heard the screen door slap shut, her head snapped over, her eyes flying to the man coming out of the house.

Just Rhys.

"Did you get my keys?" Reagan demanded.

Rhys tossed them toward her. Reagan caught them.

"Thank you." Her tone didn't have a lot of sincerity, but Amy could tell she was grateful. "Damn it."

"You need to leave for good this time," Rhys told her.

Amy felt him move closer to her side and she welcomed his presence. She wasn't sure when she'd gotten so comfortable with him, but she was.

"Trust me, I'm done."

"Good."

Reagan grabbed her suitcase and hefted it into the bed of the truck.

"Where're you gonna stay?" Rhys asked his sister.

Reagan shrugged. "No clue."

"You can stay in my guest room," he offered.

Amy noticed the way Reagan's nose scrunched up. "Although I appreciate the offer, *Sheriff,* I think I'll pass." Her blue eyes reflected more humor than frustration. "I love you and all, but I damn sure don't wanna live with you."

"You could always go stay with Mom and Pawpaw. I'm sure they could use the help."

"Yeah. And listen to Pawpaw tell me every day that I've fucked up my life. No thank you."

Amy looked at Rhys, then Reagan. "I've … uh … got an extra bedroom."

Reagan's eyes widened. "Seriously?"

Amy nodded.

The next thing she knew, Reagan was throwing her arms around her, hugging her tight. "Thank you. Oh, my God. Thank you!"

Reagan jumped back, practically skipping to her truck.

"Where're you goin'?" Rhys asked.

"Work." As though that made perfect sense. Reagan's attention turned to Amy. "It'll be late when I show up. You don't mind, do you?"

Amy shook her head. "Of course not. Do you … uh … know where I live?"

"McKenzie Catlay's old place, right?"

"Yeah."

"I know where it is. I'll shut the bar down a little early tonight." Reagan's smile was bright. "You're a lifesaver, Amy. Thank you."

Feeling as though she'd been hit by a tornado, Amy didn't say anything more as Reagan backed out of the driveway, then tore out onto the road, leaving rubber on the asphalt behind her.

Rhys chuckled. "I hope you know what you're in for."

She seriously didn't. But that was okay.

At least this way, she didn't have to stay in her house alone.

An hour later, Amy was walking into her house, Rhys and Wolfe directly behind her. She and Rhys had driven back to Reagan's bar so Amy could get her car. When they arrived, it looked as though half the town had showed up to see what had happened. She'd realized then just how quickly the news spread in a small town. Before they'd pulled out of the lot, Wolfe was pulling in, his truck blocking both of their vehicles.

This time, when Amy offered to cook dinner, he didn't hesitate in agreeing. Of course, she'd made the offer to both of them.

The problem was, she really didn't know what she could cook. She had very little in her fridge and even less in the pantry. It only took a second to get a full menu of options and they consisted of… "I don't suppose y'all like grilled ham and cheese?"

Wolfe was the first to grin, followed quickly by Rhys.

"It's our favorite," they both lied in unison.

"Whatever." Amy sighed.

Wolfe moved over, his hands curling over her shoulders as he pulled her into him. Amy went willingly, resting her head against his chest.

As he brushed his hand over her hair, he said, "How 'bout we let Rhys make grilled ham and cheese and we'll supervise?"

"*Me?*" Rhys sounded appalled. "Have you ever known me to cook?"

"There's a first time for everything," Wolfe noted.

Amy laughed, pulling back. "I can cook, it's just—"

Before she could finish the sentence, Rhys moved past her, swatting her on the butt and chuckling. "I've got this, girl. Never underestimate the power of law enforcement."

"Trust me, I won't make that mistake ever again." Although she'd said the words under her breath, Amy hadn't meant for them to come out. And she especially hadn't meant for Rhys and Wolfe to hear them.

"*What*?" Wolfe's emerald gaze slammed into her, his tone hard, his concern apparent.

As she stared at them, she felt heat creep into her cheeks. *What had she done?*

"Amy? What do you mean by that?" Rhys's tone was more pained that angry, but she saw the worry on his handsome features just the same.

"Nothing. Oh, God." Amy covered her face and tore out of the room, going straight for the guest bedroom.

She needed to get it ready for Reagan.

Yes. That was what she needed to do.

How could she be so stupid? She'd managed to keep her mouth shut for a solid year, and suddenly she'd let out her greatest secret. Not to mention, her biggest fear.

It had to be because of what Reagan was going through. The mere thought of Reagan's boyfriend hitting her had been a fear Amy had wrestled with all day.

Staring at the empty guest room, she tried to think what she should do first. Anything to keep her mind off the past and to keep the men in her kitchen from asking questions. She didn't have anything except for a futon for Reagan to sleep on, but she was sure she and Reagan could figure that out. Amy had never anticipated actually having guests.

"Amy?"

Wolfe.

Unable to move, she stood facing away from the gruff voice behind her. She figured there were two imposing men standing there, wanting some answers. Answers she wasn't ready to give because she didn't want to relive the past. It was bad enough she continued to have nightmares.

She didn't want those memories imposing during the day.

Hell, she didn't want the memories at all.

WOLFE WANTED AMY to turn around and spill her guts, to tell him what the hell was going on. Why she'd say something like that.

No, he *needed* Amy to talk to him. It was no longer a mere want.

And he knew that Rhys would demand it. The man couldn't possibly sit back and allow a statement like that to slide. It was clear something had happened to her and it was obvious it had to do with law enforcement.

Glancing over at Rhys, Wolfe nodded toward Amy, signaling for him to address the situation.

Rhys moved past him into the room, coming to stand behind her, his hands resting on her shoulders. "Talk to me, Amy. Please."

She shook her head. "I can't."

"You need to."

"No. I don't. Please, just let it go."

Rhys turned Amy around, tilting her head back to force her to look at him. Wolfe moved in beside him.

"What happened?"

She shook her head again and this time there were tears in her eyes.

"Please don't make me talk about it. Can't we just…?" A sob tore out of her. "Please, Rhys. I can't. I really can't."

Wolfe's heart ripped to shreds as her tears began to fall. This wasn't a woman prone to dramatics, and it was clear she did not want to talk about this. As much as they needed to know what was going on, he also knew forcing her wouldn't help the situation.

Putting one hand on Rhys's shoulder, the other on Amy's, he urged them back toward the doorway. "Come on. I'll cook and we can … talk about somethin' else."

Rhys clearly wasn't happy about that, but he gave a jerky nod, wrapping his arm around Amy and steering her back into the kitchen. He pulled out a chair, but she refused to sit.

"I'll cook," Amy insisted. "I need something to do. Why don't y'all … I don't know. Go outside or something."

Outside?

Wolfe hoped like hell she wasn't trying to get rid of them, because it would take a hell of a lot more than that to make him leave right now.

"I just need a minute," she pleaded.

Nodding his understanding, Wolfe grabbed Rhys's arm and tugged him back through the living room and out the front door.

As soon as the door was between them and Amy, Rhys let loose a string of curse words that would've made Wolfe's father blush. And that was saying something.

"What the fuck did he do to her?"

"He?" Wolfe was lost.

"Oh, come on." Rhys stomped across the porch, his voice low, probably so Amy couldn't hear. "Someone hurt her and I'm inclined to believe it was a man. A police officer."

Yeah, that was the conclusion Wolfe had come to as well. Although, at this point, he had no fucking clue.

"Why won't she let us help her?" Rhys turned to look directly at him.

"Give her time."

"You know, she asked me if Billy hit Reagan," Rhys informed him.

Wolfe nodded, waiting to see where Rhys was going with this.

"I told her no. Told her Reagan would never put up with that shit. I think it was the wrong thing to say."

"But it's true," Wolfe agreed.

Wolfe knew Reagan's relationship with Billy wasn't healthy by any means, but he did know that the little shit didn't hit her.

"It is. But you should've seen the look on her face. It was as though I'd personally offended her."

Interesting. "So, you think…?"

Rhys shrugged. "I don't know what to think, but yeah, I think it's safe to assume someone abused her."

Wolfe nodded, considering this. It made sense. It certainly explained how tense she was, always looking over her shoulder.

"I can't fucking sit here and do nothin', Wolfe. It's not who I am."

Wolfe knew that. It wasn't easy for him, either. "We don't have a choice."

Rhys gripped the railing and bent over, bowing his back as his knuckles turned white around the old wood, his entire body tight with his anger.

He didn't know why he did it, but Wolfe moved over and put his hand on Rhys's back. "We'll figure this out."

Rhys stood, pivoting to face him.

Wolfe found himself face-to-face with a very pissed-off sheriff.

"You're right. We will." Rhys didn't sound convinced. "Which is why I need to go. I need—"

In an effort to distract him, Wolfe grabbed Rhys and slammed his mouth over his. Jerking the man against him, he released all the pent-up frustration through that kiss.

"Fuck," Rhys moaned, his fingers digging into Wolfe's waist, their mouths separating only briefly. "God, I need you."

Wolfe knew exactly how Rhys felt. This thing between the three of them, it was building. Wolfe knew he had to be careful with Amy, but he didn't have to do the same with Rhys. He could be as rough, as passionate as he wanted to be.

And boy did he want to be.

Wolfe pushed Rhys up against the wooden post that held up the porch's roof. He held Rhys's jaw in place, roughly kissing him, thrusting his tongue into Rhys's mouth. It didn't matter that they were outside, or that it was still daylight and anyone who came down Amy's driveway might see them. He didn't give a fuck about that. He wanted this man too damn much.

Rhys was the first to pull back, but not completely. Wolfe remained close, their lower bodies still touching.

"I can't wait much longer," Wolfe admitted.

He could wait forever for Amy because that was what she needed, but he knew Rhys was as tired of putting this off as he was.

"What do we do about that?"

Wolfe didn't know the answer to that yet. But he got the feeling that he'd know by the time he went home tonight.

One way or the other, he was going to have Rhys. Whether they were alone or Amy was with them, Wolfe wasn't putting it off any longer.

RHYS WAS DOING his best to keep his temper in check. Wolfe's distraction had helped. Well, sort of. It had also riled him in a completely different way. Now he needed something to sate the urges that had been building and building. His hand was no longer doing it for him. He needed more. Wolfe, Amy… Rhys needed to feel them, to touch them, hold them. It was slowly driving him to the breaking point.

"Be patient," Wolfe said, throwing Rhys's words from the other night back at him.

Patient. Right. His patience was so fucking thin at the moment. Still, he managed to laugh and relaxed a fraction.

That lasted until Wolfe backed away from him. Once the heat of the man's body was no longer pressing against him, the source of his initial frustration made a reappearance.

After Amy's comment, he was itching to know just who had fucked with her and what they'd done. She clearly didn't put a lot of faith in the police, which led him to believe that whoever had hurt her was in law enforcement. But who? Was it someone back in Houston? Or had she met him somewhere else?

Unfortunately, his searches so far had netted absolutely nothing. He needed more information to go on. At some point, he figured she would tell him more or he would hit Wolfe up for the personal details from her employee file. Rhys couldn't sit back and let her continue to fear someone who might be out for her.

He wanted to fix it. It was who he was. Not something he could change, either.

The door opened and Amy appeared. She looked as though she'd washed her face, probably dried up the tears that had managed to escape. Rhys had noticed how rough that was on her. She was trying to push it all down, put it behind her. The fact that she still lived in fear told him that it wasn't something that would just go away.

"Dinner's ready." She forced a smile. "Although I'm not sure this can really be called dinner."

"If it's got meat on it," Wolfe said as he stepped into the house, "then it'll work for dinner."

"I'll have to remember that," Amy said with a genuine laugh.

Rhys stopped in front of her, brushing her hair back from her face and watching her as she watched him. Rather than say anything more to upset her, he leaned down and gently kissed her. He wouldn't apologize, but he would give her a little space.

For now.

"I guess we should be goin'," Wolfe prompted, two hours later.

They'd had dinner, scarfing down the grilled ham and cheese in a matter of minutes. After they'd helped her clean the kitchen, Amy had curled up on the couch between the two of them. Rhys figured she'd purposely put on a movie to keep from having to talk. Although it frustrated Rhys, he managed to let it go.

"I have to get up early," Amy said, far too agreeable for Rhys's taste. "Plus, Reagan'll be here around midnight, so I'll have to be up when she arrives."

Wolfe looked between the two of them. "Reagan's stayin' here?"

Rhys nodded. "She left Billy. Hopefully for good this time."

"You think Billy'll come out here and start shit?"

That had crossed Rhys's mind, but if Billy was consistent, he was going to spend a couple of weeks screwing any female who'd give him the time of day before he decided he wanted Reagan back. "Doubtful. Not for a while, anyway."

Wolfe nodded, but he didn't seem satisfied.

"I'm sure Reagan can handle herself," Amy told them. She looked at Rhys. "Plus, you said he never hit her. So you won't have to worry about that."

Rhys didn't say anything. He remembered that conversation in his truck. Amy had seemed offended by his statement that Reagan wouldn't put up with that shit. Add to that Amy's fear and her comment from earlier and he was starting to put all the pieces together.

It didn't make him feel a damn bit better.

Wolfe was the first to get to his feet. He took Amy's hand and led her to the door, stopping to kiss her before he stepped outside. "I'll see you at work in the mornin'."

Amy nodded, holding on to Wolfe's hand for a second before releasing him.

Rhys took his turn, kissing her gently, wishing he could keep her in his arms for the rest of the night. Unfortunately, that wasn't going to happen.

They both knew it.

"Good night," he said, keeping his voice low. "If you need anything, call me. Or Wolfe."

She nodded, but she wouldn't hold his gaze.

As soon as he stepped outside, she closed and locked the door.

"Is it just me, or did it seem like she was anxious for us to leave?" Rhys asked as he followed Wolfe down the porch steps.

"It's not just you."

They both stopped at Rhys's truck, Wolfe turning to face him.

"You're on days this week, right?"

"Yeah." He alternated weeks working days and nights. It wasn't always easy, but it worked for him. Allowed him to interact with everyone in the community.

"Come out to my place."

Rhys glanced up at Amy's house, then back to the sexy man in front of him. "I'm not sure…"

Wolfe stepped in closer. "I wasn't asking."

"Fine."

Wolfe gave a curt nod and walked over to his truck.

Swallowing hard, Rhys battled back the natural urge to argue. He wasn't going to win this one.

But then again, he didn't really want to.

14

WHEN WOLFE WALKED into his house a half hour later, he instantly wished he'd brought Amy with him.

Oh, sure, she would've declined the offer, but he hadn't been ready to leave her yet. It seemed the more time he spent with her, the *more* time he wanted to spend with her. Which was crazy. Hell, he'd loved his job before she started working there. Now that she was with him all damn day, he hated when it was time to leave.

A knock sounded on his front door a second before it opened.

"Was startin' to think you weren't comin'," Wolfe told Rhys when he waltzed into the kitchen, where Wolfe was leaning against the counter, drinking a beer.

He hadn't bothered turning on the overhead lights, knowing he'd just be turning them off again, so he stood in the dark, the light above the stove providing a white glow that didn't reach far.

"Almost didn't."

Wolfe tilted his bottle to his lips, waiting for Rhys to elaborate.

He didn't.

Clearly they had some things to discuss.

"Scared?" Wolfe taunted. Hell, it was as good a conversation starter as any.

"If I said a little, does that bother you?"

No.

In fact, Wolfe understood.

"So, how does this work?" Wolfe figured if anyone would know, Rhys would. It seemed the guy had some experience with these situations. If some of the rumors were true, anyway.

"How does *what* work?"

Crossing one ankle over the other, Wolfe took another swig of his beer. "This thing with you, me, and Amy."

"Like, you want to know which tab goes in which slot?"

Wolfe flipped Rhys off. "No, smartass. I've got that one figured out."

"Do you?" The taunt in Rhys's tone was evident.

Setting his beer on the counter, Wolfe pushed away from the cabinet and stalked across the room. As usual, Rhys stood his ground, not budging even when Wolfe got up in his face. Wolfe liked that about Rhys. He liked that the man wasn't intimidated by him, that he was willing to stand up to him. It was fucking hot.

Wolfe leaned in, his lips hovering mere centimeters from Rhys's. "Trust me, I'm not questionin' what I want from you."

"What about what *I* want from *you*?" Rhys asked, his low tenor sending a chill down Wolfe's spine.

"If you're man enough to take it, you can have it," Wolfe told him.

Okay, it had been a dare. However, Wolfe hadn't expected Rhys to call him on it.

The next thing Wolfe knew, he was up against the refrigerator, Rhys's lips fused to his, their tongues dueling. The man was a hell of a lot stronger than Wolfe gave him credit for.

This was exactly what Wolfe needed.

"I'm definitely man enough," Rhys murmured against Wolfe's mouth. "And I'll take everything you're willin' to give."

Wolfe was breathing hard, his fingers digging into Rhys's lower back as he held him close, their chests and hips pressed together, his cock becoming intimate with his zipper.

"I get this part of it," Wolfe admitted, pulling back slightly. "And jeezus, fuck, I want you more than I want my next breath. But I want Amy so fuckin' bad. I want her here with us. I want her between us. I want her *beneath me*." Releasing his death grip on Rhys, Wolfe thrust his hand through his hair, glancing up at the ceiling. "I don't know how this fuckin' works, Rhys. I just don't."

The warmth pressed against him disappeared as Rhys moved back.

"What you're askin' is whether she'll accept us bein' together without her?"

"Yeah. Maybe." It seemed like a logical question. Would it bother her? Would she be hurt? Or did she expect it?

"Will you question if I'm with her without you?"

Wolfe thought about that for a minute. There was some dark, devious side of him that liked the idea of knowing Rhys and Amy might be fucking, that one or both of them would tell him about it at some point. Perhaps they'd tell him in vivid detail.

He found himself shaking his head. "I wouldn't question it. But I'd want you to tell me what happened in detail."

Rhys cocked on eyebrow, his breaths deeper. He was clearly thinking about that, too. "I'd want that, too."

They stared at one another for several seconds before Rhys spoke again.

"And I'd expect the same … if you're with her without me there." Rhys turned away.

"You want me to tell you how I touched her? Kissed her? Licked her?"

"Fuck yes," Rhys hissed, his hands balling into fists. He was obviously holding himself back the same way Wolfe was.

"Is that how it works?" Wolfe asked, genuinely curious. "Are there parameters? Only at certain times? In certain situations? Are there rules?"

Rhys turned to face him. "Do you want there to be?"

Wolfe didn't know. He only knew that he wanted Amy there with them. Tonight. He didn't want to wait for her. He wanted to feel every inch of her against every inch of him. He wanted Rhys naked beside him, touching him, tasting him. He wanted to do the same to them.

But he didn't fucking know how it worked.

Rhys sighed and Wolfe forced all the shit from his brain. He was overthinking this.

"I should go," Rhys said. "It'll happen when it's supposed to happen. *If* it's supposed to happen."

When Rhys turned toward the door, Wolfe debated on whether or not he should stop him. He was torn, but if he let Rhys walk out that door, he'd go fucking crazy.

Hell, he was already halfway there.

"It's supposed to happen," Wolfe assured him, talking to Rhys's back as he moved toward the door.

Rhys put his hand on the doorknob. "Is it? Because I'm startin' to wonder."

Wolfe put his hand on the door above Rhys's head, keeping him from opening it. "Turn around."

There was a slight pause before Rhys turned, looking directly in Wolfe's eyes.

"You're makin' me crazy," Wolfe told him.

"Funny." Rhys chuckled, a gruff, frustrated sound. "I was thinkin' the same thing about you."

Wolfe let his eyes travel over the smooth lines of Rhys's face. "I need this," he admitted.

Rhys nodded, obviously understanding Wolfe's pain.

"I need *you*, Rhys. I need you to take the edge off. To keep me in check. That way when we have Amy, we can go slow, give her everything she needs."

Wolfe noticed the way Rhys's eyes widened. The man needed the same thing, but he clearly wasn't going to admit it.

"Don't go," Wolfe whispered. "Stay with me tonight."

Rhys dropped his head against the door. "I think you're gonna have to convince me."

"Think I won't?"

One shoulder lifted as Rhys gave one of those expressions that said *Who knows, where you're concerned.*

But Wolfe knew.

He knew what he wanted.

Sure, he was conflicted, but that didn't change the fact that he wanted Rhys.

Right here.

Right now.

I NEED YOU, *Rhys. I need you to take the edge off. To keep me in check. That way when we have Amy, we can go slow, give her everything she needs.*

Those words ran on repeat in his head, making his dick throb as the doorknob dug into Rhys's back when Wolfe crushed him to the wood, their mouths aligning, tongues moving together. The kiss was brutal. It was every damn thing he needed, every damn thing he'd thought about, dreamed about for too long now.

He was tired of thinking, tired of worrying, tired of trying to figure it all out.

He just wanted to feel.

"Holy fuck," Rhys groaned when Wolfe's rough hands slid beneath his T-shirt, forcing it higher. Callused palms abraded his skin, making his nipples harden, his dick throb impatiently.

Rhys helped the man along by grabbing a fistful of T-shirt behind his head and pulling it up and off. Rough hands moved over his skin and he sucked in a breath.

"Goddamn, I want you," Wolfe whispered roughly. "So fucking much."

"I'm right here."

Wolfe suddenly stepped back, his eyes raking over Rhys's chest, lower, then back to his mouth. "Take the damn clothes off, Sheriff."

Rhys realized then that he wasn't going to be in control here. As much as he wanted to be, there was no dominating Wolfe. The man wouldn't allow it.

Not yet, anyway.

Wolfe raised a hand and pointed to the hallway. "Bedroom."

Nope, no way was Rhys going to be able to control how this played out.

Not that he really gave a shit. Right now, he just wanted Wolfe to touch him.

Sure, it would've been damn near perfect if Amy was there, even if she was simply watching, but Rhys needed this. He needed what only Wolfe could offer him. And Wolfe was right. It would take the edge off. They couldn't take from Amy, couldn't bombard her with the need fueling them. They had to take it slow with her, so this…

This was what they both needed.

Evidently, Rhys didn't move fast enough for Wolfe, because the man gripped Rhys's belt buckle and jerked him forward, the backs of his fingers brushing Rhys's stomach. He had no choice but to move his feet, following Wolfe as the man walked backwards down the hall and into his bedroom.

Rhys had never seen the man's bedroom.

He didn't intend to do much looking now, either, because Wolfe was once more kissing him, those long fingers working open Rhys's belt buckle, then the button on his jeans, and finally the zipper.

"Boots gotta go," Wolfe informed him.

Rhys toed off his boots while Wolfe stepped back and did the same.

He'd barely managed to get the second one off when Wolfe grabbed him, pulled him forward, then took them both to the bed. Rhys grunted from Wolfe's weight, but he held on, refusing to let go. He ran his hands beneath Wolfe's shirt, feeling smooth, warm skin against his palms. It took only a second to get the shirt off, and when he did, Rhys resumed kissing him, holding Wolfe to him while rough fingers twined in Rhys's hair, pulling hard as Wolfe devoured him.

Fuck. He was going to detonate if Wolfe kept this up.

A growl rumbled up from Wolfe's chest and the sound had Rhys's dick pulsing, desperate for the man's touch.

Rhys was breathing hard, his chest heaving when Wolfe released him, kneeling on the bed and jerking Rhys's jeans down his hips. Emerald-green eyes met his briefly before Wolfe turned his attention on Rhys's cock.

The second Wolfe fisted him, Rhys's hips jerked up off the bed. "Son of a bitch."

"Like that?"

Rhys liked it so damn much he couldn't speak. Any word he might've said got lodged in his throat and came out as a long, tortured moan.

"Open your eyes."

Rhys's eyes flew open. He hadn't even realized he'd shut them.

"Watch me." Wolfe stroked him again. "Watch what I do to you."

That was a damn near impossible task when Wolfe leaned down and took Rhys's cock between his lips, his tongue swiping over the swollen head. It took effort to relax, to pull himself back from the edge. He couldn't come yet. Fuck. They'd just gotten started and he wanted to enjoy this for as long as he could.

Rhys put one hand behind his head so he could keep his eyes focused on the way Wolfe took him to the root. His other hand slid into the short strands of Wolfe's hair. He didn't apply pressure, just held on.

Sweet jeezus. The man's mouth… "Aww, fuck… Wolfe…" That perfect fucking mouth was going to do him in.

Another moan escaped, his hand tightening in Wolfe's hair as his cock pushed deeper into the sweet haven of Wolfe's mouth. The man teased and tormented him for long minutes, then abruptly stopped, making Rhys's head spin.

He watched as Wolfe got to his feet, effectively shedding his jeans and boxer briefs. Rhys's gaze instantly homed in on Wolfe's cock. He remembered the feel of him in his hand, the wide, thick shaft beneath his fingers.

Wolfe cleared his throat, dragging Rhys's eyes up to his face. That was when he noticed Wolfe was crooking his finger, motioning Rhys to come to him.

Summoned.

Damn.

Not that Rhys was going to object.

His abs tightened as he sat up. He scooted to the end of the bed, letting his feet touch the floor as he gripped Wolfe's giant dick, bringing it to his mouth without hesitation.

Opening his mouth wide, he wrapped his lips around the broad crest.

"Oh, fuck yes," Wolfe hissed, his fingers tangling in Rhys's hair.

Unlike Rhys, Wolfe did apply pressure. He pulled him forward, driving his cock deep into Rhys's throat. It took effort to take him, and he damn sure couldn't take all of him, but he gave it his all, not stopping until he gagged.

"Again," Wolfe demanded. "Take all of me."

Rhys made another attempt, which resulted in the same, but that didn't seem to bother Wolfe. The man began pumping his hips, fucking Rhys's mouth in a steady rhythm. It wasn't long before Wolfe pulled back, his cock falling from Rhys's lips.

"Don't move."

Wolfe disappeared into what appeared to be a bathroom. He returned with condoms and a pump bottle of what he assumed was lube. Wolfe tossed one condom to Rhys.

"Put it on me."

Wasting no time, Rhys tore it open and rolled the latex over Wolfe's thick shaft.

When he was suited up, Wolfe leaned over him and Rhys fell back onto the bed.

"I'm gonna take you right here, just like this. And I want you to look in my eyes when I fuck you."

Rhys had heard rumors that Wolfe liked to watch and be watched. It turned him on, or so he'd heard.

He understood why because … *fuck!* … it turned Rhys on, too.

Wolfe wasn't gentle when he positioned Rhys, forcing his legs up, Rhys's knees coming toward his chest. Rhys groaned when Wolfe inserted two lubed fingers in his ass, pushing in deep, retreating. He didn't think Wolfe meant to be as rough as he was. The tension coiling Wolfe's muscles tight said the man was holding on by a thread.

"So fucking hot."

Rhys didn't know what Wolfe was referring to, but he didn't give a damn. He wanted to feel the man inside him even if the thought briefly terrified him.

"Ready?"

Nodding, Rhys fought the urge to close his eyes. Wolfe leaned over him, their faces close. The fingers disappeared and the blunt head of Wolfe's cock took their place.

"Relax."

Yeah. Easier said than done.

"Fuck, you're tight." Wolfe grunted, his teeth clamped together.

Rhys reached for Wolfe. He needed more and he was tired of waiting.

Seconds later, Wolfe was lodged to the hilt inside him, completely still. Rhys breathed through the initial pain, allowing his body to accommodate the intrusion. It wasn't that he'd never bottomed, but he didn't usually. It wasn't his preference.

Except with Wolfe.

Rhys knew when it came to Wolfe Caine, he'd take the man any way he could get him.

Wolfe situated himself so that his feet were on the floor, yet he was practically covering Rhys, thrusting in hard and deep, grunting and groaning. Rhys kept his eyes open, locked with Wolfe's.

"Rhys … fuck … you feel so damn good." Wolfe slammed into him over and over.

Rhys held on, allowing the sensations to send him soaring higher and higher until he couldn't take any more.

Without any friction on his cock, Rhys came harder than he'd ever come in his life, his back bowing, body tensing, a strangled moan rumbling in his throat.

"Fuck, yes." Wolfe slammed into him again and again. "Always knew…" Wolfe breathed deeply. "Always fucking *knew* it would be this good." Their eyes met. "With you," Wolfe hissed, then slammed home twice more before following Rhys right over the edge. "Oh, fuck, yes!"

THE PLATE CRASHED against the wall, shattering.

A glass followed.

"You stupid bitch. Why can't you just do what I ask you to do? You'd think after nearly five years of this you'd figure out how to get it right! I'm tired of having to beat some sense into you."

Amy stared blankly at the space above his shoulder. She didn't dare look at him. She didn't want to provoke him any more. He'd obviously had a bad day and he was taking it out on her. Which was par for the course. If history was to repeat itself, he would take his anger out on her next.

"Get up!"

Amy's eyes shot to his face. "What?"

He glared at her, his face a mask of rage. "Don't make me tell you again."

Swallowing hard, Amy pushed to her feet. She was trembling; she couldn't help it.

He was on his feet in an instant, his hand coming toward her.

Amy flinched, expecting the blow to land on her face just as it had so many times before. Instead, he grabbed her hair, jerking her toward him. She stumbled, falling, her knees slamming into the tiled floor. Pain, hot and fierce, bolted through her, making her gasp.

"I said get up!" His voice was getting louder as he yanked her to her feet. "Don't make me pick you up, goddammit!"

Amy cried out, trying to move to ease the fire burning in her scalp.

"The only thing I ask is that you do what I tell you. How hard is that, Amy? You don't have to work; you don't have to take care of any fucking brats. You stay at home all goddamn day while I'm out there working my ass off. The least you can do is make sure my dinner is warm when I get home. How can you expect to be my wife? You're too stupid to be my wife."

The tears streaked down her face, but Amy didn't say a word. She knew better. The one time she'd told him she didn't want to be his wife, she'd ended up with a broken arm. Since then, the beatings had gotten worse, not better, no matter how much he apologized afterward. He still insisted it was her fault.

"This is for your own good, Amy. Remember that."

Amy jerked awake, sitting up straight.

She was on the couch, the television on.

A knock sounded on the door, making her heart leap into her throat.

"Amy? You in there? It's me. Reagan."

Reagan.

Oh, God.

Jumping to her feet, Amy scrubbed her hands over her face, wiping the tears away. She hoped Reagan didn't notice. With the lights off, maybe she wouldn't.

"I'm coming," she called out, moving fast, the adrenaline from the nightmare still flooding her system.

Amy stumbled, tripping on the rug beneath the coffee table. Fortunately, she remained upright, her shoulder bumping the wall beside the door. She unlocked the deadbolt, then the knob before pulling the door open.

"Hey." Reagan studied her briefly, a mix of confusion and concern registering on her face. "You okay? I heard screaming."

Amy quickly looked away, stepping back so Reagan could come inside. "Sorry. I was … uh … watching a movie. I must've fallen asleep. You probably heard the television."

Reagan glanced at the TV, then back to Amy. "Yeah. Okay."

"I hope you weren't out there long." Amy closed the door when Reagan dragged her suitcase inside.

"No, just a minute or two." Reagan was studying her intensely. "You sure you're all right? Looks like you were cryin'."

Amy nodded. "I'm fine."

The sympathy she saw in Reagan's eyes made her stomach twist. She hadn't had a friend in so long and now it seemed she had some everywhere she turned. That alone made her want to curl into a ball and sob.

"If you need to talk about anything," Reagan prompted, "I'm here."

"Thanks." Wiping her face to keep more tears from falling, Amy pointed toward the hallway. "I … uh … got the guest room set up. As best I could, anyway. I only have a futon, but we can get you a bed if you'd like." She knew she was talking too fast, but she couldn't stop herself. Her heart was pounding.

"A futon works," Reagan said, looking around the house. "Hell, I'd be happy to sleep on the couch. Or the floor. I'm just grateful you offered. I promise not to stay too long."

"Stay as long as you like," Amy told her. She didn't care if Reagan wanted to stay forever. Provided Amy could keep the nightmares at bay, she figured she would enjoy the company.

"You're too sweet."

Amy took a deep breath, tried to calm down. "And I'll get you my spare key to the house so you can come and go. I'm working for Wolfe and Lynx now, so I'll be gone before you wake up."

Reagan nodded, but Amy didn't meet her eyes. She could feel the waves of concern coming off of Reagan.

"Sure."

Amy walked toward the hallway. "The … uh … guest room is that way. There's a bathroom, too. It's not big, but…"

"I appreciate this, Amy. I really do."

Amy nodded. "Okay. I … uh … I'm just gonna go to bed now."

Without waiting for Reagan to say anything more or, God forbid, ask any questions, Amy turned and walked to her bedroom.

Okay, maybe it was more of a walk/jog.

Whatever.

God, she needed to talk to someone, to let some of this out. She knew holding it back wouldn't help. It was only getting worse. Her fear, her paranoia. The annoying panic attacks. She probably should've taken Reagan up on her offer to listen, but Amy knew telling Reagan would only put the woman in danger. She didn't dare do that.

No, if she was going to talk to anyone, she would tell someone who could protect themselves against the monster who was haunting her.

There were only two people she knew who'd be capable of doing that.

The question was, could she really burden them with that?

And if she did, would they still be able to look at her the same way?

15

WOLFE WOKE UP pressed up against the sun.

It took a second for his eyes to focus, for him to realize it wasn't the damn sun, just Rhys.

Fuck.

If they were going to be sleeping in the same bed, he was going to have to get a fan for the room. Between them, they'd generated a significant amount of heat.

His mind drifted back to last night. Yeah, they'd certainly generated some heat. His cock, already tenting the sheet draped over his legs, was ready for a replay. Glancing over at the clock, Wolfe realized he had fifteen minutes before he had to get in the shower.

Fifteen minutes was just enough time to...

Spooning behind Rhys, Wolfe positioned his cock so that he could grind himself against Rhys's ass, his body hardening, his need growing infinitely stronger.

The sleeping man shifted, his body moving closer to Wolfe as he mumbled, "Mmm. Mornin'."

Wolfe nipped Rhys's shoulder, his voice thick with sleep as he whispered, "I need to be inside you again."

The mere thought of burying his dick inside Rhys's hot fucking body had precum pooling on the tip.

Reaching over Rhys's hips, Wolfe took the man's rigid erection in his hand, slowly stroking, enjoying the sleepy moans coming from Rhys. "Thinkin' about me, are ya?"

"Wolfe…" Rhys's hips rocked forward and back, his shoulders pressing against Wolfe's chest. "Feels good."

That was an understatement. Everything about this man felt damn near perfect. And this … waking up to Rhys in his bed… It was better than Wolfe had expected.

"Want me to blow you before or after I fuck you? Because as much as I wanna be inside you right now, I wanna taste you, want you to come down my throat."

They groaned in unison.

"Holy fuck," Rhys moaned, his hips pumping, ass grinding against Wolfe's aching dick. "After."

Releasing Rhys's cock, Wolfe flipped over and grabbed a condom. He rolled the latex on and lathered lube over himself before turning back to find Rhys on his stomach, his hips grinding against the mattress.

Goddamn, the man was fucking hot.

Moving over him, Wolfe kissed Rhys's naked back, running his tongue along the smooth skin and rigid muscle, dragging his lips up to Rhys's neck. He rubbed his stubble-lined jaw along Rhys's shoulder, enjoying the warmth beneath him.

"No foreplay." It wasn't a question. Wolfe needed to be inside him right now.

"No foreplay," Rhys echoed.

Within seconds, Wolfe had lodged himself balls deep, the heat of Rhys's ass enveloping him.

"Christ," he breathed, holding himself completely still while his body tightened painfully hard.

Rhys moaned, his hand coming to rest on top of Wolfe's, their fingers twining together.

Wolfe rocked his hips. Rather than race to the finish line, he took his time, relishing the feel of Rhys's ass as it strangled his dick. A steady tingle started at the base of his spine, but Wolfe willed it back, rocking forward, lodging himself as deep as he could go.

"Fuck, I could get used to this," Wolfe whispered, holding himself still for a second before retreating, then pushing in again. Slow … deep… "You feel so damn good."

The tingling warning of his impending orgasm intensified. Wolfe increased his pace, his cock tunneling in and out of Rhys's tight hole, hips punching against Rhys's ass, while he tightened his fingers around Rhys's, holding on to the man as he drove himself to completion.

Wolfe didn't linger once he was spent. He had something else in mind, something he'd dreamed about last night. Wanting to take care of Rhys, Wolfe immediately pulled out, then flipped Rhys onto his back before sucking the man's steel-hard cock into his mouth. This time he didn't take his time; he wanted Rhys to come.

Rhys's fingers twined in his hair like they'd done last night, but this time the man wasn't gentle. He pulled Wolfe's hair, rough groans echoing in the dark room as he fucked Wolfe's mouth.

Wolfe cupped Rhys's balls as he sucked him, applying more suction every time while he fisted the base, stroking.

Rough.

Hard.

"Oh, fuck… Wolfe… It's too much. Oh, God."

Rhys's body bowed as his release took him. Wolfe drank him down, cleaning him with his tongue before crawling up his body and kissing him for the first time that morning.

Yeah.

It was safe to say Wolfe could get used to waking up like this.

**

An hour later, Wolfe was pulling into the shop. Amy's car was in the parking lot already, and he had to glance at the clock to make sure he wasn't late.

He wasn't.

Which meant she was early.

Before he could get his truck door opened, Amy had sprinted around to the driver's side. And the instant Wolfe put his boots on the gravel, she was in his arms, her body crashing into his.

Fear hit him harder than she did.

"What's wrong?" Panic clutched his chest, a painful constriction that made it difficult to breathe.

She didn't respond, a sob the only sound she made.

"Amy." Wolfe tried to pull back, tried to push her away, desperate to look at her face, but she was locked to him, her arms around his waist, her face buried in his chest. "Damn it, Amy. Talk to me."

The sound of her crying nearly had his knees giving out, dread filling him, stealing at least ten years off his life.

"Amy!" Wolfe wasn't known for panic attacks but the woman had him coming unraveled. He had no idea what was wrong, but it was something. Frantic to get answers, Wolfe tried to push her back again, wanting to look in her eyes. "Did something happen?"

She shook her head. "No."

"Are you hurt?"

Her face rubbed against him as she continued to shake her head.

Only then did some of the ball-shriveling fear deflate. With his ass leaning against his truck seat, Wolfe wrapped his arms around her, clutching her tightly. She was trembling, her shoulders shaking, her body heaving with every breath she took. There was no way she could miss how tense *he* was, yet she still didn't let go. He rubbed her back, letting her cry.

As they stood there, Wolfe continued to slide his palm over her back as he reached for his phone. With one hand, he shot a text to Rhys. *Need you over at the shop. Now. This is personal business. About Amy.*

He tucked his phone in his pocket and tried to stand upright. "Let's go inside, baby."

Amy inhaled deeply, exhaled slowly, her hands releasing his T-shirt. It took some effort, but she finally let go. When she stood straight, she didn't make eye contact. Her head hung low when he wrapped his arm over her shoulder and steered her toward the building. It took a minute for him to unlock the door and disengage the alarm. A little longer since he kept one arm around her, keeping her pressed up against his body.

His phone buzzed, but he didn't check it. If Rhys could get away, Wolfe knew he would. If he couldn't, then Wolfe would fill him in later. Right now, he could only focus on one thing, and that was getting Amy to tell him what happened.

He maneuvered Amy over to a chair and eased her into it. He squatted on his haunches in front of her, trying to get down on her level, wanting her to look at him.

"What's goin' on, Amy?"

She buried her face in her hands, but she'd stopped crying.

Wolfe waited as patiently as he could for her to pull herself together.

A few seconds later, Amy was wiping the tears from her face with the heels of her hands, her breaths returning to normal.

With his hands on her thighs, Wolfe looked her over, trying to assure himself that she wasn't hurt.

She finally lifted her head, her dark eyes meeting his. "Can you call Rhys?"

The request had his heart slamming into his sternum. "In an official capacity?"

Another head shake. "No. I just…" She wiped another tear from her cheek and exhaled heavily. "I don't want to tell this story twice."

Oh, fuck.

As much as Wolfe needed to hear this, he wasn't sure he was ready.

More importantly, he wasn't sure he'd be able to refrain from killing someone once he had.

AMY WAS TIRED, slightly hysterical, and a little on edge.

Okay, so, the *little* part was the understatement of the century.

More like she was vibrating with anxiety and she had to do something to relieve the pressure.

After Reagan had showed up at her house last night, Amy had hidden out in her bedroom, terrified, unable to close her eyes no matter how exhausted she was. The nightmares were getting worse and she was afraid to close her eyes. She had no one to turn to. No one.

Except Rhys and Wolfe.

Although she dreaded telling them what had happened, Amy knew she had to tell someone. It was getting worse. The terror-filled dreams, the looking over her shoulder, the walking around expecting *him* to show up at any moment.

The only thing stopping her was not wanting to see the pity in their eyes when they realized how incredibly weak she was.

She still heard Rhys's words ringing in her ears.

She puts up with a lot of shit, but she would never tolerate him laying a hand on her.

He'd sounded so confident, complete faith in his sister that she wouldn't do what Amy had done. Wouldn't be a victim.

What would Rhys think of her once he knew the truth? That she had spent nearly five years living in fear, suffering daily, beaten into submission almost from the second she'd moved in with *him*. That she'd allowed it.

Not that she'd had much of a choice. Even on her worst days, Amy knew she hadn't had a choice.

But even now, more than a year later, the tears wouldn't stop and the fear wouldn't subside and Amy was tired of both. She was tired period.

So, last night, when she'd been clutching the blankets to her chin, staring up at the ceiling, waiting for a sound, something to signal that he'd found her, that he had come back to finish the job, Amy had come to a decision.

It wasn't *if* he would find her. It was *when*. And when that day came, when he did succeed in doing what he'd attempted already, Amy wanted someone to know. If for no other reason than hopefully they'd be able to put him behind bars when he did succeed in killing her.

It was the least he deserved.

Wolfe pulled his phone out of his pocket and glanced at the screen. "Rhys is on the way."

Amy nodded, trying to pull herself together. She would get through the next hour if it killed her. Maybe then she'd be able to sleep. Something had to give, because she was feeling the repercussions of the constant terror. She'd thought that having Reagan in the house would make it easier, lessen the anxiety, but it hadn't.

In fact, the only time Amy felt relatively safe was when she was with Wolfe or Rhys. They made her believe that they could keep the devil from finding her. And that was what he was. The devil. Pure evil.

The door was open, allowing the sound of gravel crunching beneath tires to filter in through the door. Amy didn't jump, she didn't cower, she merely looked up, staring at the empty space. Wolfe was a few feet away. He wouldn't let anything happen to her.

It felt like an eternity as she stared blankly at the doorway before a figure finally appeared. She was surprised and slightly disappointed when Lynx walked in, Copenhagen at his side.

Both dog and man instantly took in the scene, their entire focus on her.

No doubt she looked like hell. She *felt* like hell.

"What's wrong?" Lynx asked, sounding just as concerned as Wolfe had. He glanced from Wolfe to Amy, then back to Wolfe, waiting for a response.

"I'll be right back." Wolfe stood and headed for Lynx, nodding for him to go outside.

"Go give her some lovin'," Lynx instructed the dog before stepping outside.

"It's okay, boy," Amy said softly as the dog sized her up. "I'm okay, I promise."

Copenhagen sauntered over, putting his big head in her lap, his eyes imploring her, as though seeking confirmation that she would be all right.

"Or I will be. One day," she added. "Maybe."

Amy stroked his head, scratching behind his ears, gently sliding her thumb over his nose. They sat there like that for a few minutes before Wolfe returned. He wasn't alone. Rhys and Lynx were behind him.

She could tell by the look on Lynx's face that he wasn't going to leave. Amy wasn't sure she could tell him her story. It would be hard enough to share with Rhys and Wolfe.

Lynx clicked his tongue twice and Copenhagen was promptly at his side, sitting obediently. Amy held Lynx's stare. "Amy, if you want me to go, I'll go. But I want you to consider somethin' first. If you're with my cousin, that makes you family. And when it comes to family, I don't sit idly by. I'll get the details, one way or the other. And I'll be there for you and for Wolfe. So, it's up to you how this plays out."

Swallowing hard, Amy tried to come up with a reason he should go. He was stone-cold serious, his eyes hard. She didn't know him all that well, but she knew Lynx was a protector. He didn't tolerate anyone messing with the people he cared about.

And to think that he might care about her like family...

The tears began to fall again, but she nodded, resigned to do this no matter the audience. "You can stay." She looked at Wolfe, then at Rhys. "You might as well pull up a chair. This is a long story."

RHYS KNEW HE wouldn't be able to sit down, so he didn't even pretend. He was already tense and that was from Wolfe explaining how he'd arrived to find Amy sitting in her car, waiting for him.

It took everything in him not to rush over to her, pull her into his arms, and ensure her that he would never allow anything to happen to her. It was clear by her body language that she wouldn't believe him.

He shifted his feet outward a bit, crossed his arms over his chest, and tried to keep the anger from reflecting on his face. Rhys was pissed for a number of reasons. The first one being that Amy had been sitting outside the building for God only knew how long waiting for Wolfe to show up rather than seeking one or both of them out. The second being the fact that Rhys had slept soundly in Wolfe's bed last night while Amy had been alone.

Rhys wanted to kick his own ass for leaving her last night.

When he'd first read Wolfe's text, he'd nearly driven his truck off the damn road. When he'd been summoned to the shop, his heart had tried to break free of its cage in his chest. Personal or not, Rhys hadn't liked not knowing what the hell was going on, and the cryptic message had caused a million worst-case scenarios to flash in his brain. It didn't help much knowing that Wolfe hadn't known anything, either.

Wolfe grabbed a chair and dragged it over beside Amy while Lynx hopped up on the table directly across from her. Copenhagen resumed his position at Amy's feet, his head resting on her shoe as he curled up close to her. The dog was obviously in tune with her pain, her fear. He had set himself up as her protector.

That made three of them. Four, if you counted Lynx, and based on the look on his face right now, Lynx Caine wasn't going to let anything happen to the woman.

Amy looked between each of them before her gaze came to rest on Rhys's face.

"You're not the sheriff right now," she said, her tone matter-of-fact. "You're … my friend."

Friend, his ass. He was a hell of a lot more than that, but Rhys clamped his lips together tightly.

"I'm telling you this because I need someone to know." She sighed. "I need to get it off my chest, but I'm not expecting you to … save me. I just want you to listen. To know."

"I'm still the sheriff," Rhys told her. "Regardless."

She nodded, as though she had expected him to say that. "I'm not gonna tell you his name."

Wolfe growled, a warning sound that had Amy looking toward him.

"I can't, Wolfe. It's too dangerous. For me. And maybe everyone in this town."

Rhys knew they could hold their own, but he wasn't going to interrupt. There'd be time for that later.

"Tell the story, Amy," Lynx prompted. "We'll determine how to handle things after we know what happened."

Her eyes darted over to Lynx's face. She seemed to consider that for a moment.

Amy took a deep breath, steeled her shoulders, and clamped her hands together in her lap, her gaze straying toward the door. "My parents died when I was sixteen. Car accident. Four-car pileup on the highway." She swallowed hard. "I went to school that morning saying good-bye to the two people who meant the most to me, and I came home that afternoon an orphan."

Rhys noticed her tone was matter-of-fact, but her eyes were sad. As though she had to push forward to keep from thinking about that day.

"At that point, I went to live with my mom's sister and her husband. They welcomed me with open arms. My aunt and I worked through our grief together. She took me to counseling. Herself, too. We talked a lot, shared memories of my mom and dad… Basically, she got me through it. Mostly.

"I finished the last month of my sophomore year at the high school near my parents' house, then transferred to the one in my aunt's district after that. I didn't make many friends, choosing to focus on my school work. When I graduated, I decided to go to a local community college. My aunt and uncle were footing the bill. They even told me I could stay with them as long as I wanted. I didn't want to leave at that point. No way did I want to live by myself." Her gaze dropped to the floor.

"During my second semester at the college, I met a guy in a political science class. I was taking it as an elective because it sounded interesting. Anyway, he was a nice guy. We talked a lot, usually at the cafeteria, sometimes at the coffee shop at the school. He was really passionate about politics and I liked being around him. During one of those conversations, about a month after we met, he invited me to a fundraising dinner. Not as a date but as a friend. It was a political thing, something he was interested in. I agreed. We went. We had a fun night. He took me home and that was that."

Rhys listened, cataloging every detail.

"I saw him in class after that and we had coffee a couple more times, but it was obvious we were never going to be more than friends. We were just too different and the semester was almost over. I was okay with that. I was nineteen years old, and certainly not looking for anything serious. I didn't even know what I wanted to do with my life and I was still trying to get over my parent's deaths." Amy looked up at Wolfe. "One day after class, he pulled me aside and said there was someone who wanted to meet me. I was confused at first, not understanding. He said the guy had approached him at the dinner and he'd been hesitant to tell me. Of course, he didn't elaborate, but it didn't matter, I wasn't interested."

"This guy you were semi-dating told you about another guy who wanted to meet you?" Lynx questioned, his voice causing Copenhagen to lift his head. "Just trying to make sure I'm on the same page."

"We were never dating, but yes." She nodded, reaching down and petting the dog's head. "I told him thanks but no thanks and went about my business. Another week went by and he approached me again. Said this guy was a big deal in the political arena and that it would benefit me if I at least talked to him. Apparently, the guy had contacted him again. I tried to tell him that I wasn't interested in politics the way he was, but he didn't listen." Amy took a deep breath. "A couple of days later, the man called me."

Rhys shifted his feet. He didn't like this already.

"How'd he get your phone number?" Wolfe asked.

"I assume the guy in class gave it to him. There was a study group and I'd signed up. We had to put that information on the sign-up sheet so we could be contacted. My uncle had gotten me a cell phone, said he wanted me to have it in case I ever needed anything. You know, if my car broke down or something."

Wolfe nodded, seemingly content with that answer.

"Turns out, I'd been introduced to this man at the party, but I didn't remember anyone specifically. I'd been introduced to so many people that night, but I hadn't tried to tie names with faces. The first time we talked, he described himself, and then I definitely remembered him. Good-looking man, distinguished, well-dressed, exuded power and authority. I think I was flattered that he was interested in me. Up to that point in my life, other than the few coffee shop visits with the guy in my class, I had never been on a date."

"You never dated in high school?" Lynx sounded incredulous.

Everyone in town knew that the Caine cousins had been dating since a very early age. And by dating, Rhys meant they were having sex.

"No. I was a straight-A student, and when I wasn't studying, I was spending time with the few friends I had or with my parents. I was really close with them. When they died, I didn't care about boys or dating … or anything really." Amy looked at Rhys. "This man who called me … he was and still is in law enforcement. But that's all I'm gonna tell you."

Rhys gave her a brief nod, his teeth grinding together. He would find out more, in time.

"So, we talked on the phone for about a week and then he asked if he could take me to dinner. I agreed, excited that he would want to take me out. Like I said, I'd never dated. I told my aunt and uncle what was going on. They were a little leery, but they didn't try to stop me. Not at first.

"He took me out to a nice restaurant on a Saturday night, then brought me home, kissed me on my front porch. We started talking on the phone all the time, started going out frequently. For about three weeks, he took me out at least four times a week. Movies, dinner, bookstores, museums, the rodeo. He never tried to push for anything more than a kiss, and only when he took me home. I started spending a lot of time with him. After one of our dates, my uncle was at the door when he dropped me off. I could tell my uncle wasn't happy, and after my date left, my uncle questioned me."

Amy paused, took a breath. She looked up, meeting each of their eyes quickly.

"The man I was dating was nineteen years older than me."

Lynx gave a whistle, Wolfe growled, and Rhys did his best not to come unglued. A fucking thirty-eight-year-old man had taken advantage of a naïve, grieving, nineteen-year-old girl. The fucker.

"I was still a teenager, although I didn't feel like one," Amy continued. "Not until then, anyway. When my uncle tried to interfere, I felt the need to rebel. I argued, told him that everything was fine. I was an adult and could make my own decisions. I also told him it wasn't serious." She glanced over toward the door again. "But it was. Serious. He was already talking about marriage." Her eyes dropped to her lap. "I thought I was in love with him. He'd wined and dined me, made me feel like I was something more than a kid, the way my aunt and uncle still saw me. He told me I was beautiful, made me feel like I was."

Rhys knew where this was headed and he only hoped he made it through the story without putting his fist through the wall.

Then again, as he glanced at the dangerous expression on Wolfe's face, he might be spending his time trying to keep the man from going postal.

It was anyone's guess who would lose it first, at this point.

16

REMAINING IN THE chair was far more difficult than Wolfe was making it look, he hoped. Amy had hardly told them anything at this point, and already, Wolfe was vibrating with fury. What the fuck could an almost-forty-year-old man see in a teenage girl? They couldn't've possibly had anything in common.

"My uncle … he … well, to put it kindly, he didn't like him at all. Said he was far too old for me, that he was using me. My aunt didn't say much, but I could tell she wasn't supportive of me dating him, either. She tried to talk to me a few times, but I always went off on these dreamy tirades about how great he was. I know she wanted to see me happy, but she didn't want me to get hurt. My uncle never held back. We started to argue all the time, until one day, he told me—"

Amy stopped abruptly when the door opened.

Reagan stepped inside, her eyes instantly taking in the scene before her. Wolfe gave her a brief head nod, then glanced at Amy. "Let me talk to her for a second."

Amy gave a nod of agreement, her hands clasped tightly in her lap.

As Wolfe was walking over to Reagan, he heard Rhys say, "Amy, the same goes for Reagan. Like Lynx told you. Family."

Wolfe glanced back in time to see Amy swallowing hard as she nodded.

"Is she okay?" Reagan's expression was one of confusion and concern.

Wolfe nodded toward the door and Reagan preceded him outside.

"When I got to her house last night, she seemed upset," Reagan explained, her face etched with worry. "I heard her leave really early this mornin'. I guess I got concerned."

"It's … complicated. When I got here, she was waitin' in her car."

Reagan seemed to process that information and Wolfe suspected she was waiting for him to say something more.

Finally, she met his gaze, held it. "Please don't make me leave," Reagan pleaded. "She needs a friend and I … I want to be there for her."

She did need a friend, but whether or not Reagan stayed was not his decision to make. "That's up to her."

Reagan nodded, glancing at the door briefly, twisting her hands in her shirt. She seemed to come to a decision because she headed back inside. She walked right over to Amy, sitting in the chair beside her and reaching for her hand.

"I was worried when I heard you leave so early," Reagan explained.

To Wolfe's surprise, Amy clutched Reagan's hand, watching the woman intently. "I'm…" Amy shook her head. "No. I'm not okay."

Wolfe moved farther into the room, coming to stand beside Rhys and petting Copenhagen when the dog trotted over to him.

When Amy met his eyes again, he nodded. "Lynx and Rhys are right, Amy. The people in this room have your back. Keep goin'."

She swallowed hard, her attention on Copenhagen when the dog came and put his head in her lap again. "Like I said, my uncle didn't like him. At first he said it was because he was so much older than me. I tried to tell him that age didn't matter. That we were happy together. My uncle didn't care. He held his ground.

"One night, when *he* came to pick me up for dinner, my uncle met him at the door. They had a conversation that resulted in my uncle slamming the door and telling me that if I went out with him again, I wouldn't be able to stay under their roof. He wouldn't put up with it."

Tears welled in Amy's eyes. Reagan reached for her hand again, holding it tightly.

"Did you ever find out why he didn't like him?" Lynx inquired.

Amy nodded. "My uncle was a 9-1-1 operator. Apparently, he'd heard some things about him. He didn't know him personally, but he said he had a reputation."

Wolfe didn't need her to explain. If the man had a reputation and the uncle didn't like him, he hadn't been a choir boy, that was for damn sure.

"I rebelled." She sniffed, a tear falling down her cheek. "Told him I didn't care. That I loved this man and I was gonna be with him no matter what. I went out to dinner anyway, and that night, he convinced me to stay at his house for the first time." Amy seemed to fold in on herself as a sob broke up her words.

Unable to help himself, Wolfe was instantly at her side. Reagan took the hint and moved, giving him space. Wolfe dropped into the chair beside her, then pulled Amy against his chest as she broke down, her body jerking from the strength of her sobs.

It took inhuman effort to relax his arms, to not squeeze too tight. The thought of this bastard taking her virginity made every cell in his body gear up for a fight.

While Wolfe consoled Amy, Lynx moved across the room to the coffeepot, Reagan right behind him. The sink ran, which meant they were making coffee as they spoke in hushed tones. Wolfe couldn't make out everything Lynx was saying, but he figured he was giving her the CliffsNotes version of the story thus far.

Wolfe made eye contact with Rhys. He had no idea what the man was thinking. He was angry, there was no doubt about that. But he was patiently waiting for Amy to continue. Wolfe knew he was keeping his distance because Lynx and Reagan were there. Evidently, he wasn't interested in anyone finding out about their relationship. If what they had could even be called that.

When Lynx and Reagan returned, they passed out coffee cups. Lynx resumed his position on the table and Reagan pulled another chair over near him and sat. Wolfe was reluctant to release Amy, but when she pulled away, he didn't hold on.

Resting his elbows on his knees, Wolfe dropped his head, staring down into his coffee cup. He got the feeling this story was going to get a lot worse, and probably never better.

Amy hiccupped. "I'm sorry … I…"

"Don't be sorry," Rhys said, coming to stand in front of her before dropping to his haunches. "We need to know what happened."

Setting his coffee cup on the floor, Wolfe watched them.

Amy nodded, squeezing Rhys's hand as she stared into his eyes. Her words came out on a tortured sob. "That night, my aunt and uncle died."

Once again, Amy cried, her hands covering her face.

Wolfe saw Rhys's face harden, the no-nonsense sheriff replacing the laid-back country boy. He knew Rhys couldn't disconnect himself from his job. He'd taken an oath to protect people, and he took it seriously. No matter what he told Amy, Wolfe knew Rhys would have to look into this. Whether he'd do it officially or off the books, it wouldn't matter. He'd do it, regardless.

Rhys waited until Amy calmed down.

She was wiping the tears from her face when Rhys asked, "How? How'd they die, Amy?"

"A fire." She sniffled. "It destroyed their entire house. They died. I was told it was probably smoke inhalation—I hope to God that's true. Their burned bodies were found in their bed."

Wolfe realized his hands were balled into fists. He got up, pushing the chair back as he did. He couldn't sit still.

"They said it was an accident," Amy continued.

Wolfe spun to face her. "And you believe that?"

If it was an accident, why were they in bed? Surely they hadn't slept through it. What about smoke detectors? Or even the smell of smoke? Or the heat? Something should've woken them up.

"No. I don't believe it." Her eyes locked with his. "Not anymore, anyway. Eventually, he told me that no one would stand in the way of us being together. I…" She sobbed again. "I don't know how he did it, but he killed them. I know he did. He never openly admitted it, but it was the little things he said."

Rhys held Amy's hand until she got control of herself again. Wolfe could tell she wanted to get this over with. Probably the only reason she pulled herself together.

"Son of a bitch." Rhys stood, pacing the floor. "Keep goin', Amy. We need to know the whole story."

Wolfe agreed, although he didn't want to hear any more. He wanted to go back to not knowing the hell that Amy had lived because it was eviscerating him. And he knew it'd been hell even without hearing the rest.

AMY FELT AS though she had a four-hundred-pound weight sitting on her chest. That was how it felt every time she thought about her aunt and uncle and the horrific way they'd died.

"The worst part about it," she said, breathing deeply, "is I didn't go home for two days after the fight with my uncle. I didn't even know. He finally took me home and it was then I found everything gone. The house, everything in it, but most importantly, the only family I had." She sniffed, refusing to break down again. She had to get through this. "Those few days were a blur. He consoled me, told me everything would be all right, held me while I cried. I remember the police station, someone telling me how they died, that they'd ruled it an accident. According to the fire inspector, there had been a leaky gas line."

"Convenient," Lynx muttered, his voice hard as steel.

"I lost my parents at sixteen, and three years later, I was burying my aunt and uncle. I had nothing. Nowhere to go, no one to turn to. I was all alone." She looked at Wolfe. "Except for him. He was there. Always there. He made me feel safe, told me he would take care of me, that I had nothing to worry about. And from that point on, I lived with *him*." Amy cleared her throat. "I lived with him for the next four years, seven months, and twenty-two days."

Yes, she had counted every painful day that she had suffered with him.

Amy straightened her back, feeling the need to show them she wasn't as weak as they probably believed she was. Not that it wasn't true, but she didn't want them to know.

"During all that time, I suffered ten concussions, a broken ankle, elbow, three fingers, my right arm, left wrist. My nose was broken twice." As she said the words, she realized how bad it looked that she had stuck around, continued to endure. She knew for a fact that Reagan never would've put up with a man hurting her like that.

"There were no questions from the hospital?" Rhys asked.

"A couple of nurses seemed concerned, but he was never less than two feet away from me. I couldn't tell them anything. Then, he stopped taking me to the hospital. A couple of times he took me to an emergency clinic. When he broke my fingers, he splinted them himself, said I'd be fine."

Amy glanced down at her fingers, wiggled them as the memory took hold.

"It's your own goddamn fault, Amy. If you'd just listen, I wouldn't have to hurt you."

"I'm sorry," she told him.

"You should be. Next time you won't fight back."

That was always his excuse. If she wouldn't fight back, he wouldn't have to hurt her. It was a lie because the couple of times she hadn't fought back, he'd still beaten her.

God, she fucking hated him.

Shaking it off, she sighed and sat up straight. "At first, he was nice afterward. He would hit me, then apologize profusely. A few times he even cried. I would forgive him, even though I knew I shouldn't. As time went on, I wanted to leave, but I had nowhere to go. I had no one else. I would work myself into a panic, worried that no one would ever love me, that I would always be alone. So I stayed. I endured."

She didn't bother to tell them about how he'd raped her damn near every day. After the first time she had tried to resist his sexual advances, he had demanded sex from her. Although she didn't fight him off, she didn't consent, either. That was rape; even she knew that. It got to the point she simply lay there while he did what he needed to do. In the beginning, he had tried to whisper romantic words, but Amy had closed her eyes and willed him to finish so he would leave her alone. Then, he stopped trying to make it good for her at all. He simply took what he wanted, whenever he wanted it.

He was the only man she'd ever been with and sex had never been a pleasant thing. Still, Amy had never been disillusioned. She knew it could be good. With the right man.

The only positive in all of it was that he'd insisted she be on birth control because he didn't want children.

The mere thought of a child living in fear the way she had…

Amy felt the tears spill down her cheeks, but more importantly, she felt the anger that had become so much a part of her for so long. "I fucking hated him," she said, her voice getting louder. "He was the devil. He beat me and beat me and no"—Amy looked directly at Rhys, the strength of her fury pointed at him—"I *didn't* try to stop him! I *did* put up with it. I *wasn't* strong enough."

"Bullshit!" Rhys yelled, moving right over to her.

Amy wasn't at all threatened by him. He wasn't going to hurt her. She felt the strength of his anger as much as her own and she understood it.

He squatted down before her. She sucked in air, her teeth clenched as she fought the tears back. She'd spent so many years living in fear, the hatred festering … sometimes she couldn't hold it in.

"That's bullshit, Amy. You were strong. You fucking lived through it. You got out."

Amy shook her head, the tears pouring down her face as the sobs won, tearing from her chest as the truth ripped her heart apart. She wished she'd been strong, that she'd gotten out. But she hadn't.

Rhys pulled her against him and she threw her arms around his neck, letting it all out. "I wasn't strong enough," she repeated against his neck.

"You're stronger than you think," he whispered, his hand sliding over her hair, cupping the back of her head, his lips pressing against her forehead. "It was never your fault, Amy. Never. The blame is on him. Never you."

Amy wasn't sure she believed that. No, he shouldn't have hit her, but she should've found a way out. Every time she tried to come up with a plan, she got scared. She'd convinced herself that she loved him. That he loved her. Deep down, she knew she wasn't at fault, but sometimes it was hard to acknowledge.

Amy pulled back from Rhys, sniffling and once again wiping the stubborn tears from her face. "I have to finish."

She felt Reagan at her side once again. Amy was glad she was there.

She looked up to see Wolfe and Lynx standing beside one another. In that moment, she understood why so many people feared them. Individually, they were intimidating. But together…

Shaking her head, she took a deep breath and looked at Rhys. "I didn't get out. Not purposely anyway." She swallowed past the lump in her throat.

Rhys stood, then held out a cup of coffee. She waved it off. She couldn't stomach anything right now.

Forging ahead, she clasped her hands in her lap, her voice steadier this time. "One day, I decided I was gonna leave him. For an entire week, I planned it out in my head. How I would do it, where I would go.

"Then on Friday, he went to work and I packed up as much of my stuff as I could. I hesitated, I'll admit it. I think that's the only reason it happened. If I had left as soon as he went to work, I probably would've been home free. But I was scared. I had no car, no credit cards. I had some money in the bank. At the time, I wasn't sure it was still there, but I'd received money after my parents' death. I had never told him about it, scared he would take it.

"He didn't allow me to have any of those things. I wasn't allowed to go anywhere alone, wasn't allowed to buy anything. The only time I left the house was when he took me somewhere. After I moved in with him, he stopped taking me out unless it was to a business function. I was only there to look pretty, he told me. I'd become his prisoner. He picked out my clothes, told me how to do my hair, what makeup to wear, how long I could sleep. I ate what he wanted me to eat, watched shows he approved of, but only when he was home. He didn't let me use the Internet, wouldn't give me a phone. There were security cameras in every room, including the bathrooms and closets, and on all the doors outside. He kept me under his thumb every minute of the day.

"He had taken over my entire life and I wasn't sure how to survive without him. I debated on whether or not I was safer with him, despite the damage he inflicted. After all, I wasn't dead. He told me he loved me and that I would always belong to him. That I would never survive without him." Amy met Rhys's eyes. "He wasn't lying. About the last part, anyway. Only, he'd meant it in an entirely different way than I took it."

She looked over at Wolfe. "Before I could get the nerve up to leave that day, he came home. He saw that I had my stuff packed, had watched me pack it, in fact. I tried to tell him that I was done. That I wanted out. I told him I didn't love him anymore, that I needed to move on with my life. That I would survive without him. That I *could* make it on my own. I even promised I would never tell anyone that he was a complete monster. Not in so many words, of course. I knew not to talk to him like that."

As she told the story, Amy saw the trend, realized how she had grown to hate him more and more with every passing day. Sure, she'd felt the anger at the time, but as she told the story, she had to wonder what had stopped her from killing him. She hated him *that* much, and prison would've been a step up from the hell she'd been living.

"What did he do, Amy?" Wolfe asked, his tone reflecting how hard it was for him to hear this.

She locked her eyes with his. "When he said I wouldn't survive without him, he didn't mean I wasn't capable." She sucked in air, glancing between them all. She could see they'd figured it out, so she kept going. "He meant he wouldn't *allow* it." Amy felt all eyes pinned on her, so she took a deep breath and blurted out the worst of it all. "He tried to kill me."

"Son of a motherfucking bitch," Lynx roared, stomping across the room.

Copenhagen whimpered, clearly worried about his human.

Amy ignored Lynx.

"He told me that if I was serious, if I was planning to leave, he was going to kill me. He told me there was no way he would let me leave him. He wasn't about to give up his life, his career for some stupid bitch—his words—who was too stupid to keep on breathing." Amy glanced at Reagan, then back down at her hands.

"Of course, he didn't have any mercy on me. He wasn't about to simply shoot me in the head, put me out of my misery. No, he used his hands, his feet, a crowbar." She sucked in air. The room seemed to be closing in on her, but she kept pushing forward, her words coming out faster. "He beat me, then dumped my body in a drainage ditch just outside of Embers Ridge. It was June and the temperatures were already soaring. That's how I ended up here. He drove more than four hours from the house where we lived. By the grace of God, an old couple had a flat tire on that long stretch of highway that day. They found me, called an ambulance."

"You're Jane Doe." Rhys was staring at her, his eyes wide.

"What?" Lynx's confusion rang loudly.

"There was a story about Jane Doe. About a year ago. I read it. It went out to the local agencies, asking for information that might lead to an arrest." Rhys never looked away from her. "They found the battered and beaten body of a woman in a drainage ditch. There were no pictures of you because..."

"Because my face was so damaged I wasn't recognizable," Amy finished for him.

Rhys nodded, pain in his eyes. "The list of injuries was extensive."

Amy nodded. They needed to know how cruel this bastard really was. "That day he broke my jaw, both wrists, my left clavicle, three ribs, and both bones in my lower right leg. My cheekbones were fractured, and the swelling on my brain was extensive." Amy shifted on the chair, the memory of the pain still fresh. "I honestly think he believed I was dead or that I would be shortly after he dumped my body. And if those old people hadn't found me..."

As those words left her mouth, her energy wavered, her body suddenly so weak, so tired she could hardly sit up anymore. Now that they knew the story...

Amy felt as though she could breathe again, like some of the weight had been lifted.

But as the exterior door slammed behind Wolfe, she wasn't sure how long that feeling would last.

RHYS PROBABLY SHOULD'VE gone after Wolfe, but he noticed Amy sagging, her entire body listing to the left as though every ounce of her energy had faded. Based on what it took to tell a story like that, he could imagine it had. So, instead of making sure Wolfe didn't beat someone to death, Rhys picked Amy up, carried her up the metal stairs and into the break room on the second floor, while Lynx went after his cousin.

After depositing Amy in the recliner and perching on the arm, he brushed back the strands of hair that had pulled free from her ponytail.

"You need to find Wolfe. Calm him down," she told him as she curled into a ball.

"I will," he assured her. "In a minute."

"I'm sorry," she whispered. "I wasn't strong."

He hadn't cried in years, but at that moment, Rhys could feel the tears forming behind his eyes. He wanted nothing more than to go back in time and change the course of Amy's life. All the way to when her parents died.

Unfortunately, he couldn't do that.

However, he could find this bastard. It might not be easy since he had no doubt she would refuse to tell him the monster's name. But Rhys *would* find him.

And when he did…

He only hoped he got to him before Wolfe did.

"When you finally left the hospital, where did you go?"

Amy rested her head on the arm of the chair. "I never told the nurses my name. I knew he wasn't going to report me missing, so no one would ever search for me. They called me Jane and I got used to it. The day finally came when they told me I was being released. I was terrified. One of the nurses—Annette—helped me for a few days after. I stayed at her house in her daughter's bedroom. Then, one day when she was at work, I left. I knew I couldn't stay. I didn't want him to hurt her if he found me.

"I went to the bank, withdrew the money my parents had left me, bought a car, then decided I needed to get far, far away from him. I stayed in various motels for months. I would stay for three or four days, then move on to another, slowly working my way up north. I got almost to Arkansas and decided I couldn't keep running forever, but I wasn't about to go back to Houston. So I made my way back here. When I found the house for sale and realized I could pay for it with cash, I decided that was a sign I should stay in Embers Ridge."

Rhys continued to slide his hand over her hair.

Amy yawned. "I didn't know where else to go."

His heart broke for her. The damaged woman who had no one to turn to for help.

Rhys sat there, watching Amy until he realized she had fallen asleep. He leaned over and kissed her head. "I'll be back in a bit."

She didn't stir, so he left her in the chair and made his way back downstairs.

Reagan was standing at the bottom of the stairs, watching him.

"Who the hell is the bastard, Rhys?" she demanded, her eyes hard. His sister had always been the protective sort. When she was little, they had a hard time stopping her from taking in every injured or homeless animal they came across. In school, she had always been the one to stand up to the bullies, no matter who their target had been. She might be a hard-ass, but the girl had a huge heart.

Rhys shrugged. "I don't know. But I intend to find out."

"Why won't she tell you his name?"

"She's scared shitless, Reagan. She fucking can't even walk in her own damn house without freezing up. I'm sure she jumps at every damn shadow, worried that he'll be back for her."

"Will he?"

"I fucking hope not." Rhys honestly didn't know. "Depends on the political power he wields and whether or not he feels truly threatened by her."

"You think he knows she's alive?"

Rhys nodded. That he did know. "If he's in law enforcement, I'm sure he knows. He would've gotten the same information I did. The media was all over it. And since he was the one who dumped her body…"

"How did he not find her in the hospital?"

"Because God was watching over her," he said. That was the only reason he could think of.

Reagan nodded. Thankfully, her interrogation was over.

"I need to go find Wolfe."

"Yeah. You do."

Rhys glanced around the warehouse. "Where's Lynx?"

"He tore ass outta here. You know him. He doesn't deal well with this … emotional stuff."

No kidding.

As he was turning toward the door, it opened and Wolfe stepped into the building.

Reagan glanced over her shoulder, then passed Rhys. "I'm gonna head over to the diner. Grab some food. Can you call me later? Let me know how she's doin'? And let her know I'm here if she needs me."

Rhys nodded. He knew his sister wouldn't let this go. Once she latched onto someone, she was like a dog with a bone. Like Lynx, Reagan was fiercely protective of those she cared about.

As soon as Reagan was out the door, Rhys moved toward Wolfe. "You all right?"

Wolfe frowned. "Are *you*?"

No. No, he wasn't. He wasn't sure he would ever be all right after hearing that.

Wolfe glanced up at the second floor. "She up there?"

"She's asleep. In the recliner."

For a second, Wolfe didn't move. His eyes remained locked on Rhys's face. It was the first time he'd ever seen Wolfe fall apart. Right there before his eyes, tears formed in Wolfe's eyes. Rhys moved toward him, but Wolfe sidestepped him before he could console him.

Wolfe reared his fist back and aimed it toward a wooden post but stopped just shy of hitting it, growling through clenched teeth. Rhys figured it had more to do with not wanting to wake up Amy than fear of shattering his entire hand.

"I want to kill that bastard," Wolfe ground out. "I want to beat him to a pulp, then do it again and again. And then I want to watch him die a slow, painful death."

Rhys understood Wolfe's anger. He felt it.

"You need to find out who the fuck he is," Wolfe demanded.

"I'll do my best. But I can't broadcast this information. It's not like I can send out an APB on the guy. Amy doesn't want him to find her. And so far, she's managed to evade him."

"You think he's lookin' for her?"

"I do. If he's as powerful as she says, he doesn't want the loose end. It's possible he's sitting back, buying time." Rhys took a deep breath. "I know you don't want to, but I need as much information as you have on her. It's the only way I'll be able to back track and find him."

Wolfe nodded, but whether he was agreeing to give him the details or simply saying he understood, Rhys wasn't sure.

He waited.

"I'll get you a copy of her application."

"She filled it out?"

Another nod. "I think she trusts me now."

Rhys didn't doubt that. She'd opened up to all of them, more so than she'd probably wanted to. It seemed trust was the least of their issues at this point.

Wolfe released a breath, his gaze straying to the second floor once more. "I'm gonna close up shop and take her back to my place. Let her sleep for a while. I don't think she slept at all last night."

Rhys nodded. "I've got to get to work. I've got Dean fillin' in, but I have to relieve him."

"Call me or better yet, just stop by the house when you get done." Wolfe reached out and touched his hand. A gesture that Rhys hadn't expected, but one that he needed more than he'd realized.

"And call me if you find out anything."

"Will do." Rhys took a couple of steps toward the door. "Oh, and Wolfe?"

"Huh?"

"Rein Lynx in before he gets himself in trouble."

A small smile tilted Wolfe's mouth. "Right. Like anyone has the power to do that."

Unfortunately, no truer words had ever been spoken. Rhys only hoped Lynx found a constructive way to release the pent-up frustration, otherwise Rhys's job was going to get that much harder.

He had enough on his plate as it was.

17

ONE THING HIS momma had taught him was how to use a Crock-Pot.

Wolfe put that skill to good use after he got Amy to his house and tucked her into his bed. He closed the blinds, turned off the lights, kissed her forehead, and told her she was safe now. He hoped she believed him. Regardless, she drifted back to sleep in no time, and he'd spent the past few hours flipping through channels and messing around on the Internet.

His brain wouldn't shut off. Amy's story and the gruesome images he'd mentally conjured up were on repeat in his head, making him crazy. He could still see her sitting stoically in that chair, reciting in horrifying detail the things that bastard had done to her. The worst part … Wolfe knew she felt responsible, as though she'd actually had a choice in the matter. He knew better. It wasn't her fault, and she damn sure wasn't weak. He hadn't walked in her shoes, and from the outside looking in, it would've been easy to say what she should've done. None of that mattered because she had done what she felt was necessary for her survival. No matter how much pain she'd had to endure.

After she'd told the story, Wolfe had stormed outside, a rage unlike anything he'd ever known fueling him. The anger had had nowhere to go, though, and he'd found himself bending over, trying to catch his breath as tears slammed him so hard he could barely stand up. Lynx had come over, put a firm hand on the back of Wolfe's neck, and told him that they would ensure that bastard never got near her again.

He appreciated the sentiment. And Wolfe knew Lynx meant it.

Over the years, Lynx had taken it upon himself to protect the people of this town, often from themselves. It had all started a decade ago when Lynx had been eighteen years old and his momma died. The tragic news had devastated their family, but over time, they'd picked up and moved on. However, Lynx and his old man had never been the same. Cooter had locked himself up in the house; Lynx had gone off the rails, becoming even wilder and crazier than he already was. It was a wonder he was still with them after some of the stunts he'd pulled.

But all in all, Lynx had become the man they all depended on to have their backs.

And he would; Wolfe didn't doubt him for a second.

As the hours had passed, some of Wolfe's rage had subsided, and the only thing he wanted for Amy was justice.

Whoever the man was who had violated her in every conceivable way for nearly five years…

Not even God could help him now.

Wolfe was brought back to the present when he heard his bedroom door open. He looked up from his spot on the couch to see Amy coming out of the room. Her hair was down around her shoulders and…

"Holy fuck." The words were expelled on a rough breath.

She was wearing his T-shirt and nothing else, from what he could tell. The shirt came down to her knees, the sleeves resting on her forearms, her nipples pebbled beneath the white cotton, and she was the hottest goddamn thing he'd ever seen.

"That's now my absolute favorite shirt," he told her as she moved toward him.

A small smile curved her pretty mouth.

Wolfe held up his arm for her to sit by him, allowing space for her to get as close as possible. She tucked her knees up close and curled against his side. He wrapped his arm around her, pressing his lips to her forehead.

"Feel a little better?" He glanced at the clock. "You slept for about six hours."

She yawned. "Yeah. I do feel better." She turned her head slightly, her eyes darting around the room. "Your house is beautiful."

"Thanks. Exactly the look I was goin' for."

Amy swatted his stomach.

He kissed her head again, chuckling.

"Where's Rhys?"

"He had to go into work. Said he'd be over when he was done."

"What's that smell? It's making my stomach growl."

"Pot roast in the Crock-Pot."

Amy tilted her head up at him. "And you tried to tell me you couldn't cook."

Wolfe laughed. "Technically, I never said that."

"You implied."

"No, not really. You assumed."

"So, you *do* cook?" She looked hopeful.

"In the Crock-Pot, yes. I'm not too bad on the grill, either. Anything else, it's a gamble."

Amy dropped her head back to his shoulder. She was quiet for a few minutes, and Wolfe thought she had fallen back asleep, but then her hand started to move, gliding beneath his shirt, her fingers grazing his stomach.

He tried to keep his heart rate under control. Not an easy thing to do when she was touching him while wearing nothing but his shirt.

"I'm sorry about this morning," she said softly.

"Nothin' to be sorry about."

"I didn't mean to dump everything on you. I just…" Amy sighed. "I'm so tired of being scared. I have nightmares. Bad ones. I have to go through it over and over again. Then when I wake up, I'm terrified he's gonna show up. One day he will; I know it."

Wolfe didn't say anything. He didn't know what to say. He couldn't imagine the hell she'd lived through.

Amy tilted her head back and Wolfe turned his, their mouths close together.

"I'm glad I'm here," she whispered.

"Me, too."

She pulled back a little, propping herself up on her arm. Her face contorted slightly. She looked confused.

"What?" he asked, unable to read her mind.

"Do you still … you know … *want* me?"

Wolfe jerked back, keeping his eyes locked with hers, his eyebrows lowering. "Why would you ask that?"

"Because…" She didn't move, but her eyes left his. "I'm damaged, Wolfe."

He reached for her, curling his hand behind her neck, turning her head so she was looking at him again. He brushed his thumb over her cheekbone, met her gaze and held it. "You're perfect," he whispered.

She snorted. "Not by a long shot."

Wolfe leaned forward, shifting their positions as he leaned her back on the sofa, his hand remaining behind her neck as he laid her down. "You're perfect for me."

Tears glistened in her eyes. "I want that to be true. You don't even understand how much."

"It is true. I don't lie."

He kissed her. No rushing, no pressure, just a long, leisurely kiss. She smelled so damn good, tasted even better.

Her hands were on him, cool fingers roaming beneath his shirt, making his breath lodge in his chest. When she attempted to remove it, he broke the kiss, allowing her to pull the shirt over his head. Her eyes drifted down to his chest, his arms, back up.

When she met his eyes again, there was heat there, and Wolfe knew damn well where this was headed. He was hesitant, but he knew if she asked, he wouldn't be able to deny her anything.

Hell, at this point Wolfe was pretty damn sure he'd do anything for her.

Any damn thing.

WOLFE AND RHYS were the right men, Amy knew.

The ones who would make her understand how good making love to someone could feel.

And Wolfe was here now.

As much as she wanted that, Amy was scared to ask him. She didn't want him to feel sorry for her, didn't want him to think she was using him to shove the memories away.

She wasn't.

Not at all.

She wanted him with a passion she didn't even understand, one that consumed her when she was around him.

"What are you thinkin' about?" he whispered, his voice rough.

"I like touching you," she admitted, allowing her hands to move over him slowly, gliding across the muscles that flexed and bulged as he held himself above her.

Wolfe smiled, his eyes darkening as he watched her face, seemingly content to remain right there, letting her explore.

Amy had no idea how long she spent simply trailing her hands over his warm skin. It wasn't until a light knock at the door broke the spell that she stopped. She didn't move, but neither did Wolfe.

"Who is it?" he called out, his eyes never leaving hers.

"Rhys."

"Door's unlocked."

Wolfe lifted one eyebrow and Amy deciphered it as him seeking approval to remain where he was. She nodded in response, her body heating, the ache between her legs intensifying. Knowing Rhys was there…

It was exactly what she wanted.

The door opened, then closed. When a shadow fell over her, she tilted her head back, looking up at Rhys, seeing him upside down.

"Am I interruptin'?" he asked, his voice gruff. But it wasn't with anger, it was something else. Something that sounded an awful lot like the way she felt on the inside. Needy, aching, almost desperate for the three of them to come together as one.

"Not at all," she told him.

He moved out of her line of sight, so Amy returned her focus to Wolfe. He was still watching her, still hovering above her. That was when she realized she was still touching him.

Rhys joined them again, perching on the arm of the couch above her head. Amy reached up, sliding her hand over his thigh, dividing her attention between the two men. She wanted Rhys down there with them. Closer. Touching her while she touched him.

When his hand covered hers, she tugged his arm. He moved, kneeling on the floor beside her head. Wolfe shifted, too, lying on his side next to her, placing her between him and Rhys.

She saw the moment Rhys realized what she was wearing. Or more accurately, what she *wasn't* wearing. His blue eyes lit with what she definitely knew was desire this time. He wanted her.

The shirt had obviously been a good idea.

When Amy awoke the first time in Wolfe's bed, she'd been sweating. When she got up to use the restroom, she'd wandered into his closet and pulled one of his T-shirts off a hanger, stripping down to her panties and then pulling it on. Then she had crawled back in his bed and slept like the dead.

Of course, when she woke up the second time, she had figured wearing the shirt might not be such a bad thing. Based on the look she'd received from Wolfe and the way Rhys's eyes flared as he blatantly ogled the length of her body, it certainly wasn't a bad thing.

The heated looks empowered her.

"Touch me," she whispered, looking from Rhys to Wolfe. "Please."

Wolfe's Adam's apple bobbed in his throat when he swallowed hard.

He didn't come out and ask her if she was sure, but Amy knew he was wondering. She didn't reassure him, wanting him to know without her having to say it.

And she was sure.

As a matter of fact, she'd never been more certain about anything in her life.

Wolfe leaned down and kissed her, and this time, Amy didn't let him get away with treating her like blown glass. She grabbed his head and kissed him back, her tongue thrusting into his mouth, her head lifting off the cushion as she crushed her breasts against his chest. Her body instantly caught fire when his hand splayed on her thigh. She knew she was affecting him because his hand tightened, his fingers pressing into her skin. Not painfully so, but enough that she could tell he was still holding back.

"Touch me," she pleaded, kissing down his jaw. "Now, Wolfe."

He growled low in his throat, the sexiest sound she'd ever heard in her life.

Amy turned her head, then pulled Rhys in for a kiss. She didn't want him to sit this one out. She wanted him right there with them. Never in her life had she imagined she'd be sandwiched by the two sexiest men on the planet, yet that was exactly where she found herself.

Right where she wanted to be.

WALKING INTO WOLFE'S house and finding the two of them laid out on the couch had made his dick roar to life. Seeing Amy in Wolfe's T-shirt… *Lord have mercy.* Rhys's jeans had become damned uncomfortable in an instant.

And now that she was kissing him, her urgency was apparent and his need grew exponentially.

But Rhys didn't want urgent. He wanted to savor her—*this*—for as long as possible. He wanted to show her just how good the three of them could be together. After the horror she'd relayed to them this morning, Rhys wanted to show her how it felt to be worshipped, appreciated. Loved.

Granted, the couch probably wasn't the best place, but it would work for the time being.

Rhys had to break the kiss because Amy was quickly driving him insane. She was making it hard to think. And thinking was critical because there were a million ways he wanted to drive her out of her mind.

Wolfe must've been thinking along the same lines because when Amy turned to kiss him, he held back, grinning at her.

"Relax," Wolfe said, his voice gravelly.

He wasn't as unaffected as he wanted them to believe, that was for damn sure.

"I think we need to move this to the bedroom," Wolfe suggested.

Rhys agreed. He got to his feet, then helped Amy up. When she was standing, he wrapped his arms around her and lifted her off her feet. She squealed, wrapping her legs around his hips, her arms around his neck. Not bothering to look where he was going, Rhys managed to make it to Wolfe's bedroom without any incidents. Seconds later, he bumped the bed with his knees. Without releasing her, he laid Amy out on Wolfe's bed, hovering over her for an extra heartbeat. When Wolfe joined them, Rhys relinquished his position and dropped to her other side.

"More touching," Amy whispered, smiling. "Quit making me wait."

"But waitin' is part of the fun," Rhys replied.

Amy rolled her eyes, making them both laugh.

Her laughter died on a raspy moan a second later as Rhys put his hand on one thigh, Wolfe placing his on the other. Her eyes flew open, darting back and forth between them.

"Yes," she pleaded.

Rhys dragged the backs of his knuckles up over her hip, making sure to take the T-shirt as he went. Wolfe mirrored the movement, revealing a pair of white cotton panties.

Air became scarce.

It wasn't that Rhys hadn't seen plenty of women's panties in his lifetime, but there was something so fucking sexy about those damn panties.

"Fuck," Wolfe groaned.

Apparently he thought so, too.

They worked the shirt up over her breasts—small, perky, and fucking perfect breasts—then helped her take it off. Wolfe threw it across the room, his eyes focused on her tits.

Rhys brushed Amy's shoulder with his lips, then trailed his mouth lower, pressing kisses to the scar there—likely where they'd gone in to repair her clavicle—until he came to one rigid nipple, which he took between his lips, dragging his tongue over the pebbled tip. Amy's sharp inhale seemed overly loud in the otherwise silent room. Her hand flew up into his hair, holding him to her.

"Oh, my…" Amy's chest heaved, her back bowing as they laved her nipples, teasing her slowly.

Wolfe lifted his head first, then shifted lower on the bed before kneeling by her legs. In one swift move, he made her panties disappear, leaving her laid out naked between them.

"Holy. Fuck. So fucking pretty," Wolfe rasped as he shifted her legs apart, shouldering his way between her thighs.

Evidently they were fast-tracking this.

Wolfe's hungry gaze focused between her legs, his thumbs gently caressing smooth, bare skin as he opened her pussy lips, revealing the wet, pink flesh.

Rhys could admit he was a little jealous when Wolfe lowered his mouth to taste her, his tongue sliding through her slit as he stared up the length of her body, watching her reaction.

"Wolfe!" Amy jerked, her fingers grabbing for Rhys's arm.

He leaned over her, kissing her gently. "Let it feel good, Amy."

"It's too much." Her head dipped down into the mattress, her stomach muscles quivering beneath his hand as Wolfe's tongue worked her into a frenzy.

"Open your eyes, baby," Rhys urged. "Watch what he's doin'. The way his tongue slides over your clit."

"Rhys … oh, God…"

The next thing he knew, Amy unraveled, crying out as her climax hit her.

If he didn't know better, Rhys would've sworn that was the first time she'd ever…

Holy fuck.

18

WHEN AMY CAME, she seemed completely shocked by it.

That was when Wolfe realized, having only had sex with one man—a fucking monster, at that—she'd probably never had an orgasm before.

Not that his ego needed much more of a boost, but… Yeah. Wolfe would be taking this accomplishment with him to the grave.

As she settled, her breaths racing in and out of her lungs, Wolfe moved over her. He didn't stop until his mouth was centimeters from hers.

"Kiss me, darlin'," he whispered. "See how fuckin' good you taste."

Her eyes widened momentarily, but then she was kissing him, a soft moan vibrating against his mouth. Wolfe pulled back, looked at Rhys, then reached for him. Crushing his mouth to Rhys's, Wolfe was more forceful with him, allowing some of the tension to escape with the rough thrust of his tongue. As worked up as he was, Wolfe was not going to do anything more than this. Although he wanted to make love to Amy, that wasn't going to happen. Not this time.

However, that didn't mean they couldn't make her come again.

Letting Rhys go, Wolfe fell back onto the bed, pressing up against Amy's side as he stared down at her face.

"You ready for more?"

Her eyes opened and she gave him a beautiful, radiant smile that stole his breath. Then she nodded.

Wolfe trailed his hands over Amy's bare stomach, but he didn't move where she wanted him to. Instead, he reached for Rhys's hand, then guided it down between her legs. Rhys didn't need any more guidance though.

They both watched her as Rhys teased her with his fingers, stroking her clit for long minutes before he pushed one digit inside her.

"Oh, God…" She groaned long and loud, her back bowing off the bed.

"So tight," Rhys muttered, his attention between her thighs. "So wet."

"You like that?" Wolfe asked Amy. "Like feeling Rhys inside you?"

She moaned, her body undulating as Rhys fingered her.

"Come for us, Amy." Wolfe lowered his mouth to her breast while Rhys worked her into another frenzy, driving her close to the brink again.

Unable to help himself, Wolfe watched the way Rhys's finger disappeared, then returned, slick with her juices. It was so fucking hot to watch, listening to her gasps of pleasure. Wolfe wanted this to go on forever.

"More," Amy whispered. "I need more."

Rhys inserted two fingers and increased his pace.

Wolfe felt his body humming, his cock so fucking hard he could've drilled holes in concrete. But this wasn't about him. It was about making Amy feel good, showing her how it was supposed to be, how a man was supposed to pleasure a woman.

Rhys's hand moved faster, his fingers driving into her.

"Come for me, Amy," Rhys whispered. "Let me feel you come."

Wolfe watched Amy's face, saw the exact moment she let her orgasm take her.

"Perfect," Wolfe whispered, sliding his finger over her cheek as he repeated what he'd told her earlier, with one slight deviation. "For *us*."

Half an hour later, after drawing Amy a bath and helping her into the tub, Wolfe found Rhys standing in the kitchen, looking out over the back pasture.

Rhys hadn't bothered to put on a shirt, his back muscles tense as he stood motionless. Walking up to him, Wolfe pressed his bare chest to Rhys's back, then slid his arms around him. He'd never imagined himself doing this. Holding a man in his house. Certainly not Rhys Trevino.

Wolfe pressed his lips to Rhys's shoulder. "You okay?"

"Yeah." Rhys turned his head so that Wolfe could reach his mouth. He kissed him once, twice. "She in the bath?"

"Yep. And she has informed me that she wants food when she gets out." Wolfe chuckled.

Rhys turned in Wolfe's arms, his voice low as he spoke. "Did you see her back?"

Wolfe looked past Rhys, out the window and into the pasture, the image of what he'd seen when he helped Amy into the bath coming back to him. It was a sight he would never forget, one that made him want to castrate the bastard who had done that to her.

"Either he whipped her or he cut her," Rhys said softly.

Or both, Wolfe thought.

Rhys frowned. "She didn't mention that part."

Wolfe figured there was a lot she'd left out. Rightfully so. For one, the details she had given them were more than any one person should've had to suffer. Having seen the jagged scars all over her back, from shoulder blade to shoulder blade, neck to ass … Wolfe had realized then that it was far worse than Amy had let on. Although she certainly hadn't spared them the details.

"She's strong," Wolfe told Rhys. "Far stronger than she even realizes."

Leaning forward, Rhys rested his forehead against Wolfe's. They remained like that for a few minutes. It was comforting to have him there. More so than Wolfe would've thought.

"You ever think that this whole time, we've been waiting for her? That *this*—the three of us—was supposed to happen?"

Wolfe understood what Rhys meant; however, he wasn't sure he wanted to see it that way.

Because if it was true, while they were *waiting*…

Amy had been suffering. So, no, Wolfe didn't want to think about it that way. Instead, he wanted to think that it was meant to be. That Amy was meant for the two of them. Twice the protection to keep her safe and ensure she never had to endure anything like that for the rest of her life.

The two of them stood there for a long time, neither of them moving. Wolfe liked that they could, that they didn't have to be doing anything at all to be content.

"Please tell me the food's ready."

Wolfe pulled away from Rhys as Amy stepped into the kitchen. Once again, she was wearing his T-shirt, her legs bare.

"Are you tryin' to kill me, woman?" Wolfe smirked, kissing her quickly as he moved toward the Crock-Pot on the counter. "And yes, you can eat. Find a chair and put your cute little ass in it."

Rhys pulled out one of the chairs at the table for her, then went to the refrigerator. It was as though the man knew his way around Wolfe's house. He didn't. In fact, until yesterday, the sheriff had never been inside Wolfe's house.

Oddly enough, Wolfe liked that he was making himself at home. It seemed natural.

"I need to call Reagan," Amy said. "I'm sure she doesn't care whether or not I'm home, but I want her to know when I'll be there."

That sounded like a question to Wolfe. Almost like Amy was asking when he was going to take her back to her place.

"Tea or water?" Rhys asked Amy. "Do you wanna go home right now?"

"Tea would be great. And no, I don't. But that doesn't mean I shouldn't. I don't want to overstay my welcome."

"That'll never happen," Wolfe mumbled under his breath. She could stay there as long as she wanted. Forever, in fact.

Shit.

When the hell had he started thinking like that?

AMY WASN'T ABOUT to ask Wolfe if she could stay the night.

Not that she didn't want to, but it felt a little awkward right now.

She didn't want them to think she was trying to hide out, although now that she thought about it, maybe she was. A little.

There was no denying that she felt safe at Wolfe's house. Especially with Wolfe and Rhys there with her. She figured if they weren't there, she'd feel just as exposed as she did at her own place. Ultimately, Amy knew there was nowhere she could hide forever. Eventually, he would find her. She only hoped she had a little notice so she could be ready.

Wolfe brought her a plate with beef roast, potatoes, carrots, and baby onions. On the side, there was a slice of cornbread. She had to fight back the tears. She wasn't one to break down and cry all the time—in her nightmares, that was another story—so it embarrassed her a little.

"What's the matter?" Rhys asked.

His concerned tone almost made her cry more, but she managed to wipe her eyes and choke out a laugh. "I'm sorry. I'm not usually such a wimp. It's just… No one has cooked me dinner since…" She looked up at the two men. "Not since my aunt."

"Well, if you can stomach my food," Wolfe said with a teasing grin, "I'll be more than happy to cook for you. But don't get all teary-eyed until you try it."

She laughed again, obviously his intention.

"And about tonight…" Wolfe brought a plate for Rhys and himself, then joined them at the table. "I'd like you to stay here. You can call Reagan and let her know. But I want you to get a good night's sleep, and that's the only way it's gonna happen."

It was true. Then again, she wasn't sure she wouldn't have a nightmare after having spilled her guts this morning. She didn't want either of them to see that, but she would deal with it if it came to that.

"I…" She was going to argue, but she really didn't have a case, so she smiled. "Thank you. I'd like that."

"Good. That's settled. Now try the food. And if you don't like it, lie to spare my feelings." Wolfe grinned, that sexy smirk that heated up her insides.

God, the man really was devilishly handsome in that bad-boy sort of way. And Rhys … he was quite possibly the opposite. Devastatingly handsome, but almost like … well, like a good boy.

Hmm.

She liked the idea of having a bad boy *and* a good boy.

Then again, she thought about the things they'd done to her earlier and there wasn't anything "good" about them. They were both dirty in the best possible way.

"What're you thinkin' about?" Rhys asked, taking a sip of his tea.

Amy blushed, the heat rising from her neck to her face. "Nothing."

Rhys smiled knowingly. "Thinkin' about more orgasms?"

His bluntness made her suck in a sharp breath when a lightning bolt of desire crashed into her.

Amy focused on her food, trying her best not to look at them. They'd know exactly where her thoughts had wandered to if she did.

Oh, who was she kidding?

They already knew if their chuckles were anything to go by.

After dinner, Amy called Reagan at the bar.

"Hey." There was a hint of concern in Reagan's tone. "How're you doin'?"

"I'm … better."

"Good. That's real good."

"I wanted to call and let you know that I won't be home tonight. I'm … uh … staying with a friend."

Reagan laughed, a hearty sound that had Amy blushing again. "Wolfe Caine is a *friend*?"

"You know what I mean," Amy said, smiling despite her embarrassment.

"I've got a question for you…"

"Sure."

"Is my brother there?"

Amy could hear Rhys and Wolfe talking in the living room. "He … uh … I … yeah. Yes. He's here."

"That's what I thought."

Amy wasn't sure if she should defend herself or Rhys or even Wolfe. And if she needed to, she didn't have the first clue what she would say.

Reagan laughed again. "Don't worry, girl. Your secret's safe with me."

"What? No. It's…" Amy sighed.

"He's my brother, remember? I know all about what he's into. And hey, it's none of my business. Are you happy?"

"Yes," she blurted, not even having to think about it.

"Then that's all that matters. As long as everyone's on the same page, you're not hurtin' nobody."

Amy had no idea if she was supposed to reply to that, so she didn't. "Since I won't be home, you're more than welcome to sleep in my bed if you want. You know, if the futon's not comfortable."

"The futon's great, but thanks for the offer."

"Sure. And I'll … uh … see you tomorrow night."

"Yep. See you then. Be safe. And Amy?"

"Hmm?"

"If you ever need to talk, I'm here."

Reagan probably didn't realize just how much that meant to her. "Thank you."

"No problem."

The phone disconnected and Amy stared at it for a minute, wondering what she'd done. Rhys had mentioned that he was bisexual but that he didn't broadcast it. Then there was the tension between their families. What if Reagan said something? What if word got out?

Amy fell back on the bed with a heavy sigh.

"Everything cool in here?"

Amy opened one eye and peeked over at the door. Rhys was leaning against it, his eyes on her.

"Yes." She sighed again. "*No.* I don't know."

"What's up?"

Turning her head, Amy looked at him. "I talked to Reagan. I told her I wouldn't be home, that I was staying with a friend. She guessed about Wolfe and I didn't deny it. Then she asked if you were here and…" Amy covered her face with her hand. "What have I done?"

Rhys joined her on the bed, sitting down with his knee bent, foot tucked beneath his opposite thigh. "It's fine. My sister doesn't share my personal business."

Amy uncovered her face. "What about the Caines and the Trevinos? If they're rivals, how is this"—she waved toward the other room where Wolfe was—"supposed to work?"

"Well, it's not like it's the Wild West. There won't be a shootout at high noon."

She couldn't help but smile at the mental image that drew.

"And besides, if it's meant to happen, it'll happen. That's the way the world works."

"Are you the philosophical kind?" she asked, trying to put some accusation in her tone.

"Not on your life, but that's one thing I know for certain." He tapped her nose. "Now, for the reason I came in here."

"You didn't come to sneak a peek under my shirt, did you?" Amy laughed when he tickled her thigh.

"No and yes. No, that isn't the reason I came in here initially. But then I saw you on the bed and…" He reached for the hem, but Amy grabbed his hand, stopping him.

Rhys laughed. "Wolfe wants to know if you wanna go out to the range for a bit. The sun's goin' down, so it's not quite as hot. Maybe you can get in some practice."

Amy bounced up off the bed.

"I'll take that as a yes."

With a little squeal, she ran to the bathroom to put on her own clothes.

THE THREE OF them had spent two hours on the range and the time had flown by.

Amy had been open to learning how to shoot more than just a shotgun, eager even, and they'd been more than happy to arm her and show her how to protect herself. Had she known long ago…

No, Rhys didn't even want to think about that. He couldn't change history, no matter how much he wanted to.

Wolfe had picked up a compact Ruger at a pawn shop that he told her would be perfect for her. It was, and once Amy understood how the sight worked, the woman was a damn good shot. Rhys had been impressed.

Now that they were back at Wolfe's, Rhys was showing her how to clean her gun while Wolfe was in the shower.

"So, can I carry the gun with me?" Amy asked, looking up at Rhys.

"You'll have to take the state-required course to carry open or concealed, but yeah. If you get the license, you can carry it with you. But that doesn't mean you don't need more practice."

She openly studied the gun lying on the table, her finger trailing over it. Rhys liked that she wasn't afraid of it, but he definitely wanted her to get more comfortable. Rhys had grown up shooting, and he was sure Wolfe had, too. That was how their families were. Shotguns, rifles, handguns. They'd been a part of Rhys's life for as far back as he could remember. Hell, he'd gone on his first hunting trip with his dad and grandfather when he was four.

Wolfe came out of the bedroom wearing a pair of basketball shorts riding low on his narrow hips, no shirt, and bare feet. He was rubbing a towel over his hair as he came into the kitchen. He looked between them, both of them openly staring.

"What's up?"

Rhys glanced down at Amy and they smiled at each other. Clearly their brains were on the same wavelength.

"*What?*" Wolfe asked again, laying the towel over the back of a chair. "What did I miss?"

"It should be a crime for you to walk around without a shirt on," Amy said, her tone sweet yet mischievous.

"Is that right?"

She giggled. "Luckily for us both, we've got the sheriff here with us."

Wolfe and Rhys both laughed.

"You spend a lot of time comin' up with that one?" Wolfe teased.

"Nope," she answered easily. "I'm just witty like that."

"And sassy," Rhys noted. "I like it."

Amy seemed to like that he'd called her that. He assumed she hadn't been teased much over the years. With the devastation of losing her parents, then her aunt and uncle, and having to live with a monster, she probably hadn't laughed much, either.

"But sassy might require some punishment," Wolfe noted.

The instant the word was off Wolfe's tongue, Rhys was sure he realized what he'd said. However, he didn't take it back, didn't stumble over it the way Rhys probably would have.

As for how Amy took it…

Rhys watched her, wondering whether or not she understood for most people, it wasn't referring to the pain that had been inflicted upon her. After all she'd been through…

"Hmm," she said, a playful gleam in her eye. "What did you have in mind?"

Wolfe looked at Rhys, then back at Amy. "I was thinkin' more orgasms."

"Yep. Me, too. I think that's the perfect punishment," Rhys added.

"Well…" Amy got to her feet, stretched leisurely, her T-shirt baring her stomach. She looked as though she was gearing up to go to bed. Of course, then she grinned. "You'll have to catch me first."

Before she could get two steps, Wolfe had tossed her over his shoulder and was carrying her to the bedroom. She giggled, her hands gripping his shorts, tugging them down and baring Wolfe's ass as the big man made the distance to the bedroom disappear in as few steps as possible.

Rhys was right behind them.

Wolfe put her on her feet, tugged up his shorts, then took a step back, his heated eyes trailing over her. "Shirt has to go," Wolfe instructed.

Amy seemed to accept his instruction as a dare, reaching down and deftly removing her T-shirt.

Rhys was content to watch the action, admire the woman standing before them in a pair of jeans and a plain white bra.

"Now the jeans," Wolfe added.

She was a little more seductive as she watched the two of them, slowly unbuttoning the jeans, then easing the zipper down. She shimmied them over her hips before letting them fall to the floor.

Good God, the woman was so fucking hot. He didn't think she even realized *how* hot. Her sweet innocence only added to the smoldering look in her eye.

"So damn hot," Rhys groaned.

"Might as well lose the bra and panties while you're at it," Wolfe rasped. "It'll save us time later."

"I will if you lose the shorts," she countered, hands on her hips.

In the blink of an eye, Wolfe had his shorts off and was standing buck-ass naked, his cock bobbing excitedly. Rhys couldn't help but admire him, too. Lean and ripped, Wolfe Caine made Rhys's mouth water.

"Oh, my God," Amy said under her breath, her eyes focused on Wolfe's very hard, very imposing cock.

Yep. That was what Rhys had thought the first time, too.

"Keep lookin' at him like that and he's gonna get too excited," Wolfe said, that warning growl accompanying his words as he gripped his cock in one big hand, stroking slowly.

Amy turned to him. "Now you, Sheriff." She smirked. "I think Wolfe would like to help you out."

Rhys was going to have to do some work to catch up with them since he still had his damn boots on.

"You first," Wolfe told her. "Then I'll strip him while you watch."

As though that was one hell of a prize, Amy removed the bra and panties, tossing them to the side of the bed.

Rhys focused on breathing when Wolfe moved in behind him, his arms wrapping around Rhys's waist as he worked on his belt buckle. Knowing this would take a while, Rhys helped them along by toeing off his boots.

"Oh, fuck," he hissed, leaning into Wolfe when the man pulled his cock from his boxers, his rough grip sending shockwaves through his insides.

Before he could process what was happening, Amy was in front of him.

On her knees.

And holy fucking hell…

It was a damn good thing Wolfe was behind him. Otherwise, Rhys would've been on the floor.

She looked so damn sweet, so innocent kneeling before him, her hands sliding up his jean-clad thighs. Rather than go for his dick, she reached for the waistband and tugged the denim down.

Rhys didn't move a muscle, his attention on remembering how to breathe when she did slide her soft hand over his erection. Between her soft touch and Wolfe's rough, callused fingers, Rhys was sucking in air, his eyes fixated on their hands.

"Taste him," Wolfe instructed from over Rhys's shoulder, sliding the head of Rhys's dick over Amy's bottom lip.

"Oh, hell," Rhys hissed.

Wolfe pressed closer to Rhys's back, his dick grinding against Rhys's ass. As if that wasn't distracting enough, Amy took the head of Rhys's cock in her luscious mouth. He hissed, unable to look away, unable to breathe.

She was watching him as she hesitantly sucked, then licked the swollen head before taking him between her lips once again.

"Don't stop doin' that," he said, the words coming out strained. "Feels so good, baby."

That seemed to encourage her, because she repeated the motions over and over again, driving him absolutely crazy.

While Amy gave him the sexiest—albeit most inexperienced—blow job he'd ever received, Wolfe managed to rid Rhys of his remaining clothes.

When Wolfe came to stand on Amy's other side, she turned, keeping one hand on Rhys's cock while she reached for Wolfe's. Rhys grinned when Wolfe growled. Now the man knew how it felt. Her simple touch was enough to blow a man's head clean off his body. Both of them.

"Damn, baby." Wolfe set his hand on the top of her head when she leaned in and licked the tip of his cock. "I've dreamed about that mouth on me."

Again, she seemed to need the encouraging words, because she became more confident, alternating between taking them each in her mouth. But the next time she focused on Rhys, Wolfe went to his knees, giving Rhys an evil grin.

They were going to double-team him.

As much as he wanted it, Rhys wasn't sure he'd survive it.

Not that he wouldn't give it a shot.

After all, he wasn't a quitter.

19

AMY AND RHYS were naked.

In his bedroom.

Wolfe was pretty damn sure it wasn't his birthday yet, but son of a bitch, he'd never in his life received anything as incredible as this gift.

Thinking about how Amy had come to work for them not even two weeks ago, then he'd taken her to the range for the first time only five days ago made his head spin. Things were moving fast. Okay, maybe not as fast as Wolfe's previous encounters considering one-night stands were usually his M.O. Two weeks wasn't a lengthy period of time to go from talking to fucking, but hey, Wolfe was the go-with-the-flow kind of guy.

He'd take it.

Watching Amy suck Rhys's cock was the only thing keeping Wolfe from picking her up and setting her on his dick. He was desperate to feel the heat of her pussy wrapped around him, but he knew it would be in bad taste to rush it.

They'd get there.

Eventually.

Hopefully, sooner rather than later.

"Your turn," Amy whispered, her hand wrapped around the base of Rhys's cock.

Wolfe leaned in, taking Rhys's dick all the way to his throat. He did it for two reasons. One, he fucking wanted to. And two, he wanted to gauge Amy's reaction. This was what she was signing up for. Although Wolfe had every intention of giving her plenty of attention, he intended to do the same with Rhys.

Amy's hand cupped the back of his head, her breath warm against Wolfe's cheek as she guided him up and down on Rhys's cock.

"Fuck…" Rhys groaned. "Y'all are gonna kill me."

Wolfe pulled back, allowing Amy a turn. They continued the trade-off until Rhys put a stop to it, mumbling something about death and taxes and coming before he was ready. While Rhys tried to get himself under control, Wolfe turned his focus on the sexy naked woman kneeling beside him. Wrapping one arm around her back, he pressed his lips to hers, then lifted her off the floor and deposited her on the bed, never breaking the kiss.

Her hands cupped both sides of his face, her breasts crushed to his chest, the heat between her thighs pressed against his leg. While he devoured her, Wolfe allowed her to ride his thigh. Her moans intensified and he was forced to break the kiss, anxious to watch as she made herself come.

"Wolfe…" Her eyes closed, her body undulating, hips grinding as his thigh provided friction against her clit.

"That's it, darlin'. Rub your pussy on my leg."

"I'm…" Her nails dug into his biceps.

"Come for me," he demanded softly. "Then I'm gonna watch Rhys eat that sweet pussy till you're screamin' for him to let you come again."

Amy cried out, her hips stilling, chest heaving. He would never tire of watching her come apart. She was so fucking hot, so sensitive, so uninhibited. He loved that she could trust them enough to let herself go like that.

Reluctantly, Wolfe rolled off her, sliding his hand beneath her knee and spreading her legs. Rhys was right there, leaning down, his tongue diving to that sweet spot between her thighs.

Her soft moan seemed to go on forever, her hand digging into the comforter as her back bowed slightly.

"I like that," she whispered hoarsely. "So much."

Her eyes were on Wolfe's face.

"One of these days," Wolfe said, inching closer to her, cupping her breast and rolling her nipple between his thumb and forefinger, "you're gonna call me."

One dark eyebrow lifted and she moaned again.

"You and Rhys are gonna be somewhere—maybe his house or yours, perhaps in his truck, it won't matter… Wherever you are, he's gonna be eatin' your pussy just like he is now. And you're gonna tell me in explicit detail exactly what he's doin' to you."

"Oh, yeah?" she rasped, her eyes rolling back in her head.

"Definitely. And while you're tellin' me how his tongue is flickin' your clit, how he's makin' you beg for him to fuck you, I'm gonna stroke my cock."

"Rhys…" Amy's back bowed, her hand reaching for Rhys's hair. "That … oh, my God … feels so good. Don't stop. *Please* don't stop." Amy took a deep shuddering breath, let it out. "Why wouldn't you be with us?"

"Because it makes me hard just thinkin' about the two of you together without me."

Amy released a long, slow moan, her eyes closing. "I'm so close…"

"Make our girl come, Rhys," Wolfe instructed, never looking away from Amy's face.

Amy's breaths came fast, her hand sliding behind Wolfe's head, her short nails digging into his neck. He was pretty sure this was his new favorite pastime, watching the sexiest woman alive when she came.

Seconds later, she did just that.

"That was … amazing," she whispered, her arms and legs relaxing.

Rhys chuckled as he crawled up onto the bed with them.

"We're not finished with you yet, darlin'," Wolfe told her.

Amy cocked her head as though thinking. Wolfe waited to see what was on her mind.

"You said I would call you while Rhys is … you know."

A smirk curved his mouth. She was so damn cute.

"Yeah," he confirmed.

"What about you and Rhys? Will one of you call me?"

"When?" Wolfe wanted to hear her say it. "When would you want one of us to call you?"

Amy's gaze shifted to Rhys. "When you're together."

"What would we be doin'?" Rhys inquired.

Wolfe leaned down and brushed his lips against her ear. “Tell us. What would we be doin’ to each other when we called you?”

Amy sucked in a breath but didn’t speak.

“Would Rhys call you while I’m suckin’ his dick?”

Amy moaned, her eyes closing. Wolfe continued to fondle her tit.

“Or would I call you while my dick’s slidin’ in and out of his hot fucking mouth?”

“Yes…” She opened her eyes. “And touching each other.”

“How?” Wolfe wanted her to elaborate. Sure, he might come without ever having the pleasure of being inside her body, but holy shit, it might just be worth it.

Something passed through her eyes, and Wolfe was almost positive she was imagining the two of them together, on the phone with her.

When she didn’t say anything more, Wolfe knew he couldn’t wait much longer. He ached, his dick throbbing.

“Think about it, darlin’,” he told her. “And when you’re ready, you can tell us. In the meantime…”

Wolfe rolled onto his back, bringing her with him, his hand cradling the back of her head as he held her pressed to his body. She straddled his hips, her hands resting beside his head.

Keeping his voice low, soft, he decided to tell her exactly what he wanted.

“I WANT TO feel your pussy milkin’ my cock.”

Wolfe Caine had a dirty, filthy mouth.

And—something she had just learned about herself—Amy freaking loved it. The dark cadence of his voice, his rough, dirty words … they made her want things she’d never dreamed of wanting.

And she wanted them now.

“Come on, darlin’. Ride me.”

A tremor raced through her, lighting up her insides.

Feeling slightly self-conscious, Amy pressed her mouth to Wolfe’s, needing a distraction. While she was exploring his mouth with her tongue, Amy felt hands near her butt. She turned her head, trying to see what was going on.

“Condom,” Rhys informed her.

Oh, my God.

Rhys was putting a condom on Wolfe and it was … hot. Like, seriously hot.

When Wolfe gasped, Amy peered down at him. His eyes were closed, his teeth clamped together.

Apparently he liked it.

“Put my cock inside you,” he ground out, still not opening his eyes.

Amy shifted and with Rhys’s help, she eased down on Wolfe’s cock.

Lordy. He was … huge.

When she’d first glimpsed his package, Amy’s mouth had fallen open. She’d never seen anything so big, so … intimidating. The thought of taking him in her body… Would he even fit?

She was about to find out.

Amy’s muscles tightened as he inched inside her. He was stretching her painfully tight.

“Too much,” she whispered, slightly embarrassed that she couldn’t do as he wanted.

“Relax, darlin’.” His eyes were open and focused on her face.

“It won’t fit,” she conceded.

“It’ll fit, I promise,” he said, that sexy smirk making her wetter than she already was.

When he pulled her down against him, her breasts flattened to his chest, Amy relaxed into his kiss, loving how warm his hands were as they slid over her back. When he gripped her butt and started rocking her forward and back, easing deeper and deeper inside her, pleasure unlike anything she'd ever known infused her. From her head to her toes, Amy's skin tingled, her core tightening as he pushed inside, sliding over nerve endings she hadn't even realized she had.

"You okay?" he whispered.

"So okay," she said, pressing down on him.

"You're in control, baby."

Amy liked the idea of being in control, even if it was slightly off-putting. She knew Wolfe was being gentle with her. She'd learned that was how he was. No matter what she wanted, he was going to take care of her. In fact, Amy figured if she wanted more, she would have to tell him.

One day she might be able to do that. Until then, she wanted them to guide her, to show her what to do, because she had no experience with this.

Suddenly Rhys was next to them, kneeling beside Wolfe's head, his cock in his hand.

"Suck me," Rhys instructed Wolfe.

Wolfe's head turned, his tongue darting out and licking the swollen crest.

Amy couldn't help but sit up, rocking her hips to keep the friction going, her hands planted flat on Wolfe's chest. When Wolfe took Rhys in his mouth, she shuddered, a violent tremor racking her entire body. These two men together… It blew her mind how much she liked watching them.

Rhys wasn't gentle with Wolfe, driving his cock into Wolfe's mouth, pretty much fucking his face. Amy didn't realize she was rocking faster on Wolfe, the friction of him inside her doing amazing things.

"I'm gonna come from watching you ride him," Rhys said.

Amy nodded, although she wasn't sure why she was. She wanted to watch Rhys come.

His hips began pumping faster as he fucked Wolfe's mouth. His chest heaved, his grunts and groans echoing in the room. God, she was going to be the one coming from watching *them*.

"Fuck, yes," Rhys hissed, his hips stopping suddenly, his cock jerking as he came.

Amy paused, transfixed by the erotic sight.

The next thing she knew, she was on her back, Wolfe hovering over her. He kissed her and she tasted Rhys on his tongue. It was slightly surreal and intensely sensual. Not something she'd ever imagined she'd experience.

Wolfe's hand slid behind her knee, lifting her leg and holding it near his hip as he took complete control. This was what she'd wanted. To make this man lose control. She was inundated by intense pleasure. Between the solid length of him inside her, his grunts and groans, and the way his beautiful body looked when he was above her, Amy knew it couldn't get much better than this.

"Wolfe! Oh, God!" That was all it took. Him taking control… Suddenly Amy was spinning out of control, her body detonating as he impaled her over and over.

"Oh, hell," Wolfe growled. "Fuck, baby… Milk my cock. Just like… Ahh, God!"

Amy opened her eyes and watched as Wolfe came, his body tensing, his muscles flexing as his cock pulsed inside her.

Seconds later, sheer exhaustion consumed her.

Amy didn't even wait until Wolfe pulled out before she gave in to sleep.

RHYS AWOKE TO a warm body pressed against him. A soft, warm body.

It took a second for him to remember he was still at Wolfe's and the sweet thing curled up against his side was Amy. Her thigh was draped over his leg, her hand rubbing circles around his navel, the outer edge of her palm grazing the head of his semi-hard dick every so often. That was probably what had woken him.

He remained motionless, enjoying the feel of her hand on him, the way she touched him, her lips brushing his shoulder. Rhys had noticed that she liked to touch both of them. It seemed her hands were always somewhere, as though it was a security for her. Whatever her reason, he liked it.

She continued for several minutes before her soft voice whispered, "Are you awake?"

Rhys turned his head.

The room was dark except for the sliver of moonlight streaming in through the blinds, highlighting Amy's face. Her eyes were wide, her mouth slightly open. She looked like she'd been well fucked and was ready for round two.

God, please let her be ready for round two.

"I am. But why are you awake?"

Her answer didn't come in the form of words, and admittedly, Rhys was a little shocked by her actions. Not disappointed but definitely stunned.

"What're you doin'?" he asked, his tone teasing as she crawled over him, her naked thighs straddling his naked hips. Her long hair draped over his chest, tickling his skin, making his cock swell and lengthen.

"Hopefully you," she answered.

Simple, straightforward. She knew what she wanted, and good heavens, Rhys certainly wanted to give it to her.

He chuckled, but she cut off the sound by pressing her mouth to his. Rhys grabbed two handfuls of her incredible ass, pulling her against his cock. Her smooth, wet flesh slid over him and he sucked in a breath.

He groaned, then released her and fumbled on the nightstand for a condom. He didn't know for sure there was one because he had tossed them haphazardly earlier, but if he was lucky...

His fingers slid over a foil packet and he sent up a silent thank you to the man upstairs.

Rhys wasn't sure what had gotten into this woman, but he wasn't about to resist her. Last night, after Wolfe had practically screwed her into the mattress, Amy had quickly fallen asleep. That had only been four hours ago. Apparently the woman had caught up on her sleep.

"Rhys?"

"Hmm?"

Her mouth trailed down his jaw, then his neck. Her warm breath had his cock twitching.

"Make love to me?"

Fucking hell.

"Sit up." He had to put the condom on and there was no way to do it with her sitting on his dick.

Amy sat, moving back so his cock bobbed against his stomach. She surprised him again by snatching the condom from his hand and rolling it down his length. It took her a little longer than it would've taken him, but again, he wasn't about to protest.

When she leaned back over him, Rhys took her mouth with his, then rolled her onto her back.

Wolfe was sleeping beside them. Or he had been. Rhys was almost positive he was awake now. His deep, even breaths had quickened, which meant he was likely taking in the show. If the man was going to feign sleep in order to sneak a peek, who was Rhys to argue?

Amy's legs wrapped around his hips and Rhys wasted no time aligning their bodies. He knew he had to go slow. She had to be sore from Wolfe earlier. Rhys wasn't small in the penis department, but Wolfe was well above average, no doubt.

Rhys slid his latex-covered dick through her slit, grazing her clit while he kissed her. He continued until her nails dug into his back, a signal that she was tired of him playing around. Rhys reached between them and guided his cock where they both wanted him. Seconds later, he was pushing in deep. Slow and deep. The smooth walls of her pussy gripped him, drawing him in.

"Aww, hell," he whispered, leaning down and pressing his lips to Amy's.

The kiss was soft, gentle, her fingers sliding into his hair. She didn't try to rush him and Rhys wasn't in a hurry. She was perfection, her body molding to his. He could've stayed just like this forever and never needed anything more.

A warm hand landed on his back. A much bigger, rougher hand. A tremor shot through him at the knowledge of Wolfe watching them.

The warm hand disappeared, replaced by a warm body. Rhys pulled his mouth from Amy's when he realized Wolfe was behind him, the man's arms bracketing Rhys's shoulders.

Just when he thought it couldn't get any better.

"You want this?" Wolfe's deep voice rumbled against his ear.

"So bad," he replied.

Bracing himself above Amy, Rhys pushed in as deep as he could go, then stilled when Wolfe's hands separated his ass cheeks.

"Oh, fuck," he hissed when a warm tongue grazed his asshole. "Oh, holy fuck."

Amy's inner muscles flexed, tightening around his dick. The combination of that and Wolfe's tongue on sensitive flesh had him shuddering.

"What's he doing?" Amy asked, her voice soft, seductive.

Rhys sucked in air. "He's… Oh, fuck, that feels good." He met Amy's gaze. "He's licking my ass."

Her pussy tightened, squeezing him. She obviously liked the idea of that.

Amy pulled his head back down, and Rhys sank into the kiss, keeping his weight off her, not wanting to crush her although he was being assaulted by pleasure. Wolfe's tongue disappeared, then something pushed in his ass.

A finger.

Slow and easy, Wolfe teased him while Rhys rocked forward and back. The sensation was fucking incredible. Driving into Amy, then back against the intrusion in his ass. He wanted Wolfe to fuck him, to drive all three of them to completion.

When Wolfe moved again, Rhys shifted, holding himself still, preparing for Wolfe's weight.

The moonbeams bounced off Amy's face, her eyes shimmering as she watched the two of them above her. The expression on her face told him she knew what was happening, and she wasn't put off by it.

Rocking his hips gently, he kept them both hovering on the edge until finally, the blunt head of Wolfe's cock breached his ass. Rhys sucked in air as the initial pain took him, but he let it out, focusing on the incredible feel of Amy's pussy clutching him, her inner muscles locking on his dick.

Her hands played with his hair, her eyes shining as she held his gaze. Rhys couldn't move, pinned between them. Once Wolfe was seated to the hilt, Rhys relaxed as much as possible, allowing Wolfe's momentum to do all the work for him.

Amy sighed deeply. "Rhys … oh…"

He watched her watching him, suspended in a state of complete helplessness, but he still felt in total control. Rhys was right where he wanted to be.

Wolfe's hips punched against him, his cock driving inside him until he was fucking him harder, faster, deeper. Their combined moans drifted in the air around them for long minutes until Rhys's release built, damn near knocking him down. He continued to rock against Amy, hoping like hell he could bring her to orgasm before he came.

Clearly aware of Rhys's inability to do anything more than endure, Wolfe's hand slipped between Rhys's body and Amy's. How the man managed, he didn't know, but the next thing Rhys knew, Amy was panting.

"Wolfe … Rhys … I'm… Oh, God, that's so good." Her head tilted back, neck straining as she cried out their names over and over.

Her orgasm triggered Rhys's, and seconds later, Wolfe was following them right over the edge.

20

"SINCE WHEN DID we become delivery drivers?" Calvin grumbled for the fiftieth time since they got in the truck. Just twenty-seven fucking minutes ago.

"What *I* wanna know is why you made my ass ride in the back seat," Lynx bitched from behind them.

Wolfe peered at his cousin in the rearview mirror. "'Cause that's where your ornery ass belongs."

Lynx flipped him off.

"Why'd she refuse delivery again?" Wolfe's father questioned, his head leaned back, eyes closed.

"She insisted I bring it," Wolfe explained.

"She hot?" Lynx inquired.

"I ain't touchin' that with a ten-foot pole," Wolfe said, using some of Lynx's favorite words.

Amy had attempted—at Wolfe's insistence—to get a regular delivery set up for Melissa Stephenson. So, they'd changed the original delivery to the next available one. Wolfe had thought Mrs. Stephenson would simply accept the table and go on her merry way. Oh, how he'd been wrong. Apparently, she'd answered the door in a bikini—which their normal delivery drivers hadn't minded one bit—then adamantly refused the table because Wolfe hadn't been there.

Wolfe wasn't any happier about the situation than Calvin or Lynx was. However, Wolfe damn sure didn't intend to deliver the table by himself. For one, he wasn't going to carry the damn thing inside without help, which was why he'd brought Lynx. And two, he needed someone there to keep the woman from jumping him. Hence the reason his father was along for the ride. Wolfe had no doubt she would come on to him, given the opportunity. Even if he wasn't completely caught up in Amy and Rhys at the moment, Wolfe wasn't going to go anywhere near that woman without backup.

"She's married?" Calvin asked, one eye opening as he peered over at Wolfe.

Wolfe nodded as he turned the truck down the street he'd been directed to by the navigation system.

"And she's interested in *you*?" Lynx sounded skeptical.

Asshole.

"Is she blind?" his father joked.

Wolfe glared over at his father, then back at his cousin. "Y'all just wait. You'll see."

"Aww, hell," Calvin retorted. "This oughta be good." Calvin glanced back at Lynx. "I'll get to watch you work your magic on this ol' gal."

"Damn straight," Lynx hummed.

"Oh, come on, old man," Wolfe teased his father. "I bet you got some magic left in them old bones."

Calvin flipped him off.

Wolfe chuckled.

"This chick got money?" Lynx inquired, leaning forward and resting his forearms on the front seats as they turned into Mrs. Stephenson's ostentatious neighborhood, both sides of the street lined with oversized mansions.

"Oh, yeah," Wolfe told him.

A minute later, that was proven when they were pulling up the stone driveway toward the enormous white-stone monstrosity with an immaculately manicured yard, palm trees galore, and stonework that had to cost a pretty penny. Yep. The woman had money. Or her husband did.

Not that Wolfe gave a fuck either way. He wanted to drop off this table and be on his way. He had a girl waiting for him back at the shop. Although he'd wanted to bring Amy with them, he'd figured Mrs. Stephenson would find a way to be rude, and that was the last damn thing he wanted to deal with today. So, he'd left Amy working with Copenhagen standing guard. He'd given her the instruction not to answer the door for anyone, then he'd locked the doors behind them.

"We gonna flip a coin to see who rings the bell?" Lynx asked. "You said she was in a bikini last time?"

Wolfe glanced in the rearview mirror. "The job's all yours, boy. Have at it."

Lynx was out the door in a second, whistling as he sauntered up the front steps. He hit the doorbell, then cast a grin over his shoulder.

A second later, the door opened.

Lynx pulled off his straw hat and shot the woman a full-fledged grin. "Hey, sweet thang. We got a delivery here for ya."

Wolfe peered up at the door and nearly fell over.

Melissa stood staring at Lynx, her eyes wide, her red lips shiny. She didn't look even slightly frightened by the intimidating cowboy covered in tattoos from his neck to his knuckles. Nope, she certainly wasn't scared. More like … hungry. And if he was closer, he'd probably see the hardened points of her nipples peeking beneath the thin lace of that black teddy. She even had four-inch stilettos to go along with it.

"Hot damn," Calvin muttered. "She's married, you say?"

Wolfe lifted an eyebrow, then headed around to the back end of the trailer. He unlocked the door, lifted it, then grabbed one of the chairs.

"Yes, ma'am," Lynx was saying when Wolfe approached, "he's my cousin. Clearly, I'm the better-lookin' one."

Mrs. Stephenson giggled.

Of course she did.

Lynx had a way with the ladies. Old, young, married, divorced, single. Didn't matter. The guy knew how to sweet-talk his way right into their hearts.

When Wolfe moved up onto the porch, Lynx glanced back at him, a shit-eating grin plastered on his face. "She's got lemonade."

"Right this way," Mrs. Stephenson crooned sweetly, turning and adding some additional swing to her hips.

Wolfe wanted to get this shit over with.

And fast.

Twenty minutes later, they had the table set up in the dining room and Wolfe was wiping it down with a cloth.

"Come on, boys," Mrs. Stephenson called. "Come get some lemonade while it's cold."

Calvin leaned in. "Does it get hot?"

Wolfe shrugged. "I'll see y'all out at the truck."

"Nope. Sorry, son." His father grabbed Wolfe's arm. "You got us in this mess. You're gettin' us out."

Fuck.

AMY WAS SITTING in her office when she heard the boys come in. Copenhagen was out the door and down the stairs in no time.

They'd left almost three hours ago to deliver the table to Mrs. Stephenson and hadn't been sure when they'd be back. Amy had been so engrossed in coming up with ideas for their online store that she hadn't even realized the time.

"Amy! Hey, girl! Come on out here!" Lynx shouted.

Laughter ensued.

Getting up from her chair, she couldn't help but smile, loving the sound of so much happiness. She'd spent so many years alone, trapped in her house. No friends, no family, no one to talk to. It was nice to have Wolfe and Lynx around. Not to mention, Calvin. And Copenhagen. She couldn't forget him.

Stepping out of her office, she peered over the railing.

"Hey, darlin'," Wolfe's father greeted.

"Hi, Mr. Caine." She smiled brightly, happy to see him. She'd only talked to him a few times since she started working at the shop, but whenever she did, he always made her feel as though she was a part of his family.

She glanced over at Lynx. He was holding something up toward her. "I brought you a donut."

Amy grinned.

"Don't lie, boy. Wolfe got her the damn donut," Calvin grumbled as he smacked Lynx on the back of the head.

"Yeah, but I went with him; therefore, I'll take my thanks in the form of a kiss."

Wolfe swatted Lynx on the back of the head.

"Hey!" Lynx laughed, passing the donut to Wolfe.

Amy's eyes flew over to Wolfe. He was smiling up at her and her heart twisted tightly in her chest.

It had been two days since she'd stayed the night with Wolfe and Rhys. Wolfe had driven her to work the next day and she'd stayed at her own house last night. Of course, she'd spent nearly every waking moment wishing she were back with them.

Granted, it was nice having Reagan at the house, and she'd felt slightly more comfortable now that she'd told them about what happened. Amy knew they would be on the lookout, and Reagan had even brought her shotgun back to the house. Rhys had told her he'd keep extra patrols going by her house to help her feel safer.

But for Wolfe to bring a donut…

Amy was going to fall in love with this man if she wasn't careful.

"Stay there," Wolfe insisted. "I'll bring it to you."

Amy nodded, then returned to her office.

"How come you get to have all the fun?" Lynx whined, laughing. "I'll talk to y'all later."

"Don't you call that woman," Calvin hollered, following Lynx toward the door. "She's married."

"Trust me. I wouldn't get near that with a ten-foot pole."

"I wouldn't be surprised if she doesn't start stalkin' you," Calvin told Lynx. "See her eyes get all bugged out when she saw those damn tattoos?"

"I wasn't lookin' at her eyes," Lynx noted.

The front door closed with a bang and the entire warehouse was silent.

Wolfe appeared in her office doorway and Amy smiled at him. "How'd it go?"

One dark eyebrow lifted. "Well, the good news is she's latched onto Lynx."

"And the bad news?" Amy's heart swelled to overflowing when Wolfe handed her the single glazed donut. It was her favorite.

"She's latched onto Lynx."

"So, how's that bad? Well, other than, you know … she's married and all."

"It means she'll likely be stoppin' in for visits."

"But at least she'll be keeping her hands off you," Amy told him.

Wolfe closed her office door, flipped the lock, then moved toward her.

"There's only one woman's hands I want on me."

Setting the donut on the desk, Amy allowed Wolfe to turn her chair so that she was facing him.

"Is that right?"

Wolfe relocated the donut to a safer place up on the filing cabinet. It made Amy wonder what his intentions were. Her body had already heated about ten degrees since he stepped into the room.

When he reached down and easily lifted her from her chair, Amy squealed. Her butt was planted on the edge of the desk and Wolfe took a seat in front of her.

"I think you should wear skirts to work," he said as his hands slid beneath her T-shirt.

"Yeah?" Okay, so she was breathless, but that was because this sexy cowboy was touching her, his warm hand grazing her side, sliding higher. "You thinkin' about implementing a new dress code?"

"Oh, yeah."

"Why's that?"

Wolfe pulled her head down with his other hand, his mouth meeting hers, his lips firm yet soft. She accepted his kiss, leaning into him as his hand traveled higher on her rib cage. It was warm, rough against her skin. Her nipples hardened; her sex clenched.

When he pulled back, he groaned. "Because it would make burying my face between your legs so much easier."

Her clit pulsed at his gruffly spoken words.

She'd never been on the receiving end of a dirty-talking man. Amy had never given much thought to whether or not she'd like it.

Boy, did she like it.

When his hands trailed down her stomach, his fingers resting on the button on her jeans, Wolfe's green eyes met hers and she could tell he was seeking permission.

The idea of him doing that here seemed so taboo. But her body ached for him. Since the other night, she'd thought about him and Rhys constantly. Day, night. Didn't matter. It was as though they'd stoked a flame inside her, and she wanted more of what they'd offered that first night.

With a jerky tilt of her head, Amy gave him permission to proceed. And in case he misunderstood, she hopped off the desk and stood directly in front of him.

Another growl rumbled in his chest when he leaned forward and pressed his mouth to her stomach. Amy cradled his head, her body trembling when he unhooked the button, then lowered the zipper. He continued to kiss her stomach while he reached down and removed her boots, then helped her shimmy out of her jeans.

The wood desk was cold on her butt when he picked her up and put her on it again, but she welcomed the chill because her body was on fire.

"Damn," Wolfe hissed. "So fucking pretty."

Amy's face flamed with embarrassment as his fingers trailed between her legs, his thumb grazing her clit.

"Need you naked," he said, his free hand pushing her shirt up.

Amy helped by removing her shirt, then her bra. It was *definitely* taboo to be in her office completely naked while Wolfe was fully dressed.

"I'm gonna have to get you a bigger desk," he grumbled as he moved the laptop out of the way, then eased her down onto her back.

Wolfe dropped to one knee, then propped her legs over his shoulders as his warm breath fanned her pussy lips.

Her back bowed off the desk when his tongue teased her sensitive flesh. "Wolfe…"

"I fucking love when you say my name," he mumbled before resuming his feast on her.

He licked and sucked, nipped and flicked her clit; all the while her body coiled tighter, her nipples painfully hard, in desperate need of his touch. When his tongue speared her, fucking her, Amy's breath caught in her throat and she cried out, unable to stop it as she came in a rush. She was getting used to how easily they could make her orgasm. It hadn't even occurred to her that she'd never had an orgasm until Wolfe used his mouth on her. After the first time, that incredible feeling was something she longed for.

She was writhing and moaning when he lifted his head, then leaned over her. His hot mouth descended on hers and Amy wrapped her arms around his neck. She wanted to hold on to him forever.

He must've sensed her need because he pulled back, grinned. "Not done with you yet."

The man was going to drive her completely insane with pleasure.

He stood tall, his fingertips trailing over her chest, then both big hands cupped her breasts, squeezing as he pinched her nipples, his eyes following his movement. Amy watched his face. Seeing the way he looked at her, as though she was all he ever wanted, did strange things to her insides. She liked this side of Wolfe.

His hands continued lower, his thumbs parting her lips again, his finger trailing over her clit, making her moan.

Wolfe's gaze lifted to hers. "God, Amy... You're so fucking beautiful."

When he said stuff like that, she could almost believe it.

"More," she whispered. "Please."

"What do you want?" His thumbs pushed inside her, his finger still teasing her clit, his eyes never leaving hers.

"You. That's what I want."

"Tell me," he urged, fucking her with his thumbs, pushing in deep, retreating slowly.

It took a second for her to build the confidence to tell him what she wanted. He continued to tease her, fondling her so intimately. Amy grabbed her breasts, squeezing them roughly. She needed more than this.

"Fuck," Wolfe hissed. "You're gonna kill me, woman." His eyes locked on her hands intimately teasing her nipples. He looked up at her face. "Tell me, darlin'."

She held his stare. "Fuck me, Wolfe." She inhaled sharply when his thumbs thrust into her again. "Fuck me now."

What felt like hours was probably only a couple of minutes, but Wolfe managed to push his jeans past his hips, cover himself with a condom, and then he was filling her.

He jerked her toward him, her butt on the edge of the desk, her legs straight up in the air, her thighs resting against his stomach, his thick arms holding her in place while he pounded into her.

Amy had never felt anything as amazing as this. Wolfe fucking her on her desk, his heated gaze locked with hers, his rough groans echoing in the small space. Her orgasm built within seconds and then exploded. She bit her lip to keep from crying out, a whimper escaping instead. Wolfe was still watching her, still fucking her hard and deep.

"You have to come for me again," he told her.

The man was certainly a generous lover. Not only did he make her come one more time, he didn't stop until she'd nearly passed out from multiple orgasms.

Three more, to be exact.

"WHERE YOU AT?"

"Headin' home," Rhys told Wolfe as he turned onto his street.

"Want company?" This time Amy's voice came through the phone.

"Y'all out and about?"

"Yep," Amy said. "So, is that a yes?"

She sounded so damn sweet he couldn't bring himself to say no. Not that he really wanted to. Sure, he was exhausted, but when it came to spending time with them, he was sure he could forego a few extra hours of sleep.

"That's a yes."

"Okay. See you in a few."

The phone disconnected at the same time Rhys's house came into view.

Not only his house but the big black Chevy parked in front of it.

He smiled.

For whatever reason, it eased something inside him that Wolfe and Amy came to him this time. So far, he'd been the one tagging along wherever they went. Although he knew that came with the situation, he didn't want to always feel like the third wheel.

He pulled his truck into the driveway and parked beside Wolfe's truck.

"'Bout damn time," Wolfe greeted as he got out of the truck.

Rhys opened Amy's door and helped her out, accepting the quick peck on the lips she offered.

For a woman who was new to this threesome thing, Amy didn't seem to be having a hard time with it.

She took his hand, linked their fingers, her other hand wrapping around his bicep as she followed him up the porch steps. Again, he was hyperaware of how much she touched him.

"I like it out here," Amy told him. "It's peaceful."

He didn't live on the amount of land the Caines had, but the four acres he did own were enough for him. The house was small, just an old farmhouse that needed some more work, but Rhys was short on time these days, so he hadn't put as much into the renovations as he'd wanted to. However, he'd done the major work already. New floors, replaced the appliances, upgraded the cabinets and countertops, replaced the rotted boards on the front porch. He still needed to tackle the bathrooms and get the small barn so that it was functional.

After unlocking the door, he stepped back out of the way and allowed Amy and Wolfe to go inside. Wolfe offered a mischievous smirk, which had Rhys wondering what the guy was up to.

"Rhys, this is so nice," Amy said, her voice echoing in the relatively empty house. "Very masculine."

Wolfe grunted. "How come he gets masculine and you called mine beautiful?"

Rhys grinned.

Amy shrugged. "Your house *is* beautiful."

Wolfe rolled his eyes, but he smiled while he did it.

"How was work, honey?" Wolfe teased, turning toward the living room.

Rhys ignored his sarcasm, making his way to the kitchen. He couldn't remember the last time he'd had anyone in his house. Well, other than Reagan. His sister stopped by from time to time, but he figured that was mostly so she could get a break from that deadbeat dumb ass she'd been dating.

"What did y'all do today?" Rhys asked as he rummaged through his refrigerator. "Want somethin' to drink? Beer? Water?"

"I'll take water," Amy said sweetly.

"Beer's good."

Rhys retrieved two beers and a bottle of water, then joined them in the living room.

"We had sex on my desk," Amy offered when Rhys handed over the water.

Completely floored by her statement, Rhys stared at her, unable to release the bottle of water. He noticed Amy was smirking up at him, her cheeks rosy from her blush.

Sweet little Amy had just stolen his breath with that out-of-character comment, and she seemed to realize it, too.

"How's that?" he asked, clearing his throat.

"Sex. On my desk." The corners of her mouth turned upward.

Rhys's cock was already growing at the thought of the pair of them on Amy's desk.

He managed to release the water bottle, then passed a beer to Wolfe before dropping into the oversized chair across from the sofa.

"I'm thinkin' he might not understand fully," Wolfe stated, his voice rough.

"No, I get it," Rhys clarified, glancing over at Wolfe. "I just wish I'd been there to watch."

Wolfe's grin widened. "Baby, you should give him a demonstration."

Amy glanced between the two men and Rhys noticed the color on her cheeks deepened. Yep, the woman might have a dirty streak, but underneath it all, she was still sweet and innocent.

"Do to him what I did to you," Wolfe instructed, leaning over to take Amy's water bottle.

She passed it over without hesitation, then got to her feet.

Rhys was riveted by the sight of her approaching, that formfitting T-shirt doing little to hide the fact that her nipples were hard.

"You'll have to stand up first," Amy said, a slight tremble in her voice.

It was obvious she was trying to be bold, daring.

He liked that she was, but he also liked her hesitation. She was so damn sweet.

Rhys set his beer on the side table and got to his feet.

Amy's fingers dipped into the waistband of his jeans as she smiled up at him. "First, we have to get you naked."

His cock jerked behind his zipper.

This was one hell of a way to come home after work. Never in his life would he have expected it.

While Wolfe watched and Rhys tried to remember to breathe, Amy unhooked his belt buckle, then unbuttoned and unzipped his jeans. When Rhys went to toe off his boots, Amy stopped him. She knelt on the floor in front of him and his stomach muscles tightened in anticipation.

He watched as she tugged and pulled on his boots until they gave way, then she dumped them on the floor beside the chair. Once those were out of the way, she yanked his jeans and boxers down his hips, over his thighs, then to the floor. Before he knew what she was going to do, Amy pushed him and he fell back into the chair with a grunt.

She laughed. "Wolfe's a little dominant," Amy noted. "In case you haven't noticed."

Rhys chuckled, his gaze straying to Wolfe. The man was sitting on the couch, his eyes focused on the two of them, heat making the dark green glitter.

With his dick hanging out, Amy pushed Rhys's shirt up and instructed him to remove it.

He did.

Then she leaned in and kissed his stomach, trailing her lips down, down…

"Holy Jesus," he rasped when she took him in her mouth. "Such a sweet mouth."

Amy teased him for long minutes, licking him like a lollipop then sucking him as deep as she could. She was still hesitant, but there was significantly more confidence in her movements. She'd obviously paid attention to what he liked and she was implementing her new skills.

"Lower," he urged, reaching down and pressing his cock to his belly.

Amy looked at him, uncertainty in her eyes.

"Lick my balls," he told her.

When she leaned down, her tongue gliding over his ball sac, Rhys hissed.

"Suck them into your mouth. Easy though."

She did as he instructed, her hand curling around his cock while she slurped and laved his balls.

"Fuck, baby," he groaned, leaning farther into the chair as she continued to torture him with her sweet fucking mouth.

If she kept that up, he was going to come.

As though reading his mind, Amy stopped. She lifted her head and crawled up his body until she was straddling him. Her mouth covered his and Rhys cupped the back of her head, his other hand grabbing her ass as he pulled her closer, his cock pressing against the denim between her thighs. He swiveled his hips, intensifying the friction on his dick. Amy realized what he was doing and helped him along by mirroring his movements.

He liked this feisty woman. He liked her innocence and the sassy woman beneath that sweet exterior. She was a perfect blend of both.

When she pulled back, both of them breathing hard, Rhys had to rein in the urge to take control.

"What did Wolfe do next?" he questioned, watching her.

Without a word, Amy crawled off of him, toed off her boots, then stripped off her jeans before turning to Wolfe. Rhys glanced over to see Wolfe watching them intently. The heat burning in those emerald-green eyes could be felt from across the room.

"Naked," Wolfe instructed.

"You kept *your* clothes on," she countered, her voice raspy.

"Yeah. But you look a hell of a lot better naked than I do."

In Rhys's opinion, they both looked damn fine naked.

Amy quickly disposed of her shirt, panties, and bra while they both watched her raptly. As though she'd expected him to have it, Amy held out her hand and Wolfe tossed her a condom, then she turned her attention back to Rhys.

She repositioned herself on his lap, straddling his thighs while she rolled the condom down over his aching dick. Before he could ask her to hurry, Amy lifted up and settled herself right on his cock, guiding him inside her.

"Pretend this is a desk," she whispered, grinning.

He sucked in air as though it was becoming extinct.

When she started riding him, her hips lifting and lowering, he gripped the arms of the chair and groaned.

"God, baby … so fucking hot." He could hardly breathe, but he managed to encourage her with words. "That's it. Ride me … fuck me … oh, gawd, baby."

Her internal muscles clamped down on him, squeezing intimately, making his breath catch.

When her movements slowed, Rhys helped her out, gripping her ass and lifting and lowering her on him, driving his hips up every time her thighs hit his. Her short nails dug into his shoulders, her eyes closed, and those sexy little moans continued to escape her.

Knowing Wolfe was watching, combined with the velvet friction of her pussy against his cock, Rhys was racing to the finish line. Using his thumb, he rubbed her clit, circling over the hard nub until Amy was panting. He didn't stop until she cried out his name over and over as she came.

Only then did he let himself go.

21

One week later

"SO," LYNX PROMPTED, hip propped against one of the seven-foot dining tables Wolfe had been working on for the past two days with very little progress. "I stopped by your place last night."

Wolfe glanced over at his cousin. The guy was smirking, clearly planning to bust Wolfe's balls about something. Pretending he didn't notice, Wolfe swiped the sandpaper over a rough spot.

"Wanted to check on you. Haven't seen you out and about in town, thought maybe you were becomin' a hermit. So, I hopped my happy ass in my truck, drove *all* the way out to your place, and what did I see?"

Lynx wasn't usually prone to dramatics, and Wolfe wasn't prone to tolerating them, so he offered his cousin a glare, urging him to get to the fucking point.

"When I got there, I chose not to stay. Figured since Rhys's truck was *out*side and you and Amy were *in*side, y'all were probably doin' fine, so I took off."

Shit.

Lynx uncrossed his arms and held his hands up. "You ain't gonna get no judgment from me, hoss."

Sighing, Wolfe went back to work on the cedar chest he'd been restoring for an older couple who were having their house remodeled. Wolfe's family didn't just create new things at the shop, they also restored the old.

"Am I right?"

Wolfe flipped him off.

His cousin chuckled.

Lynx sipped from a cup of coffee as he watched Wolfe work. "You talk to your old man lately?"

"Not in a coupla days, no. Why?"

"No reason. I went by there this mornin'. All's good."

"How's Cooter?" Wolfe asked, referring to Lynx's father.

"Same. I think that damn garden's gonna overtake the house one of these days."

"Yeah? It doin' well?" Wolfe wasn't sure how it could be considering the temperatures had been hovering at the one-hundred-degree mark for the last week.

"No. More weeds than garden, but that doesn't stop the old man from tryin'."

No, Wolfe didn't figure it would. Cooter might've been a shut-in—although maybe not in the extreme technical sense because he did venture outside of his house, but no farther than the garden in the backyard—but he also enjoyed spending time in the sun. Most days when Wolfe went by there, the man was sitting in a rocking chair on his front porch, reading a book. They still worried about him, but Cooter Caine was a tough old bird.

"Any news about…?" Lynx tilted his chin toward the offices upstairs.

Wolfe shook his head. "Not yet."

"Sheriff doin' somethin' to find that asshole?"

"It's slowgoin'," Wolfe admitted. "He doesn't want to draw attention to her if the guy hasn't yet figured out where she is."

"The old man said he heard gunshots out there last night. Y'all teachin' her to shoot?"

"Yep." As much and as often as they could. Amy seemed to truly enjoy it, and Wolfe couldn't deny it made him feel a hell of a lot better knowing she could handle a firearm.

"Good. At least she'll be ready for the fucker if he does come 'round."

They would *all* be ready for him. And if Wolfe had anything to say about it, the bastard wouldn't get within five miles of her before he met the business end of Wolfe's shotgun.

"I hear Reagan's still stayin' at Amy's place."

Wolfe straightened, cocked an eyebrow at the interesting change in subject. "Yeah? Where'd you hear that from?"

Lynx shrugged.

Wolfe knew Lynx had a thing for Reagan Trevino. It wasn't public knowledge and the guy made damn sure most people thought otherwise, but Wolfe could tell he was sweet on her. It seemed that every time Reagan and that dumb ass Billy Watson broke up, Lynx's mood improved. Then, of course, it would go downhill once she took his sorry ass back.

If they were lucky, she was done with him for good this time. Nearly two weeks apart was a record for the two of them, so anything was possible, but Wolfe wasn't going to hold his breath.

"So—" Lynx began, but Wolfe cut him off this time.

"Don't you have somewhere to be besides in here yakkin' my damn ear off?"

Lynx chuckled. "All right, cry baby man."

Wolfe laughed. He should've known that was coming after his breakdown the day Amy shared her horror story. Granted, Lynx wouldn't dare call him that when anyone else was around to hear it, and because of that, Wolfe wouldn't kick his ass.

"I'll check ya later. Tell Amy to holler if she needs somethin'." Lynx grinned. "Not that she will since it seems she's got you *and* the sheriff at her beck and call."

"Shut the hell up," Wolfe said, grimacing.

He didn't want people up in his business, even his cousin. Right now, this thing with him and Amy and Rhys was new. He didn't need any outside forces interfering. Shit never worked out when that happened.

Hell, Wolfe liked his uncomplicated life. And with Amy and Rhys, he felt as though things were going exactly the way they were meant to.

"Talk at ya later," Lynx called out as he sauntered toward the door, clicking his tongue twice to get Copenhagen at his side.

"Later," Wolfe grumbled, then grabbed the sandpaper and got to work.

It seemed he'd been dealing with one interruption after another all damn day. Between the leak he'd found after last night's storm, then his power sander blowing a breaker, him fixing that, and Calvin calling to tell him he'd be taking the day off so the store would be closed until one of them could get over there, plus Lynx's need to dish like a fucking girl, Wolfe hadn't gotten shit done.

His gaze strayed to the offices above him. He was tempted to check on Amy, see if she needed anything, but he knew she was fine. Probably glad to put a little space between her and the rest of the world for a little while.

For the past few days, she'd spent most of her time with Wolfe or Rhys, or both. They'd alternated between staying at Wolfe's and Rhys's. Twice he'd taken Amy home and she still froze outside, despite the fact that Reagan was staying at her place. Her reaction only pissed Wolfe off. Not at her, at the bastard who'd put that fear in her eyes.

Last night, after her insistence that she could spend a night alone in her own bed, despite what Rhys or Wolfe wanted, Wolfe had driven her out to her place. The second Wolfe had pulled up to her house, Amy had shifted from the easygoing woman she'd been for the past few days to one who hesitated to get out of the truck.

While she'd gone inside to grab more clothes after his insistence for her to stay with him again, Wolfe had walked the perimeter of the house, checking it out. Nothing looked tampered with. Didn't stop him from shooting a text to Rhys, asking the man to quit dicking around and find out who this bastard was. Wolfe wasn't going to tolerate Amy having to walk around fearing for her life indefinitely. He fully intended to put a stop to it, but he wanted to give Rhys a chance to check it out first. If that didn't work, Wolfe would take matters into his own hands. He knew people who would be more than happy to help him out, namely his cousins who lived not far away in Coyote Ridge.

If push came to shove, Wolfe wouldn't hesitate to reach out to his cousin Travis for help. He'd caught up with him at a family reunion a while back and they'd kept in touch. But Wolfe wanted that to be a last resort.

With a sigh, Wolfe decided to leave it all alone for a bit.

After all, he did have a job to do.

More importantly, he needed to stay busy. That way, the day would go by quickly. It wasn't usual for him, but these days, he had something else to look forward to. Something that would put a smile on his face *after* they locked up the shop.

Didn't mean they would leave.

AMY WELCOMED THE opportunity to go to work at Reagan's. After spending all day tucked in her office, staring at a computer screen, she was grateful to be able to move around. Didn't even matter that Wolfe was watching her from the far corner of the bar like he did on nearly every night she worked. He claimed he just wanted to be close. She wasn't sure that was the case, but since she felt safer with him, Amy didn't argue.

It was Thursday but, oddly enough, the place was relatively busy. Most of the tables were occupied, along with several seats at the bar. Nothing seemed to be happening, but the conversation was going nonstop. And as would be expected in a small town, there was a lot of gossip taking place.

"Ol' Billy's got him a new girl. Did you see that?"

"Sure did. Not sure what to think about that one though. Her eyes are shifty."

Amy had to fight the urge to laugh.

She wasn't sure who Billy had hooked up with, or whether the woman had shifty eyes, but she knew for a fact that these people were protective of Reagan. By the end of the night, this new mystery woman would likely end up having a third boob and maybe a sexually transmitted disease. The first would be made up, of course. The second … well, it could go either way.

Not that Amy cared.

Nor did it seem that Reagan gave a shit, either.

Amy hadn't seen the woman smile as much as she had these past couple of weeks. She seemed less stressed, more relaxed. Genuinely happier.

Well, that was usually the case until Lynx Caine showed up. As soon as he stepped into the bar, Reagan always tensed up.

There had to be something going on there that Amy didn't know about. From what she could remember, she'd never heard any rumors about Lynx and Reagan, but the way the two acted around each other said enough. She wasn't sure whether they secretly liked each other or if they hated each other. Maybe a little of both. Whatever it was, Amy hoped they worked it out. She liked them both too much to see them at odds.

"Hey, sweet thang. How 'bout a beer over here?"

Amy stopped wiping the bar and nodded to a group of men sitting at a table against the wall. They'd been there for about an hour and so far hadn't gotten too rowdy, despite the fact their voices continued to rise as the minutes ticked by.

At the bar, Amy requested three Bud Lights from Reagan, then stood waiting for her to deliver. While she was standing there, Wolfe came over, his eyes hard.

"What's wrong?" she asked, concerned.

Leaning down so that his mouth was close to her ear, Wolfe whispered, "You know how hard it is not to beat a man for calling you sweet thang?"

Amy chuckled, her eyes dropping to the bar. "He didn't mean anything by it."

"Maybe not, but I bet if I kissed you right here, he wouldn't dream about sayin' it again."

Lifting her face to his, Amy's lips twitched with the urge to smile. "Feel the need to mark your territory?"

As soon as the words were out of her mouth, a strange feeling stirred inside her. One she didn't like all that much. She hadn't given much thought to how much time she was spending with Wolfe and Rhys, but the idea of being their possession was something she hadn't considered. She'd endured being someone's property for so long she had no desire to ever go back to that.

Then again, when she was with Rhys and Wolfe, she felt whole for the first time in her life. She felt … well, protected. They allowed her to be who she really was, and they made sure she knew how much they wanted her. It was a good feeling.

Which meant it was nothing like her previous experience. In fact, it was the opposite, and perhaps that was why she liked that Wolfe got all dominant and possessive.

"Damn straight, darlin'."

She had spent the better part of five years "belonging" to someone. However, she'd been a prisoner, unable to make decisions for herself. That wasn't the case with Wolfe and Rhys, she knew. They didn't make her feel smothered, trapped. Plus, she actually liked people knowing that she was with Wolfe. They'd kept things on the down low mostly because she wasn't just with Wolfe. She didn't think Wolfe or Rhys cared what people thought, but Amy still worried what people would think if they knew she was with both men. More so because she didn't want it to cause problems for Rhys. If it were up to her, she would shout it from the rooftops.

It wasn't up to her though.

And she understood where Rhys was coming from. When she really thought about it, she realized how unnatural the three of them together was. But when she was with them, she realized how right it felt. She was conflicted.

Her biggest issue was that Amy did not want to rush into something because they offered her a sense of purpose, of belonging. Of security. Most importantly, she didn't want to be dependent on them. She wanted to live her life, be who she wanted to be. And it was true, they hadn't tried to change her, but Amy knew they wanted to wrap her in cotton and protect her from the world.

"Here you go," Reagan said, passing over the beers. "Give the girl some breathin' room, Wolfe."

Amy took the three beers over to the men, leaning in and setting them on the table.

When a firm hand landed on her backside, Amy straightened suddenly.

"Sorry, sweet thang," the man who'd asked for the beers said. "Hard to keep my hands from wanderin' to somethin' that fine."

"Well, you better find a way to keep 'em to yourself before I rip them from your fucking body."

The rough rumble of Wolfe's voice from behind her had Amy taking one step back from the group.

"Ah, hell, Caine. Why didn't you say somethin'? If I'd known you were sweet on the girl, I wouldn't've touched."

"Shouldn't be touchin' anyway," Reagan called from the table next to them, where she was grabbing two empties. "Why do you dumb cowboys think we want your filthy hands all up on us?"

Reagan sounded as though she was teasing, but Amy had to wonder.

"Keep your fuckin' hands off my girl," Wolfe demanded, then steered Amy back to the bar.

His girl?

For whatever reason, there was a churning in her belly. The sweet kind. The kind that made her want to jump on Wolfe, to kiss him right there in front of everyone. She'd never thought she'd feel that way about anyone who wanted to claim her. But when Wolfe said it…

"My girl," he declared again. "And the whole fucking bar should know that."

Amy let out a squeal when Wolfe pulled her into his arms and crushed his mouth to hers. She tried to resist him at first, but she gave in quickly. The man's mouth could do wicked things to her, make her forget her manners or where she was.

When he finally pulled back—after a couple of catcalls and whistles—they were both breathing hard.

"Well," Amy huffed, stepping back. "I think you effectively staked your claim."

"I'd say so," Reagan said with a laugh.

"Now, if you don't mind, I need to get back to work. You can sit right there and watch."

"Oh, darlin', you know how I like to watch."

Heat infused her. Yeah, watching was one of the things Wolfe did enjoy. And Amy had to admit, she liked it, too. Especially when…

She shook off the thought before her mind went directly into the gutter. She was at work and did not need to be thinking about all the deliciously dirty things Rhys and Wolfe had done to her over the past week.

Feeling slightly guilty for letting her mind wander, Amy peered up at Wolfe. He was watching her. A crooked smile tilted his lips and he winked.

She sighed.

What else could she do?

"SHERIFF TREVINO, MY name is Joanna Tannenbaum. I'm a detective with the Houston Police Department. I'd like to speak to you about a missing person I've been personally looking into. When you get this, please give me a call back."

Rhys jotted down the phone number the detective rattled off, a nervous tension tightening his gut. After disconnecting from the voice mail, he dialed the number.

"Joanna Tannenbaum," the woman greeted, her tone curt, professional.

"This is Sheriff Rhys Trevino. I'm returnin' your call."

"Thank you for calling me back, Sheriff. I've been working a cold case, and I came across some information I thought you could help clarify."

Rhys didn't respond.

"Anyway," she continued, "let me start by saying that this case is not official."

"Not official?"

"An actual missing person's report hasn't been filed; however, there is a case file," she clarified. "It's regarding a Jane Doe, who... You know what? Would it be possible to meet with you in person to discuss this? It's ... well, it's something I'd rather not talk about over the phone."

Inviting the detective to Embers Ridge could pose a problem. Then again, she had contacted him, which meant she knew exactly where to find him if she chose to. Odds of her finding whatever it was she was looking for were about fifty-fifty, regardless of whether he brought her to town or she came on her own.

"Tomorrow mornin'," he suggested. "At my office."

"What about Sunday? Say, nine o'clock. That's the only time I'm off for the next week."

"All right. Sunday mornin'. Nine a.m."

"Thank you, Sheriff. I think this is information you'd be interested in having."

He would agree, even though he couldn't guarantee her unofficial case involved the Jane Doe from a year ago—a.k.a. Amy Smith—but he had a feeling that it did.

"See you Sunday morning at nine," she concluded, then disconnected the call.

Rhys hung up the phone and stared down at it. Although the woman hadn't mentioned anything about Amy, Rhys had a strong suspicion that her past had just caught up with her.

By the time Rhys was off shift, he was exhausted. Rather than go over to Reagan's and get shit from the local hotheads, he opted to go home. He hadn't spent a whole lot of time there lately, and it seemed like a good night to sit back and relax by himself.

He hadn't been in the front door three minutes when his cell phone rang.

"What's up, Sheriff?" Wolfe questioned, his tone steely.

"Nada. Just got home."

A heavy pause hung between them for a second, and Rhys started to wonder if Wolfe had expected Rhys to simply spend all his time at his place. As much as he enjoyed the time he'd spent with Wolfe and Amy, Rhys still needed time to himself. Plus, he had a million things on his mind. The least of which was not the fact that he had a meeting with a Houston detective on Sunday morning, and sure as shit, if he had to face Wolfe, Rhys would give himself away. Until he knew exactly what it was about, he didn't want to share the news with anyone.

"Okay then. I'll let you go."

"Wait," Rhys blurted. "What's up?"

"Nothin'. Just thought you'd stop by the bar on your way home. That's all."

"Sorry. Got a lot of shit on my mind right now."

"No worries. I'm gonna take Amy home tonight. She said she really wants to sleep in her own bed."

Rhys didn't know what to say to that. He understood Amy's need to go home. She'd spent a significant amount of time with both of them, and things had been steadily intensifying between them from the get-go. The woman was probably in need of some alone time, too.

"Is Reagan gonna be there?" Rhys asked.

"Yep."

"Tell 'em to call if they need anything."

"Sure. Later."

The call disconnected abruptly and Rhys leaned against the counter with a heavy sigh. It was evident Wolfe did not like when things didn't go as he'd planned. Not that Rhys was privy to the man's plan. They'd taken things one minute at a time for the past couple of weeks, and truthfully, Rhys was having difficulty trying to figure out what he should do next. This thing between them—as hot as it might be—was moving a little fast.

Rhys was all for the sex. No arguments from him on that front. However, the rest was new for him. Rhys hadn't had a relationship since his early twenties, and that one hadn't been nearly as time-consuming as this one was.

Truth was, Rhys didn't know how to do relationships. Especially not with two people, although that was what he wanted in the long run. He just hadn't expected things to escalate so quickly. He knew a big part of that was due to Amy and her past, but someone had to put the brakes on, and Rhys figured it might as well be him.

Plus, it would do Wolfe good to see that Rhys wasn't going to jump through hoops for him. He'd never been that guy, and no matter how hard or how fast he was falling for Wolfe and Amy, he refused to ever be that guy.

Now he just needed to figure out how to balance it all out.

If that was even possible.

"SIR?"

Kelly Jackson peered up from his desk, his eyes scanning the man who'd rudely interrupted him. "What is it?"

"Remember how you told me to let you know if that Jane Doe file was ever opened?"

An icy tremor raced down Kelly's spine as he sat up straight. "Yes."

"Looks as though someone's been checking into it."

Kelly masked his expression, not wanting to let on that this was possibly the worst news he could've received.

"Do you know who?" he asked, keeping his tone casual.

"Detective Joanna Tannenbaum."

Son of a bitch.

He should've known that woman was going to be trouble. She'd only asked him about Amy at least half a dozen times since he'd concocted the story of Amy going to take care of her sick grandmother. He had no idea why Jo was so interested, and he didn't like the fact that she was so fucking nosy.

"Did she say what she was looking into?"

"No, sir. She actually claimed she *hadn't* looked into it, but her IP address was used to access it."

"Thank you, James."

"Yes, sir."

When James turned and left the doorway, Kelly leaned back in his chair, his chest burning. He knew he shouldn't have let this go on this long. He should've taken care of her long before now. But after he'd been promoted to Houston police chief, Kelly had gotten a little lax. He had more to worry about than the stupid woman who should've been six feet under.

And maybe lax wasn't the right word. Kelly had to admit he could've taken care of her long before now. He'd tracked her from the day she left the hospital near Embers Ridge. He'd kept tabs on her when she stayed with that nurse, then when she hopped from motel to motel. There for a while, he thought she was going to leave the state, but she never had. Instead, Amy backtracked to that damn small town. She bought a house and settled in not too long ago. He figured he had time to deal with her. After all, a year had passed and no one had tied the Jane Doe back to him.

So, he had backed off these past couple of weeks. He wanted to let her get comfortable, to think he wasn't going to come after her. There'd been some masochistic pleasure in knowing that he could get his hands on her whenever and wherever he wanted. She couldn't run from him, and she damn sure couldn't outsmart him.

But the fact of the matter was, she should be dead.

It was true, from the second he'd laid eyes on her way back then, Kelly had wanted her fiercely. He'd been excited to take her virginity, to ride her hard, to make her submit to him. Only that damn uncle of hers had caused problems from the beginning. And after he'd had to take care of them, Amy had changed. She'd become a headache over the years, and he had no idea why he'd kept her as long as he had.

And then she'd thought she could just leave him.

He could still feel the rage burning just under his skin. It had never gone away completely since the day he'd sat at his desk and watched as she moved through the house and packed her things. But she had hesitated. Kelly knew she wouldn't leave him. She didn't have the gumption. She was too stupid to make a decision like that on her own. But he'd been tired of waiting for it. Admittedly, she'd gotten braver. So, he'd followed his instinct that morning when he had hightailed it back to the house.

And that was when the rage won out. He'd been blinded by fury to the point he hadn't been able to stop beating her. But she just wouldn't die. It was as though she had something to live for, but he knew better.

When she had finally stopped fighting back, Kelly had knocked her unconscious. She'd suffered so many broken bones, and he figured the broken ribs had punctured her lungs. Hell, he'd figured if her injuries didn't kill her, the elements alone would have. That was the only damn reason he'd dumped her out in the middle of fucking nowhere. He knew she didn't have any family, no friends. No one would be looking for her. And when he'd been asked about her, he'd fabricated a story about her moving up to Pennsylvania to take care of her ailing grandmother. It had been hard to let her go, he'd explained, but necessary.

At least the last part had been true.

"Shit," he grumbled, glancing out the window.

Looked as though he was going to have to put a plan in place. He'd known it would come to this one day, and he'd actually looked forward to it. However, he wasn't a man to react. He had to have a plan. He might not be able to get his hands on her right away, but it would be soon.

And this time he would make sure she was dead before he dumped her body.

Hell, he'd bury her himself just to make sure.

And if he needed to take care of Joanna Tannenbaum, he'd take care of her, too.

No woman was going to alter his course. Not now. Not ever.

22

WOLFE SPENT THE majority of his Saturday working. With Amy at home doing girl shit with Reagan and Rhys being standoffish, Wolfe had figured some time alone would do him some good, too. Seemed to be what everyone else was aiming for, so why the hell not.

Didn't matter that it was his fucking birthday.

The day had gone by fast and he'd finally managed to get some shit accomplished. Amazing how a little time without interruptions could get things back on the right path. And now, the only thing he wanted to do was head home, grab a shower, then maybe head over to Reagan's for a beer with his cousin and hopefully his old man.

After cleaning and locking up, Wolfe headed home, calling Calvin on his way.

"'Yello."

"Hey, old man. You up for a beer in a bit?" Wolfe asked.

"Uh. Shit. What time?"

"Coupla hours, maybe? I'm headin' home to clean up. Then I thought I'd head over."

"Okay. I've got some shit to do, but I'll try to make it by there."

"See you if I see you." Wolfe disconnected and then dialed Lynx's number.

"Wassup, hoss?"

"You wanna meet for a beer at Reagan's?"

"Yup. What time?"

"Give me an hour or so to shower and I'll see you there."

"Make it around seven and I'll see you there."

"Perfect."

At least someone had some time for him today.

Not to sound like a broken record or anything, but it was his fucking birthday.

Two hours later, Wolfe was climbing out of his truck in front of Reagan's. The damn parking lot looked like a ghost town. The only vehicle there was Reagan's. He knew Amy was working tonight but figured she'd caught a ride with Reagan since she'd been doing so frequently lately.

As he stepped up to the door, he briefly wondered if someone was playing a trick on him. Sure, it was a little early, but seven o'clock wasn't too early for a beer in this small town.

Opening the door, he noticed Reagan standing behind the bar and Amy leaning against it. Both women's eyes cut to him when he made his way inside.

"We were startin' to wonder if no one was gonna show up tonight," Reagan noted, sounding somewhat relieved that they had a customer.

"Where's everybody at?" he asked.

"Thought maybe you could tell *us*," Reagan replied.

Wolfe glanced over at Amy. He noticed she was trying really hard not to smile.

"Okay, what's goin' on?" No fucking way was this bar completely empty on a Saturday night.

Amy giggled but tried to mask it. She was too late.

Wolfe moved toward her. She backed up, still grinning from ear to ear.

"What'd you do?" he asked her directly.

"Me? What makes you think *I* did something?"

"You're blushin', darlin'. I know you're up to somethin'."

He crowded her between his body and the wall. Planting one hand over her head, he leaned down and cupped her jaw. When he went to kiss her, Amy giggled again but was quickly silenced when he slipped his tongue past her lips.

A soft moan escaped her and Wolfe realized what he wanted for his birthday.

Her.

And Rhys.

Naked.

Before he could tell her as much, the door opened behind him. He slowly broke the kiss, then turned just in time to see…

"Happy fuckin' birthday, hoss!" Lynx shouted.

Holy fuck.

People started filing into the room one by one, all following Lynx, who was carrying one hell of a cake.

"You seriously didn't think we'd forget, did you?" Lynx asked. "I mean, you're thirty and all. Not an important birthday or nothin'."

Wolfe couldn't help but smile. He put his arm around Amy and pulled her to his side. When he looked down at her, he noticed she was still smiling.

"Did you have somethin' to do with this?"

"Maybe. I noticed the date on the calendar in the break room, so I asked Lynx about it."

"You got a keeper there."

Wolfe looked up to see his father moving toward him, a huge grin plastered on his face.

"Yeah?"

"That girl worked her butt off to get all these people to keep a secret."

"Not an easy thing to do in a town this small," Reagan added.

"Definitely not," Rhys said when he joined them.

"A free round of beers helps when tryin' to bribe people though," Lynx added.

Wolfe glanced around at all the people. Friends he didn't see that often, his father, his cousin, Rhys, Amy. Shit. Everyone who meant anything to him was there.

Hell, he hadn't had a birthday celebration like this one since he turned twenty-one.

Peering down at Amy, Wolfe tilted her chin up, then leaned closer. "Remind me to thank you properly later on."

"Okay. I'll remind you."

He just bet she would.

IT REALLY WAS hard to keep secrets in a small town. Amy had learned that firsthand over the past week.

The day she realized Wolfe's birthday was coming up, she had recruited Calvin, Lynx, Rhys, and Reagan to help her surprise him. She hadn't thought it would work, but she'd figured they could give it a shot anyway.

Turned out better than she thought it would, actually. Seeing Wolfe walk into Reagan's, completely confused over why there was no one there, had proven to her that people were willing to go the distance for someone they cared about. The people in this town were top notch in her book.

And now, everyone was drinking beer, laughing, joking, and telling stories about Wolfe. Amy was technically working, but Wolfe continued to pull her into his lap, refusing to let her go, so she wasn't getting much done.

"For his tenth birthday, he wanted a shotgun of his own," Calvin said from his perch on a barstool. "His momma wasn't on board with the plan. But she knew how much it meant to him, so she took him out on the range and worked with him. Turned out, Wolfe taught his momma a few things about guns that day."

Wolfe smiled, his eyes warm. Amy liked the way he interacted with his father; the love and admiration between the two was apparent. Not to mention the respect. And they both obviously missed Wolfe's mother.

It made Amy miss her family. Her parents had been taken from her so suddenly. There was still a void deep inside her, one that would forever be empty. Then her aunt and uncle… The thought of how they'd suffered. *Why* they'd suffered. The ache in her chest had never gone completely away, and times like this, it intensified. She felt short of breath because of it.

"What's wrong?"

Amy jerked her attention to Wolfe. It took her a minute to shake off the thoughts. "Nothing. Why?"

Wolfe frowned, clearly not believing her.

Feeling too many eyes on her, Amy dislodged herself from Wolfe's grasp. "I need to take care of some customers," she murmured, then headed for the bar.

Amy took a deep breath, tried to compose herself. This was a party. She was supposed to be having a good time, not getting trapped in the past.

"The surprise party turned out great," Reagan said. "You did good."

The unexpected praise helped to ease some of the longing that had consumed her. "Thanks. I couldn't've done it without your help."

"Pfft. Whatever. It was all you."

Amy rolled her eyes. It wasn't all her. Not by a long shot. Sure, it might've been her idea initially, but she suspected someone would've come up with it if she hadn't. Wolfe was popular in this tight-knit community. They would've pitched in to celebrate his thirtieth birthday without her.

The thought didn't sit well though.

Amy hadn't realized how much she'd come to love this small town, the people, the interaction. It was so much more than she'd ever had. She almost felt like family, and she didn't want to think about how it would be if she wasn't here.

A warm hand curled around her hip and Amy turned to see Rhys standing behind her. "You okay?"

She nodded, wishing she could lean in and kiss him. Wolfe was all about public displays of affection when it came to her, but she and Rhys had to remain distant. He had never out-and-out said anything, but Amy had gotten the sense when they were in public. He always seemed to keep a safe distance between them. With them but not *with* them.

She briefly wondered if it would always be like that. Should this thing between them become permanent, how would that work out?

Geez. She needed to get her head back in the game here. Why she was thinking about things that didn't matter, she wasn't sure. This thing they had going was great. It was simple and easy and…

It wasn't either of those things, she realized.

Not simple.

Certainly not easy.

However, now was not the time to be dwelling on shit like that. She had more important things to do.

Like celebrate Wolfe's thirtieth birthday and enjoy herself. There'd be time to get lost in her own head later.

Much, much later.

WHEN WOLFE ASKED Rhys to check on Amy, he wasn't sure what to expect. He'd been sitting at a table on the far side of the room when Wolfe came over. The first time since he'd arrived, in fact. Although Rhys hadn't known what the man would say, he admitted he'd been a little disappointed when Wolfe had mentioned she was acting funny. Rhys had figured Wolfe was being overly dramatic, but now that he was looking at her, he could tell something was bothering her.

"I'm good," she said, although her eyes seemed far away.

"Sure?"

"Positive." She paused for a moment, studying his face. "Well, that's mostly true."

Rhys frowned, hoping she would elaborate.

When she leaned in, her mouth close to his ear, he tried to ignore the chill that raced down his spine. The woman turned him on simply by breathing.

"I'd be better if I could kiss you right now."

Rhys jerked back, his eyes locking with hers. The sexy smile on her face had him tempted to give her exactly what she wanted. Except half the town was in that bar right now, and the last thing Rhys needed was for people to start talking about the three of them. In all the time he'd held out for a permanent relationship with a man and a woman, he hadn't thought about the logistics. How it would play out in public. He still wasn't sure what to do about it. And he'd admit, he'd been giving it some serious thought these past few days, but he hadn't come to a conclusion.

"How 'bout a rain check?" he offered. "When we leave here, I'll be sure to cash it in."

Amy smiled but it didn't quite meet her eyes.

Did she want this thing to go public?

Was that even possible? Being sheriff was an important role. One he hadn't really considered until the people of his county voted him in. That meant something. If he came out in a ménage relationship, how would they take it?

Shit.

That wasn't something he even needed to be thinking about right now. For one, this thing between him and Wolfe and Amy was new. It wasn't serious. They were having a good time. A damn good time, actually. And based on that gleam in Amy's eyes, they would be having more fun tonight.

"Rain check it is," she said before turning away to deliver a beer.

Rhys peered down the bar to where Wolfe was perched on a barstool beside his old man. Beside them were Lynx and a couple of buddies Wolfe had gone to school with. They were laughing at something Calvin said. Wolfe was smiling when he looked up, his eyes meeting Rhys's.

It wasn't that Rhys felt like an outsider when it came to the Caines. Not usually anyway. However, tonight he did feel a little separated. With the feud between their families a real thing, it wasn't like Rhys could sidle up to them and join in the conversation. Not to mention, he was the law, and those boys had never been much into interacting with him in a social setting.

Even if he wasn't on duty tonight.

And he didn't even want to think about what would happen when the town figured out he and Wolfe were bisexual. God only knew how people would react to that. Theirs was a conservative town. Marriage was a sacred thing. Between a man and a woman. And once vows were spoken, only death could come between them.

Hell, Lynx's divorce had caused a slight stir, and that had been nothing in the grand scheme of things.

Fuck.

Rhys took a sip of his beer and tore his gaze from Wolfe's, choosing to watch Amy as she maneuvered around the room. Funny how he'd been a huge part of making this party happen, yet he felt as though he shouldn't even be there. And Wolfe damn sure wasn't trying to make it easier on him, either.

Sure, Rhys had put some distance between himself and Wolfe these past few days, but that was because he felt like things were moving too fast. That didn't mean he wanted it to come to a screeching halt.

Amy moved back to the group, leaning into Wolfe as the Caines continued to laugh and joke. When another round of laughter erupted from the group, Rhys decided it was time to go. He damn sure didn't need to be the third wheel here tonight. And he'd rather sit at home by himself than stand on the opposite side of the room and watch the two people he cared most about enjoying themselves while he was forced to keep his distance.

"Where you headed, Sheriff?" Reagan called out when Rhys dropped a twenty on the bar and headed toward the door.

Raising one hand over his head in a half-ass wave, Rhys didn't look back.

"Hey!" Wolfe's deep baritone rang out behind him, but Rhys continued out the door and into the warm evening air.

He had something important to take care of in the morning anyway. Might as well call it an early night.

23

WHAT. THE EVER-LOVING. FUCK.

Wolfe set Amy aside when Rhys walked out the door without so much as a backward glance.

"Give me a minute," he told her, then followed the sheriff out the door.

Rhys was already climbing into his truck when Wolfe spotted him.

"What the fuck? Where you goin'?" he called out.

The son of a bitch had the nerve to shut his damn truck door. Wolfe had to wait for him to lower the fucking window.

"You got a curfew or somethin'?" Wolfe asked, scanning Rhys's face to see if he could read him.

"Got an early mornin' tomorrow."

"Tomorrow's Sunday," Wolfe informed him.

"Some of us work on Sunday," he said defensively.

Wolfe put his hand on the door and moved closer. "What the hell's your deal?"

"*Me*?" Rhys's expression hardened. "I'm goin' home, Wolfe. What the fuck do you want me to do? Sit in the goddamn bar and stare at you and Amy from across the room? No fuckin' thank you. I'll pass. But happy fuckin' birthday."

Wolfe had no idea what had gotten into the man these past few days, but something was clearly bothering him. While Wolfe had tried to include him in any plans he'd made with Amy, Rhys had been coming up with one excuse after another.

Taking a deep breath, he considered all the things he wanted to say, but he opted to keep them to himself. He'd never been big on complications or drama and he damn sure didn't intend to start now.

"Fine," he said with a sigh, releasing the door. "Later."

Without a word, Rhys tore out of the parking lot, his tires kicking up gravel. Wolfe turned to see Amy standing near the door, watching him.

"Is he okay?"

Wolfe shrugged. "No fuckin' clue."

"What did he say?"

"Nothin'."

Amy studied his face, concern forming a deep groove in her forehead. "Are you gonna go talk to him?"

"Fuck no." Why the hell would he do that? If Rhys wanted to play childish games, he could do so alone.

When Wolfe reached for Amy's hand, she pulled back.

"What the hell?" He stared down at her. "You're gonna pull this shit, too?"

Amy flinched like he'd backhanded her. Of course, he then felt like an asshole. Which was probably fitting. But it was his birthday, for chrissakes. Where the fuck had the night gone wrong? And why tonight of all nights?

Wolfe studied her face momentarily. He could see she was concerned about Rhys. And he couldn't really blame her. The sheriff was acting strange. Even for him.

With a sigh, Wolfe reached for her again. "Fine. When you get off work, we'll go talk to him."

She seemed to process that information and then nodded curtly. Wolfe wasn't sure what she was thinking, but he wasn't about to get into it with her here. It was his fucking birthday, damn it. Why the hell did everyone want to start a damn fight tonight?

Two hours later, they were closing down the bar. Literally.

Wolfe waited for Reagan and Amy to finish up, lock the doors, then join him outside. The two women spoke quietly, then Amy came over to where he stood by his truck.

"You ready?"

She nodded, but he noticed she wasn't smiling.

Placing his hand on her lower back, he walked her around to the passenger door, then helped her in the truck. What he wanted to do was strip the woman naked right here in the parking lot and spend the next hour of his life feasting on her.

Instead, they were likely going to get into an argument when Amy realized he wasn't going to go chasing after Rhys. He'd considered it for a while, but then came to the conclusion that they both needed some space. If the man wanted to talk, they could do so tomorrow. After they'd both slept on it for a little while.

"Did you have a good birthday?" Amy asked as he was pulling out of the parking lot.

"I did."

She was silent for a few minutes, her eyes scanning outside. "I thought we were gonna go talk to Rhys."

Wolfe shook his head. "He said he didn't wanna be bothered. He's gotta work in the mornin'."

Amy's eyebrows lowered, her eyes locked on him.

He cast a sideways glance her way, then turned his attention back to the road.

"I think we need to go to his house."

"And what?" he asked, his tone rougher than he intended. "Beg him to give me the time of day? Not interested."

Wolfe felt as though Rhys was purposely trying to push him away, and if that was the way the man wanted to play it, then Wolfe could certainly oblige him.

"Did you stop to think about how Rhys felt tonight?"

Jerking his attention to Amy, he tried to process her question. "What?"

"At Reagan's. When he was sitting on the opposite side of the room. Alone."

Rhys hadn't been alone, he'd been…

Son of a bitch.

Sighing, Wolfe pulled the truck off onto the side of the road. "What are you sayin'?"

Amy was staring at her hands clasped tightly in her lap. "He was by himself, Wolfe. While you were with your family. And me." She met his gaze in the dark cab of the truck. "Do you know the lengths he went to to help set up that party? It wasn't just me. He played a huge role in getting people together, convincing them to keep their mouths shut."

Tightening his grip on the steering wheel, Wolfe stared out the window. Honest to God, he hadn't even thought about it tonight. He'd been happy that Rhys was there, but he truthfully hadn't considered what it felt like for him to keep his distance. He'd thought Rhys was doing it on purpose, not because he felt he had to in order to keep this thing between them out of the public eye.

"Fuck."

"You need to go talk to him."

Amy was right. Wolfe did need to talk to Rhys.

And he knew exactly what he needed to say to the man.

AMY WASN'T SURE what was going on between Wolfe and Rhys, but she figured it had a lot to do with ego. That and maybe a little confusion about how this thing between the three of them was going to play out.

There was no doubt about it, she'd seen the hurt in Rhys's eyes tonight when he'd been sitting alone at the back of the bar. And it had damn near broken her heart not to be with him. She wanted to be with both men. Not just Wolfe and not just Rhys. She hadn't signed on to this thing one on one, and she didn't like the fact that they couldn't go out in public together. Although it was an unconventional setup, for Amy, it only seemed to work if the three of them were together. She hadn't given much thought to why that was, but she felt it deep inside.

Sure, she would go along with it if she had to—if this was what both men wanted—but that didn't mean she liked it. So, when it came to their private spaces, she didn't see why the three of them couldn't spend their time together.

She was surprised that Wolfe didn't call Rhys to give him a heads-up that they were coming. Instead, he pulled his truck back out onto the road, only this time he turned in the opposite direction. *Toward* Rhys's house.

They drove in silence, and Amy felt the nervous tension ratchet up a few notches the closer they got to Rhys's house. She could practically feel the emotion bubbling inside Wolfe, and she wanted to ask him what he was feeling, what he intended to say when he saw Rhys, but she managed to keep her thoughts to herself. One thing she had noticed about both Rhys and Wolfe was that neither man was big on conversation. Not the deep, personal kind, anyway.

As usual, when they pulled into the driveway and he shut off the truck, Wolfe climbed out first, then came around to her side and opened her door for her. She grabbed his hand, linking their fingers together as he marched toward the front door.

Before Wolfe knocked, the door opened and Rhys stood in the open doorway, no shirt, no boots, just a pair of jeans riding low on his hips.

The man really was a fine specimen. Sleek, muscular, sexy. He made her mouth water.

"Not done readin' me the riot act?" Rhys questioned, leaning his shoulder against the doorjamb.

Knowing these two were going to go toe to toe, Amy released Wolfe's hand, marched right up to Rhys, and waited until he looked at her. When he did, she reached up, jerked his head down, and kissed him right on the mouth. She didn't let it linger, though, choosing to release him before sidestepping him and going inside. If they wanted to act like fools, they could come find her when they were finished.

Taking a seat on the leather couch, Amy made sure she had a front-row view of the showdown about to take place on the porch. Both men had squared off, staring at one another. She could feel the waves of emotion pouring from each of them although she wasn't exactly sure what emotion that was. Anger, frustration … maybe love. Who knew. But sooner or later, they were going to have to man up and figure this out.

Otherwise, this thing between them was going to detonate long before it ever hit solid ground.

And wasn't that going to suck?

Because one thing Amy knew with absolute certainty…

She'd fallen in love.

With two stubborn men.

RHYS WAS SURPRISED to see Wolfe and Amy on his doorstep.

He figured their arrival probably had more to do with Amy insisting they solve this problem rather than let it fester. He seriously doubted Wolfe would've backed down quite so easily.

Rhys was gearing up to say something, but Wolfe beat him to the punch.

With two steps, the big man closed the distance between them. Rhys held his ground when Wolfe reached for him, surprised when Wolfe wrapped his big hand around the back of Rhys's neck and pulled him closer.

"I don't wanna do this," Wolfe said, his voice low, tone rough. "I'm not gonna fight with you."

"Who said you had to?" Rhys countered.

"I'm sorry," Wolfe stated firmly.

Rhys pulled back, meeting those dark green eyes. "For what?"

"For makin' you feel like an outsider."

Okay, so Rhys had been gearing up to accuse Wolfe of not knowing what the hell was going on. Clearly he didn't have a leg to stand on because Wolfe had nailed it right on the head. And damn it to hell, it took all the wind right out of Rhys's sails. Not that he wanted to fight with the man, but he had felt like an outsider.

And not just tonight.

Wolfe leaned in, his hand still cupping the back of Rhys's neck, their foreheads touching.

"That wasn't my intention. Not by a long shot."

Rhys took a deep breath, released it.

"I told you," Wolfe continued, "I don't know how this fucking works. I don't know what I'm supposed to do or say … or … fuck. I don't even know what I'm supposed to *feel*."

Those words shocked Rhys momentarily.

"But I know one goddamn thing," Wolfe growled, moving even closer, their lips practically touching. "I'm not about to let you shut me out. I'm all in where you and Amy are concerned. I want every damn thing you'll give me. Not just tonight. Not just tomorrow night. I want every goddamn night, Rhys. From here on out."

Swallowing hard, Rhys fought the emotion that clogged his throat. He hadn't been sure what he'd wanted from Wolfe. Not even what he'd wanted the man to say. However, this was a damn good start.

"I don't know how it works, either," Rhys admitted.

He knew he felt something for Wolfe and Amy. Whether it was love or simply lust, he hadn't yet figured that out, but it was serious, whatever it was. It was the very reason he'd needed time and space. To think. To work it out in his head. To come to terms with it.

"We can figure that out together," Wolfe whispered.

They could. But that would require them to talk about it, and Rhys damn sure wasn't good at that. He'd never been the kind to open up. Having had a hard-ass for a father, Rhys had learned long ago to keep his feelings locked up tight. He didn't know how to express himself, and half the time, he didn't even know what he fucking wanted.

But he knew what he wanted right now.

Wolfe and Amy.

That was what felt right to him.

This.

Here.

These two people with him. They made him feel whole. Complete.

"So, does that mean y'all are gonna kiss and make up?"

Rhys grinned, reaching for Amy when she moved up beside him, her cool hand sliding over his bare chest.

"Is that what you want us to do?" Wolfe asked, pulling back.

"Oh, yeah."

"Well, we should probably take this party inside then," Wolfe suggested.

Rhys stepped back, keeping Amy locked to his side as Wolfe moved inside the house. He shut and locked the door behind them. When he turned around, he found Wolfe standing as close as he'd been on the porch. Only this time, neither of them said a word before Wolfe's mouth crashed down on Rhys's.

An overwhelming surge of adrenaline powered through his veins, fueled by a desperate, all-consuming need and something a hell of a lot stronger. He grabbed Wolfe, fisting his shirt as he pulled him closer, letting the kiss consume him. The way Wolfe plundered his mouth stole his breath and all of his thoughts.

Realizing he was still holding on to Amy, Rhys managed to break the kiss, but as soon as he did, her mouth was on his. Or maybe it was vice versa.

Her soft moan vibrated through his entire body and he grabbed for her, lifting her until she had no choice but to wrap her legs around him. Once she was securely against him, Rhys carried her to his bedroom, then deposited her on his bed.

Amy chuckled as she got to her knees, pulling her mouth free from Rhys's.

"I know it's after midnight," she whispered, "but you think we could pretend it's still Wolfe's birthday for a little while longer?"

Rhys felt the smile tugging at his lips while it grabbed hold of his heart. This woman never ceased to amaze him. He felt as though she was what he'd been waiting for his entire life.

And okay, yeah. He probably owed Wolfe that much.

"What'd you have in mind?"

They both turned to look at Wolfe. The man's eyes were dark with desire as he watched them, one shoulder leaning against the wall, hands in his pockets as though he was completely unaffected.

Right.

The bulge in his jeans said otherwise.

"Don't mind me," he said gruffly. "I certainly don't mind watchin'."

"I think it's my turn to watch."

Rhys's attention turned to Amy instantly.

She smiled shyly. "What?"

"You wanna watch, darlin'?" Wolfe sauntered toward them.

"I do."

Rhys glanced back at Wolfe.

"Come here, Sheriff."

There wasn't an ounce of request in Wolfe's gravelly tone. Without thinking, Rhys turned to face the sexy cowboy who had driven all the way to Rhys's house in an attempt to salvage this thing they had. He wasn't sure what the next steps were after tonight, but right now, Rhys knew exactly what he wanted.

And he damn sure wasn't about to do anything to jeopardize that.

24

THE SECOND WOLFE'S eyes landed on Rhys out on that front porch, he knew that this thing between them was about to explode. He'd spent the past few weeks twining his world with theirs to the point he knew he wanted them in his life. Permanently.

Not that he was the type to ever think about the future or anything long-lasting, but the mere thought of losing either one of them damn near made him crazy. Tonight had been a hell of a lot harder than he'd let on. He had wanted to spend his birthday with Amy and Rhys. They were the brightest points in his life right now and without them he felt empty. Lost.

And this ... the intense lust that coursed through his veins, that ignited like diesel fuel when they were together was only a fraction of it.

Wolfe came to stand between Rhys's legs, staring down at the man as he sat on the edge of the bed. Unable to help himself, he ran his hand down the side of Rhys's face, the rough stubble abrading his palm as he studied him, tried to read his mind.

Love.

That was what Wolfe felt for Rhys and Amy. Strong, powerful, all-consuming love. Something he'd never felt for one person, let alone two. Not like this. It was a need, a hunger, a desperate yearning that only seemed to be sated when he was with them. And he was serious when he said he was all in. He wanted it all.

Rhys's eyes were searching his face in turn, and Wolfe met and held his gaze as he slipped his hand behind Rhys's neck, shifting higher and palming the back of his head as he leaned down.

When their lips met, Wolfe forced himself to take this slow. As hot as the fire inside him was burning, he didn't want to rush this. He still remembered the first night he was with Rhys. The two of them alone. It had been more than he'd anticipated. Truth was, it had scared him a little. Made him want more than he knew he should want.

And though he'd found the same feelings churned when he was with Amy, he could never imagine his life with one and not the other. He needed both of them.

Amy moved closer, kneeling behind Rhys, her hands on his shoulder, her breasts pressing against the back of Wolfe's hand. She was watching them and he fucking loved that.

Strong fingers tugged on his jeans and Wolfe pulled back, staring down the length of his body as Rhys unbuckled his belt, then released the button. He sucked in a breath when Rhys's hands slipped beneath his shirt, curling around his waist, warm fingers pressing into his flesh. He fucking loved the way Rhys touched him. So sure of himself, so strong, powerful. It settled him in a way he'd never expected.

Wanting to feel more of him, Wolfe reached behind his head and tugged his shirt up and off, tossing it to the floor. Rhys's hands moved higher. Rough, warm. Wolfe's abs contracted, his breath lodged in his chest as sensation after sensation consumed him. When Amy's hands joined Rhys's, Wolfe drew air deep into his lungs. Soft, smooth. So different, yet they both touched him with reverence, in a way that made Wolfe feel like the luckiest bastard on the planet.

Rhys leaned forward, pressing his lips to Wolfe's stomach. Wolfe kept Rhys's head cradled in his hand, holding him, desperate for more of his touch.

Amy pulled back, her eyes on them as she kept one hand on Wolfe, the other on Rhys. Wolfe fucking loved that she was always touching them, as though she didn't want to be too far away.

Wolfe pulled Rhys to his feet, then leaned in for a kiss while they both fumbled to get the other's jeans off. It took several minutes, but they managed to disrobe, still groping, still kissing.

When Wolfe laid Rhys back on the bed, Amy moved out of the way, but she didn't go far. Wolfe reached for her, placing his hand on her thigh, needing to feel her, too, wanting her close.

"Wolfe…" Rhys pulled him down, then crushed their mouths together. The kiss went from simmer to boil in seconds, and Wolfe was lost to it, drowning in the sensation of having Rhys beneath him. Warm, hard, eager.

His brain was processing all the things he intended to do to Rhys, but before he could put a plan in motion, Rhys flipped their positions. Wolfe found himself flat on his back, Rhys's weight blanketing him, their mouths once again coming together, tongues dueling, hands roaming. For a brief moment, he considered giving in to what he knew Rhys wanted.

"Let me," Rhys groaned. "Let me give you this."

Wolfe shook his head, instinct saying he couldn't give in. Not that he didn't necessarily want to, but he wasn't sure he could handle it. If he gave up that last piece of himself, he wasn't sure he'd ever get it back. And despite his feelings for Rhys and Amy, Wolfe wasn't sure he could allow himself to be that vulnerable. After all, Wolfe had admitted how he felt to Rhys—told him he was all in, that he wanted everything—but the man hadn't responded in kind.

Rhys pulled back and stared down at him. Wolfe met his gaze, held it.

"Let me love you, Wolfe."

The tightening in his chest threw him, the acceptance, the need. His self-control was being battered from all sides and he knew if Rhys pushed him, he would give in. He couldn't help it. He wanted everything these two were willing to give him. He'd always been the one in control, the one others depended on. To have them focused completely on him…

Rhys's mouth trailed down his jaw, his neck. Wolfe closed his eyes as the warmth moved south, pausing to torment his nipple before shifting lower. He sucked in a sharp breath when Rhys's mouth descended over his cock.

A warm body moved beside him and Wolfe opened his eyes to see Amy lying on her side, warm and so fucking beautiful. While Rhys teased him with his lips and tongue, Wolfe pulled Amy down to him, kissing her. Gently, leisurely. He forced himself to relax even when Rhys's mouth moved lower.

When Rhys's tongue slid lower, rimming his asshole, Wolfe's entire body jerked.

"Does it feel good?" Amy whispered, her eyes on his face, her fingers sliding down his cheek.

It amazed him that she understood his hesitation.

He nodded.

She kissed him again, and Rhys's mouth sent him into hyperspace, his tongue thrusting inside his ass, fucking gently. When his finger replaced his tongue, Wolfe sucked in air, his arm banding around Amy.

"Let it feel good," Amy said softly, her hand sliding over his chest, his neck, cupping his face.

He gave her a jerky nod, but he wasn't even sure what he was agreeing to. This was too much. If Rhys wasn't careful, Wolfe was going to come before they made it to the next phase of this birthday seduction.

Sensation after sensation slaughtered him as Rhys fucked him with one finger, then two. The man brushed that sensitive spot inside him and Wolfe damn near came off the bed.

"Oh, fuck … oh, fuck…" Wolfe drew air deep into his lungs.

As though he knew how close Wolfe was, Rhys paused, his mouth moving over Wolfe's cock once again.

"Naked," Wolfe commanded Amy. He needed her naked. He needed…

Amy nodded. While Rhys continued to blow him, Wolfe watched as Amy shed her clothes until she was gloriously naked. Then she was back on the bed, her hands on him. It was clear she was distracting him, and it was working.

"I want to feel you inside me," Amy told him, her lips sliding along his jaw. "Deep inside me."

Wolfe growled at the same time Rhys released him. He managed to roll over, pulling her beneath him. Without thinking about the repercussions, he plunged inside her before he even realized he didn't have a condom.

His entire body drew taut as the slick warmth of her pussy clasped him.

"Fuck … oh, my … fuck…" He didn't move, staring down at her. "I … oh, God, Amy." A deep, rumbling growl sounded from his chest, more animal than man. "Feels so fucking good."

A small smile formed on her mouth.

"Need a condom," he groaned, hating the thought of pulling out of her right now.

"It's okay," she whispered. "I trust you."

It wasn't necessarily about trust. Well, it was and it wasn't. Wolfe wasn't sure where this thing with them was going. If she got pregnant…

The idea of her pregnant with his baby had his body pulsing dangerously. He stared down at her.

"I'm on birth control," she said. "Implant."

Part of him was relieved, part disappointed. Still, he couldn't move. Warm hands gripped his hips, pulling him out of the erotic stupor as he felt the mattress shift behind him.

"Kiss me," Amy pleaded, pulling Wolfe's head down.

Welcoming the distraction, Wolfe gave in.

To her kiss, to Rhys. To everything.

For the first time in his life, he was handing the reins over to someone else.

And he realized then that they were the only two he'd ever trust to hold on and not let him go.

Ignoring Rhys behind him wasn't even an option. He heard the rustle of a condom being opened, felt the shift in the bed when he joined them. The way the man leaned over him, his warm, comforting weight didn't detract from the anxiety he felt as the blunt head of Rhys's cock pressed against his asshole.

Damn.

Fuck.

Amy shifted; the friction of the smooth walls of her pussy had ecstasy shooting through him. It was almost enough to ease the sharp pain that ignited deep within him when Rhys pushed inside. His body stretched painfully around the intrusion, but he focused on breathing, letting the pain morph into pleasure.

"So tight," Rhys groaned against his ear. "So fucking tight."

Amy moved again, rocking her hips, exquisite pleasure slamming through him as his cock lodged deeper inside her body.

The next thing Wolfe knew, they were both fucking him. He could do little more than remain poised above Amy, her sweet softness beneath him while Rhys plunged deeper and deeper into his ass with every thrust and retreat. His head was spinning, his brain obliterated by the intensity of it all. He didn't know whether he was coming or going. Wolfe could easily get addicted to this. Having both of them at once. It was fucking incredible. More so than he'd ever expected.

"Oh, fuck," he hissed when Amy pinched his nipple.

"More," she pleaded on a sigh. "Fuck me, Wolfe."

Holding his hips still, Wolfe redirected his cock so that he was fucking into her every time Rhys slammed into him. Sweat broke out along his forehead as he tried to hang on, desperate to make Amy come before he let go. He wasn't sure that was going to happen.

It was too much.

Not enough.

"Holy fuck," he growled. "Fuck … me…"

Amy's nails dug into his back as she cried out his name over and over. It took a second to realize she was coming. Once he did, Wolfe's body took over, his cock swelling, his balls drawing up tight to his body.

"Rhys … oh, fuck… Gonna…" Wolfe roared his release as it barreled through him, every cell in his body overwhelmed by sensation.

Seconds later, Rhys groaned behind him, his body stilling as he let himself go.

AMY MIGHT'VE BEEN slightly jealous of Wolfe.

She'd never seen something as incredibly beautiful as that man when he gave himself completely to someone else. It had stolen her breath and her heart at the same time. Then again, the look of pure ecstasy on Rhys's face when he'd claimed Wolfe… Amy had felt that right down in her soul.

So, maybe she was a little jealous of both of them.

And now, as she lay between Rhys and Wolfe, she was scared to close her eyes. She wanted this night to last forever. She'd never felt more complete than she did right then, with these two men. It all felt a little surreal. Although the L word hadn't been mentioned once tonight by anyone, Amy knew she'd been surrounded by it since she walked into Rhys's house. Truthfully, she hadn't felt anything even remotely close to this sort of emotion since before she met *him*.

Still, she had to wonder when this happy-go-lucky feeling was going to end. She knew it wouldn't last forever. As much as she wanted it, her life wasn't mapped out that way. She was still waiting for the other shoe to drop. And that shoe just so happened to be a two-hundred-pound monster she was waiting to jump out at her around every corner.

"Come here, girl," Wolfe whispered, tugging Amy until she was curled up against his side. He kissed her forehead. "Why can't you sleep?"

She shrugged, but the movement was limited because of her position. Resting her head on his chest, Amy draped her arm over his stomach, her hand resting on his chest. She loved when Wolfe held her like this. It made her feel safe, cherished.

"I'm sorry about tonight," he added, his voice low.

Hugging him tighter, she swallowed the lump in her throat and tilted her head slightly. When he bent his, Amy kissed him softly, letting her lips linger on his.

"It ended well," she told him.

"It did." He brushed his lips across hers. "You made my birthday perfect."

Her heart squeezed.

"Only one thing could've made it better," he whispered.

Amy lifted her head and stared into his eyes. "What's that?"

Wolfe pulled her head down, his warm breath fanning her ear. "If we'd both been inside you at the same time."

A shiver marched down her spine. The kind that left her body energized, her nipples hardening. But at the same time, trepidation coursed over her skin. The two of them taking her at the same time … that would be the ultimate possession. She wasn't sure she was ready for that. She might never be ready for that.

"Amy."

She realized he was cupping her face, staring back at her. She forced a smile.

"Not till you're ready," he said, his tone reassuring. "You call the shots here, believe it or not."

She studied his face for a moment. "How do you figure that?"

Amy felt Rhys shift, her eyes sliding over to him. He was awake, watching them.

"Because that's the way it is," Wolfe answered.

Amy shook her head. She wanted to believe it, but it didn't seem as though it could be real. Her calling the shots? She'd never called the shots.

"It's true." Rhys's voice was scratchy, deep. Sexy.

When she tried to pull away, Wolfe rolled her onto her back and both men lifted their heads, staring down at her. Amy watched them, dividing her attention between the two of them. She reached up and cupped each of their cheeks.

"I'm not sure how I got so lucky," she whispered.

Wolfe put his hand over hers, then turned his head and kissed her palm. "I'm the lucky one."

Rhys smiled, linking his fingers with hers and bringing them to his mouth. "That was my line."

"Where do we go from here?" she asked. She knew it was the question all three of them wanted an answer to. "I mean … we can't do what we did tonight for much longer." She shook her head, then looked at Rhys. "I don't want to pretend I'm not with you when we're out in public."

Rhys nodded. "I know."

That didn't sound as though he had an answer.

"So, is this it? We'll be together in private?" Amy didn't like the idea of that. "Sure, I get it. But it's … it's not what I want."

"I'm all in," Wolfe stated, his tone matter-of-fact. "I have nothin' to hide."

Amy looked at Rhys again. He didn't look quite as sure. Then again, Amy knew his job could be at stake. He was an elected official. She knew from what she'd heard that he was in his first year of his four-year term. That meant he might not make it to a second term and she knew he loved his job.

"Why does it have to be so hard?" she whispered.

"It's not," Wolfe replied, leaning down and pressing his mouth to hers. "It's not hard. Not hard at all."

Amy wished she could believe him, but she couldn't shake the feeling that they were both slipping out of her grasp. One second she felt on solid ground, the next as though the earth was crumbling beneath her.

She wanted to hold on to them. Not just in the moment, either.

More importantly, she wished Rhys would commit to them both.

Because without him being all in…

It wouldn't even matter.

RHYS WAS UP before Amy and Wolfe the following morning. He'd set his phone alarm to wake him after they'd fallen asleep. He'd slipped out of his own house, leaving the two of them asleep in his bed, and knowing they were there, in his home, in his bed… It had been difficult to leave. Not because he didn't want them there. On the contrary, he realized as he was slipping out of the house that he wanted to wake up to them every damn morning, to go to sleep next to them every night.

Like Wolfe, Rhys had realized he was all in.

At some point last night—or maybe it was this morning, he wasn't sure—Rhys had realized they were *it* for him. He would never want anyone else the way he wanted them.

Not that he had time to dwell on the state of his love life. He had agreed to meet Joanna Tannenbaum this morning regarding her unofficial Jane Doe case. She'd called about ten minutes ago to say she was running late and he tried not to let it bother him. Around these parts, people tended to be early, not coming up with excuses. But not everyone was from a small town.

So, he had agreed to meet her over at the diner, where he now was with a cup of coffee and slightly less patience. He knew it was a risk being out in the open, but since Wolfe would be at church, Rhys figured it was as safe as any place in town.

He knew instantly when the white Ford Taurus pulled into the parking lot that Joanna Tannenbaum had finally arrived. Rhys watched as she climbed out of her car, smoothed down her shirt, and straightened her sunglasses. She wasn't quite what he'd expected. Then again, he hadn't really known what to expect, but the woman who resembled a supermodel more than a detective certainly hadn't been it. Her blond hair was hanging over her squared shoulders, and the shoulder holster and badge weren't concealed.

When she stepped inside, she removed the dark shades and peered around. She caught Donna's attention, and a second later, she was being pointed in his direction.

Rhys stood and held out his hand to greet her. "Mornin'."

Her grip was firm. "I'm sorry I'm late, Sheriff."

"Not a problem." He motioned for her to sit and once she did, he took his seat.

Donna strolled over. "Can I get you some coffee?"

"Yes. Please. That would be great." She turned toward Rhys, then lowered her voice. "Thank you again for meeting with me."

Rhys nodded. "You mentioned a Jane Doe case."

"Yes." She turned toward Donna when the woman set a white mug in front of her, then poured the coffee. "Thank you."

Donna nodded, then disappeared.

"I'm sorry I couldn't do this over the phone, but it's"—she held Rhys's stare, her expression serious—"sensitive."

"How so?"

She swallowed hard, then reached for her purse. A second later, she pulled out a picture and pushed it across the table.

Rhys stared down into the familiar brown eyes of the woman he'd left in his bed just a short time ago. She looked different though. Her hair was board straight and dark. She wasn't smiling as she stood next to…

Leaning forward, he snapped his eyes to the detective. "Is that Chief Kelly Jackson?"

She nodded and took a deep breath. "About a year ago, Chief Jackson's girlfriend conveniently went to Pennsylvania to take care of her ailing grandmother."

No she didn't, but Rhys didn't say as much. He figured Detective Tannenbaum knew that already since she was sitting in front of him.

"It just so happened it was at the exact same time that a Jane Doe was left in a drainage ditch not far from here."

Rhys could tell she was watching his face to gauge his reaction. He didn't respond.

"Personally, I think Jane Doe and Amy Manning are one and the same."

Manning.

Her last name was Manning.

"And how do I play into this?" he asked.

"As you're aware, Jane Doe was found not far from here."

He nodded. "She was."

The detective sighed, clearly not happy that he wasn't willing to share information. Until he knew what her angle was, Rhys didn't intend to tell her anything.

"Oddly enough, Chief Jackson has visited Embers Ridge a few times in the past year."

Rhys sat up straight. "What?"

She nodded.

"Look," she finally said after sipping her coffee. "Something felt really off to me about the relationship that Chief Jackson had with Amy Manning. I've worked for him for quite a while, even before he became the police chief."

"When did he make chief?" Rhys knew it had been headline news out of Houston, but he didn't remember the time frame.

"Eleven months ago."

Well, that was definitely coincidental since Jane Doe had made the news almost thirteen months ago now.

"Chief Jackson and Amy were together for nearly five years," Detective Tannenbaum explained. "That's a long time to simply let someone go from your life. And that's exactly what he did. If your girlfriend of five years went to take care of a family member, wouldn't you expect her to come back?"

Rhys figured the question was rhetorical. And yes, he would.

"Before she just disappeared from his life, Jackson talked about her all the time. He seemed enthralled with her." Joanna brushed her hair back from her face. "Whether or not that was genuine is another story entirely. However, he did talk about her. And then suddenly, she's gone. Simply vanished from his life and he acted as though nothing happened."

"Did he mention they broke up when she left?"

"No. And that's the strangest part. According to the story that's traveled around, she simply went to take care of her grandmother, but she wasn't coming back."

"Were they married?"

She shook her head, then took another sip of her coffee. "No. In the beginning, he mentioned they would get married, but that died off about a year into their relationship."

"And you don't think she's in… Where'd you say? Pennsylvania?"

"No." Detective Tannenbaum rested her arms on the table. "I don't. For one, Amy Manning didn't have any living relatives."

"And you know this how?"

"Like I said, the relationship seemed off to me. I was introduced to her a couple of times at various functions and she stuck with me for whatever reason. Sweet girl. Very young. Almost naïve, I guess you could say. Anyway, when the man who seemed to be so in love with this woman simply let her go and didn't look back, I had to wonder."

Rhys continued to stare at her.

"I know what you're thinking," she said, a small smile forming on her mouth. "And no, I have no personal relationship with Kelly Jackson. Never have. I've worked for him for a long time, and to be honest, there's something about him that's off."

"Off how?"

"His demeanor. The man is the no-nonsense, take-no-shit sort of guy. He's a hard-ass, but when it comes to cops, he's fair. However, that's not the case when it comes to criminals. As a patrolman, he was feared. There have been stories about him. About incidents. No charges have ever stuck and he's risen in the ranks despite the rumors. But I think he's hiding a dark side."

The man was hiding the fact that he was a fucking monster.

"And what brings you to Embers Ridge?" He already knew the answer.

"I've kept my eye on the Jane Doe case. The fact that it never went anywhere concerned me. Like I said, it was too coincidental that his girlfriend disappeared at the same time Jane Doe appeared. So, I watched him and waited for him to screw up. It's inevitable. All criminals screw up eventually."

Rhys waited patiently for her to explain.

"He turned in an expense report. A gasoline charge. From here in Embers Ridge."

Son of a bitch.

"No, I shouldn't have been snooping, but—"

"It was too coincidental," he completed for her. He got it.

She nodded. "Honestly. I think Amy Manning is…"

The bells over the door jingled and Rhys looked up as Wolfe and Amy walked into the restaurant.

The detective glanced over at the same time she inhaled sharply and then finished her sentence. "…here in Embers Ridge."

Well, fuck.

25

WOLFE HADN'T EXPECTED Rhys to be home when he woke up. He knew the man had business to take care of this morning. He'd said as much. However, Wolfe damn sure hadn't expected Rhys to be sitting in the diner with a blond woman wearing a gun and a badge, either. The only point in Rhys's favor was the fact he didn't look happy to be there.

His eyes locked on Rhys's and he could see something that looked a hell of a lot like panic set in. Wolfe's gaze snapped to the woman.

Badge.

Gun.

Not from around here.

Fuck.

It didn't take brains to figure out what the hell was going on. The blond was staring at Amy, her eyes wide with recognition, which could only mean one thing.

Wolfe had royally fucked up this time. Bringing her here.

Son of a bitch.

"Amy?" the woman called out.

Wolfe instantly put his arm around Amy and turned to lead her back out the door, his brain working a million miles a second in an attempt to reverse this clusterfuck and get Amy out of there. Fast.

"Fuck," he grumbled.

"What's wrong? Who was that?" Amy asked.

"No idea, but I don't think this is somethin' you need to be in the middle of." Wolfe was going to fucking kill Rhys. How the fuck could he do this?

"What? Why?" Amy turned to look behind them, but Wolfe continued to usher her toward his truck.

"Amy! Please wait!" the woman called out from behind them.

Rhys was right behind her and it was clear they weren't getting out of there without a confrontation.

Wolfe's body coiled tight, his need to protect Amy fierce.

"What the fuck is goin' on?" Wolfe questioned, keeping his body positioned in front of Amy when he turned to face the woman. "How do you know her?"

Before she could answer, Rhys intervened. Wolfe couldn't hear what he said to the woman, but after a few words, he moved toward them, keeping his back to the mystery woman.

"What the fuck?" Wolfe kept his voice low, but it wasn't easy.

"Who is that?" Amy's voice trembled nearly as much as her hands. Clearly she'd figured out what was going on as well.

"She's…" Rhys took a deep breath, released it slowly. "She's a detective out of Houston."

Amy blanched, every ounce of color in her face draining away.

"What the fuck is wrong with you?" Wolfe yelled at Rhys. "How could you fucking do this? You brought the bastard right to her goddamn doorstep!" His hands were balled into fists and it took every ounce of his self-control not to punch the man.

"It's not what you think," Rhys said, his voice calm.

"The fuck it ain't," Wolfe snapped. "A goddamn Houston detective? Did he send her here?"

Amy's fingers dug into Wolfe's arm and he turned to face her. She was so pale, her hands trembling, her eyes wide.

Before Wolfe could get his arm around her, Rhys put his hands on her shoulders and leaned in.

"Breathe, baby," he whispered softly. "It's not what you think. She contacted me."

When Rhys peered up at him, Wolfe tried to gauge whether or not Rhys was lying. After all, the man hadn't said a fucking word about a detective from Houston contacting him. Nor had he mentioned meeting with her.

"She wanted to talk about a Jane Doe case," he explained, glancing between them. "I agreed to meet her this mornin' to hear her out." He stood tall. "I wasn't entirely sure it was about you, but yes, I suspected. However, I had no idea you'd show up here."

"It's the goddamn diner," Wolfe countered.

Rhys swallowed hard. "I thought I had some time. I thought you'd be at church."

"Time for what?" Wolfe didn't fucking understand.

"Did *he* send her?" Amy's voice trembled.

"No. Not that I can tell," Rhys admitted. "From what she says, she's lookin' into this case unofficially. She thought it was too much of a coincidence that Chief Kelly Jackson's longtime girlfriend up and went back to take care of her ailing grandmother at the same time a Jane Doe was found battered and nearly beaten to death a few hours away."

"Kelly Jackson?" Wolfe had no idea who that was. "Is that his name?"

They both looked at Amy. It took her a moment, but she finally nodded.

Rhys clarified, "He's the recently promoted chief of police in Houston."

Fucker.

"But that's not the worst part."

Wolfe didn't know if he could handle hearing anything else.

"She's concerned because…" Rhys took a deep breath. "She has proof that he's been here. In Embers Ridge."

"Oh, my God." Amy leaned into Wolfe, and he instantly put his arm around her, tugging her close to his side. "Why is she here? What does she want?" Her words came out fast and clipped, her panic evident.

"I want to bring that bastard to justice."

All three of them turned their attention to the woman now standing a few feet behind them.

Wolfe had to give her credit. The woman had balls. She met Wolfe's gaze head on, held it. "My name's Joanna Tannenbaum and I'm a Houston detective. I've worked under Kelly Jackson for years." She looked at Amy. "Your sudden exit from his life made me suspicious. That's the only reason I'm here. I've been tracking this for the past nine months. When I found out he'd visited here, the red flags went off. I knew it wasn't a coincidence at that point. Rather than approach you directly, I wanted to meet with the sheriff. See what we could do to … protect you."

"So he knows where I am? That I'm alive?" Amy asked, her short fingernails digging into Wolfe's arm, her hands trembling.

"I'd say it's highly likely. And if he doesn't, it's not because he hasn't tried to find you," Joanna explained.

Leaning down, Wolfe pressed his mouth close to Amy's ear, speaking only loud enough for her to hear. "He won't hurt you, Amy. I swear to you. I won't let him."

Her grip on him tightened and he tugged her closer, glancing over at Rhys. "I need to get her somewhere she feels safe. This ain't it."

Rhys nodded in agreement.

"Come on." Wolfe ushered Amy into the truck and offered one final look back at Rhys and the detective.

"What if he followed her?" Amy questioned when he climbed in the driver's seat after helping her in the truck. "What if he's here?"

Knowing he couldn't answer her questions, Wolfe decided to call in backup. Grabbing his phone, he dialed Lynx's number first.

"What's up, hoss?"

"I need you to meet me at Cooter's. I want you to get my dad, too."

"Everything cool?"

"No," he said firmly. "But I'll explain everything when y'all get there." Wolfe pulled out onto the main road. "Shit. And Lynx, grab Reagan while you're at it. I want her aware of what's goin' on, too. Since she's stayin' at Amy's place, she could be in danger."

"I don't like the sound of this one fucking bit. But I'll corral 'em all and meet you there."

"Thanks."

Wolfe hung up and dialed Rhys's number. "All right. Here's the plan. I'm takin' her out to Cooter's place. If you trust that detective, I suggest you grab her and meet us out there. Just make sure you're not followed."

"Will do. See you in a few."

Tossing the phone in the center console, Wolfe reached for Amy's hand. He linked his fingers with her icy-cold ones. He fucking hated that he could do nothing to ease her fears. Nothing yet, anyway.

"Amy?"

"Yeah?"

"No one's gonna let that bastard get close to you. You hear me?"

She nodded, but Wolfe could tell she wasn't convinced.

Good thing actions spoke louder than words, because Wolfe was about to show his girl just what happened when an outsider threatened one of their own.

IT WAS A good thing Amy hadn't eaten anything. She knew for a fact she wouldn't have been able to keep it down. Not while the icy ribbons of fear were latching onto her insides, clutching painfully tight.

Even now as she sat in Wolfe's uncle's house, a solid wall of men between her and the outside world, she couldn't stop shaking. It hadn't helped that she'd had to repeat her story so that the rest of Wolfe's family understood what they were up against. And just like the first time she'd relayed the details, she watched grown men hover close to the edge of a killing rage. She'd never felt more protected than she did here, but she knew Kelly. They didn't. The man was a monster. A powerful one, at that.

The arrival of the detective had sent her world into a spiral. If Kelly didn't know where she was before, he definitely did now. Not that Amy was disillusioned enough to think he hadn't figured it out long before now. She'd always suspected he was watching her. It seemed like a perverse game he would play.

The question was, when would he show his hand?

"Hey, you okay?"

Amy jumped when Reagan put her hand on her arm.

"I'm sorry. I didn't mean..."

When Reagan tried to pull back, Amy stopped her with a hand on hers. "No. I'm sorry. I'm just a little jumpy."

Reagan had been great through all of this. She had sat right beside Amy, holding her hand through the worst of the story just like she had the first time. It was clear she was as angry as the rest of the people filling the small house, but she was hiding it better than they were.

"I'd like to say I'm fine," she said honestly. "But I'd be lying."

"You're safe now," Reagan assured her, nodding toward the group of men huddling across the room. "Look at them. They're ready to start a war for you."

Amy wanted to believe her regarding her safety. She wanted to think that Kelly couldn't get to her, but she knew him. He would stop at nothing to protect himself. And unfortunately, she was a liability.

"I'm down. Bring that fucker on!" Lynx growled, drawing everyone's attention.

Amy glanced at Reagan, but obviously, she didn't know what they were talking about.

Rhys and Wolfe both looked directly at her. Then more eyes turned her way.

A sense of foreboding crawled over her skin.

Amy knew whatever their plan was, she was not going to like it.

Not one bit.

RHYS'S GUT CHURNED.

He couldn't fucking believe how this had escalated so quickly.

What should've been a brief informational meeting with a detective out of Houston had turned into an all-out battle between the Caines and the asshole who'd tormented Amy for years.

The worst part, Rhys was torn between upholding the law, bringing the bastard to justice, and letting the Caines loose on the fucker. He knew what the right thing to do was, but the latter sounded a hell of a lot more satisfying. For one, there was nothing to say that they could bring this asshole to his knees.

"Can I talk to you for a second?" Joanna asked, her tone soft, concerned.

Rhys turned his attention to her.

"Outside?"

He nodded, then glanced over to Wolfe to let him know. The big man nodded once, then headed toward Amy.

Rhys followed the detective out onto the shaded front porch.

Joanna leaned against the railing and faced him. "I don't mean to pry and you certainly don't have to tell me, but I was…" She glanced at the screen door. "I was wondering about the dynamic here." Her aqua-blue gaze met his again.

Cocking an eyebrow, he waited for her to elaborate. He wasn't sure which dynamic she was referring to, although he had an idea.

"I'm not judging, so don't jump to that conclusion. I just need to know the relationships that are goin' on here. Initially, I thought Wolfe was with Amy, but..."

Rhys glanced out at the acres of dry grass blowing in the breeze. The sound of the screen door opening and closing behind him didn't have him looking back. He knew who it was.

Joanna's eyes flew to the newcomer, and a second later, Wolfe's hand was on Rhys's shoulder and Amy was standing beside him, her arm sliding around his waist.

"Is that enough of an answer for you?" he asked.

"So, the three of you...?"

"Love each other," Amy told her.

"Okay, then." Joanna smiled. "Honest. I'm not judging."

"Good. Now, what's the plan?" Wolfe inquired, squeezing Rhys's shoulder.

More boots sounded on the porch behind him, and Rhys figured the others had followed them outside. As much as he feared what this relationship would do to his career, Rhys truly didn't give a shit what anyone thought. Amy was right. They loved each other. And if they were going to protect Amy, it was time to focus on other things.

Rhys turned toward Amy. "Joanna believes that the best way to tackle this issue is to face it head on."

"What does that mean?"

He hated how pale she was, how scared she was, and he wanted to erase the fear from her eyes forever. Although the plan was risky, Rhys knew it was their best option. He glanced over to Joanna, allowing her to explain it.

"Amy, I respect the fact that you're moving on with your life." Joanna glanced at Wolfe, Rhys, then the others. "And it's clear you've got a strong family behind you. But if you want to make this go away forever, you are going to have to face this."

Amy was already shaking her head.

"Hear me out," Joanna added, her tone soft, soothing. "What Kelly Jackson did to you was…" Joanna shook her head. "It was horrifying. He needs to be brought to justice, to be punished for what he did."

"I just want him to go away," Amy pleaded.

"We know you do, honey," Rhys said, turning to face her. He put his hands on her shoulders and stared into her eyes. "And we can make that happen, but it's gonna require you to face him again."

She shook her head, then pressed her face against his chest. Rhys cradled her head and held her close. He could feel the eyes of the others on him. This was the first time he'd touched her since he arrived at the house. Wolfe had remained by her side and Rhys had kept his distance. He was tired of keeping his distance. He damn sure wasn't going to stand back and let her face this without him.

"You can continue to hide out here," Joanna added, "but as you said, he tried to kill you once already. He won't let you go."

"Then why hasn't he come for her yet?" Reagan asked.

Joanna shrugged. "I can't answer that. I don't know what he's up to."

"He's playing a game with me," Amy said, her words muffled against Rhys's chest. He released her enough so she could turn, but he didn't let her go. "It's something Kelly would do. He said I wouldn't live without him."

"I figure," Joanna inserted, "with his new role as police chief, he's got a lot on his plate."

"And he's the type who wants to handle things himself," Amy noted.

Joanna nodded. "Which means he's waiting until not so many eyes are on him."

"So, he'll come for her eventually?" Reagan asked.

"I think so, yes."

"And we avoid that how?" Lynx asked.

Rhys knew the man would prefer to greet the bastard with the business end of his shotgun, but that wasn't an option.

"My suggestion is that Amy go public with her story."

"No!" Amy yelled, instantly pushing away from Rhys. "I can't. I won't. He'll… Oh, my God. He'll kill me."

"He won't get near you," Calvin declared, stepping out from the group.

Rhys watched as Wolfe's father moved around to face Amy.

"You understand that, girl?" His tone was gruff, his demeanor serious. "We won't let him. This"—he motioned with his hand—"is your family now. And we protect our own. That bastard won't get close enough to touch you ever again."

Rhys knew Calvin believed every word he said. Rhys only hoped that was true.

Tears were streaming down Amy's face, and Rhys knew it gutted every man standing on that front porch.

"Come here, kid," Calvin said, motioning for her to come to him.

When Amy stepped away from Rhys and Wolfe, Calvin enveloped her in his burly arms, hugging her tight. "I promise you, girl. No one will hurt you ever again. Not on my watch."

"Or mine," Lynx stated.

"Or mine," Wolfe added.

"Or mine," Cooter and Reagan said at the same time.

"See? We've all got your back." Calvin pulled back, looking down at her face and tilting her chin up so she was looking at him. "Whatever you decide to do, you've got us right behind you."

More sobs tore through Amy, and Wolfe reached for her, pulling her against him. Rhys couldn't stop himself from holding her, too. Once again, several pairs of eyes were on them, but he didn't care.

"All right, Sheriff," Calvin addressed him directly. "I need to have a word with you."

Rhys had been expecting some sort of confrontation. Especially now that they'd come out with their relationship.

Meeting Wolfe's gaze, Rhys nodded, then watched as Wolfe led Amy back inside, Lynx, Reagan, and Joanna following.

A second later, he was facing Calvin and Cooter.

"I just want to make something crystal clear," Calvin said in that same gruff tone Rhys was used to.

Here it came. The warning he'd always expected.

"You've done a remarkable job as sheriff of this town."

Rhys shook his head slightly, trying to clear his ears. Had he heard him right?

"And we fully expect you to continue keepin' things in line." Calvin nodded toward the house. "This thing that the three of you have goin'…" Calvin met his eyes straight on. "It's the most important thing. I want you to remember that. Whatever happens, family matters."

Rhys nodded.

"And if you're with my son, then that makes you family."

Rhys's stomach had dropped to his toes. He hadn't expected that. In fact, he'd expected one or both of them to warn him off of Wolfe and Amy.

"And the feud between the families?" Rhys asked because it had to be said.

Cooter laughed, a loud, rough sound. "Your old man fabricated that feud, son. Back when we were kids."

Rhys frowned.

"He never told you?" Calvin asked.

Rhys shook his head.

Cooter laughed again, glancing at Calvin, then at Rhys. "It was over a girl. In eighth grade."

That pulled a smile from Rhys. He couldn't help it.

Of course, it made sense. His father had always thought he was top dog. If some teenage girl had chosen a Caine over him… Yeah, that made perfect sense.

"So we're good, then?" Calvin asked.

Rhys nodded.

"Good. Now, the three of you need to talk it over and let us know what you wanna do where this asshole's concerned. We're behind you on this." He leaned in. "And you'll understand that Amy makes the decision here and we're all here to watch her back. No matter what."

"I understand. And I wouldn't have it any other way."

"Now come on. It's fuckin' hot out here."

With that, Rhys followed the two men back inside.

26

WOLFE OPTED TO take Amy back to his place so that the three of them could discuss their plan in private. Now that his family was fully on board and they knew what was going on, he managed to relax. A little. Knowing they had his back helped.

Granted, it didn't seem to do a damn thing for Amy. When they'd walked in his front door a few minutes ago, she had started pacing the floor and hadn't stopped.

She shook out her hands as she stared at the floor. Back and forth. Back and forth. Wolfe sat on the couch, Rhys in the chair. He was getting dizzy watching her, but he could see her brain was working overtime, and he damn sure didn't want to interrupt her thought process. Whatever she decided to do, he was behind her. They would get through this. One way or another.

Finally she turned to him.

"What do you think I should do?"

He should've known she would ask him that. "Honey, I can't make that decision for you."

"Do you think the detective is right? That I should fight him?"

Wolfe shrugged. "It's not a bad idea. If you bring it up publicly, he's no longer the boogey man. He can't lurk in the dark, because someone's gonna have their eye on him."

Amy nodded. "Doesn't necessarily mean I'm any safer."

No, it didn't. Considering the kind of power the chief of police had—especially the chief of police of the largest city in the state—the guy could probably pull a lot of strings and make some serious puppets dance.

"On the flip side," Rhys added, "it won't be pretty, Amy. Once you make that accusation, people are gonna come out of the woodwork with questions. Your life will no longer be private."

"So you think I should stay quiet?" she asked Rhys.

"That's not what I'm sayin'. I just want you to consider all the facts. Do I want that bastard to go down for what he did? You're damn right I do. And I'll stand right behind you the entire way."

"What if people don't believe me?"

Wolfe had already thought about that. "There will be some people who don't. There's nothin' you can do but be honest."

Amy faced him directly. "Do *you* believe me?"

Wolfe got up from his spot on the couch and walked right over to her. He tipped her head back and stared right in her eyes. "Every word, baby. No one here doubts you at all. But that doesn't mean someone won't."

She shook her head. "I don't want to come out with it. I just don't. I want to go about my life without having him in it."

Unfortunately, they all knew that wasn't going to happen. No matter which decision she made. If the detective was right and Kelly Jackson had visited Embers Ridge, the man knew where Amy was. It was only a matter of time before he played his hand.

"Do I have to do this right now?"

Rhys joined them. "No. You don't. I'll make sure my department is aware of the potential danger to you and ask my deputies to keep their eyes open."

"And my family will keep an eye on you at all times." No way would any of them not be vigilant from this point forward.

Amy sighed. "So, basically, I'm gonna be a prisoner again."

Wolfe frowned. "No. Not at all."

"Will I be able to go anywhere without one of you worrying about me?"

Fuck.

"What about sleeping at night? I'm not sure I'll even be able to."

She would if she was with them. Wolfe would make sure of it if he had to stand guard over her every damn night.

Not that he wanted it to come to that. For Amy's sake. She'd been through enough already.

He fucking hated this shit. He hated all of it. He wanted to find this fucking bastard and beat him within an inch of his life and make him suffer for what he did to Amy. For what he was still doing to her.

"My point exactly," she added when neither of them spoke. She glanced between them. "On a more positive note, I think we came out to Wolfe's family today."

That pulled a smile from him. They had definitely done that.

"Do you think word will get out to the rest of the town?" Amy appeared genuinely concerned.

"Not unless the detective says somethin'," Wolfe answered. He knew his family. They weren't the gossipy type. Not when it came to things like that, anyway.

"Which I seriously doubt she'll do." Rhys glanced between them. "Lynx drove her to the diner. She had to head back to Houston."

"Do you think she'll confront Kelly?" Amy looked fearful of the notion.

"Doubtful. She's been keepin' this off the books for a reason," Rhys said. "I really believe her motives are pure. She's a detective and Kelly brought out those instincts in her. She followed a lead and it led her here. I truly believe she's lookin' out for you."

"Maybe he's forgotten all about me," Amy mused, her eyes dropping to the floor.

Wolfe knew she didn't really believe that. No one believed that.

Rhys stepped closer. "He deserves to pay for what he did, Amy. Too often victims of domestic violence don't come forward. Their abusers go without punishment. And I get why they don't. Fear, shame. Those are some powerful emotions. They cause people to pretend nothing happened when in reality, they suffered. Their abuser deserves to be punished."

Amy peered up at him.

"He won't stop," Rhys continued. "If he did this to you, he'll do it to someone else. Hell, it's possible he already has. Considering his age, you were probably not his first victim, either."

Wolfe watched as Amy processed that information. Her eyes widened in horror, and Wolfe could feel her pain. He knew she didn't want to even think about that man hurting someone else the way he'd hurt her.

"I need some time to think about this," Amy finally said, her eyes fixed on Wolfe's face.

"You let us know when you're ready," Wolfe told her, pulling her against him and wrapping his arms around her. "And what you decide. We're not goin' anywhere."

Amy nodded, her gaze bouncing back and forth between him and Rhys.

When she pulled back, Wolfe reluctantly let her go.

"And I don't want either of you thinking you have to save me."

Those words felt like a slap to the face. Wolfe took a single step back. "Why would you say somethin' like that?"

Amy didn't move. "Because … that's how it feels. I've burdened you both with my problem since day one. And I've seen the way you are. Both of you. You're looking to save me." She shook her head as though that made no sense. "No one can save me from him."

"I… Are…? Holy *fuck*." Hell, he couldn't even form a sentence. He was completely thrown by her words. Did she honestly believe that he only wanted to play the hero here?

"Is that what you really think?" Rhys asked, his tone ringing with the same confusion that Wolfe felt.

She glanced between the two of them before finally nodding her head and looking down at the floor.

Taking a step closer, Wolfe tilted her chin up, forcing her to look him in the eyes once again. "You really don't get it, do you?"

"Get what?"

"Goddamn, Amy. You *don't* get it. I'm not tryin' to *save* you…" Wolfe held her gaze, his voice hoarse with emotion. "I'm tryin' to *love* you."

THOSE WERE QUITE possibly the most powerful words Amy had ever heard.

And the conviction behind them…

She hadn't meant to hurt Wolfe or Rhys by saying that they didn't need to save her. But that was how she felt. As though she'd become a charity case. At least in the past few hours, anyway. Everyone was coming together to figure out a way to fix this for her. How could she not think that?

What they didn't understand was Amy couldn't be saved. Not from him. She knew he was out there, probably counting down the minutes until he snatched her. She knew him. He would enjoy playing this game. It was what he always wanted, for her to fear him. No matter how many people stood between her and him, Kelly Jackson would find her again.

Oh, she was certainly more than grateful that Wolfe and Rhys and the people in this town wanted to help her, but she didn't want that to be their only reason for being with her.

As she looked up at Wolfe, then at Rhys, Amy realized one thing. Obviously, she had jumped to conclusions.

The expressions on their faces were of complete shock and anguish. As though she'd called them every bad name in the book.

"Did you hear me?" Wolfe questioned, his eyes hard.

She nodded, not moving when he took a step closer.

"I *love* you, Amy."

Her breath hitched, the words making her heart constrict. She wanted to believe them. God, she even prayed they were true. Never had she been happier than when she was with Wolfe and Rhys.

"I don't want to be the goddamn hero. I want to *love* you. And yes, I want to protect you, but that comes with the territory. It's who I am. Who I've always been." Wolfe looked over at Rhys. "And you. That goes for you, too."

Wolfe shifted, moving directly over to Rhys. Amy could see the tension in his arms, his back. He was coiled tight, the spring inside him dangerously close to breaking. She held her breath, waiting for what he would say.

"I fucking love you. There. I said it. I fucking know exactly how I feel. Exactly what I want." He glanced back at Amy. "This"—he waved his arm to encompass the three of them—"is exactly what I want. Do y'all get that?"

He was yelling, but Amy could tell he was more frustrated than angry. She understood that because this was all so confusing.

Well.

Not entirely.

There was one thing she knew for certain.

She waited until Wolfe looked at her again.

"I love you, too," she whispered, still standing a few feet away. Scared to move, scared to breathe. She met Rhys's gaze next. "And I love you, too."

Maybe it was all happening too quickly, but she knew you couldn't put a time limit on love. It happened when it was supposed to happen. Did she trust her heart?

With these two men, she did.

Sure, her choices hadn't always been spot on, but with Wolfe and Rhys, Amy knew this was where she was meant to be.

However, she realized Rhys hadn't said anything. Not one single word.

She glanced over at him. She and Wolfe were both staring at him, waiting for him to say something. She could see he wanted to.

"Goddammit," he grumbled.

She saw the moment he gave in to what he was feeling. He held out his arm to her, and Amy moved toward them. Then Rhys was jerking Wolfe to him, their lips fusing together as Amy was pulled against them.

Her heart swelled dangerously large. It felt as though it would break right out of her chest. Her stomach dropped; every cell in her body was invigorated by what she felt for these two men.

Just like them, she was all in.

And for the first time in what felt like forever, Amy wasn't scared.

Not of them.

Not of herself.

Not of her decisions or of what tomorrow would bring.

Not of the possession that she felt when they looked at her.

This was what she wanted.

It was vastly different than anything she'd ever known.

It was…

Perfect.

RHYS HAD NEVER seen Wolfe like this.

Well, not when he wasn't engaged in a knock-down drag-out, anyhow.

He was practically vibrating.

Wolfe ripped his mouth from Rhys's, then gripped his head, holding him tightly, their eyes locked.

"Tell me," Wolfe demanded.

Rhys stared back, swallowing past the lump in his throat.

"Fucking tell me," Wolfe growled. "I want to hear it." Wolfe shook his head. "No. I *need* to hear it."

Rhys knew exactly what Wolfe wanted to hear. And if he was honest with himself, the words were burning his tongue, desperate to get out. But he held himself back.

Fear gripped him.

Fear of what this would mean for him.

His entire life could be flipped upside down by admitting that he loved these two. Hell, admitting that he loved Wolfe alone could pull the rug right out from underneath him.

Could he do it?

Could he risk everything he'd worked so hard for?

For a chance at a life he'd always dreamed of, a love he'd never thought he would find?

"Fuck," he grumbled as his heart pinched tightly, his abs contracting as a wave of emotion ripped over him, stealing his breath.

"No?" There was a sadness in Wolfe's eyes, one that said he could read Rhys's mind, knew the war he'd waged with himself.

"You can't say it?"

Rhys didn't move.

"Because it's not true?" Wolfe questioned. "Or because you're fucking scared?"

Still, Rhys sucked in air, his chest expanding as the breaths came faster.

"Because if it's the latter, we'll work on that," Wolfe explained, his tone softening. "We don't have to make every damn decision right this second. But goddammit, if you fucking love us, I. Have. To. Hear. It."

Rhys nodded. It was pure instinct. "I do." His voice was a raspy whisper forced out of his body by nothing more than pure emotion. "Yes, damn it. I love you." He looked at Amy. "I love you, too. I'm just…"

"Scared," Wolfe finished for him. "We all are."

All three of them stood there, staring at one another. In that instant, words weren't necessary. They meant little compared to what was obviously going on here. Whether they admitted it or not, this was where the three of them were meant to be. Rhys's entire life had been leading to this very moment.

"Goddamn," Wolfe bit out, jerking Rhys to him, their lips slamming together.

And then Wolfe was moving the three of them toward the bedroom. Wolfe broke the kiss and turned to Amy, grabbing her, lifting her, holding her to him as Wolfe pressed his lips to hers. Her arms went around his neck as she kissed him back.

Rhys could feel the energy swarming them. The tension was intense; the emotions were fueling every movement. Passion, need, and yes, love.

No one could predict what tomorrow would bring, but in this moment, with these two people, Rhys knew there was no place he'd rather be. And if his entire world came crumbling down on him when the sun came up in the morning…

So be it.

Because, as he stared at the two of them, he knew deep in his soul that nothing in this world would ever feel right again without them in it. Not his job, his house, his independence. None of it meant a fucking thing without them.

Wolfe turned back to him and Amy's eyes locked on his face. It was obvious they were trying to figure out what was holding him back.

"I love you," he whispered, his eyes darting from one to the other as the words came out easier that time.

"Get over here, Sheriff," Wolfe commanded. "And put your fucking money where your mouth is."

Well, when he put it that way…

"WHAT DO YOU think she'll decide to do?" Reagan asked Lynx as he drove her back to Amy's.

They'd dropped the detective off at the diner, waited until she got in her car and pulled out before Lynx turned his truck in the direction of Amy's house.

"No idea," he answered curtly.

During the drive from his father's house, the two women had talked softly about what they thought would happen if Amy did go public with what had happened to her.

If he was being honest, Lynx would rather they take care of the threat themselves. No reason they should sit back and wait for the bastard to make another move. And sure, Amy could go public with her story. But what would that do? Rile up the reporters? Have them storming Embers Ridge with their questions and curiosity? Lynx didn't like that idea.

Nor did he like the idea of this bastard still walking around out there. He needed to be put in the fucking ground for what he did. Any man who put his hands on a woman or child out of anger deserved to be shot. Or hung. Better yet, shot while they were hung.

Lynx must've been quiet for too long, because as he pulled down the drive to Amy's, he saw Reagan turn toward him. He cut his eyes her way briefly. "What?"

"Are we ever gonna talk about what happened?"

He tapped the brakes a little harder than he should have, forcing her to throw her hand out to brace herself on the dashboard. He then brought the truck to a complete stop, his knuckles tightening on the steering wheel. "Nothin' to talk about."

"Oh, that's horseshit and you know it," she countered hotly.

Goddamn, the woman turned him on when she let her temper get the best of her. Fuck, every damn thing she did turned him on.

"You kissed me, Lynx."

He cocked an eyebrow and turned toward her, dropping one hand to his lap. His dick was like an iron bar, desperate for this woman. All it took was one whiff of her perfume, one glimpse of her perfect fucking body and his dick took complete control of his thought process.

She was right though. He had kissed her. But…

"That was ten years ago," he argued. "And you were fucking sixteen years old, damn it."

That's what he hated about that fucking memory. Reagan Trevino had been his for the taking, right there sitting on the tailgate of his truck. It had been the day of his mother's funeral, and she was the only person besides his family who had come to check on him. She had sat by the lake with him for hours. They talked about growing up, about his mother specifically, about the memories they both had of her.

And before the damn night was over, Lynx had kissed her.

He'd been eighteen fucking years old and had no business putting his hands on a naïve sixteen-year-old girl. Didn't matter if Reagan had kissed him back. He should've never done it.

So, he'd told himself he would wait until she turned eighteen.

"I'm not sixteen anymore, Lynx."

No, she wasn't. But she had a damn boyfriend—

Only she didn't have one anymore. The day she finally quit that bastard, Lynx had considered chasing her down and convincing her to give in to him, to give in to how fucking good they could be together. The only thing that had stopped him was their history. Reagan always took Billy Watson back. For nearly a decade, Lynx had sat back and watched as Reagan took that dumb little fucker back every damn time, and he figured this time was no different.

"What about Billy?" he asked because he couldn't help himself. If he was even going to consider putting his hands on this girl, he had to know that Billy was in her past, that he would never be in her future.

"What about him?" Her dark eyebrows angled down, her confusion apparent.

"You gonna take his sorry ass back?"

Her frown turned to a grimace and he could tell he'd pissed her off with that question.

"What does that have to do with this?"

He sat up straight. "Every goddamn thing, Reagan."

She put her hands on her hips. "How?"

Lowering his voice, Lynx decided to be honest with her. If she thought she could handle him, she needed to know exactly what she was dealing with.

"Because the second I put my hands on you, the instant my mouth touches yours … that makes you mine, Reagan."

She huffed. "I belong to no man, Lynx Caine. You should know that now."

"Then it's a damn good thing I've never touched you."

"No," Reagan replied hotly. "You've only touched every other female in this county."

Not entirely true, but yeah. He wasn't a damn saint, and truthfully, he'd been fighting his need for this one woman for so long Lynx could admit that he'd searched high and low for someone who could eliminate her from his thoughts.

He'd yet to meet that woman.

He doubted she existed.

As far as Lynx was concerned, there was only one woman meant for him.

And she was sitting right there in his truck, her lips pursed, her eyes blazing.

And once again, he seriously doubted he would end up getting what he wanted.

Because as much as he wanted to think otherwise, Reagan Trevino was too hard to handle, too much to tame.

Reagan reached for the door handle. "Fuck you, Lynx. Fuck you and the horse you rode in on."

Lynx didn't say a word.

She turned to face him once she was out of the truck. "And it's not like I wanted your hands on me, anyway. I've already had one bad boy. I damn sure don't need another."

Lynx leaned over and smiled, baring his teeth. "Darlin', you don't know what a bad boy is. Billy is a dumb ass who didn't deserve to be in the same goddamn room as you."

"But you do?" Her hand flew to her hips again.

"Darlin', you can't handle me."

"Try me, Lynx."

He shook his head and sat up, turning to look out the front window. "That's the problem, Reagan. I'm not interested in a taste test." He looked directly at her. "If I get my hands on you, it will be forever. And until you accept that—"

The door slammed and he chuckled as he watched Reagan and her cute little ass march right up to the front door.

One day, that hellcat was going to give in.

It was just a matter of time.

27

WOLFE WASN'T SURE how he was going to make it through the next few minutes. He was hanging by a thread, frayed and ready to snap.

Not to mention, completely naked.

"Wolfe…" Amy moaned, pulling his head back down to her breast. "Don't stop."

Taking her to the mattress, Wolfe came down over her, his tongue swirling around her nipple before he sucked it into his mouth. He wasn't gentle. Hell, he wasn't sure he could be. His need was too great, his body on fire, a desperation unlike anything he'd ever known consuming him. There was an undeniable need to possess, to claim and he had them right where he wanted them.

Growling, he pulled off of her breast, then trailed his mouth down her stomach, dipping his tongue in her navel, before stopping at the apex of her thighs.

"Need to taste you," he groaned.

And that was the God's honest truth. Wolfe craved Amy's taste. His tongue itched to caress her sweetness. Hell, he could spend hours driving her wild by burying his face between her thighs. He was addicted, pure and simple.

Sliding his tongue along her slick slit, Wolfe hummed as Amy's sweet taste lit him up from the inside out. She was liquid fire, squirming against his mouth while Rhys feasted on her tit, sucking hard, his hand flat on Amy's stomach.

They were both holding her. Not forcefully, but enough to keep her from jerking off the bed. Her hands were fisted in the blankets as though she was attempting to hold on, too. Wolfe knew the feeling. In a minute, once they were both lodged deep inside her body, he was pretty damn sure he was going to fly apart.

And he couldn't fucking wait.

Crawling back up her body, Wolfe slipped two fingers into her warm, wet pussy, gently fucking her as he laved her other nipple.

"Wolfe … Rhys…" Amy moaned. "It's too much."

No, it wasn't enough. It never would be.

When Rhys lifted his head, Wolfe mirrored his movement, then kissed the man as Amy grabbed for them. Her short nails dug into his shoulders, and he could tell she was as eager, as anxious as they were.

There would be plenty of time for more foreplay later.

Breaking his mouth from Rhys's, Wolfe rolled to his back, pulling Amy with him.

"Put me inside you," he commanded roughly. "Need to feel that slick pussy on my cock."

Amy was panting as she ground her cunt against his rock-hard length.

"God, baby," he groaned. "I fucking love when you do that, but if you don't sit on my cock, I'm gonna lose my mind."

She moaned as she guided him right where they both needed him. He swallowed her soft moans, kissing her as she took him inch by inch into her body.

Wolfe hissed as pleasure consumed him. The warm, tight clasp of her pussy sent shockwaves slamming into him, electrical pulses firing beneath his skin.

Amy moaned, pulling her mouth back as she pressed her pelvis against him, lifting her ass. Wolfe knew Rhys was behind her, teasing her ass with his tongue.

"Oh, God!" Her eyes closed, her muscles tightening.

"You like that?"

Her head bobbed as she nodded. "Y-yes-s-s."

Wolfe watched her face, the way she closed her eyes, her mouth open as she gave herself over to the pleasure.

When she started moving again, Wolfe pulled her down to him, her breasts crushed to his chest.

"Take us both, Amy. At the same time." Although he didn't phrase it as a question, Wolfe wanted her to agree. He would never do anything she didn't want.

Her jerky nod had his breath slamming into his chest.

"Tell me," he instructed. "Say it."

Her eyes opened and she held his stare. "Yes," she ground out, her hips lowering over him once more, then rocking forward and back. "I need to feel you both."

Wolfe met Rhys's gaze over Amy's head. The man's dark eyes were glazed and Wolfe knew he was thinking the same thing. There was no turning back from this. What she was giving them, what they were taking from her was something that would hold them together forever.

Gripping Amy's hips, Wolfe guided her, pumping his hips as he fucked her from underneath. Her soft moans were fucking music to his ears.

The bed shifted between Wolfe's legs as Rhys got situated behind her. Wolfe wrapped his arm around Amy's back, holding her tight to his body.

"Relax for us," Rhys instructed.

Amy's head lifted, her breaths sawing in and out of her lungs.

"Just a finger," Rhys told her.

"Mmmm." Amy's nails dug into Wolfe's shoulders.

"Kiss me," Wolfe commanded.

Amy lifted her head and Wolfe met her mouth, his lips merging with hers, his tongue delving past her teeth. He was rough, needy, unable to help himself. The thought of him and Rhys inside her at the same time, possessing her in a way no one else in the world ever would, had his body trembling.

Desperate for everything they were willing to give him.

Every damn thing.

WOLFE'S BIG HAND cradled the back of her head and Amy allowed him to shift so that he could own the kiss.

She had accused him of not being dominant enough before, but that certainly wasn't the case now. He was holding her together, keeping her from shattering in a million pieces, and she wanted more. She wanted them to show her what it meant to be claimed by them. Owned in a way that she wouldn't run from, she wouldn't fear. And she knew Wolfe and Rhys were going to do just that.

She welcomed it.

Craved it.

Rhys's finger pressed into her ass and her body caught fire. It was a feeling she'd never thought she would enjoy, but it was hard to deny as Wolfe filled her pussy and Rhys caused electrical currents to pulse through her from his gentle probing touch.

"More," she groaned. She was tired of waiting.

The bed shifted and Wolfe once again began fucking her from underneath, his hand gripping her hip, his fingertips digging into her flesh as he pushed up and pulled her down simultaneously. Her clit pressed against his pelvis, supplying the right amount of pressure to have her head spinning.

She heard the sound of a condom wrapper being opened, but she didn't look back. Her stomach muscles quivered in anticipation, spasms of pleasure racking her entire body as Wolfe continued to fuck her. An effective distraction.

And then the mattress dipped again and Rhys's lips were on her shoulder. She felt the blunt head of his cock pressing against her back entrance.

"Relax," he whispered, his lips trailing to her neck. "Let us love you, baby."

She nodded, although it wasn't necessary.

Wolfe had stopped moving, but his mouth found hers again, his tongue thrusting against hers, his hand tightening at the back of her head. He was holding her together again and she knew he wasn't going to let go. He would never let go. They would both keep her in one piece no matter how much she worried otherwise.

The pressure on her asshole sent pain slamming into her, her body tensing.

Wolfe's hips rocked beneath her as his hand slipped between them. When his thumb pressed on her clit, she focused on that sensation as the pain lessened. The pressure was intense, causing her lungs to seize up.

"Oh, God," she cried out. "Too much."

Rhys stilled behind her.

The three of them were breathing hard and she knew they were waiting for her to give the green light.

Turning her head, she found Rhys's mouth with her own, kissing him, adding another distraction as she pushed back against the intrusion in her ass, taking more of him. He groaned into her mouth and the vibration sent chills racing down her spine. Although she was crushed between them, Amy knew she was in control. That in itself had her body warming again, her pussy clenching around Wolfe's cock still deep inside her.

"Oh, fuck," Wolfe hissed. "Milk my dick, darlin'. Oh, yeah. Just like that." He groaned, his fingertips digging into her hips again.

Pulling back from Rhys, Amy pushed her hips back hard.

She cried out as she took Rhys's cock deep into her ass. Both men stopped moving as her body stretched painfully tight. The pain was unlike anything she'd ever known, humming through every nerve ending. But she still wanted more. She couldn't explain it, probably never would be able to. She was in the moment, overcome by sensation. Pain and pleasure warred within her, but having Rhys and Wolfe there… It was everything. It made her fearless, frantic for everything they would give her.

"Fuck me," she whimpered, desperate to give herself over to them.

They'd allowed her to control this and now it was their turn. Amy wanted to know what it felt like for these two men to possess her in the most basic way.

Glancing down at Wolfe, Amy sucked air into her lungs. "I'm ready for … everything."

RHYS'S COCK WAS lodged to the hilt inside Amy's tight ass. The pain it caused was both heaven and hell, but he never wanted it to end.

Shifting his hips slightly, he pulled back, pushed in. In, out, he began a slow rocking motion as an all-out assault on his body happened from the strangling grip of her ass. He could feel Wolfe's cock through the thin barrier inside her body and it was unlike anything he'd ever felt.

Not like this.

Never like this.

"More!" Amy cried out, her hips slamming back against him.

Rhys gave her more, punching his hips forward while Wolfe moved beneath her.

"Yes…" She whimpered again. "Please … don't stop. I need … more."

Her words alone were bringing Rhys dangerously close to the edge. With his hands on her hips, Rhys began pumping into her, pulling her back against him. He met Wolfe's stare over Amy's shoulder, saw the pleasure glittering in Wolfe's eyes. The man was feeling the same thing Rhys was.

Pure fucking ecstasy.

The best damn drug in the entire world.

This woman between them, begging for more, her body hot, demanding, and so fucking sweet.

She was going to send him over the edge before he ever got going.

Knowing he was dangerously close, Rhys began fucking her, driving in deeper, harder. Her soft moans echoed in the room, combined with his rough breaths and Wolfe's soft words of encouragement.

"That's it, darlin'. You feel so fucking good. Aww, God, yes…" Wolfe jerked his hips, driving up into her.

Rhys couldn't keep a steady rhythm as his body caught fire, soaring on a plane of sheer sensation. It coursed through his veins, thrummed beneath his skin, buzzed in his ears.

"Fuck..." he groaned. "Amy ... baby..." Rhys fucked her for all he was worth as her body milked him, tightening around his cock.

"That's it, darlin'. Come for us," Wolfe crooned. "Come for us so we can come inside you. *Deep* inside you."

Amy screamed, her body trembling, her muscles clamping down.

Her orgasm triggered his own, and Rhys could hardly breathe as Wolfe reached down, his hand gripping Rhys's thigh as he, too, let himself go.

Half an hour later, after Rhys had caught his breath and Amy had drifted off to sleep, Rhys realized he couldn't keep still. They had just engaged in what was the most intense, life-altering sex of Rhys's entire life. He needed to burn off some of the energy and sleeping wasn't an option.

So, after disposing of the condom, then gently cleaning Amy with a washcloth and tucking her beneath the blankets, Rhys had slipped out of the bedroom with Wolfe right behind him.

As though thinking the same thing, they made their way into the kitchen. Rhys grabbed a bottle of water, and Wolfe proceeded to pull out the ingredients for sandwiches.

"How do you see this playin' out?" Rhys asked as Wolfe placed bologna and cheese on the counter. "I mean really playin' out."

Rhys needed to know. Was this forever for them? Were they moving forward? Permanently?

Turning to face Rhys, Wolfe studied him while Rhys waited patiently for the wisdom the man would impart.

"One day at a time," he said, his tone ringing with honesty.

It shouldn't have surprised him that Wolfe would say that. The man was a laid-back country boy. Their motto seemed to be *one day at a time.*

"Is it that easy?" Rhys didn't believe it was. How could it be?

If he went public with a relationship with these two, he would stir up a world of shit in their small town. People talked, they judged, they assumed shit they had no business assuming.

Wolfe shook his head but moved closer, cupping Rhys's face with his hands. Admittedly, Rhys loved when he did that, exerting his dominance, making Rhys feel as though control was not his to have. He'd never wanted that before, so he didn't understand why he wanted it from Wolfe, but he did.

"It's not supposed to be easy," Wolfe stated firmly. "It's supposed to be worth it."

"It is," Rhys agreed. "Worth it, I mean."

He could admit that much. He hadn't been blowing smoke up their asses when he said he loved them. He did. That didn't mean he wasn't scared shitless about where this was headed or how it would play out.

"It's not like we'll take out a billboard ad," Wolfe stated, his tone reassuring. "Let's go about our business. One day at a time."

Wolfe leaned in and kissed him before Rhys could come up with a rebuttal. Rhys would've come up with something; however, he got the feeling Wolfe wasn't finished talking.

The kiss lingered for a minute, maybe two. Long enough that Rhys relaxed somewhat.

"I want more than sex," Wolfe told him. "I want you and Amy in my bed every damn night."

"Your bed? Why not my bed?"

Wolfe pulled back, locking his eyes with Rhys's. "Is that what you want? Because I'll do it. We don't have to live here."

"You'd really do that?" Rhys had figured Wolfe would have balked at the idea.

Wolfe took a step back and Rhys waited for the argument, for the man to tell him it wasn't what he wanted.

"I'll do whatever I have to in order to hold on to you and Amy. That's all there is to it." He waved his hand around his house. "This is nothing more than brick and wood, Rhys. It's not what's gonna keep us together."

Rhys sighed. Damn it. Why did Wolfe have to be so damn logical? "I know it's not. And I'm not hell-bent on my house. I'll sell the damn thing. It makes no difference to me. But…"

It wasn't even really about the house. He had no personal attachment to the damn thing. What he really wanted to know was, "Do you think we're movin' too fast?"

One minute it felt like they were; the next Rhys felt as though they weren't moving fast enough. From the instant Wolfe had called and invited Rhys to the range with him and Amy, things had been moving at the speed of light. Add to that the fact that Amy was running from a crazy fucker, and Rhys felt as though he was swimming in quicksand, fighting to get his feet beneath him but it never happened. Yet when they were apart, he wanted to be with them.

Wolfe shrugged. "Maybe."

"Think maybe we could slow the horse a bit?"

"Me, personally?" Wolfe shrugged. "I don't want to slow down. I want to let the momentum carry me where it's supposed to."

Rhys saw the truth in Wolfe's eyes. When the man had said he was all in, he hadn't been bluffing.

"I'm gonna ask Amy to move in with me," Wolfe admitted. "I want you here with us, but I get it. I do. You're the sheriff; you've got a reputation to uphold. I'm not lookin' to destroy that."

"Goddamn," Rhys bit out as he turned away from Wolfe, sliding his hand over his hair. "Why am I makin' this so damn complicated? It's not, is it?"

When Rhys turned back, Wolfe was grinning. "It's not."

Neither of them moved for several tense seconds.

Rhys had to spend some time working this out in his head. That's how he operated. He couldn't make a decision right now. If he followed his heart, that would be easy, but he needed to give it some serious thought.

"One day at a time," Wolfe said. "That's all we can do."

Rhys nodded.

Turning away from Rhys, Wolfe chuckled. "And I expect you'll start to enjoy goin' to sleep in my bed every night and wakin' up there every mornin'."

Rhys barked out a laugh. It was always so damn easy for Wolfe.

Wolfe glanced over his shoulder. "After all, I fully intend to make it worth your while."

"Do you now?"

"Oh, I definitely do."

No doubt Wolfe would.

"So, how many—"

Before Wolfe could ask whatever he wanted to ask, Rhys's phone rang. He glanced down at the screen, noticing it was one of his deputies.

"Sheriff Trevino," he answered quickly, glancing over at Wolfe.

"Sir, we've got a fatality accident. Car plowed into a tree out here on 95. She's wearin' a shield. I figure you're probably gonna want to come out here for this."

Fatality accident? In his town? Even if Dean hadn't mentioned the badge, Rhys would've questioned it. Sure, they had plenty of accidents on their stretch of 95. With a speed limit of sixty-five on the winding road, it wasn't always pretty. But a fatality? It would be the first since he took office, and a sense of dread skated down Rhys's spine when he asked, "What's the make and model of the car?"

"White Ford Taurus. Single female driver."

The breath rushed out of his lungs as he stared at Wolfe.

"How long ago did this happen?" Rhys asked.

"It looks like … Well, it looks like she's been here for a little bit. An hour or so? Chris was out patrolling and saw skid marks."

Shit. "I'll ... I'm on my way."

"What's wrong?" Wolfe asked, standing directly in front of him

Hanging up, Rhys swallowed hard. "It's … uh…"

He couldn't even get the words out before he leaned over, breathing deep as he tried to keep from losing it.

28

"HEY," WOLFE GREETED Lynx when Rhys took off out the door like his ass was on fire.

It had taken a couple of minutes to get the man to share the details of the call, and once he had, Wolfe understood his sudden panic. In fact, it had triggered his own.

"What's up?"

"Where you at?"

"Home. Why?"

"We got a problem." Wolfe went on to explain what Rhys had told him, trying to keep his voice low so that he didn't wake Amy. He and Rhys had decided they'd try to find a way to explain this to her without sending her spiraling into a full-blown panic attack. He knew he probably needed to do so now, but until Rhys confirmed what was going on, they'd decided it was better to keep her in the dark.

Not that either of them liked it, but he knew it was necessary.

"Son of a fucking bitch," Lynx roared. "I need to call Reagan. Fuckin' A."

Without another word, Lynx disconnected the call and Wolfe stared at his phone. Less than a minute later, the damn thing was ringing again.

"You get ahold of her?"

"Fuck no. I just hope like hell it's 'cause she's pissed at me. I'm on my way to Amy's right now."

Wolfe heard a familiar *ding-ding-ding* that said Lynx was getting into his truck.

"Let me know when you get her."

When the call disconnected that time, Wolfe tossed his phone on the counter.

His eyes slid to the shotgun sitting in the corner, and he pushed off the counter and headed over to it. He double-checked to ensure it was loaded, then set it back down.

If the devil himself showed up on Wolfe's doorstep tonight, he was going to regret ever fucking with the woman Wolfe loved.

And if by chance he didn't show up, if he was merely playin' a game, Wolfe knew it would be time to implement plan B. After all, his aunt had married into a pretty powerful family. A family who would take no shit from anyone. And he knew exactly which cousin he needed to call to help him on this.

Grabbing his phone, Wolfe skimmed through his contacts until he found the man he was looking for.

Time to give Travis Walker a call.

The phone rang twice before his cousin's gruff voice answered. "'Lo?"

"Hey, Trav. It's Wolfe."

"What's up, man? Things good?"

"Not really, no. I need your help."

"You got it."

That was what Wolfe loved about family. They were willing to help without even knowing what it was you needed.

"All right then. Here's what's goin' on…"

"GODDAMN IT," LYNX yelled, slamming his phone down on his leg. "Sorry, boy," he told Copenhagen when the dog peered over at him.

Reagan wasn't answering the damn phone and he was still five miles out. It was making him fucking crazy. If that crazy fucking lunatic bastard had made an appearance in Embers Ridge, the woman was a sitting duck.

There was no doubt about it, the asshole knew right where Amy was. Or rather, where she should be. Had probably known all along. There was no other explanation for the detective who'd arrived here to die here the same day. He didn't even need Wolfe's or Rhys's confirmation that it was her.

It was her. And that bastard was lurking somewhere. Maybe he'd come to snuff out the detective, but he wasn't leaving without finishing what he came for. The accident wreaked of desperation, which meant Amy damn sure wasn't safe. And in turn, neither was Reagan.

"Fuck." He white-knuckled the steering wheel. "We have to get to her, Cope. Have to. If that motherfucker thinks Reagan's Amy…"

He didn't want to think about that.

But it was possible.

It damn sure didn't help that Reagan looked similar enough to Amy before she had dyed her hair. In a dark house, the asshole wouldn't be able to tell the difference.

"Goddammit!" Lynx roared, hitting the steering wheel.

He hated this helpless feeling. Fucking hated it.

With his foot to the floor, Lynx fishtailed off the main road and onto the dirt road that led to Amy's place.

Three minutes.

He'd be there in three fucking minutes.

Right now, that felt like an eternity.

REAGAN HEARD THE noise when she was washing her face.

She slipped out of the bathroom, hand towel pressed to her cheek. Glancing left into the guest room where she'd been sleeping, she checked to see if it had come from there. She didn't see anything.

That didn't stop her from setting the hand towel down and picking up her sawed-off shotgun. This was her no-nonsense gun. It made grown men's eyes widen and their nuts shrivel. That was the very reason she loved it.

The rest of the house was dark, so she turned to her right, moved slowly down the hall.

She heard it again. The sound of the lock on the front door.

Her phone rang again, but she ignored it.

She knew Amy wasn't the visitor at the front door. No way would she come home this late. For one, she couldn't drive herself since her car was parked out front.

Reagan stopped at the mouth of the hallway, shotgun up and aimed at the front door.

"Just to warn you," Reagan stated firmly, loud enough to warn the would-be intruder, "my daddy taught me never to point a gun at a man unless I intend to shoot him. Open that door and I *will* put an extra hole in your body."

The noise stopped, but Reagan remained where she was. Waiting.

Several seconds passed, her heart hammering hard, blood rushing in her ears.

A pounding on the front door had Reagan damn near coming out of her skin.

"Reagan! Open the goddamn door!"

Lynx?

What the fuck?

With the gun still at the ready, she moved closer to the door. "What do you want?"

"You to answer the goddamn phone," he yelled back.

Okay, so it was definitely Lynx. She'd ignored at least one of his calls, and she figured the others had been from him, too.

Reaching over, she flipped the lock, then took a step back, the shotgun still aimed at center mass.

The knob turned and the door opened a fraction of an inch.

Taking a deep breath of relief, she lowered the gun. "Why the hell'd you try to break in?" she questioned, pissed that he'd do something so freaking stupid.

He frowned. "What are you talkin' about?"

"The lock." She nodded toward the door.

Lynx glanced down and studied the brass deadbolt.

"Fuck. Come on. Let's get the fuck outta here."

"Why? What happened?"

"I'll fill you in on the way out. Keep the gun with you. Let's go."

Lynx Caine could be a world-class asshole, but he wasn't the type to order her around unless he felt it was necessary.

And that was the only reason Reagan followed him out the door and into the night.

Without a lick of makeup on.

KELLY WATCHED FROM the shadows as the oversized tattooed cowboy took the brunette out to his truck.

His heart was slamming against his ribs, the adrenaline making his dick hard.

That had been damn close.

Too close.

If it hadn't been for the roar of that damn engine, Kelly would've been a sitting duck when that asshole showed up.

But he was so close.

Taking a deep breath, Kelly stood from the shadows when the headlights turned and aimed in the opposite direction. They were leaving.

Good.

That would give him time to come up with a plan. One that would eliminate Amy once and for all. Shit. He'd already gone too far taking out Jo, but the woman had been a menace. She shouldn't have stuck her nose in his business.

Thankfully, she was no longer a threat.

And once he got his hands on Amy, she wouldn't be, either.

But tonight wouldn't work. With the *accident,* the local cops would be busy for a while, but that also meant they were out and about. Since he was supposed to be in San Antonio on business, he would do well to head that way and be seen. Taking care of that damn nosy detective had been his main objective tonight and he'd accomplished that.

There would be plenty of time to come back for Amy later.

He'd let some of the heat die down. Maybe a day. Possibly two.

But he would be back.

And he would take care of her once and for all.

AMY HAD NO idea how long she'd been asleep, but she had a good idea of what had woken her. From Wolfe's bedroom, she could hear voices. Loud voices. More than one, at that.

She took a few minutes to get herself presentable, using the restroom, pulling her hair up in a ponytail, brushing her teeth, and putting on clothes. By the time she emerged from the bedroom, the voices had subsided.

"Hey, baby," Wolfe greeted.

When he walked across the room and came right to her, she knew something was wrong.

"What is it?"

Her attention was drawn to Lynx and Reagan sitting at the kitchen table, Copenhagen sleeping on the floor in the middle of the kitchen.

"What happened?" Her gaze darted around the house, anxiety curling in her belly. "Where's Rhys?"

"He had to go work an accident," Wolfe explained. "Come here. Sit down."

Amy pulled out of his grasp. "Tell me, Wolfe. What's goin' on?"

Wolfe sighed as he thrust his hands in his pockets. "Joanna Tannenbaum was killed tonight."

Her heart slammed against her ribs. "*What?*"

Oh, God. Oh, God.

She felt the panic bubbling up from her belly. It raced up into her throat, threatening to strangle her.

"Sit," Wolfe ordered, urging her down on the sofa.

This time she didn't resist. Her legs were too weak.

He followed her down, his arm coming around her shoulders. "She was leavin' town. Someone ran her off the road. Rhys called a few minutes ago to confirm it was her and that he didn't suspect it was an accident."

"He's here. He's in Embers Ridge." She couldn't breathe. Her chest was too tight, her lungs weighed down by some unseen force.

Amy leaned over, trying to catch her breath. She saw Lynx's big booted feet as he came to stand in front of her. He perched on the coffee table and she forced herself to look up at him.

"He tried to break into your house tonight," Lynx told her.

Her gaze swung to Reagan. "Are you okay?"

She nodded. "I was ready for him." A smile formed on her lips as she nodded toward the door.

Amy looked over to see three shotguns leaned against the wall and one big, nasty-looking gun beside them.

"Lynx must've scared him off," Wolfe said, his arm tightening around her.

"Do you think he's still here?" she asked, knowing no one could really answer that.

"Hard to tell, but I doubt it. With the accident and the cops out on patrol, he's probably hightailin' it outta Dodge."

Amy dropped her head into her hands and took deep, cleansing breaths. Poor Jo.

As she thought about the detective who had come here to warn her, anger seeped into her bloodstream, erasing some of the panic. After a few more deep breaths, Amy lifted her head and peered at the three people watching her.

"He has to be stopped," she insisted.

"That he does," Lynx agreed.

"So what do we do?" Amy asked, looking to Wolfe for answers. "How do we stop him?"

"Don't know, darlin', but we'll figure somethin' out." He pulled her closer to him and his lips pressed to her forehead. "I promise you that."

It was one thing to know he was coming after her, something else entirely for him to start eliminating random people. If he could take out a detective, Amy knew it wasn't farfetched to believe he could take out Rhys and Wolfe, too.

Her blood turned to ice, and for the first time in her life, she felt something other than fear when it came to Kelly Jackson.

No, this was something akin to a full-blown homicidal rage.

29

"NO! DON'T! PLEASE!"

Wolfe's eyes flew open, his body jerking upright as his tired brain prepared to face the threat. Reaching for the lamp, he tugged the chain, and the room filled with a soft yellow glow.

The *empty* room, that was.

Beside him, Amy jerked, her voice a whimper. "No more, please! Don't!"

Oh, fuck.

With a gentle hand, Wolfe shook Amy, trying to wake her from the apparent nightmare. With his voice little more than a whisper, he leaned closer. "Baby, wake up," he urged. "Come on. You're dreamin'."

Her body jerked and her eyes opened. Wolfe noticed she was breathing hard and tears were streaming down her face.

When it appeared she was lucid, Wolfe wrapped her in his arms and pulled her close to his side. He brushed her sweat-dampened hair back from her face and kissed her forehead. "It's okay, baby. I've got you."

While Wolfe was giving Amy time to catch her breath, he heard the sound of the front door open, then close. He knew Rhys was back and he was finally able to fully relax himself. He'd been asleep for about an hour, but it had been fitful, leaving him tossing and turning, his brain unable to shut down completely. Rhys had texted to let him know he was still working the scene and that he'd be home soon.

A few minutes later, the bed shifted.

"Hey," Wolfe greeted, his voice rough from exhaustion.

"Hey." Rhys leaned over and kissed Amy's forehead. "What's wrong?"

"Nightmare," he answered for her.

"Wanna talk about it?" Rhys asked as he got situated, his body pressing close to Amy's on the opposite side as Wolfe.

"It's one I have all the time," she said softly, her hand absently sliding over Wolfe's chest.

Neither of them spoke, and Wolfe knew Rhys was waiting the same way he was, hoping Amy would continue to open up to them, to let them in.

"I'm sure you've seen the scars on my back. I don't think about them much anymore because I rarely see them, but I'll never forget how they got there."

Wolfe sucked in a sharp breath and met Rhys's eyes in the dimly lit room.

He could see the same fury that had ignited in his gut burning brightly in the man's dark eyes. This was another story, another reason Kelly Jackson needed to be stopped. He wasn't sure prison was enough for the bastard.

In fact, he wasn't sure Hell was enough punishment for the bastard, but it was a damn good start.

HER BONES WERE frozen, the nightmare having taken its toll on her. Amy hated those damn dreams, the reminders of what she'd lived through, what Kelly had done to her. As much as she hated talking about them, it did help. More so when she shared with Rhys and Wolfe. They didn't make her feel the shame she'd been consumed with for so long.

"The first time it happened, I was in the kitchen washing dishes," she began, the memory taking over, carrying her right back to that horrific day.

"You done in there yet?" Kelly called from his spot in front of the television.

That was where he went every day after dinner. She was expected to have it ready for him and it couldn't be the same thing he'd had at any point in the past month. And he insisted it was fresh meat and vegetables. Nothing frozen, no cans. Amy hadn't been much of a cook before she met him, but after, she'd had no choice but to learn.

"Almost," she answered softly, making sure there was no heat in her tone although she hated that he questioned her all the time. The water was on in the sink; he should know she wasn't finished yet.

"I want the bathroom done next. It's filthy."

Amy rolled her eyes as she stared out the window. The bathroom wasn't filthy, because she had cleaned it two days ago when Kelly had found a drop of conditioner on the glass shower door. At that point, he had insisted that she get on her hands and knees and scrub the entire bathroom.

"Did you hear me?" he yelled.

Amy glanced over her shoulder to see him on the couch, bare foot propped on the coffee table. She wanted to tell him to clean the bathroom himself, but she knew better.

"I heard you," she answered, scrubbing the pan from dinner.

The water must have masked the sound of his approach, because Amy didn't even know he was behind her until he grabbed her hair and jerked her head back.

"Did you just talk back to me?"

"N-no. No, of course not." Fire burned her scalp as he yanked her backwards.

Then it was gone because he shoved her forward. Her soapy hand slipped on the edge of the kitchen sink, and she fell forward, her cheek hitting the faucet.

"Get in the goddamn bathroom and clean it up!"

"I…" Amy pushed herself up. "I have to finish the dishes. I'm almost done."

Admittedly, her tone wasn't as submissive as she normally was, but the anger was building and she couldn't seem to contain it.

Kelly's fist slammed down on the lever controlling the water and the sink shut off. When she reached for a hand towel, he grabbed her upper arm, his fingers digging painfully into her flesh.

"Kelly … don't. Please. I'll clean it."

"You're goddamn right you will. And when you're finished, you'll get the punishment you deserve. The punishment I should've given you a long damn time ago." He jerked her toward the bathroom.

When they reached it, he shoved her, sending her slamming into the wooden door. A sob threatened, but she held it back as she turned and slipped inside. She knew better than to close the door. She was never allowed to close the door. Not when she showered or used the bathroom. He insisted that he always be able to see her. That was the reason for the cameras everywhere.

Amy felt the two men beside her move closer, their arms holding her tightly. It was their presence that made the memory bearable. She knew she would never have to endure that ever again.

"After I cleaned the bathroom, he made me strip. Said I was dirty. I told him I would shower, but he said no. Said that would happen *after* my punishment." She took a deep breath. "When he pulled out the whip, I freaked. He had hit me plenty of times and had used various things. A belt, a flyswatter, a ruler, a wooden spoon. Whatever he could find close by. But a whip… I was terrified."

Neither man said anything, but she felt the tension in their bodies.

"I tried to run, but he caught me. I kicked and screamed, but he tied me to the bed. He kept ropes there because that was his thing. He sat on me while he secured me in place, facedown on the mattress. I never stopped fighting, never stopped screaming. I kept hoping that one day someone would hear me. The mailman, UPS driver, solicitor, Jehovah's Witness. I didn't care, I just wanted someone to hear me, someone to stop him. No one ever did.

"Anyway, that night, he whipped me until I bled. The pain was excruciating. But the worst of it came when he made me shower afterwards. He scrubbed my back with soap, and I screamed and screamed until finally I passed out from the pain." She swallowed hard. "That was the *first* time he used the whip. It wasn't the last."

Wolfe pressed his lips to her forehead. "He will never hurt you again."

She knew he meant what he said, but Amy only prayed it was true.

SLEEP DIDN'T COME easily for Rhys. And when he did finally drift off, the events of the night had caught up with him. Seeing Joanna Tannenbaum's lifeless eyes staring back at him, her car mangled beyond belief. Then Amy's story of the additional horrors she had survived.

It had roused him, making it impossible to close his eyes again.

It all made Rhys question himself, his job. Being a sheriff wasn't something he'd ever thought he would do, but he enjoyed it. Liked helping people, protecting people. Then shit like this came to light and he realized it wasn't enough.

There were monsters like Kelly Jackson out there. They came out of the woodwork all the time. And right now, as he lay in bed, staring up at the ceiling, Rhys knew someone out there was suffering the way Amy had and there wasn't a goddamn thing he could do about it.

However, he could protect Amy.

No, there was nothing to say that Kelly Jackson wouldn't find a way to get to her, but they could arm her, teach her how to protect herself. There were plenty of people who said guns weren't the answer, and perhaps they were right in a lot of cases. However, when it came down to protecting your life against a definite threat, sometimes it was the only option.

Finally giving up on the ability to close his eyes, Rhys climbed out of bed as quietly as he could, then slipped out of Wolfe's bedroom and into the living room. He thought about making coffee, but he was too keyed up for caffeine.

What he needed was something to punch.

The sound of the bedroom door opening, then closing had him turning around to see Wolfe walking out of the bedroom, wearing nothing but a pair of basketball shorts. His body hardened, some of the anger replaced by lust.

When Wolfe's green eyes met his, Rhys knew they were thinking the same thing. There was one very powerful way to release the pent-up energy, to burn off the adrenaline, to numb the pain if only for a little while.

Apparently Wolfe was on the same page, because he walked right up to Rhys, put his hand behind his neck, and jerked him forward. A not-so-gentle nip on his bottom lip told Rhys that Wolfe was strung tight, too.

They were a fumble of hands and mouths for long minutes. Groping, touching, kissing. Other than their combined grunts and groans, the room was silent, warming significantly the more they touched.

"Need you," Wolfe growled. "Right fucking now."

Rhys nodded.

When Wolfe pulled a condom from his pocket, it was clear this had been Wolfe's intention all along.

"Don't suppose you have lube to go with that?" Rhys teased, biting Wolfe's lip gently.

"Of course I do." Wolfe pulled back and a small tube of lubricant appeared in front of him. "But before we get to that, I want you in my mouth."

Rhys didn't even have a chance to say anything before Wolfe was on his knees in front of him. Rhys's boxers met the floor and the heat of Wolfe's mouth consumed him. He grabbed Wolfe's head, his fingers twining in his short hair as he held on. The suction, the heat, it slammed through him, his body tensing as the glorious sensation assaulted all of his senses. Unable to help himself, Rhys jerked Wolfe to him, driving his cock into the man's throat. Wolfe allowed Rhys to use him, to fuck his mouth. In, out, deeper, harder. He was blinded by the lust that took over, the overwhelming pleasure obliterating everything else from his mind.

"Fuck," Rhys hissed. "Love your mouth." He continued to fuck Wolfe's face, not being gentle, but Wolfe didn't seem to mind. He remained on his knees, his perfect fucking mouth giving him more pleasure than he thought possible.

Rhys held on as long as he could, but eventually his orgasm won out and he came in a rush, his legs nearly giving out. Wolfe's arm banded around him as he surged to his feet, their mouths crashing together momentarily. He knew his feet were moving, his legs carrying him somewhere, but he didn't know where. He allowed Wolfe to guide him, to do what he needed to do.

"Kneel on the couch," Wolfe demanded, a gentle nudge sending Rhys onto the cushion.

He turned away, kneeling as instructed and gripping the back of the couch. He was grateful he didn't have to hold himself up any longer. More so when Wolfe pressed two lubed fingers into his ass. His cock twitched, but it wasn't going to come fully back to life. Not that he cared.

Wolfe's fingers disappeared moments before the man's cock impaled him, Wolfe's hard chest pressing against his back. A firm hand gripped his hair, pulling his head back. Rhys went with the movement, turning his head and allowing Wolfe to kiss him as he drove into him from behind. It was rough and so fucking good, the blood in his body returned to his cock, thickening it.

"Need this," Wolfe whispered against his mouth. "Need you."

Rhys knew how he felt.

"Gonna fuck you hard now," Wolfe warned.

A strong hand landed in the middle of Rhys's back, pushing him forward. He lowered his chest to the cushion as best he could. Wolfe gripped his hips and began slamming into him, fucking him harder than Rhys had ever been fucked before. It was brutal and so fucking good.

Unable to help himself, he reached between his legs and gripped his cock, jerking roughly, chasing another release. A few minutes ago, he would've sworn it wasn't possible, but he could feel it, another orgasm building, cresting.

Seconds later, as Wolfe was impaling him over and over, harder and harder, Rhys came with a strangled cry. Mere seconds after that, Wolfe slammed into him one last time, following him right over into the abyss.

30

"TRAVIS, THIS IS Sheriff Rhys Trevino. Rhys, Travis."

Wolfe watched as Rhys and Travis shook hands.

"Nice to meet you, Sheriff." Travis's blue-gray gaze was assessing as he glanced from Rhys to Wolfe, then back.

"You, too."

"And this is Amy. Amy, meet my cousin Travis and his husband, Gage."

Amy offered her hand, but Wolfe could see she was hesitant.

"Our wife is back at home with the little ones," Gage noted. "She wished she could've been here."

Amy's eyes slammed into Wolfe and he fought the urge to smile. "Now you can't say you've never met anyone like those books you read… Who did you say the author was again?"

Amy's cheeks turned a pretty shade of pink and Wolfe chuckled as he pulled her close.

Wolfe had already filled Travis in on the situation on the phone, so he didn't feel the need to run down it again.

"Would it be possible to grab a bite to eat?" Travis asked, glancing between them. "I was up early and I'm starvin'."

"The diner's just around the corner," Rhys informed him.

"Perfect." Travis stepped back and waited for Gage to move in front of him before following the man out of the building.

Wolfe let Rhys and Amy precede him so he could lock the door behind them.

A few minutes later, the five of them were seated at the diner, coffee in front of them and food ordered.

"We've got a couple more comin'," Travis told Donna. "They'll have the same thing."

"Who else is comin'?" Wolfe asked, hearing this for the first time.

"Ryan Trexler and Zachariah Tavoularis. RT owns Sniper 1 Security. Z's his partner slash husband. I wanted to bring them in on this, see if we couldn't knock this out rather than sit on our thumbs and wait for this bastard to make a move."

"You think that's possible?" Rhys inquired, his eyes traveling to Amy briefly. "Without putting her in danger?"

Travis's gaze remained on Rhys for long seconds.

"She's my main priority," Rhys added. "Mine and Wolfe's."

When Travis looked his way, Wolfe nodded. He hadn't clarified the relationship because it hadn't come up, but he didn't feel any need to hide it. And since Rhys had been the one to mention it…

"Understood," Travis said firmly. "And the goal is to get him out in the open without putting anyone in the line of fire."

"Not that it'll work," Gage added. "But it's always the plan."

"So, I did a little research on Kelly Jackson," Travis prompted, his gaze sliding to Amy. "Were you aware that he was married before?"

Amy shook her head. "He never mentioned anything."

Travis leaned back in his chair, his hand resting on the table, finger tapping slowly. "He's a widower. First wife … they were married for nine months." Travis met Wolfe's gaze. "She was twenty-three years old when she drowned in the bathtub."

Amy gasped and all eyes turned to her.

"You said *first* wife?" Rhys stated.

"You caught that?" Travis smirked. "His second wife presumably overdosed. She lasted a little longer than the first. Eighteen months they were married. No toxicology report was ever run to confirm; however, it was ruled a suicide. She was twenty-two."

Holy fuck.

"This guy is bad news," Gage noted. "He's gotten away with it all this time. Figure it has something to do with his position. The fact that he's in law enforcement." Gage peered over at Amy. "I think it's high time we take him down."

Wolfe didn't think Gage would get any arguments on that one.

The only question remaining seemed to be: How would they go about doing that?

AMY HAD NO idea who Travis Walker was aside from being Wolfe's cousin or what he did for a living, for that matter, but she had to admit, the air of authority he had told her he was someone you didn't want to mess with.

And his husband... *Lord have mercy.*

Gage Matthews-Walker was the take-no-shit type who was clearly ready to jump in and wipe out the problem before it went any further.

Not that it could get much worse than it was now.

Her stomach churned every time she thought about Detective Joanna Tannenbaum. The woman had gone out on a limb to notify Amy, to help her, and she'd died for her efforts. No doubt Kelly had forced her off the road, causing her to slam into that tree. According to Rhys, she had to have been going damn fast for that type of impact. However fast she'd been going, and for whatever reason, it had been enough.

And to find out Kelly had two previous wives. Both of whom died during their marriage to the crazy man... Amy couldn't help but consider herself damn lucky.

"Were you able to locate his whereabouts?" Gage asked Rhys. "At the time of the fatality crash last night?"

Rhys frowned. "San Antonio. Or so it appears. I've reached out to see if I can get someone to confirm they actually saw him there. He could've easily checked into his hotel online so it was assumed he was there."

"True," Travis noted.

The bells over the door jingled and all eyes turned that direction.

Two men strolled inside, one ridiculously large. In fact, he had to duck so he didn't hit his head on the doorjamb.

Amy had thought Travis Walker was a giant of a man, but this guy made Travis look small.

The men removed their sunglasses and peered around the room before coming their direction.

"RT and Z, this is my cousin, Wolfe Caine, Sheriff Rhys Trevino, and their girl, Amy Manning."

Their girl?

Warmth infused her at those words. She hadn't expected to be introduced that way, but she found she liked it. More so because neither Wolfe nor Rhys seemed bothered by the title.

"Nice to meet you," RT said, shaking all proffered hands before Z did the same.

The two men then took the extra seats at the table, and Travis proceeded to fill them in while the food was delivered and everyone chowed down. Everyone except her, that was. Amy picked at her food, her stomach too unsettled to eat.

"Not only was the detective run off the road last night," Wolfe added when Travis finished speaking, "but someone attempted to break into Amy's house. She currently has a roommate, and my cousin Lynx showed up over there. We think he scared Kelly off."

"Highly likely," RT noted. "But no sightings of him?"

Rhys shook his head. "Unfortunately, due to the tourists we see coming through to Dead Heat Ranch, people aren't as vigilant as they could be. We see a lot of strangers, so most people don't notice them unless they stick around for a while."

Which meant Kelly could've come into this very diner and had breakfast and no one would've been the wiser. The thought made Amy's stomach churn.

The bells over the door jangled again, and once more, all eyes strayed to the door.

Amy looked up to see Lynx making his way over. He stopped and greeted Travis and Gage, then they went through the introductions once more before Lynx grabbed a chair from a neighboring table, then took a seat beside Amy.

"You okay?" Lynx asked, nudging her knee with his.

She peered over at Wolfe's cousin. She couldn't even force a smile. This was all too much.

She wanted to cower into a corner and wait for this all to be over. Unfortunately, that would never happen. She knew she couldn't hide anymore. Part of her wondered if she should hop in her car and take off, find somewhere else to go, another place to hide for a while. It might've sounded tempting if it weren't for Rhys and Wolfe. Amy loved them. No way could she envision her life without them in it. Sure, if it came down to their safety, that might be one thing, but it wasn't something she wanted to contemplate right now.

"We'll take care of it," Lynx stated, his voice reassuring.

Amy didn't believe him. She didn't believe any of them. She knew their intentions were good by offering the empty platitude, but they didn't know Kelly. She did. He was the devil in human form.

"Trust me, kiddo," he stated, leaning closer as though reading her mind.

His arms were covered with tattoos, from his knuckles all the way up to his neck, even behind his ears. It was an interesting mix of designs, some of which she could make out, even possibly understand, but others she knew were personal to him.

"He's too powerful," Amy forced out, her gaze dropping to her lap.

Lynx chuckled. "There's no such thing."

"He's right," Travis noted. "There's no such thing."

Lynx nodded to the four men sitting across the table. "My cousin's got some serious pull. He knows some pretty powerful people himself."

Amy glanced over at Travis Walker. The guy was massive. Not to mention, intimidating.

"And these two…" Travis motioned a thumb toward RT and Z.

Amy's gaze strayed to the two men.

"They're not gonna let anything happen to you. This is their specialty."

Amy didn't know what *this* was referring to, but she nodded anyway.

"So, they're not related?" she asked, glancing between the men.

It seemed everyone was related in some way. She didn't even know how many cousins Wolfe had, but it seemed there were quite a few of them.

The men at the table laughed, some of the tension easing.

"Not related, no. Z grew up in Coyote Ridge, though," Travis explained. "His brother works for my family."

"My aunt Iris married into a really big family," Wolfe added, "and it only seems to get bigger every time we turn around."

Travis smiled at Amy. "I've got six brothers. And every damn one of them wanted to be here today. So, if push comes to shove, I'll bring them in." Travis's face sobered as he glanced back at Wolfe and Rhys. "But I don't expect it to come to that."

The group of men got quiet and Wolfe turned to look at her. A shiver of unease made goose bumps pop out on her arms and legs.

Lynx patted her knee. "It'll be fine. Ain't nothin' gonna happen to you on our watch," Lynx assured her.

Amy wished that were true. She wished it could all just go away. She was tired of watching over her shoulder. Especially now, when it seemed her life was coming together. She had a great job, she had friends, and she had two men…

Everyone started talking, and there were too many people for Amy to keep up, so she continued to move her food around her plate until finally Travis cleared his throat.

"We do need to get back," Travis said, his tone deep, authoritative. "Our wife's holdin' down the fort."

Amy glanced over at Rhys, then at Wolfe. She still found it hard to believe that Travis had a husband and a wife. And two children, she thought she remembered them saying. It was surreal. But in the same sense, it gave her hope.

"We'll be plantin' a few agents in the area," RT explained. "Just to keep an eye out."

Agents? What was this?

"Keep your eyes open, Amy," Gage told her. "It'll be over soon."

Another thing she didn't believe, but she nodded because she knew that was what they expected from her.

"Walk us out?" Travis said to Lynx. "We'll be in touch."

And with that, most of the testosterone vacated the building.

WHEN THE FIVE men cleared out, Rhys changed seats, moving to Amy's other side so that she was between him and Wolfe.

Oddly enough, now that Travis Walker and Sniper 1 Security were involved, he felt a little better.

Not great, no, but at least he felt as though there would be eyes on the situation. The biggest issue was that Rhys couldn't even alert his deputies to keep an eye out for Chief Jackson. It would raise suspicion, and until Amy decided to go forward and speak up, Rhys knew it would only cause problems.

Which left him with his hands tied.

Unless, of course, Kelly Jackson showed up again. Then all bets were off.

According to Travis, this situation wasn't going to simply go away and talking to Kelly Jackson wasn't going to be an option.

Good news was, Kelly Jackson wasn't going to get away with what he'd done.

Bad news was, Kelly Jackson wasn't going to go away anytime soon if they couldn't pin him down.

"Not hungry?" Wolfe asked Amy, nodding toward the food she had hardly touched.

"No."

Obviously that meant her food was fair game, because Wolfe reached over and snatched her bacon. Amy smiled and for the first time that morning, Rhys didn't think it was forced.

They sat silently for a few minutes after Rhys signaled for the check. Wolfe beat him to it, though, only to find out that Travis Walker had picked up the tab anyway.

"I've come to a decision," Amy said suddenly, her eyes fixed on her hands, which were clasped tightly in her lap.

"About?" Rhys glanced at Wolfe, who shrugged.

Those dark eyes lifted to meet his, and Rhys saw something in them that told him Amy was about to show just how steely her backbone was. He had never thought of her as weak. Not for a single second. Sure, on the outside, Amy was sweet and innocent. However, deep down, there was a tough woman.

"Jo came here to help me," Amy stated, her eyes darting back and forth between the two of them. "She died because she thought there was something off about Kelly."

Wolfe nodded.

"I'm done sitting back and waiting for him to kill me."

Rhys cringed at her choice of words.

"And I can't sit back and let Jo's death be in vain."

Rhys leaned forward and took her hand, linking their fingers. Yes, they were in public. In the diner, for crying out loud. Probably no more of a public place right in the heart of the gossip grapevine than right here, but Rhys didn't care. He could still hear Calvin's words ringing in his ears. Family. That was what was most important.

Which meant he would deal with the fallout when it came, and he knew Wolfe and Amy would be right there beside him.

"You are the strongest woman I have ever met," Rhys told her, his voice rough, his chest aching from the churn of emotion that built whenever he thought about all she'd been through.

Amy shook her head, but Rhys silenced her by pulling her closer. He pressed his mouth to hers. "It wasn't a question," he told her. "It's the truth. And whatever you wanna do, we're right here. At your side."

Wolfe leaned in and took her other hand.

Of course, he happened to do so at the exact moment that Donna walked up to refill their coffee.

"Sheesh," the older woman said, chuckling. "I shoulda known." Donna peered down at Amy. "Girl, if anyone can keep these ol' boys straight, I think it'll be you." She topped off two of the cups, then patted Amy on the shoulder. "Good luck, hon."

A smile formed on Amy's lips and it grew wider as she stared back at the two of them.

"I'm not sure anyone can keep you boys in line." She leaned in closer. "But I'm damn sure willing to try."

Wolfe lifted an eyebrow and glanced over at Rhys.

"Amen."

31

Two days later

"YOU READY TO head home?" he called up to Amy.

"In a minute!"

What in the world was that girl working on? She'd been locked away in her office for almost two hours straight. He hadn't seen her since the last time she came down to use the restroom and clean out the coffeepot.

The most confusing part was the fact that she had called Rhys to come over, and he'd been up there for the past half hour with her, doing God only knew what.

Figuring they'd be down in a minute, Wolfe started reorganizing his work area for tomorrow. He went to the far corner and grabbed a small can of stain—red oak—for an armoire he was working on. As he was walking back, his cell phone rang.

He glanced down to see that it was…

Wolfe stopped walking. "Hello?"

"Hi," Amy greeted, her voice smoky and seductive.

Oh, hell.

"Remember how you told me one day I'd call you when Rhys and I were … you know?"

"Yeah." His throat was dry as he tried to swallow.

"Well, this is that day."

He breathed out heavily, then leaned against one of the tables that needed to be taken over to the store. "Is it now?"

"It is and … oh, God," she hissed softly. "Rhys…"

Son of a bitch.

Wolfe's dick hardened instantly at the sound. "What's he doin' to you, darlin'?"

"He's…" Amy moaned softly. "I'm on the couch. Naked. And … and Rhys is kneeling on the floor in front of me… He's … oh, yes."

"Don't stop," he insisted. "Keep talkin'."

Wolfe's gaze swung up to the second floor. He could see the break room door was closed, and he could practically picture the two of them in there. Amy laid out on the couch with Rhys's head between her splayed thighs.

"His tongue is…" Another moan.

"Is Rhys dressed?" Wolfe had to know.

"Yes. Fully. But I'm…"

Naked. He knew.

Holy fuck.

"What's he doin' to you?"

"His tongue is licking me and … God, it feels so good."

"Where's he lickin' you?"

"My … my pussy." Her words were softly spoken and Wolfe could hear the embarrassment.

He had to give her credit for trying.

"I wanna watch, Amy," Wolfe told her. "I wanna watch while he licks your sweet pussy."

"Oh, my … Rhys … don't stop."

"Can I watch, baby? Can I come upstairs and watch while Rhys eats your pussy? While he makes you come?"

Wolfe didn't move from where he was, despite what he said. He wasn't sure his legs would hold him up, and the friction from his jeans against his dick would likely have him coming. Probably not a wise move here in the warehouse.

"Talk to me, baby," he urged. "Tell me how it feels. How his tongue feels sliding against your clit."

"Good … so good. Oh, God! Now he's… Rhys … your fingers … they feel so good."

"Is he fingering you? How many fingers is he usin'?"

"Two. He's … fucking me with two fingers and his tongue is flicking my clit. Wolfe … it's … it's too much."

Amy was panting through the phone and the sound was so damn sweet, it was as though she were breathing right on his dick.

"Rhys … oh, yes … right there. Right there!" Amy cried out and Wolfe closed his eyes, picturing how fucking hot she was when she came.

Son of a bitch.

And to think, all this torture had been his own damn fault.

Not that he was complaining.

Not one single bit.

When Wolfe heard the door open at the top of the stairs, he was still leaning against the table. As soon as they both appeared on the landing, he waved toward the door.

"Time to go home," he said gruffly.

"Yeah?"

"Oh, yeah." He smiled at the pair of them. "Then it's my turn."

KELLY SAT IN his SUV, watching as Amy and two men came out of the oversized warehouse. He had watched the tattooed cowboy he'd seen the other night come out about an hour ago. A little searching on his phone and he found out who the owners were and what it was they did there. It didn't take much to realize Amy was working there now.

He had been a little surprised to see the sheriff disappear inside a short while ago. And now the three of them were walking out together, the sheriff's arm around Amy.

Granted, that wasn't all he'd noticed during his trip to Embers Ridge today. There were a couple of additions to this town since the last time he'd been there in the form of security agents.

Kelly figured they were there to protect Amy, possibly even looking for him specifically.

He should've known she had opened her big fucking mouth.

He'd known it was only a matter of time before she went spilling her guts to anyone who would listen.

Kelly tilted his head down, cell phone to his ear as he mouthed a pretend phone call when two guys walked out of the gas station directly across the street from the furniture warehouse where Kelly was parked. They looked like cowboys, but their eyes were trained to take in their surroundings.

Yep. These guys certainly weren't amateurs.

But even so. What could they do? Approach him? It wasn't like Amy could prove anything. If she did decide to speak up, it wasn't like anyone was going to believe her over him, anyway. Hell, he was the chief of police of Houston. He had the entire fucking department behind him.

However, it did mean he was going to have to lie low for a while.

But not for long.

After all, he'd never been the kind for loose ends.

♥□□□□♥□□□□♥

Don't hate me!

I know, I know. You're probably thinking: The story ended there? What? She can't be serious!

Sometimes, that's what happens when you know that a storyline is going to continue. The next book – Hard to Handle (Lynx & Reagan) will be out in July 2017, so you won't have to wait long to see what happens.

In the meantime, I hope you enjoyed Wolfe, Amy, and Rhys's story. Hard to Hold is book 1 of this 2-book series, which you might've noticed is a spin-off from my Alluring Indulgence and Coyote Ridge series'.

Want to see some fun stuff related to the Caine Cousins series, you can find extras on my website. Or how about what's coming next? Find more at: www.NicoleEdwardsAuthor.com

If you're interested in keeping up to date on the Caine Cousins or the Walker Brothers as well as receiving updates on all that I'm working on, you can sign up for my monthly newsletter.

Want a simple, *fast* way to get updates on new releases? You can also sign up for text messaging. If you are in the U.S. simply text NICOLE to 64600 or sign up on my website. I promise not to spam your phone. This is just my way of letting you know what's happening because I know you're busy, but if you're anything like me, you always have your phone on you.

And last but certainly not least, if you want to see what's going on with me each week, sign up for my weekly Hot Sheet! It's a short, entertaining weekly update of things going on in my life and that of the team that supports me. We're a little crazy at times and this is a firsthand account of our antics.

Acknowledgments

Sometimes a story simply comes. This was one of those times and I have to say, I am so lucky to have such a great group of people who back me when it comes to my crazy thought process.

First and always, I have to thank my wonderfully patient husband who puts up with me every single day. If it wasn't for him and his belief that I could (and can) do this, I wouldn't be writing this today. He has been my backbone, my rock, the very reason I continue to believe in myself.

Chancy Powley – If you don't like something, you tell me. And that, my friend, makes a truly fantastic beta reader. It's hard to believe that we've been doing this for 4 years now. I can't wait to see what the next 4 has in store.

Allison Holzapfel – Girl, I am so lucky to have you along on this crazy ride. Thank you for being there for me and for making me laugh.

Amber Willis – I'm not sure what I would do without you. You've been through a lot lately, yet I know that you are there for me whenever I need you. So, thank you for that.

Karen DiGaetano – Thank you for telling it like it is. I'm looking forward to the friendship growing.

Wander Aguiar and Andrey Bahia – You two are class acts in every way. Thank you SO much for giving my characters life. Working with you is a true pleasure and I look forward to what the future has in store for us.

Thank you to my proofreaders. **Jenna Underwood, Annette Elens, Theresa Martin, and Sara Gross.** Not only do you catch my blunders, you are my friends and it is an honor to call you that.

I also have to thank my street team – Naughty (and nice) Girls – Your unwavering support is something I will never take for granted. So, thank you **Traci Hyland, Maureen Ames, Erin Lewis, Jackie Wright, Chris Geier, Kara Hildebrand, Shannon Thompson, Tracy Barbour, Nadine Hunter, Toni Thompson, and Rachelle Newham.**

I can't forget my copyeditor, **Amy at Blue Otter Editing**. Thank goodness I've got you to catch all my punctuation, grammar, and tense errors.

Nicole Nation 2.0 for the constant support and love. You've been there for me from almost the beginning. This group of ladies has kept me going for so long, I'm not sure I'd know what to do without them.

And, of course, **YOU, the reader**. Your emails, messages, posts, comments, tweets… they mean more to me than you can imagine. I thrive on hearing from you, knowing that my characters and my stories have touched you in some way keeps me going. I've been known to shed a tear or two when reading an email because you simply bring so much joy to my life with your support. I thank you for that.

About Nicole Edwards

New York Times and *USA Today* bestselling author Nicole Edwards lives in Austin, Texas with her husband, their three kids, and four rambunctious dogs. When she's not writing about sexy alpha males, Nicole can often be found with a book in hand or making an attempt to keep the dogs happy. You can find her hanging out on Facebook and interacting with her readers - even when she's supposed to be writing.

By Nicole Edwards

The Alluring Indulgence Series

Kaleb

Zane

Travis

Holidays with the Walker Brothers

Ethan

Braydon

Sawyer

Brendon

The Walkers of Coyote Ridge Series

Curtis

Jared

Hard to Hold

Hard to Handle

The Austin Arrows Series

The SEASON: Rush

The SEASON: Kaufman

The Bad Boys of Sports Series

Bad Reputation

Bad Business

The Club Destiny Series

Conviction

Temptation

Addicted

Seduction

Infatuation

Captivated

Devotion

Perception

Entrusted

Adored

Distraction

The Dead Heat Ranch Series

Boots Optional

Betting on Grace

Overnight Love

The Devil's Bend Series

Chasing Dreams

Vanishing Dreams

The Office Intrigue Duet

Office Intrigue

Intrigued Out of the Office

Their Rebellious Submissive

Their Famous Dominant

The Pier 70 Series

Reckless

Fearless

Speechless

Harmless

The Sniper 1 Security Series

Wait for Morning

Never Say Never

Tomorrow's Too Late

The Southern Boy Mafia/Devil's Playground Series

Beautifully Brutal

Without Regret

Beautifully Loyal

Without Restraint

Standalone Novels

A Million Tiny Pieces

Inked on Paper

Writing as Timberlyn Scott

Unhinged

Unraveling

Chaos

Naughty Holiday Editions

2015

2016

BECAUSE NAUGHTY CAN BE OH SO NICE®
NE
LTD

Made in the USA
San Bernardino, CA
24 May 2018